The Hunter
Awakening

Nicholas Arriaza

Cover Design by Nicholas Arriaza

Printed in USA by Rio Dulce Books (www.RioDulceBooks.com)

First edition

ISBN: 0-9987933-0-2
ISBN-13: 978-0-9987933-0-6

DEDICATION

For my son. You inspire me every day.

PROLOGUE

Yellow eyes aglow in the pitch black, a beast maneuvers through a cave that has been hidden away for over two hundred years. The stagnant air is thick and heavy and tastes of death. Saliva drips from the creature's razor-sharp canines. Over seven feet tall, it walks upright, its massive, prominent rib cage expanding with each breath. Ripped and stretched, its clothing barely covers the massive creature.

Careful to not leave any marks from its long, hard claws, the beast slides its hands along the cave walls as it makes its way through the narrow corridors, ignoring the beautiful and ancient cave art on either side of the passageway. Its focus is purely on the mission, to retrieve a hidden artifact without leaving a trace.

A hundred yards in, the path opens to a grand excavation. Unlit torches hang from the hollow's walls. In the center sits a massive wood cathedra, hand carved with religious depictions of classic Christian tales, and a large cross. A mummified body sits upon it, shackled, a large, wooden-handled blade protruding from its chest. Though the beast knows not to disturb the throne or its inhabitant, it cannot resist. Carefully, it walks toward the cathedra; its curiosity and the allure is too strong to resist. The beast moves in close to examine the man.

Reaching out, it touches the skin; he is well preserved and hard as stone. Looking at the blade, it dares not touch it. The beast positions its massive head within a foot of the man's leathery body and takes a quick whiff. Surprisingly, there is no smell.

The beast shakes its head and returns to its task. Quickly walking through the main area to the far wall, it reaches a large, marble-like stone that stands seven feet tall and five feet wide. The beast extends its massive arms, gripping the sides of the stone. With brute force, it pushes the slab, exposing another, secret chamber.

A loud popping sound explodes from the newly opened area, as the air is sucked into the room, passing in a rush. Lowering its head to get past the lintel, the beast must squat to move around within the room.

A large wooden pulpit stands in the center of the small space. Upon the pulpit sits a leather-bound book, covered in two centuries' worth of dust. As the creature wipes the book, the symbol it has been searching for is exposed. The creature pulls out a small cloth from its waist band, wraps the book in it, and heads out, making sure everything is left exactly as it was. It passes the mummy and walks along the narrow corridor, until it is free of the cave. The beast's heart pumps rapidly, its body wanting more of an adventure, but it knows not to linger or deviate, as the punishment is not worth the risk.

The sky above is covered in clouds, and no light can be seen from the moon. The creature can smell rain in the air. Summoning all of its might, the beast forcefully pushes the large boulder back in front of the entrance, once again concealing the cave. Finding and retrieving the book safely has been its primary concern. It neglects to secure the latches that once held the heavy boulder in place. Pressing hard on the massive boulder, which gave it so much trouble, the beast decides it is secure enough for now. The latches can be secured later. The book must be safely delivered to its new owner.

CHAPTER ONE

"Chris? Are you sure you can't stay home today?" Melisa rises from the bed, mischievously moving the covers and exposing her naked body. "I thought we could have a naked day, spending it in each other's arms." She seductively rubs her fingertips along her bare thigh. She can't remember a time when she felt so attracted to her fiancé.

Chris, pushing his arm through his dress shirt, looks at Melisa in the mirror's reflection and smiles. "Oh babe, I wish I could."

"Why do you have to go, anyway? I thought your brother was supposed to handle the meeting?" Melisa rolls her eyes, irritated by the whole situation.

"So did I." Chris raises his right eyebrow, looking down at his overnight bag. He lets out a soft sigh. Pulling his tie out, he quickly wraps it around his neck, knotting it into a perfect cross knot.

"I don't get why you asked him, if you knew he was so unreliable?"

"Alex, is young, is all. And my dad asked me to. Said if I give him more responsibility, he'll start to shape up." Chris tightens his jaw at his own words.

Melisa doesn't know his brother, Alex, all that well. But from what Chris has told her in the past, she can't fathom how Chris can continue to allow Alex to work with him. He has six brothers, and Alex was the only brother he complained about.

"Then make him and get back in bed with me." Melisa pats the bed.

1

"Mel, I can't. I need to meet the inspector."

"I thought you were the boss." Melisa tries to goad him. Chris pauses, as he grabs his blazer off the nearby chair, his knuckles turning white, as he holds it.

"I am," he says softly, turning to her.

"Then?" She shakes her head with attitude looking out the massive floor-to-ceiling window.

"Then nothing. I'm going to take care of my business. Then, I'll come back here. And that will be the end of this conversation about my brother."

"Whoa, I was just playing." She turns back to him. Chris, realizing his frustration is being directed at the wrong person, quickly smiles at Melisa. She tries to hold back the tears. He's never spoken to her in such a way. He was mean, and that wasn't him. Something else is going on.

"Oh babe, I'm so sorry. It's not your fault my brother is such a dumb shit." Chris's voice breaks as he speaks. "I should have never spoke to you that way. I just hate that you are right." He pauses and looks down at the floor. "I hate that my brother continues to challenge me."

"Then do something about it. Stop allowing him to interfere with our life and your business." The tears build in her eyes. She loves Chris so much, and hates to see him being taken advantage of.

"It's not so simple."

"Chris, I don't understand your family. You all seem so close, except for that little shit," she says, while slyly wiping her tears.

"Alex is young. I will get through to him. I know it." Chris looks himself over, adjusting his tie.

"I really hope you do. Sooner rather than later," she says, looking up and down his lean, muscular frame. "You really wear a suit." He is tan, but only lightly. With a quick glance back toward her, he smiles. She dines on his features. His cheekbones are high and well-defined, while his neck is muscular without being stocky. His short, wavy, dirty blonde hair is perfectly layered. But it is his eyes, his beautiful light blue eyes that she can never get enough of.

"It's the suit you got me." Looking into the frameless floor-standing mirror that leans against the wall, he gives himself an approving wink. Standing just shy of six foot two, he has to squat to zip his suitcase closed.

Melisa can't help but smile. She has always found his confidence alluring. And today he is wearing it well. Melisa turns away and looks out the windows again.

"I know," Melisa says and wipes a tear. Focusing on the hillside, she thrusts her lower lip out in an exaggerated pout and pulls the covers back over her body. She knows what suit it is. She was happy to spend the money on it. He needed a new suit, so he could handle meetings like this. He is such a hard worker, and she just wanted to help. Now, it just looked like the suit he was wearing to leave her alone, when she wanted him to stay.

"I need to get out of here," he says, giving himself a final look in the mirror.

"I know." She smiles but can't hide the tears in her eyes anymore. She knows how important the meeting is. He worked so hard getting the lease, going against some of the top restaurateurs in the city. Chris thinks he got the lease due to her connection with Mr. McCarthy, her boss. But she knows it was all Chris. He could sell anything, and he never had to lie to do so. He had that "it" factor. He transferred enthusiasm like no one else, his passion undeniable. Chris hated to hear people talk about their passion for something. He believed if you had to tell people you have passion, you had already failed to demonstrate it. When Chris spoke, you couldn't help but listen.

Seeing her emotion, he moves to comfort her. "You have a career that requires a lot from you. And I'm trying to make a business. Do you realize that if all goes well, we will have three of the hottest bars in Los Angeles?" Chris takes a seat on the bed next to her.

"I know. I guess I'm just feeling a little hormonal is all."

"How many times have I asked for you to take a few days off, and you couldn't because you had some deadline, or you were on the verge of a breakthrough?" Chris can't stop the feeling he has to defend himself.

"I know."

"Look, you relax here, and I'll be home before you know it," he murmurs as he caringly rubs her back. "Then we can lie in bed all day." Very lightly, he kisses her covered shoulder. "We can even discuss names. Even though I'm sure we are going to name him after his father," he whispers into her ear and gently brushes her brown hair away. He softly kisses her earlobe. "Don't you agree?" he asks as he tenderly rubs her shoulders through the comforter.

"I don't think I like his father's name; let's name him after you," she teases, playfully bumping her head against his chin.

"Okay, funny guy," Chris laughs, softly biting at her earring, tugging at it. "I'll be back in two hours."

"Don't worry. I'm over it. I'll head into the office today. I still have a few reports that I need to finish." Melisa pushes him away.

"Mel, you will not." Chris gives her his stern face. "You have finally taken a few days off. You are going to stay here and wait for me." He focuses only on her eyes. Looking at each other for a moment, Melisa can't help but laugh.

"Fine," she says and gets up from the bed. "Did you tell your brothers?" she asks as she saunters across the room, her olive skin glistening under the sun revealing her perfect nude form. Her small baby bump just showing, added to her allure.

"I told Vincent and Aaron; I'm sure they told the rest." Stopping her movement, she looks back at her man.

"Did they say anything?" she asks.

"What do you mean?" he asks, turning his head in wonder.

"I don't know, maybe congratulations? Geez." She continues toward the bathroom.

"Oh, of course they did. They are super excited." Chris looks away from her when he makes the statement.

"Did they say anything about me getting fat?" Giving a quick shake of her butt, she looks back at him with a smirk. "Who knows how long I'll have this body; are you sure you don't want to get one of your brothers to take care of the meeting?" she flirts, softly tapping her firm tush.

"Err," he growls and buries his face in a pillow. "You know I have to. Don't be cruel," he pleads and throws the pillow at her.

"You made this bed, now you have to sleep in it," she says and scampers off into the bathroom.

"Why don't you take a dip in the pool and cool off? I'll be back in time to make you brunch," he hollers to her.

"What was that?" she asks as she returns to the room. The sun offers Chris a picturesque view of her features. Her cute round nose. Her full dark lips. Her almond eyes seducing him as she gazes back at him. The highlights in her shoulder-length brown hair, which shimmers gold. Her pheromones are calling to him, making it hard to control his animal instinct, and Chris sultrily walks to her; she gives him her back.

"It's going to be a beautiful day; it's always perfect after it rains." He holds her nude body tight. He wants to laugh; she has been trying to be sexy with him the whole morning as he got ready. But, it was when she was acting like herself, that's when he saw her in that way. "Why not stay home and relax, go swimming?" Turning to face him, carefully not breaking his hold of her, she looks up at his firm, masculine features. "The warm pool water is always exhilarating in the cold mornings. I'm sure the baby will love it."

"Chris, I love you. I'm not going anywhere," she whispers. "I'll be okay, just go to work. I'll see you later." She caresses his firm chin. Looking deep into her brown eyes, Chris can't control himself. His lips meet hers with such power that she lets out a soft moan. The passion is so strong that she can't resist matching his force. Chris picks her up with his powerful yet gentle hands. Carrying her effortlessly, he takes her to the bed, where he lays her down and looks her over, reveling in her beauty yet again.

Melisa looks up at this man she loves. "Babe," she says and reaches up and softly touches his face. "Thank you." Chris turns his head, and raises his eyebrows in wonder.

"What for?"

"Go to your meeting, I know how important it is. You can't be late."

"But . . ."

"No, honey. I'm sorry I pushed so hard. I know how important this is. All I wanted was to know you loved me, and you just showed me. Go to work, I'll be fine." She pushes herself up and kisses him.

"When I get back, we will spend the day in this bed. I promise."

"Oh, yes, we will." She drops back down on the comforter. She watches him pick up his bags. He blows a kiss to her as he walks out the door. Melisa closes her eyes, and falls back to sleep with a smile.

She wakes up an hour later, her body tingling all over with lust; oddly, it's not all directed toward Chris. She can't remember the dream she had but something has made her very excited. She feels her body; it is calling to her. She has never felt like this before, but she has never been pregnant before, either. Getting out from under the covers, she grabs her phone off the nightstand. Two unread messages wait for her. One is from Chris:

> *"I'll be home soon. Then we will*
> *continue what we started, I love you.*
> *Please don't go to work."*

The second message is from Dr. Weinstein:

> *"Mr. McCarthy is looking for you. Please call."*

"Fuck!" Melisa lets out. Leaning her head on her shoulder and pushing her hand deep into the mattress, she calls in to the office. "Dr. Weinstein," a throaty-voiced man answers. He is one of the many doctors who work under Melisa. Melisa's job title is Executive VP, Chief Medical Officer, an amazing position for one so young. Dr. Weinstein is among those staff members who do the tasks she doesn't have time for. "Hi Doctor, it's Dr. Castro," she says, trying to hide her annoyance.

"Where are you? Mr. McCarthy has been asking for you," he asks. "He was asking about your email in response to the letter from the FDA. I told him you were still working on it."

"I have the week off," she states. "I sent out a memo," she reminds him.

"What would you have me tell Mr. McCarthy?" he asks.

"Nothing. Transfer me to his line." Rolling her eyes, she shakes her head.

"Of course, hold on. Enjoy your time off," he says and disappears from the line. The sound of a sharp quick tone followed by a ringing comes next.

"Hello," a deep smooth voice answers.

"Mr. McCarthy, it's Dr. Castro."

"Dr. Castro, good morning," the smooth voice says, rolling the "r" of her name. By the sound of his voice, he is happy to be talking to her.

"Good morning," she replies, her tone matching his. "I heard you were looking for me?"

"Yes, I have a meeting with the FDA on Thursday and need the preliminary results from the trial."

"I'm still going over the data. I think we still have some time before we

6

should be talking with the FDA, sir."

"Oh, I'm a little surprised."

"When did you make the appointment? I didn't see it on the calendar," Melisa asks.

"I made it yesterday. I was having lunch with a colleague and he helped get it for me."

"I don't think we should be rushing into anything, but I can get the results mid-day tomorrow."

"Great, where are you? I didn't see you on campus."

"I'm home. I have the week off, but . . ."

"Wait a second," he interrupts her. "You are on vacation? I'm so sorry to bother you on your time off. I can't believe I didn't know."

"Yeah, it was a surprise to everyone," Melisa says and lets out a fake laugh.

"When is the last time you took some personal time?"

"Umm, this is the first time since I started . . . That would make it seventeen months."

"Melisa, my dear, you know how I feel about time off. It's important to keep fresh."

"Yeah, I just got caught up in my work."

"Well. To be honest, I'm a little annoyed. Now I have to move my meetings around. You need to start being more responsible."

"I'm so sorry . . ." She tries to apologize, thinking he is being serious.

"I'm just kidding. You take the time you've earned. No one on this campus works as hard as you. I'm sure those wonderful people at the FDA will be willing to move the meeting to next week, or even later. I just got a little excited." Melisa can hear the smile he is wearing. "I don't want to hear that you did any work today."

"But sir . . ."

"No buts," he interrupts again. "Now enjoy your time off. I expect you to be well relaxed upon your return."

"I will try," she says, laughing with him and ending the conversation. Placing the phone back on the bedside table, Melisa looks around. "Well, now what?" she asks herself. Begrudgingly, she gets out of bed and walks to the large floor-to-ceiling windows. Her home faces a hillside and is not easily accessible by foot, allowing her to stand nude, completely exposed as she stretches and looks out into her well-kept yard and infinity pool.

The early morning sun reflects perfectly off the blue water and ripples across her home. *I should go for a swim*, she tells herself. *You know what; you've earned this time off. A quick swim and then shower. And hopefully Chris will be home in time to join me in the shower.* She continues the thought of being able to make love to Chris all day.

Looking through her bikinis, she can't make up her mind. *I need to start wearing some of these skimpy ones before I get too fat*, she thinks, pulling out a monokini. "Oh my god! Not today, girl," she says and shakes her head. Stretching out the skimpy elastic fabric, she laughs. She continues to dig through her drawer until she finds her favorite, a Roxy bikini top, with a tropical-style pattern. It reminds her of hand-woven Guatemalan fabrics, but much lighter in color. "Now we're talking," she can't help but say aloud. Looking around, she laughs to herself. *Who cares what you're wearing. It's just you.* With that, she spends another ten minutes finding the bottoms to match the top.

She gets dressed in front of her mirror, still laughing off her strange feelings of wanting to be sexy yet understanding that no one is there to see her. Looking her body over in the mirror, she can't help but admire her figure, caressing the small pot belly showing from the baby growing inside her.

Her mind races with visions of her future. Chris playing with a young boy, teaching him how to play soccer. Going to the beach together. Chris running in the water, holding hands with his son. Watching the man being a father is the sexiest thing she has ever imagined. This feeling of sexuality is almost overwhelming. She can't remember a time when she felt as turned on or for as long as today. Chalking it up to hormones, she shakes it off and heads for the pool.

The sun is bright, engulfing the landscape around her. Looking down at the water, she can hear the soft splashing of the ripples hitting the edges of the pool. The blue floor of the pool dances with yellow sparkles of sunlight, which shimmer like fire under the water. The sounds of nature surround her. She can't believe how happy she is. Giddy, she smiles at her reflection. A sense of freedom, almost juvenile in its intensity, comes over her. The urge to just jump in nude strikes her. *God, I haven't done this since college,* she thinks. Looking at her surroundings, she realizes that she has no reason not to indulge herself. Without another thought, she does it. Shucking her bikini, she dives into the water. The rush causes a sudden gasp reflex. Rushing to the surface, she breaks through with a deep breath. Treading water, she pulls her hair back from her face. Feeling the water on her exposed breasts and buttocks makes her tingle in anticipation of Chris's return. She couldn't be happier.

The water is perfect. With every stroke she feels herself becoming calmer, more in tune with a self that she hasn't connected with for too long a time. Her body feels invigorated, almost stronger even than when she was a teenager. Remembering a time when she could hold her breath and swim underwater for two lengths of the pool, she goes for it. Her body responds perfectly; the second lap feels easy and she goes for a third, almost going for a fourth. Not wanting to tempt fate, she races to the surface and gulps in another huge breath.

Reaching the edge of the pool, she pulls herself out easily. A euphoric feeling surrounds her body. The bird song is crystal clear, the perfume from the roses intoxicating, each rose having a different scent. Her nude body shining in the sun, Melisa for the first time in her life feels one with the earth. Wringing out her hair, she looks out and up to the hills. The thought of people being able to see her on the trails above brings a tingle, but her modesty comes back.

She hurries to her bikini and puts it on quickly. Looking around, she just can't be sure no one is looking at her. Her clear eyes take in more beauty than ever before. The roses stand out with an unaccustomed vibrancy. Breathing in deeply, she can't believe the fragrance. How has she not noticed how wonderful these colorful plants are? Standing, looking out at the hillside, she exhales, completely at peace. She closes her eyes and places her hands on her belly. Listening, she hears a faint sound from high above on the trails. It sounds like a struggle of some sort.

Squinting to sharpen her eyesight, she scans for the source. It's the undeniable sound of someone in pain. Following the lines of the trails, she doesn't see a soul. Then, suddenly, it appears; someone is holding onto the edge of one of the trails roughly a hundred feet above. Focusing, she tries to make out the person. As she watches, he loses his grip and falls, tumbling down toward her.

Screaming, Melisa covers her eyes. She can hear every thud and scrape the man's body makes as it tumbles down the loose gravel of the steep hillside. The echoes are haunting as the man's body crashes through the bushes above her. Then she hears the solid thump of a body falling on her property. Her body moves on instinct, following the main retaining wall, which is lined with long thin horsetail reeds. Finding a section that has been broken, she follows the trail of crushed stalks to the man.

Pushing through the bushes and small trees, she finds him. He lies motionless, his body a mangled mess. A sudden gasp for breath startles her. Head to toe, his body is covered in dried mud, with blood running brightly down the hardened surface. His clothes are mere strips, barely covering his body. Carefully, she moves the foliage, exposing the man. "Sir, I'm here to help. If you can hear me, I'm going to touch you," Melisa calls out.

She carefully places her hand on the man, who lies face down, his hair caked with mud and plastered to his head. His skin feels like old cracked leather, which surprises and confuses her. Even as she recoils from his stench and grotesque appearance, she knows she needs to help. Returning her hand, she carefully moves his limbs.

His neck is in a very peculiar position; she has to move around him in order to check his pulse. She doesn't want to cause more injuries, but needs to get close enough to check his vitals. His body is bent like a pretzel, and she straightens out what she can without affecting his back or neck. Upon feeling her touch upon his neck he moves, turning his head and gasping for air. "Sir, please stay down. You had a horrible fall. We need to make sure you're okay," she tries to explain, using her hand to slow him.

"*Agua*," he calls out, trying to roll over. With every move, the tattered clothes on his body peel away, exposing more of his physique. His body slides under her fingers as he rolls. She holds him firmly, keeping him from rising up. Her fingertips touch what could only be an indentation in the center of his chest. Looking down, she sees four large mutilations traveling from his upper left chest down to his lower left abdomen and a large open puncture wound in the center of his chest. But, no blood is coming out it.

Melisa can't believe her eyes. In all her years in medicine, she has never seen such a sight. He twitches suddenly, causing her finger tips to touch the wound, and a strange feeling comes over her. Heat builds inside her. Her mind wanders, and she is transported to another time, a place she has never been before. It's dark except for two torches lighting the area. A man sits in a large chair, arms shackled with spikes stabbing into his forearms. Blood drips down. A man in a long leather overcoat walks up to him holding something sharp in his left hand. Without warning, he plunges the object into the restrained man. His whole body flexes in pain. He looks up in Melisa's direction. His eyes are focused directly on her before he slumps over. A loud howl erupts from behind and frightens her back to reality. She looks around making sure what she heard was from the vision and not real.

The brightness of the day overwhelms her for a moment. Unsure what has just happened, Melisa pulls away from the man's body. Opening his eyes, he stares at Melisa for a moment. "*Chel?*" he asks. His chest wound is gone. His four scars remain. "Chel?" he calls out again

"Excuse me?" She is shocked by the man's word. It is almost as if he is calling her by name, but it's one she has never heard before. "You need help; I need you to stay here," she tells him. *Did I imagine the chest wound? Was the sun playing tricks on me?* she wonders. His skin looks hydrated, not as it was just a moment ago. *What was the vision she just saw?* Melisa closes her eyes and counts to ten with controlled breath. Focused, she opens her eyes. She doesn't have time to figure out what she saw or if it was even real. The need is to concentrate on what's real right now.

"*Aqua.*" The man asks again for water, this time looking her in the eyes. She can't believe that his eyes match those of the vision. His topaz eyes stare innocently.

"Water? Okay. But you need to stay here," she tells him. The man just looks at her. "*Espere aquí,*" she states. The man nods gently. As she gets up, the man's face changes; he looks at her belly and reaches up to touch it. "*¿Qué es eso?*" he asks, his tone angered. He asks two more times, each with more anger behind it. "What? What is what?" she asks back, confused. She stands to walk away, but the man grabs her arm tightly. "*¿Qué han hecho?*" he hollers.

"I haven't done anything; I'm trying to help," she screams at him, breaking away from his grip. She hurries away and back to her house, picking up her robe as she passes the pool. Reaching the back entrance, she has to pull open the heavy slider. Looking back to make sure the man is not following her, she enters, locking the slider behind her.

She can't help but watch the man as he rises. The agony on his face almost causes her to open the door to help again. Thinking better of it, she just watches.

His body quivering all over, shakes growing with every step he takes, the man stumbles through her yard toward her pool. He never looks in her direction; he just moves forward in pain, dropping at the edge. He cups the water with his hand and starts to drink. Melisa is frozen watching the man. He gets up, water dripping from his chin. He looks in her direction. Melisa ducks, not knowing the reflection of the glass makes it hard for him to see her.

He heads to the side of her house. Once he is out of view of Melisa, she dials nine-one-one. She turns to a ten-inch monitor on the wall that activates once she swipes her finger over it and pushes on the button that reads "Cameras," which in turn displays nine images. The whole exterior of her house is now viewable. Pushing on the screen marked "Orchard," she sees the man now displayed full screen.

"Nine-one-one, what's your emergency?" The operator startles Melisa.

"Oh, yes. I have a man who has fallen onto my property. He is weak and malnourished," she explains.

"Is he responsive?" the operator asks.

"Yes, but he is confused and somewhat aggressive," she reports.

"Did he try and harm you?" the operator asks. "Are you in a safe location? Can you see the man?"

"No…he did grab my arm. But it was not to harm me." She looks down at where he had grabbed her. She doesn't feel any pain, but a mark is plain to see. She knows it will be a bruise tomorrow.

"Ma'am. Please keep your distance."

"I am, I have a security camera system. I have been watching him. He is heading toward the street."

"Are you alone?"

"Yes, but I'm fine. I don't believe he is dangerous. I think he is just lost and in pain." Quickly, the operator gets Melisa's information. Melisa is not happy with the way the call is being handled but is relieved when the operator finally informs her that she is sending the police

"Miss. Please stay inside and wait for the officers, they will be there shortly."

"Please send an ambulance; he needs help."

"Miss, we will do what's best for the man. Please wait inside until the officers arrive."

"Look, my name is Doctor Melisa Castro, I will not go outside, but I'm telling you. He needs an ambulance. He rolled at least one hundred feet down the hillside," she insists. The operator doesn't take the conversation any further. Melisa hangs the phone up and sees the man is leaving the screen, moving to another area. Quickly changing the display, she now sees him appear on the driveway camera. "Don't leave, help is on the way," she says and taps on the frame of the screen with her finger tip.

The man stops his forward movement and looks around in a panic. In obvious distress, he reaches for his head. A faint siren can be heard from outside. Watching the man, she can see it is affecting the man. As the piercing sound comes closer, the man falls to the ground grasping his ears. Melisa can't help herself. Her every muscle is telling her to wait inside, but her moral code will not allow her to. She grabs her cell, puts on her robe and heads outside.

The police arrive a moment before she can reach the man. "Stay right there, miss!" one of the officers orders from outside of her metal gate.

"Then get in here and help him," she screams, pushing a button on her phone to open the gate.

The man is lying in pure agony. His hands cover his ears, from which small streams of dark red trickle. "Sir, do not get up!" the other officer instructs. They approach with caution, guns drawn.

"He is in pain. Put those guns away," Melisa yells at the officers.

"How long has he been like this?" the first officer calls out to Melisa.

"He just did that; I think it was the sirens," she explains. "He had a horrific tumble from the trails," she adds.

"We're going to need an ambulance." The first officer speaks into his shoulder walkie-talkie. The second officer approaches the man and kneels near him. "Holy shit, this guy smells horrible," he says and backs off. Using his blue gloves, he carefully touches him. "Hey, I'm going to touch you. Do you have any weapons on you?" Slowly he turns the pain-stricken man over. A splatter of dark thick blood pours out of the man's ear. "Oh shit!" the officer blurts and jumps back. The man starts spitting the same tar-like blood, saying something that no one can understand.

Melisa rushes in to investigate. "Stay back, ma'am," the first officer orders, but Melisa doesn't listen.

"I'm a doctor; this man is in desperate need of help," she says as she reaches him. "Give me your jacket," she orders the second officer, who responds to her firm order. "Come here, help hold his head up," she continues to direct him. The siren of the ambulance can be heard. "Get them to turn off that siren; this man won't be able to handle it," she says and looks to the first officer who just stands there. "Now!" she yells and the officer reluctantly obeys.

"*Usted va a estar bien,*" she says, telling the injured man he'll be okay. The man opens his eyes and locks eyes with her. Melisa continues to stroke his hair. "*Chel, perdóname por favor,*" he is able to push out of his lips before he faints. The dark blood coming out of his ears thins and then stops.

Why is he asking to be forgiven? Melisa wonders. She leans her head to see into his ears. But the thick black residue makes it impossible for her to see inside. She doesn't want to move his head too much, before they get a brace on it.

"Who's Chel?" the officer asks her.

"I don't know."

The paramedics arrive and, after a brief exchange, Melisa reluctantly allows them to take over. She asks the EMTs which hospital they will be taking him to. Her home sits on the border between two hospitals. The EMT informs her that they can only take him to County, because the other hospital doesn't take head traumas.

Melisa watches as they take the man away. The officers take her information and a statement. When everyone has left, she walks back inside. She notices the blood on her robe sleeve. A rush of emotions comes over her. Melisa collapses to her knees and sobs.

Pulling out her phone, she calls Chris. He doesn't answer. She texts him: "*Please come home, I need you.*"

CHAPTER TWO

On the other side of the hill, an older man is opening his small shop: "Tobias Hudson's Rare Antiques." The sign is faded and easy to miss if you're not looking for it. As luck would have it, John Sullivan almost did. He was in such a hurry to get to the shop right when it opened he passed the building, but luckily saw the sign in his rearview mirror.

That was an hour ago now. The nervous man in his early twenties has been sitting in his beat-up, red, eighty-seven Volkswagen Golf, getting out every few minutes to see if the man has arrived. The hours of operations state he doesn't open until nine, but John hoped it would be like other shops, and he would show up early to get things in order.

But, with the shop being what it is, and the old man being Mr. Hudson, he would have no such luck. As any of the neighboring shop owners could tell him, Tobias Hudson would arrive five minutes before opening and leave five minutes after closing without fail. Those same shop owners would also agree that, despite his eccentricities, he knew his business.

Mr. Hudson was truly one of a kind. He had dark skin. His head was shaved, something he did every morning. Standing just under six feet tall, he retained the broad shoulders of a much younger man. His sense of style was classic, yet unique. Every item of his clothing had a set time and place to be worn. He had clothes for work, clothes for going out, and even clothes for watching movies.

When the lights of the shop turn on, for John to see, it is at exactly the

15

same time he does every morning. John jumps out of his car and hurries into the shop from the parking lot. He carries a small towel-wrapped object tucked under his arm. The bell on the door catches the old man by surprise. "Oh dear, good morning," he greets the young man. His almost-British accent catches John off guard. "I'm sorry, do you have an appointment?"

"Hi. I have something you might be interested in," John stammers.

"Oh?" the old man responds. "And what might that be?"

"Here," John says and clumsily places the towel down. "I got this from my uncle." He unwraps a dirty, rusty blade. Mr. Hudson notices the nervousness in the man's trembling hands. John tries to figure out the man's origins. He knows he's not English. Maybe somewhere in the Middle East or Africa.

"Your uncle?" the old man replies with a raised eyebrow. "Are you sure you're in the right place? Maybe a pawn shop would be better for you, my young man. I usually deal with clients who make appointments. I'm not accustomed to random gentlemen rushing in here so early trying to unload items they feel I may be interested in," he explains without looking up at the man.

John tries to show the old man's words don't affect him. "Are you interested?" he asks, putting his hands in his pockets and hiding any uneasiness. The old man walks away to the back office without saying anything.

Trying to look around the corner, John disappointedly covers the tarnished metal object. Picking it up, he puts it to his chest. He recognizes the signs of depression coming on strong. He turns and heads for the door. He had spent over an hour researching a place where he could sell this item.

He didn't want to go to a pawn shop. Having dealt with them a lot, these past few months, in his mind they are all crooks. He had no desire to allow them to take this amazing gift he had found, and give him nothing in return. They would give him pennies on the dollar, just like they have done with his other personal items, he kept telling himself.

When he came across the item, he felt it was a sign from God. This old, rusted blade was going to get him out from the rut he's fallen into recently. Get him back on track, back to the confident man he would tell people he is. Reaching the glass door, he opens it but doesn't want to give up. The feeling of hope returns, with thoughts of having been meant to find the blade. Something good was going to come from this, he just knew it deep in his bones.

"Let's have a look at what you have got there," Mr. Hudson calls out, returning from his back area carrying a small box of tools. "Place it over here," he says, pointing to a spot on his display case. There is a magnifying glass with a light on it. John looks up to the sky, thanking God for his intervention.

John watches the old man's hands, trembling softly as the other man works. His care and patience is mesmerizing. John focuses on every delicate move the old man makes, cleaning and revealing the truth about the item. "Do you have any idea what you have here?" the old man asks.

"A blade of some kind?" John answers quickly. "Its old, that's for sure," he jokes.

"A dagger, actually. They call this little beauty a Bollock Dagger," he glances up at John to see if he is paying attention. "You see these two round shapes at the bolster," he says, glancing up at him once more, reading the young man's face. "It's like a pair of bollocks," he laughs, fully aware that John has no idea that bollocks means testicles. "It can also be called the kidney dagger," he goes on, his chuckle continuing at his little inside joke. "Where did you find this? And don't say you got it from your uncle."

"I found it in the hills," he answers.

"When?"

"Is that important?" John spurts out.

"I suppose not." Mr. Hudson deliberately looks up over the rim of his glasses making eye contact with John. "Does anyone know you found it?"

"No." John holds the stare. A bead of sweat falls from his hair line.

"Are you sure?"

"Yes, I'm quite sure," he replies, trying to match the old man's coolness.

"I can't understand why an item like this would be in the Griffith Park hills . . ."

"I didn't say anything about the Griffith Park hills," John interrupts.

"I beg your pardon, I just assumed," Mr. Hudson evenly adds, looking the young man up and down.

"Well, please don't do that." John clears his throat as he replies.

"I see. Well, we're done here. You can take your blade and leave my shop now," Mr. Hudson calmly says while gathering his tools. "Have a good day."

"What, wait. I'm sorry, I didn't mean to be rude," John pleads, grabbing the old man's arm. Mr. Hudson looks down at John's hand. John quickly lets go. "I'm sorry." He sees he has over stepped. "Can you please help me?"

"I will only help if you tell me the truth and no longer lie to me. Where did you get this blade?" Mr. Hudson's stone face isn't reassuring to the young man.

"I didn't do anything illegal," John informs him, a rush of panic causing him to spit as he speaks.

"That's not my question. I'm no angel; I just don't want to be tricked. If you're trying to unload something that can get me in trouble, I promise you, you will get the raw end of this deal," he explains coldly, causing chills to run up John's back.

"But I didn't, okay, you need to understand that," John hastily continues on about his innocence.

"My dear sir, please tell me where you got this item, or be on your way," the old man says, taking control with a soothing charm.

"Okay. I'll tell you." John adjusts his shoulders; a peace comes over him. He can trust this old man. "I was with my friend early this morning. She and I went for a hike in the hills, and yes it was Griffith Park." He pauses to collect his thoughts. "I knew that today would be a great day, especially since it rained last night. We met at the bottom around six and got to the top by seven. One of the reasons I like going after it rains, no one else is on the trails." Telling the story, he over communicates, adding insight into his motives, proving his intentions were innocent.

He goes on for a while, explaining every detail of the trail. "Once we got to one of the peaks we decided to stop and have a snack. It's my favorite spot. There are a few trees that fell some time ago, and we can sit there and look out onto the city. It's truly one of the greatest views of downtown Los Angeles. Anyway, as we sat there my friend noticed a boulder lying up against a newly broken tree. The size was massive. At least ten feet wide," he says, stretching out his arms to embellish the story.

"Following the boulder's path of destruction, we found where it came from. At first I thought it was just a cave, but upon further investigation, I knew it was manmade. It was a mine of some kind, or at least that's what I thought then."

"What was it?" the old man asks. John has Mr. Hudson's complete attention.

"Well, after a long debate, Bernadette and I went in . . . My friend is named Bernadette, sorry," he informs the old man. "So, using our phones to light the way, we traversed the mine. Once inside we found that it was incredibly deep. It didn't take long for us to discover it wasn't a mine at all." He pauses. "It was an ancient Mayan tomb."

"A tomb? Mayan tomb?" the old man raises his eyebrow.

"Well, I can't say I know it was Mayan for sure. But I have been to Cancun and it looked just like them."

"Cancun?" Mr. Hudson chuckles. "So it wasn't native American?" Mr. Hudson holds back his smirk.

"I don't know. I guess it could have been," John concedes. "Whatever it was, it was ancient," he adds, frustrated. "Anyway, that's where we found the knife."

"Was it just lying there? Wasn't there anything else?"

"What?" John leans back making distance between him and the old man. "What do you mean?"

"I mean, this blade is an odd item to be in an ancient burial cave," Mr. Hudson explains.

"Oh, well, yeah. There were other items, but I didn't like anything but this."

"And so you took it?"

"Yeah."

"That's fine." He motions for John to place the blade back down on the counter. "And this woman, this Bernadette. Will she want to make claim to this or tell people that you found it?"

"What, no. No way."

"Even if I tell you that this blade is worth thousands of dollars?"

"What?" John blurts out in excitement.

"If it is what I assume it is, yes it could fetch such a price." He uses a little solution on the blade, revealing a brilliant silver finish.

"You're kidding me," John says, beginning to wobble. "Is that real silver? I thought it was rusted metal."

"Take a seat, my boy. I have a lot of work to do before we can be certain. I just want you to be prepared for the fact that you may be a little richer, and this friend of yours would be left wondering where her share is."

"I would of course give her half," John states without being able to look the old man in the eyes.

"Well, give me some time. I have a lot of work to do here," Mr. Hudson informs him. "Why don't you take a seat," he motions his head to the small couch by the window, never taking his eyes off the young man.

Mr. Hudson spends twenty minutes cleaning the blade. John sits impatiently, stretching every few minutes to see what the old man is doing.

"I have a question; I'm sorry: What is your name, young man?"

"John."

"Well John, I have a question."

"Go ahead," John says and walks up to the counter.

"Did you happen to take any pictures? You said you were using your phones to light your path."

"Yeah, I took a few; Bernadette took a bunch."

"Can I see them?"

"I can show you mine. I won't ask Bernadette for hers, though," John explains.

Mr. Hudson nods with understanding. "She doesn't know you're here, does she?" he plainly asks.

"No," John admits. "She was against me taking the blade." He lowers his head.

"I would be remiss, if I didn't implore you to tell her what you are doing. These things can get out of control quickly." Mr. Hudson looks deep into John's eyes. He sees that the young man is full of anger and sadness. He knows his words are falling on deaf ears.

"Here." John shows the images on his phone. "Just swipe to the left for the next image," he explains. The first is of the entrance. It's no taller than six feet, with perfectly smooth stone carved into a perfect arch stretching out four feet wide.

"Brave," Mr. Hudson says, looking up at John. "I don't believe I would have entered," he adds. John just looks at him with a smile.

The next image is from within. It a great shot of the cave art. A few swipes more and Mr. Hudson now has a close-up of one of the cave drawings. "Interesting," he lets out. "This is Mayan; what a great guess," he tells John, continuing to scroll through the images. "This here, this is not Mayan," he adds, showing the screen to John.

"What is it?"

"It's Catholic."

"What do you mean, Catholic? I've never heard of Catholic cave drawings." His disbelief is almost rude.

"I'm sure there are a lot of things you do not know." Mr. Hudson's response puts John in his place. "Look up the Catacombs of Rome. Maybe that will help your unfamiliarity," he adds.

"I didn't mean anything." John tries to back off but is interrupted by Mr. Hudson's gasp.

"Oh my," he says, and shudders.

"What?" John asks.

"It's a cathedra. How odd." Mr. Hudson pauses and looks out into space.

"What's a cathedra?" John asks, giving in to his lack of knowledge.

"Amazing, you may have found him," he murmurs. John, unsure of what he has heard, leans in to catch anything else the shopkeeper may whisper. "This will change Los Angeles," Mr. Hudson softly adds. John, hearing this, takes a step back.

"Well, what is it?" John asks.

"A chair for a bishop."

"A bishop?" John asks with a hint of stress in his voice.

"Yes." Mr. Hudson can feel that the young man is hiding something.

"What about this?" He shows Mr. Hudson another image.

'Puesto aquí descansar es el cazador,' he reads aloud. "Oh, my," Mr. Hudson expresses. The old man's dark complexion whitens. He turns away in thought. "Here laid to rest is the Hunter," he whispers.

"Is everything okay?" John asks. But all he can see is the dollar signs.

"Oh yes, forgive me." The old man turns back around, smiling. "You have found something very special."

"What is the Hunter?"

"It's not a what, it's a who," the old man says through tightened lips. He points to the blade. A small image is carved into the blade. It's a deer's antlers with a cross atop it. "This is the symbol for many saints; one that comes to mind is Saint Eustace. He was a Roman soldier who while hunting came across a stag. The image of Christ appeared to him between the stag's antlers and the man changed his faith at that exact moment."

"What happened to him?"

"No one knows for sure. There are writings of him being bull bronzed or something along those lines."

"Bull bronzed?"

"Yes, it's when they burn you alive in a bronze bull. The Greeks started it, but the Romans also used that form of torture."

"Why would they do that?"

"Because he wouldn't follow the pagan gods of his Roman empire. But it has been refuted by the church." He pauses. "The only thing that is for certain, he is a martyred saint."

"That sucks," John says and shakes his head.

"I guess that would. If it happened."

"So, what of this blade? What's it worth?" John asks. His greed is not lost on Mr. Hudson, but he responds to it.

"It's from a small group of special soldiers. More like knights. Actually they were knights," he corrects himself. "I'm sure you've heard of the Knights Templar, or the dagger men of the Jewish–Roman War?" He looks to John, making sure he has not lost him. "Well, these knights were so secretive only a few knew of their existence."

"And who are they?" John is fascinated by Mr. Hudson's words.

"The Knights Prosperitas," he glares. "Good Fortune," he clarifies. "It's a group of men, who helped the Inquisition dispose of those marked as heretics, witches, and werewolves." His face and attitude show his indifference toward them. "They were disbanded in the seventeenth century. There is word that they still exist, but I assure you, they do not."

"How do you mean?" John asks.

"Because the knights were not needed anymore."

"I'm confused; how do you know that?" John asks.

"Well, after the Basque witch trials, the Inquisitor-General found that, no, there is no clear evidence that witches are to be believed, and the judges should not pass verdict on anyone, unless external and objective evidence satisfactory to persuade everyone who hears it can be established." He pauses. "That was in the year of our lord, sixteen-fourteen. After that, many European countries stopped their so-called witch hunts."

"Wow," John whispers. "So what do you think of this dagger?"

"Daggers like this were given to knights. But how it got here I haven't the faintest."

"What do you think it's worth?"

"I would guess twenty to thirty thousand." Mr. Hudson smirks, finally giving the impatient young man a number.

"You're kidding me?"

"No. I don't kid about things like this, John."

"Are you interested?" John looks the old man in the eyes.

"My dear boy, I do not have those kinds of funds here. I wouldn't even be willing to sell it on consignment."

"Why not?"

"This is a very dangerous item. The people looking for items like this can be very radicalized. I will not have any business regarding this item," he tells him. "Witch hunting lasted in the Americas for much longer than any other place on earth. If it was still happening in Los Angeles, who knows why it was put there," he says, matching John's stare. "That cave was only covered by a boulder. Did it look like anyone else had been in there before you?"

"No," he states quickly. "I just saw some animal tracks."

"Animal? What kind?"

"I don't know. B, thought it was a coyote. But the mud was so loose, it was hard to tell. Plus, they seemed too large to be a coyote's."

"And you still went in? Having a young woman with you." The old man can't help but question the young man's thought process.

"Well, yeah. Why not?"

"Well, it's just odd. Didn't you wonder, how did that boulder get dislodged?"

"What do you mean?" John asks, trying to think back. "The earth was still muddy; it looked like it just slipped."

"Hmm. Without something giving it a nudge, I can't see how it moved, though. Even if the earth gave way, it still seems odd." Looking back at the blade, he says, "I wouldn't be surprised if someone was using that place for some kind of ceremony." He picks up the dagger in his hand and caresses the handle. "The wood is in surprisingly good shape. How could this be?" Mr. Hudson asks himself.

"What do you mean? I thought you liked it."

"I love it, but I hate it too," Mr. Hudson clarifies.

"I don't understand."

"I would guess you wouldn't. This item you have is something that has so much blood on it. And I suspect it will have more very soon. People will hurt for this item, even kill. I would recommend not trying to sell this item. You should put it back where you got it. Let the historians find it. Or take it to the proper authorities."

"Like who? The cops?"

"Maybe the antiquities department of the LA Museum?" His uneasiness becoming more clear, Mr. Hudson watches every move John makes.

"I don't get it. It's just a blade." John is irritated by what Mr. Hudson is telling him.

"Oh, it's so much more. It stands for a time that the church would love to keep hidden. It was used in some of the most horrific ways. People who know their history may think they can derive some power from it. Some people still believe in magic, and an item like this could really inspire." He looks the young man directly in the eyes. "All the blades from these knights had markings; each one was special and given for a special act."

"What was this one?"

"Was there anything else in the cave?" Mr. Hudson's hooded eyes look deep into John's eyes.

"No!" John's face gives him away. "Yes, there is one thing."

"What's that?" the old man asks nervously.

"The blade was stuck inside something?" He pauses, seeing Mr. Hudson seems to know already what he is going to say. "It was in a man's chest." Mr. Hudson takes a step back, shaking his head.

"He was sitting in the cathedra," Mr. Hudson states knowingly.

"Yes."

"Well, I was right. People still believe in magic. Please leave," he states calmly.

"I need to sell this thing, please help me," John begs. "Please, I'll take whatever you got." He pauses. "I found this, I didn't steal it. I really need the money. This year has been so hard, and by the blessings of God, I found this dagger." As the words pass his lips, his confidence in using God as his savior weakens. He can't read Mr. Hudson, and isn't sure calling on the man's faith is working in his favor.

"Young man, I will not. You lied to me. And I will not be implicated in a crime. Especially if I can't trust you." He packs up his tools.

"I know, I did." He again grabs the old man's arm. "I lied, but I thought I had to. If I would have told you I found a blade stuck in some decaying corpse you would have called the cops."

"Maybe..But not likely," Mr. Hudson says.

"Please. sir. I really need to sell this item. Maybe you could at least get me in contact with someone who would want it?"

"Young man. First, I will not have any of my associates deal with this. Second, if I was to offer you half of what this item is worth I would hate myself." He pulls his arm away. "Unlike some people, I believe in integrity."

"I would take half, no problem," John waves his arms in front of his chest shaking his head.

"That wasn't my point. I meant that I would not take advantage . . ."

"Take advantage, please," he interrupts Mr. Hudson. "I came in here hoping to get five hundred, maybe even a thousand dollars. Anything more than that would be huge for me."

"Listen, son, I can see you are desperate. It's not a pleasant sight," Mr. Hudson calmly states.

"I am, I'm sorry." John gathers himself. "Here, my last shred of dignity." He pauses. "I lost my job a few months ago. I've been trying to get back on my feet but nothing is sticking. I'm going to lose my apartment, and I can't ask anyone for help," he explains.

"How did you lose your job?" Mr. Hudson inquires, assuming the man is just trying to take advantage of his good nature.

"I spoke out of place. I've been telling everyone that they just let me go, but the truth is I said something stupid in front of the main boss. I didn't even know it was him."

"So losing your job was your fault?"

"Yeah. What can I say; I fucked up."

"John, I'm actually surprised. I thought you were going to bullshit me again." He pauses. "I can't believe I'm actually considering this," the old man lets out, shaking his head.

"So you'll take it?"

"I already know what will happen if I don't at least try. This blade needs to get into the right hands. I believe I can make that happen."

"Mr. Hudson, you are awesome." John reaches out to touch his shoulder. Visibly annoyed, Mr. Hudson moves, not allowing the contact.

"I'm not pleased with what I am about to do. Nor am I happy with you. I warn you again. Do not make me regret helping you. No one can know of what I am doing." Mr. Hudson walks to the back office leaving John full of hope.

CHAPTER THREE

"Mel!" Chris hollers out when he enters the house. "I got here as quickly as I could." Taking a deep breath, he shouts, "Where are you?" Something isn't right; her scent is off to him. There is another scent in the house. Hurrying through the entrance, he peers into the kitchen, which is to his right. He doesn't see her, but the odd smell is close. His concern for her is visible on his face; his eyes sharpen and his ears perk.

Thoughts of their phone conversation play out as he searches. He misunderstood the context of her text message, assuming she wanted him home for lovemaking. It wasn't until he finally called her back, that he got an earful from her. She told him the whole story of the man. He didn't take her anger or accusations personally. He understood that she was frightened. Once she got the anger out of her system, she told him to take his time, and everything was okay. Now he debates his decision not to drop everything and rush home. His defensive nature heats his body.

Calling out to her again, he takes in another controlled breath, using his powerful sense of smell to locate her. Turning back from where he came, he heads to the opposite end of the house. The walkway floats along the great room with glass dividers, separating it from the area below. The polished hardwood floors echo with the sound of his firm steps. The sun is shining in from the large floor-to-ceiling windows, illuminating everything as he passes.

He reaches the west wing of the house. The master bedroom is to his right, up a floating flight of stairs. Closing his eyes, he listens for her. Turning to his left, he goes down a more traditional-style hallway. He peers into the other rooms as he passes them, knowing she isn't in them. She's in the last room, her office. The lines smooth from his brow as he hears her talking on the phone behind the heavy wooden door.

"No, he was admitted sometime after eight-thirty," Melisa says to the person on the other end of the line. Chris walks in slowly, without making a sound. The solid door moves with ease, not because of his strength, but from the quality of its hinges. They are satisfyingly heavy and feel engineered to perfection. He admires the door, which is made from walnut with an inset walnut casing and stretches from floor to ceiling. He nods in approval of its build quality. *This could be great for the new restaurant*, he thinks. Melisa was always his style guru. She always had the best ideas regarding how to look elegant and modern.

He passes the many honors addressed to Melisa, all in matching black frames. These range from many college awards, to independent recognitions from the state. Having never gone to college, he truly appreciated all the accolades she had on display. She was most proud of the H. Richard Winn, M.D., Prize, the highest honor of the Society of Neurological Surgeons. Chris didn't know what she did to get the award, but loved that she was recognized for being the best.

"That's all right. I'll check back later." He hears Melisa's conversation coming to the end. "Yes, my name is Dr. Castro; do you need my number again? Great, thank you." She hangs up, letting out an annoyed release of breath. Turning around in the chair, she is startled to see Chris and lets out a squeal. "You butthole! You almost gave me a heart attack," she exclaims, panting and holding her hand over her heart.

"I'm sorry, I didn't want to disturb you. I see you're dressed for work." He uses his finger to point out her suit pants and shirt. "I thought you were going to stay and wait for me." He moves closer to her, looking down at her computer monitor. She has a document open. He doesn't understand the language but knows she's been doing research and development for some new drug.

"Are you working from home?"

"I was just finishing a thought."

"Who were you talking to?"

"That was another thought," she says and smiles.

"Melisa, are you okay?" Chris's moves in close to her, looking deep within her eyes. She is acting out of character. He still questions the scent he picked up when he entered the home. "Is everything okay? The baby okay?"

"What?" Melisa scrunches her eyebrows. "Of course. Why would you . . ." she stops herself. She had not thought about the baby this whole time. She'd been trying to locate this mysterious man, and not once had she considered him.

"Is everything okay?" Chris lowers himself.

"Yeah, I'm just a little out of it," Melisa says and looks into Chris's eyes.

"When I called back, you sounded like . . . ." he continues, trying to read her mind through her eyes. "I'm not sure what to say here?"

"Chris, everything is fine. I'm fine, the baby is fine." She laughs. "What took you so long, anyway? The club is only twenty minutes away." Melisa leans back in her chair away from Chris, looking him up and down.

"I had a few things to finish. I got here as quickly as I could. Are you sure you're okay?"

"Yup." She starts to get up.

"Why don't I believe you?"

"I don't know what I feel right now. All I know is you weren't here," Melisa answers. The vision she had when she touched the man has been playing out in her head all day. She can't think of anything else. The man being held against his will. The blade-like object being stabbed into his chest. She can't explain it, nor explain why she had it.

"I'm sorry I misread the text. I thought you just wanted me to hurry up with my meeting, not that something happened," he defends himself. He knows he shouldn't but he can't help himself.

"So, I tell you I need you, and you think I only want sex?" Melisa can't control herself.

"What?"

"I needed you here. And you didn't even answer my call."

"That's crazy, I can't be here all the time. Plus, I called you right back." He tries to explain, but Melisa isn't willing to listen. "If you truly feel that way, how come you won't move in with me?"

"Don't try and make this out to be my fault." Melisa points her finger at him. "I've already told you. I'm not going to move into that frat house, you call home. I have a brother and I wouldn't live with him. How could you expect me to live with your six brothers?"

"Whoa, whoa, whoa. I'm not sure what has gotten into you. But, I'm not trying to get into a fight. I'm here now. How can I help?"

"All I wanted today, was to spend it with you. Then all this happened," Melisa says. Tears begin to build in her eyes. "Jesus, I don't know what's wrong with me. I seem to be crying or horny every minute," she laughs.

"Well, I can help with either," Chris says and tries to hold her.

"You're not getting off the hook that easily," she says, smiling. "I'm actually mad at you. You really should have been here sooner. I could have been in trouble; it was all really frightening."

"Melisa, I see that this incident has affected you. I am truly sorry I wasn't here and you had to go through it alone." He places his hands on her waist. Looking deep into her eyes, he says, "I don't know what I would do if I lost you." He pecks her on the lips softly. "You are right; I should have thought about how scary this all was for you." Then he kisses her with more passion.

"That's all I'm asking for," Melisa says, leaning into his chest from her chair allowing him to hold her tight. "Why do you have to be such a jerk," she laughs softly.

"It runs in the family." He kisses her forehead.

"I hope our son doesn't have that trait," Melisa says, pressing her face into his chest. She remembers the wound again. She still can't explain how it was open and not bleeding. She had looked at some journals, but everything leads her to ulcers. Which that certainly was not. The sound of Chris's heart beat brings her back.

"Not with you as his mother." He smiles, and Melisa looks up at him. He brushes her hair softly away from her face with his right hand, not releasing his left from holding her tight. "Do you know how beautiful you are?" He kisses her softly on the nose.

"Sometimes."

"So, is the naked day off?"

"I don't know, is it?" she asks with the same twinkling in her eye she had earlier in the day. The phone rings. It's Melisa's emergency line from the hospital. Chris shakes his head knowingly. Moving his arm, he allows her to pick the phone up. She doesn't excuse herself. She picks it up, as if he doesn't matter right now. Listening to her tone, he realizes that the love session is not going to happen. He watches Melisa as she converses with whomever is on the other line. He stands up expectantly.

"Yes. I can be there right away." She hangs up.

"I guess you have to go into work?"

"Kind of. They found the John Doe."

"What do you mean? What John Doe?"

"The man who came here. County was having trouble locating him for me. I'm having him transferred to my hospital."

"I don't think I like the idea of you working on this man. Ever since he trespassed onto your property, you've been acting off."

"What? That's ridiculous. I haven't been acting off."

"Melisa. I don't think this kind of stress is what you need right now. It's not good for the baby."

"I beg your pardon? If I feel like I can be of help to someone, I will do just that. And as for this baby in my belly. I'm no idiot, I will never jeopardize his health and wellbeing, either." She waves her finger as she speaks.

"Wow, wait a second babe. I didn't mean that," he says and opens his arms to her.

"Yeah, I bet you didn't," she replies and walks past him.

"I'm sorry."

"It's fine."

"How about I go with you?" Chris calls out, following her.

"Go with me? To the hospital? Ha!"

"Yeah. I would love to see you in action."

"Yeah . . . I don't think I like that," Melisa says as she packs her briefcase.

"Why not?"

"Because." She doesn't even look at him.

"I don't know if I like you taking care of a guy who just happened to fall onto your property."

"Chris, he is just someone that needs help. I will do what I always do." The vision she saw comes back as she speaks.

"I just mean: you don't know him. Why would you be trying to help him out?"

"I don't know. It just is something I feel I should do. Is there something wrong with wanting to help someone?" she responds, not wanting to tell the truth that she needs to know what the vision was. And why did she get it when she touched the John Doe?

"Of course not. I'm not saying that. I just thought you wanted to have the day with me," he states, taking her briefcase from her.

"I do. And thank you for listening to me. How about we meet for dinner?" she offers. She reaches out for her case but Chris keeps it away from her.

"I have work tonight."

"I figured."

"How about coming out to the club? We can order in, watch the people dance. Maybe dance ourselves?" Chris offers, giving her a little shimmy to entice her.

"No thanks, I would rather you stay away from dancing." She tries again to get her briefcase from him, but his long arms keep it too far from her grasp. "Are you going home or do you think you can stay here tonight?"

"I'm closing; it would be too late. I'll just stay in the loft," he says, referring to the loft he had built over the club.

"All right. How about tomorrow? Should I expect to see you?" she asks.

"Of course. Are you still taking the week off?"

"I was planning to. I just want to check on the John Doe."

"How about this: Let's get out of town for the weekend." He offers the briefcase back to her.

"Where would we go?" She waits to take it.

"How about Santa Barbara?"

"That would be lovely," she says and smiles, taking the briefcase from his hand. "Can you grab my other bag, please?"

Chris helps Melisa carry her bag to the car in the garage. He loads her into the car and watches her drive off. She waves, blowing him a kiss goodbye. He walks with the car as it moves away, hiding his true worry about her actions. Something just isn't sitting right with him. She was acting so out of character and that scares him.

Slowly walking back toward the house, he sees the leftover blood from where the man must have been lying on her driveway. Kneeling down, he touches the dark blood with his finger. It's dark and thick. Bringing it to his nose, he is disgusted by the smell, so much so that he gags. Wiping his finger on the cement, he removes what he can. The smell remains on his finger, so he goes up to the house and grabs the water hose hanging on the wall. Spraying his finger, he inhales again. "What the fuck is this shit?" he asks aloud. Looking around the garage, he finds a can of powdered bleach. Sprinkling it on his finger, he rubs it almost raw until the stench is removed.

He grabs a brush and takes the can of dry bleach and hose to the driveway. Not caring about his clothes, he kneels down and scrubs the area with the detergent. The stench of the blood is heavy in his nostrils. Holding back his retching, he works hard to remove the stain. His hand viciously scrubs, breaking away bristles with the force, until the last scent is gone, and he can again breathe easily.

Getting up, he looks down at his pants. Both knees are exposed. With a soft laugh he dusts off his pants "Shit, Mel is going to be pissed". He heads back up to the house and puts everything away. Going into the laundry room, just inside from the garage, he takes off his pants and throws them into the waste basket. Looking through a pile of clothes, he finds a dirty pair of jeans he had left a few weeks back.

He shakes them out and puts them on. He heads to the kitchen. He needs to remove all traces of this horrible scent. He finds its location with ease. Melisa must have touched the wall touchscreen after helping the man. He grabs a sprayer and cloth and cleans the screen.

Once he is done, he realizes what he has been doing. This primal need to do what he did, makes him wonder. Why would he be so affected by this blood? He has never felt like this before in his life. Now that no trace is left, he wonders if he should have kept something, maybe shown it to his father.

That thought passes quickly. There is no way he would go to his father for help. That would be the last thing he should do. Knowing his father, even if he had no idea about what the causes were, he would make something up. Bring up the old days. Explain to him that he needs to learn more about his heritage. Just a whole bunch of bullshit.

Chris debates following Melisa to see the man, this John Doe that she is so hung up on. But from what she told him about his weakness, he isn't someone he should be worried about. He is just a vagabond who was filthy beyond anything he ever heard of. Melisa is a strong woman; that's why he chose her.

CHAPTER FOUR

John had to wait close to an hour for Mr. Hudson to pay him. But, it was worth the wait. Mr. Hudson was able to come up with the ten thousand dollars he had offered. Mr. Hudson would not give the money until John accepted the fact he must never tell a soul he was involved. He also warned of the consequences, from a legal standpoint, on John's actions leading up to that moment. Griffith Park being owned by the city, he would lose his claim to the dagger, and then be charged with theft. Mr. Hudson promised that John would be the only one in any trouble.

The sun overhead, John sits at a red light. Full of emotion, he looks up through his sun roof, basking in the sun's radiance. A loud horn blasts him, making him focus back on the task at hand. Driving down Victory Boulevard in Burbank, he looks out at all the shops and people. He's not really taking them in; his mind is checking off all the bills he is going to pay off and in what order.

Rent is two months late, so that's thirty-two hundred. Phone another hundred. Electrical is good, but he has to pay up on his gas. Thinking back to the last time he was in such a position, he remembers that he promised to leave if he ever got the money to do so. He could pay the bills, leaving him with six thousand, or he could do as he had pledged himself.

A smirk appears. *Fuck paying those bills. I'm leaving and will never come back. They can suck my dick*, he tells himself. "I'm out of here," he hollers out the window as he drives through the city. Someone on the streets screams back,

"Good riddance," causing John to laugh. *Yup, fuck this city,* he confirms to himself.

He pulls up to his apartment driveway and stops at the gate. He has to get out of his car, leaving it running. He walks patiently from left to right in front of the gate, squeezing the little black garage clicker on its corners, pushing the gray button with different pressure until it finally starts to roll. He rushes back into his car and drives through. Tossing the remote into the center console, he lets out a laugh. "Oh yeah . . . I am so out of here," he guffaws.

Standing at his opened front door, he takes in the surroundings of his small, one-bedroom apartment. The main area holds his dining table, covered with papers and books. A small couch faces a sixty-inch TV, and a coffee table is covered with leftover food wrappers from Del Taco, Tommy's, El Pollo Loco, and other miscellaneous food locations. Lips tightened, he shakes his head in disbelief. *What has become of me?* he thinks, looking at the mess he has been ignoring for way too long. Dropping his keys on the small corner table by the door, he heads to the kitchen to the left. Pulling out a box of large brown heavy-duty bags, he takes one out and holds it open at the end of the coffee table. "Jesus," he says aloud, as he begins to clear the littered table.

He picks up paper cups with liquid still in them, wrappers of whatever fast food he decided to have with food still in it. The smell from the greasy fast-food leftovers wafts into his nostrils, causing him to cry out in disappointment for his choices. Papers and receipts from who knows what, add to the chaos. The mess is overwhelming. "Fuck this," he says and shoves everything off the table into the bag with one swipe. One of the papers manages to miss the bag and lands on the floor.

John picks up the paper and reads it with a smirk.

September 16, 2016

John Sullivan

8845 Laurel Street

Burbank, CA, 91505

Dear John:

We appreciate that you took the time to apply for the position of Lead Game developer with our company. We received applications from many people. After reviewing your submitted application materials, we have decided that we will not offer you an interview. We appreciate that you are interested in our company. Please do apply again in the future should you see a job posting for which you qualify. Again, thank you for applying. We wish you all the best.

Regards,

Human Resources Staff Signature

Yeah, I'll be doing that, he teases himself. With even more ammunition he tirelessly goes through his house and cleans every room. He is so singularly focused he doesn't even notice that he has missed a few calls. He doesn't stop his enthusiastic cleaning until a sudden knock on the door startles him.

Opening the door, he is surprised to see Bernadette. "Where the hell have you . . ." She stops herself. Looking past him, her eyes widen. "What the shit?" she lets out and enters without asking. "What's going on here?" she asks.

"Come on in, why don't you," he taunts and closes the door.

"I've been calling, but I can see why you have not been answering. I don't think I've ever seen this place so clean," she comments.

"Yeah, thought it was time," he says. He can't help but look her up and down. Her tan cheeks are flushed, and her forehead is reddened. Her brunette hair is tied in a ponytail. Her tight-fitting workout capris and darkened sports bra show perspiration areas. Her nipples pushing through the bra and the thin material of the capris around her crotch and butt leave little to the imagination.

"Really?" she scoffs. "And what brought this on?" She turns to him, catching him staring at her ass. Rolling her eyes, she asks, "So what's going on, John?"

"What do you mean?" he replies and walks to the kitchen. "Would you like some water?" he offers.

"Yeah, thanks."

"Are you coming from the gym?" he calls from the kitchen, perfectly aware of where she had been.

"I didn't even finish. Cause I had to come here, since you wouldn't pick up your phone."

"Why?" he asks, confused, coming back into the living room carrying a can of pop, as he likes to call it, and a glass of water for Bernadette.

"I'm assuming you haven't been watching the news," she replies and turns on his TV. "Do you get headaches from being so close to this thing?" she asks. "Why would you even buy such a large TV?"

"I got it on special, plus it's great for work."

"Did you find a job?" she asks excitedly.

"No, but once I do," he adds.

"Jesus, John, you need to get your shit together."

"Hey, look around. I am," he states.

"A little cleanup is a good start. But that is nothing when it comes to you missing your rent because you bought a huge TV and a video game system," she points out.

"I've sold off enough of my things, okay," he says. "Why do you always have to challenge my choices?"

"Yeah? Like what? The things people give you as gifts?" she argues. "What happened to your dad's watch?" she adds with spite. "That was a good choice."

"Thanks for that," he says gruffly and hands her the glass of water, which she just places on the table, not drinking it. He takes a seat in his arm chair, pulling the foot rest up and rocking back. He swings his feet back and forth like a child. He taps on the top of the can before he opens it.

"I didn't mean that, it's just ridiculous that you have such a large TV in such a small apartment, and you are always low on funds. I mean, maybe if you didn't spend your money on shit like this you wouldn't be in the situation you're in," she states indifferently, still flipping through the channels

"Thanks for the pep talk. So what are you doing here? I really don't need any more advice right now. I got a lot to do before . . ." He stops himself. Bernadette didn't miss his sudden break.

"Before what?" She looks around, taking in all the trash bags and things being sorted. "You leaving?"

"Maybe," he smiles.

"Well, not before we take care of something." She points to the TV. She has found what she was looking for. The headline reads "Mysterious mine found in Griffith Park."

"Yeah, what about it?"

"What about it?" she yells at him. "Maybe the fact you stole that fucking knife. It's all over the news that they know people have been ransacking the cave and they are investigating it."

"So?"

"Um, what do you think will happen if they find out we took that stupid knife?"

"How could they? That's ridiculous."

"I don't think so. They said they have investigators taking shoe prints and asking for those who have been inside to come forward. They have already said they won't prosecute anyone who comes forward, but those who do not will be charged with grand theft."

"Please, B, you really think they can find us? It's not C.S.I. They're just trying to scare people." He takes a big gulp of his soda.

"Well, it's scaring me. Where is the knife? I want to take it in."

"I don't have it."

"What?"

"Yeah, I sold it."

"You did what?" She throws the remote on the couch.

"I sold it."

"Well, you better get it back."

"Can't do that."

"How much did you get?"

"I got three, three hundred dollars," he states, taking another drink.

Bernadette, watching his every move, takes a seat on the sofa, placing her hand on her forehead. "Are you fucking kidding me?"

"No, sorry. I was going to tell you, and give you your half."

"My half? What the fuck, man. You think I need a hundred and fifty bucks?" she moves her hands, cradling her face. "I don't believe you," she states, muffled by her hands. "I swear; you better not be getting me in trouble." She leans back on the couch, looking up at the ceiling in disbelief.

"Look, the man I sold it to will not tell anyone where he got it."

"How do you know that? How do you know that, John?" she repeats herself.

"He was a good man."

"A good man at a pawn shop, that's rich."

"He wasn't at a pawn shop. It was an antiques dealer," he states proudly.

"And he didn't want to know where you found the knife?"

"Well, yes of course, he did. But he doesn't care. I'm telling you," he says, trying to convince her.

"Did you tell him about me?" she asks. Watching John closely, she knows his every tic. He squirms for a second before shaking his head no. Had she not been watching so closely, she would have missed it. "You fucker," she calls out. "I knew I should never have gone with you."

"What does that mean?"

"Nothing." She doesn't want to point out any more of his flaws.

"B, you know how much I like you. Why are you being so mean?"

"John, you don't like me. You like the idea of me."

"That's not true. Look, I'm going to be selling off the rest of my stuff. Then I'll have enough money to do things again. Maybe we could . . ."

"Stop right there, John. There is no we. I've gone out with you once, and it was a long time ago. We are just friends."

"Wow, are you fucking serious?" John replies, angered by her words.

"John. You really have no idea how to be a friend, let alone a boyfriend."

"B, why are you being this way?"

"Because you got me mixed up in your bullshit. Now this antiques dealer knows that I was with you. When I should never have been there." She lets out a frustrated groan.

"Look, he is trustworthy. I promise. Now please, take your share." He tries to give her the little fold of money. Bernadette knocks the bills away and gets up.

"You're such a dick," she says, shaking her head and rushing for the door. She sees that he is only hearing half of what she is saying to him. John quickly beats her to the door, holding it closed.

"I'm sorry, I promise they will not be able to find us. It's not like there were cameras. And I didn't see anyone else on the hill at the time," he says, trying to soothe her.

"Let go of the door, John."

"Are you going to tell anyone?"

"No, and I'm also not going to talk to you again either." She pulls the door, striking John with it. He watches her walk down the exterior hall to the stairs, then leans over the balcony to watch her leave the main entrance. Looking up at the sky, he notices that the sun is almost down. He hadn't expected to spend so much time cleaning.

He shrugs his shoulders and goes back inside to watch the news program. "Archeologists are still puzzled by the cave. They are not letting us in yet, but have told us that they don't believe the cave is a temple, as was reported earlier," the news reporter explains. "I have the young man who found the cave earlier today. Rudolph, can you tell us what you saw?" The female newscaster interviews a heavy-set young man, wearing a yellow Laker's jersey over a white tee shirt who's grinning ear to ear.

"Oh man, it was amazing. I took a whole bunch of pictures but the rangers have my phone right now. It's all good though because I posted a bunch on my Instagram page: @rudeoff323 is my handle. Check them out and all the other cool stuff I got on there," he states, giggling.

"Why don't you explain what people should expect when they check out your page," she goads him.

"Oh yeah, well. You know, there were all these cave drawings or paintings, I'm not sure what they are called. But, there were a lot. Then I saw some books on the floor, and even a throne. Like from a movie or something. A lot of old pots and I don't know what they are called, maybe jugs. Things for water, I guess," he continues, laughing at his ignorance.

"Goodness, how exciting." She turns back to the camera. "Well there you go, @rudeoff323 on Instagram can give you some close-ups of what's in the cave." Turning to the young man, she smiles and says, "Thank you Rudolph for sharing with us today. I'm sure you'll have a lot of new followers after tonight."

"Go Lakers!" the kid screams.

John turns off the TV. *Why didn't they talk about the man?* he wonders. Reaching for his laptop, he goes to the young man's Instagram page. Going through twenty of his pictures, he finally sees one of the chair. It's empty. The kid even takes a few on it. "That is not cool," he murmurs. Closing the lid of his laptop he looks blankly in the direction of his TV, his head cocked to the side.

Opening his computer again, he types "The Knights Prosperitas" and starts a search. The information that comes back has nothing to do with what the old man had told him. It's all investment firms and other types of businesses. There is nothing even close to the same name. Pulling out his phone, he looks for the image of the blade. He finds what he needs, the marking of the deer with the cross.

He types in a new search: "Saint Eustace." The search comes back with tons of information. Scrolling through, he refines his search, "Eustace blade," which offers a few images. One image in particular really catches his attention. It's an engraving by "Albrecht Dürer"—he butchers the name as he reads it aloud. Saving the image, he opens his photo editing software. He amplifies the image and inhales deeply. "You got to be kidding," he squeals. "That is too crazy." The details of the blade on the painting are so similar to those that were on the dagger he found that he can't control himself. *Did that old man tell me the truth, or did he actually understate the importance of this blade?* he wonders.

Biting his lip, he closes the computer. Looking at his phone, he contemplates calling the old man and telling him off. But, did the old man lie? He weighs out what happened. He told him that it was worth a lot of money, and he also didn't really want to buy it. John admits that he pushed him to buy it. Or did he? He begins to suspect that the old man may have played him.

But, if he wanted to play him, he could have just told him it was worth a lot of money, but he would pay only a small amount. He did point out he wasn't a pawn shop. He begins to wonder if Bernadette was right to worry about the old man. No, the old man took care of him, John decides. And with that he continues to clean up. Grabbing the garbage bags he heads to the dumpster. Tossing the four large bags in, he lets the lid slam. "What the fuck happened to the man?" he blurts out.

CHAPTER FIVE

When Melisa arrives at the Los Angeles County Hospital in her white Audi A3, she pulls directly into the temporary parking lot. The guard on duty quickly tucks his shirt in his pants and holds his stomach a little tighter, in his mind hiding his belly flab. "Hello Dr. Castro, what brings you to the area?" he asks playfully.

"Hi," Melisa responds. She quickly looks at his badge. "How you doing, Cliff?" She greets him with a simple hand shake. "Is it okay if I park here? I should be only twenty minutes."

"Well, you know that's for pick-ups and drop-offs . . . But I think it will be okay, just this once," he smiles. "Haven't seen you around these parts in some time," he adds familiarly.

"Yeah, got to talk with Dr. Franklin. I'll be as quick as I can." She smiles, leaving him. "You are the best." The guard smiles as he watches her walk away. He can't help but check out her butt as she enters the building.

Inside, Melisa goes straight to the elevator; she doesn't even acknowledge the people working the check-in desk. She holds the door for a few people rushing to catch the elevator. Pushing for the fourth floor, she politely asks and pushes the buttons for the others who have joined her in the elevator.

There is a young girl covering her mouth with a napkin; the older woman standing next to her seems eager. "How you feeling, sweetheart?" Melisa asks.

"She has a cough and a little fever," the little old woman answers.

"Is that right? Well, you know the fever is the body's way to help fight off illness. Sometimes a fever is exactly what you need."

"Really?" The little girl looks up to the older lady. "Is that true, Grandma?"

"Sometimes, yes," she replies. The bell rings and the doors open to the fourth floor. "Feel better, sweetheart." Melisa says goodbye and exits.

Walking through the halls, she follows the signs for Neurology Center. When she enters the receptionist area, she walks right up to the admitting nurse. "Hi, I'm Dr. Castro, can you please tell Dr. Franklin that I'm here?" she asks politely.

"Oh, yes. Dr. Franklin is expecting you." The woman gets up and opens the door for her. "Do you know where his office is?" she asks.

"I do. Thank you." She walks by and through the hall passing diagrams of the brain and how it works, one of which has her name on it, "Melisa Castro, M.D, Ph.D., M.P.H.D.," with a small picture of her. She pretends not to notice it, but she knows the image so well, she couldn't miss it if she tried.

Dr. Franklin is sitting at his desk. He has short, well-kept blonde hair, an earring in his right ear, and a superior air about him. When he sees Melisa he jumps up to greet her, giving an embrace that doesn't feel genuine. He stands on tip toes to give her a kiss on her cheek. Even with her hunching down he has trouble. "Oh girl, you look fantastic," he states with a soft lisp. "There is something different about you," he adds, holding her arms out and giving her the once over.

"Nope, nothing different." Her eyes widen, as she gives off a fake laugh. *I'm not showing yet, am I? I'm only four months*, she thinks to herself. This man was the last person she would want to share such news.

"It's about time you got yourself back down here with us lowly 'County' doctors," he teases, leading her to a chair in front of his desk.

"Oh please, you would be where I am, had they offered you the job," she counters.

"Maybe, but since I'm not, I can tease you," he says, continuing in the same contemptuous tone as he walks around his desk. He takes his seat, and once seated, he appears taller than her.

"I know, Big Pharma is the devil," Melisa, says rolling her eyes and waving her hands scornfully at the thought. "But what I'm doing is for the good. And Mr. McCarthy is different; his company is different."

"Yeah, I'm sure he is the good C.E.O." The short man rolls his eyes.

"Actually, he is." Melisa hates having to defend the stigma of her profession or her boss. "I've been working on a new drug that will help millions of people with Alzheimer's."

"And cost a fortune," the doctor interrupts. "Can't wait for your reps to come and bother us."

"Actually, no. It will not. We are going to be giving this away for free."

"Bullshit," he leans back in his chair, causing it to squeak. "Free usually means the government is paying for it, which means all the tax payers are paying for it."

"No, no bullshit. Mr. McCarthy has other ways of making money. The R&D we are doing will give him insight for another project. But the actual drug we are working on will be free," she says, crossing her arms and not wanting to talk about it anymore.

"You say that now," he responds.

"Mr. McCarthy is a great man."

"I'm sure he is. I'm sure he is great in all kinds of ways," Dr. Franklin says, in a tone that is alluding to something inappropriate between her and her boss.

"Wow, jealousy is a horrible perfume," Melisa states with fire in her eyes. "Like you wouldn't have taken the job had it been offered to you," she blasts. "How many times did McCarthy decline your requests for a grant?" she asks, rising from her seat. The anger inside is something she has never felt before.

"What a minute, Melisa. I was just kidding." The little man retreats, holding his hands up in peace.

"I'm sorry. I, I don't know what came over me." She closes her eyes, calming herself. "I guess, I'm just tired of all the accusations. This hatred for what I'm doing, based on what others are doing is getting tiresome."

"Hey girl, it was me. I'm sorry. I went too far." He gives off a fake laugh.

"Why is it that when a woman gets ahead there's always someone to demean or discredit her by saying she must be sleeping with the person in charge, reducing all women to whores, who use sex as leverage. Why is it never assumed it's due to a woman's merit?" She can't help herself.

"Wait a sec, I wasn't saying that at all,"

"I bet you weren't," she says and rolls her eyes.

"So, you here for that John Doe?" He quickly changes the conversation.

"Yes. How is he?" she asks, her tone returning to normal, everything that had just transpired gone from her mind. This little man in front of her is of no consequence. The John Doe is her number one priority.

"Honestly, I do not know how to answer that question," he responds, motioning for her to take a seat.

"Really?" Her eyebrows are raised. "What did you get from the scan?"

"We didn't do a scan."

"Why not?" she takes a seat. "He had blood coming out from his ears, and loud sounds intensely affected him," she adds, deep in her own thoughts.

"Yes, they cleaned the blood. Had to clean his whole body actually . . . That's where things get weird."

"Weird?" She takes two deep breaths. "Please elaborate, Doctor."

"We couldn't find anything wrong with him," he explains. "None of the exams gave me any insight to what caused the bleeding. His ears were clear; all the dried blood was external. He didn't have any issues with lights, sounds, or anything else." He pauses for a moment, looking for the right words. "He is without memory, but from what I can tell it's not from any head trauma. He seems to be in perfect health, Melisa."

"How peculiar. Is he able to communicate?" she asks.

"Yes." He smirks as if he has a secret.

"His motor skills?"

"The man is fine."

"What do you mean?" She curls her lip. "Are we talking about the same man?"

"I sure hope so."

"Stranger and stranger," she says and shakes her head. "Can I see him?" she asks, getting up expectantly.

"Of course. Are you still planning to transfer him to your center?" Dr.

Franklin asks, getting up from his chair. *That's it.* He is angry that she is transferring the patient, she realizes.

Melisa slowly follows the doctor, peering past him over his head. The doctor offers for her to go in first. She rounds the door peeking in first. The man is not at all how she remembers him. This is a very strange feeling for her. She never talks about it, but her photographic memory is her most cherished ability. Slanting her head slightly, she looks the man over. He is looking away out the large window. He is tan, and his skin looks smooth and clear of blemishes. *Did the dirt that covered his body make him look the way I remember?* she wonders.

His arms are restrained; she looks at Dr. Franklin. "We had a little trouble when doing some of the tests," he tells her.

The man's body fills out his gown; his shoulders are wide, nothing like the boney man who she held. His chest pushes the fabric out with clock-like rhythm. "So how are you feeling?" Dr. Franklin asks the man, breaking Melisa's trance.

The man turns to the doctor in a slow, smooth motion. "I'm quite well, Doctor," he answers in perfect English, but with an elegant Spanish accent. Looking at his face, she can't help but gasp. Noticing Melisa, the man tries to straighten himself up. His cheeks begin to flush and it pains him not to be able to hide it so he turns his focus back to the window.

"You speak English?" Melisa blurts out. The man turns to her. Their eyes lock, and if not for the color and detail of them, she would not believe him to be the same man.

"I do, forgive me. I am not able to stand to greet you," he states, blushing.

"It's okay. Do you remember me?" she asks. Dr. Franklin is taken aback by her inquiry.

The man looks her up and down. "I am sorry, but I do not," he informs her.

"You were at my house; you spoke to me," she tells him and walks closer to him. She can't take her eyes off his.

"Please, your forgiveness. I have been given many a medicine; I am not that clear right now." He smiles. Melisa looks at Dr. Franklin and motions with her head to join her outside the room.

"What the hell?" she asks.

"What?" Dr. Franklin says, showing his confusion.

"That man did not look like that this morning."

"What can I say, you already forgot how good we are here at County," he teases.

"Oh please, that's not what I'm talking about. That man is noticeably heavier than when he was at my house. Was he weighed when he was admitted?" she asks, keeping her voice low, but showing her anger.

"Of course." He hands her the tablet with the patient's digital chart.

"One hundred fifty." She looks up at the doctor, then peeks her head back into the man's room. "Does he look like he only weighs one hundred and fifty pounds?" she asks rhetorically. Dr. Franklin looks at the information, befuddled.

"How odd. This must be a mistake," he replies, his mind trying to figure out what is going on.

"I don't think so; that man didn't even look to be one hundred pounds when I saw him this morning. So if he gained fifty pounds by the time he arrived here and now he looks, geez, what do you think, hundred eighty, maybe even ninety?"

"He looks extremely fit. I would guess he is up there, yes."

"How could this be?" Looking at the tablet, she checks for blood work results. "How odd. He is in perfect condition." She's talking to herself, as Dr. Franklin smirks.

"Weird, right?" Dr. Franklin smirks and glares at Melisa.

"Yes, weird," she says, rolling her eyes. Pulling out her cell phone she calls her hospital. "I'm going to have him transferred right away," she informs Dr. Franklin. She walks away from the man's room. Dr. Franklin returns to the man's room.

"It looks like you will be moved to a new hospital," he tells the man.

"Hospital? Or are you taking me to be judged?" the man asks. Dr. Franklin doesn't understand what he means by being judged.

"It's a special hospital that will be better equipped to help. You are not in any trouble, that I know of," the doctor tries to reassure him.

"The woman seems to be uncomfortable with me," the man says, looking at the door.

"Dr. Castro can sometimes come off that way," he says and smiles.

"Doctor? A woman doctor?" he asks, causing Dr. Franklin to laugh.

"Yeah, I don't know what they were thinking when they allowed a woman to be a doctor," he says and covers his mouth, still laughing.

"You're mocking me?" The other man tightens his eyes.

"I'm sorry, I just would have loved for you to have asked that question in front of her."

"I meant no offense, sir. I would rather not have her thinking I have disfavored her."

"It's okay, I won't tell her what you said." He is trying to control his giggles just as Melisa walks back in the room.

"What who said?" she asks.

"Oh nothing, our friend here just needed some clarification as to what your role is." The man's eyes grow large. "He thought I was in charge, but I've informed him you are now," the doctor adds, relieving the man.

"Oh, yes. Thank you. So the transfer will happen within the hour," she tells Dr. Franklin. Turning to the man, she says, "I'm going to be your doctor from now on. I have a transport coming up to help. Now you are restrained and I'm sorry, but we will be keeping you that way until we get you to our facility."

The man looks down at the leather straps around his wrists. "I am no danger to you, miss." He pauses. "Miss Castro, if I heard correctly," he adds.

"Dr. Castro, or Melisa if it's easier for you," she tells him with a smile.

"I will be no trouble. If the restraints, as you call them, are needed, I will not protest," he comforts her.

"Dr. Franklin, could you give us a moment?" she asks, not turning to him. "I would like to do a little exam, and if you don't mind, some privacy."

"Of course." Dr. Franklin leaves. Melisa waits for him to leave before she begins her examination. With her hands she guides the patient to raise up, so she has access to his back.

"I'm sorry if this is cold," she tells him trying to use her breath to warm the shining metal of the stethoscope before she places it on his back under his gown. As she listens, his lungs sound perfect. No signs of fluid retention. Checking around for other abnormalities, she finds him to be in perfect health. "I need to check your chest; I mean heart," she tells him.

Having him lay back, her hands are shaking with anticipation. She doesn't know what she really expects or even hopes to see. Holding her breath. She pulls his gown forward, exposing his chest. Letting out the air, she sees the scars.

She again uses the stethoscope, listening in on his heart. His beats are in perfect rhythm. The hard beats are solid and slow. Focused on his scars, she craftily touches them, hoping for something to happen, but nothing does. "How does your chest feel?" she asks.

"My chest feels normal, Doctor." Intrigued, the man watches as she works. Melisa tries not to look into his eyes. "So, what does Chel mean?"

"Chel?" the man repeats, looking away in thought.

"Yes, you called me by that name, twice."

"I'm sorry. But I do not have any recollection of such a name or interaction." He locks eyes with her. Again guiding him to move, she starts to examine his head.

"Tell me if you feel any pain."

"Your touch is very soft, Miss Castro."

"Thank you, but that won't always be the case."

"I don't understand?"

"Nothing, I thought I was being clever," she smiles. The man mirrors her smile. The smile falls from his face.

"What is it?" Melisa asks.

"Tell me, how did I come to be here?"

"Has no one explained it to you?"

"The doctors enjoy hearing themselves talk; I never really had a chance to ask any questions."

"Makes sense."

"Am I in trouble?"

"No. You had a horrible fall."

"Fall?"

"Yes. You fell down a hill, onto my property."

"Your property." He looks away, trying to remember.

"Did I hurt you?"

"No."

"I'm sorry to have inconvenienced you . . ." he starts, but Melisa stops him.

"It was not your fault. I mean, we don't know why you were on the trail in the first place. And from the looks of you, you shouldn't have been."

"I wish I could remember."

"It happens. I'm sure it will come back. Head trauma is still very tricky. All I can say, you being able to speak in the matter you have been conversing with me, gives me hope." She caringly places her hand on his shoulder.

"You believe I will regain my memory?"

"I have no doubt," she says, believing her own words. "Why don't you rest? The transfer will be happening shortly."

"Miss?"

"Yes?"

"I have another question."

"Of course."

"I'm supposed to believe I am in what I have learned is a hospital. A place for healing. But, as I look around, nothing tells me familiarity. Everything is new, and strange. Is that something that will be corrected too?"

"What do you mean?" She gently squeezes his shoulder to comfort him. The man looks up to the ceiling, focusing on the lights.

"The illumination from the ceiling? How is that possible?"

"The lights?" Melisa looks up at the square, plastic-covered lights.

"Yes," he replies.

"I'm not sure of your question."

"Those lights, are not something I understand. I see bright lights and noises that are like something I have never seen before," he adds, looking down at the foot of his bed. "I feel so lost."

"Oh my, please don't." She impulsively hugs him, holding him close. "Head trauma can do many things to confuse us. Please don't think there is anything wrong. You are just hurt, and we need to get you better," she adds. Realizing that she is acting out of line, she pulls away. She had never done anything like this before. She was known for caring, but never being affectionate. The lack of control of her emotions is starting to take its toll on her.

The embrace shocks him, embarrassing him. The woman being so forward feels taboo. Then, the feeling fades and comfort and calm wash over him, and the feeling of being lost begins to leave. Looking up at her, he sees the tears in her eyes. "I'm sorry, Miss Castro."

Melisa pulls away and does her best to hide the building tears. She has never cried in front of a patient, feeling that it would be unfair to them. But with all the hormones kicking through her, she can't control it. "Why don't you lie back? Rest up. I'll see you before they transfer you."

"Will you not be with me?"

"No, I have to do a few things before I meet you at my hospital. But I won't be there much later than you." The man looks out the window and tries to close his eyes. Melisa leaves him to rest.

CHAPTER SIX

Alex, Chris's youngest brother, is sitting in the office, at Chris's desk. He stares blankly at the computer monitor, lost in thought. His short hair is cut in a design you would see on a soccer player from Europe, high and tight, with lines shaved in decoratively. His arms are resting on the desk, knuckles slightly white from holding them tight.

Muffled music can be heard rattling through the walls. His eyes slowly turn their focus on the door. He knows one of his brothers is coming in. The door opens, and Chris appears. He pauses in the doorway when he sees Alex at his desk. The music pounding behind him, now engulfs the office. Closing the door, Chris walks in suspiciously. "What's going on?" he asks his younger brother.

"Sorry bro." He quickly gets up from behind the desk. The sound of his dangling belt hits the desk. Chris focuses away from his brother as he pulls up his pants and fastens his belt. A young girl comes out from under the desk, wiping her red-colored lips. Her short dress needs to be pulled down. Her long, full-bodied blonde hair is disheveled and she runs her hands through it. Looking down, not making eye contact with Chris, she scurries out, the sound of the club blasting in as she opens the door to make her escape.

Chris waits for the door to close before he engages his brother. "So who's doing her job while she's up here?" Chris states without emotion.

"She was doing a job," Alex says, trying to make light of the situation.

"That's not funny, Alex." Chris is in no mood to deal with his childish games.

"I'm sorry, bro. I really like this one." Alex walks to the window that overlooks the club. He can see his female friend moving back behind the bar. She looks up at him and gives him a little smile, knowing he is looking down at her. Her dark eyeliner accentuates her green eyes.

"That's what you said about the last three." Chris takes a seat in his chair. "And I'm sure this one will quit soon, after you do something inappropriate."

"Oh come on bro, that's ridiculous," Alex defends himself.

"Is it?"

"I think she's a keeper. Do you think she could be a manager?" Alex asks. To Chris, the request is out of left field.

"She's only been here for two months. She's not even past her probation." Chris's eyebrows rise at the thought.

"But you can't deny she's good at her job?"

"What job are you talking about?" Chris chuckles at his play on words, but instantly regrets giving Alex the opening to continue his vulgar communication.

"Come on Chris, just give her a chance. I already talked to Vincent and Greg about it."

"What?"

"Yeah, they said it wasn't a bad idea."

"They did, did they?"

"Of course."

"And who told you, you could speak to them about such things?"

"No one. I just . . ."

"Alex. No!"

"Fuck you, bro." Alex hates having his idea dismissed so easily. "You've changed so much since you've got with that girl." A soft knock on the door turns their attention away from Alex's request. Chris is happy for the interruption. Dealing with Alex when he is like this can be wearing on him. The door opens, and in walks a monster of a man. His long red hair, down to his shoulders, makes him even more difficult to ignore. He wears a matching, well-kept beard. He is like a Viking warrior, fearsome to behold.

He stops at the doorway seeing he interrupted his two brothers.

"Hey Vincent, what's up?" Chris welcomes him with a smile. Vincent looks at both brothers before entering.

"Hey brother. There is someone here to see you," his booming deep voice, with its ever-present Polish accent, informs Chris. Vincent is the eldest of the seven Kosmatka brothers. He and his brother Aaron both were born in Poland. With his build and hair coloring, you would never guess him to be related to either of the other two brothers.

"Are we done here?" Chris looks at Alex, who is shocked.

"I guess," he pouts and hurries past Vincent, who moves to allow his much smaller brother to get by.

"What's his deal?" Vincent asks, walking into the office.

"I don't like you and Greg indulging him."

"I'm sorry?"

"I have enough issues with Alex. I no longer want you guys listening to his ideas. If he has something to say, he needs to speak to me. Not you."

"Oh, well, Dad . . ."

"Dad?" Chris interrupts, his eyes glaring at Vincent, who lowers his eyes looking to the floor.

"It's nothing. I'm sorry. I will do as you say." He looks up through his hair at Chris but doesn't look him in the eyes. Chris shakes his head, biting at his cheek.

"Who is asking to see me?" Chris asks as he walks to the window, looking down at the club.

"Him, the one talking with Valerie," the massive man replies, pointing down to the young woman who just moments ago was pleasuring his baby brother.

"The one with all the gangster gold on and the slicked back hair?" Chris laughs. "What does he want?"

"He wouldn't say. He tried to act tough with Aaron."

"How did that go?" Chris chuckles, knowing his elder brother, Aaron, can be short tempered.

"Greg interrupted them." Vincent looks at Chris, referring to yet another brother, the fourth brother, younger than Chris. "Want me to get him out of here?"

"Nah, I'll go find out what he wants." Chris pats him on the shoulder.

"He's not alone," Vincent warns.

"That's fine. Just keep Alex away from the area. He is sweet on Valerie."

The club is loud; Chris is bopping his head to the beat of the trip-hop groove playing. The VIPs he walks past all try to get a word with him, but he just smiles and motions to them that he'll be back around. Reaching the bar, he finds the man is saying something to Valerie, who looks intimidated by the visitor's words. Chris doesn't interrupt; he just stands behind him listening to what he is telling her.

"Listen bitch, I ain't paying for nothing in this club. You may not know who I am, but trust me when I tell you—you should watch what you say." His voice barely carries with all the noise around him.

"Valerie, you can take care of someone else." Chris has heard enough. The man quickly turns to Chris, who is smiling at him. "You wanted to talk to me?" he asks smoothly.

The man jumps and splashes his drink on his hand. "What the fuck, can't you see I have a drink?" He turns, screaming, trying to be heard.

"Sorry, I'll get you another one." Chris keeps his calm, his voice being heard without the visible effort that this angry little man needs.

"Yes you will," he says and sucks on his hand. "You Chris?" he asks, leaning in to be sure he is heard.

"I am, and who are you?" Chris makes eye contact with the bartender, nodding for her to make another drink.

"I'm here to talk to you. Let's go to your office; it's loud as fuck," he orders.

"Nah, I'm cool," Chris moves his head away from the man.

"What the fuck does that mean?" the man hollers

"Say what you got to say."

"Look man." He leans in again. "I'm here for my uncle. You know him. He has noticed your club, and he wants me to make a deal with you. So now let's go up to your office."

"Who's your uncle?"

"Vladimir Taymizyan," he says and smiles with all his teeth. Chris is unfazed by the name, which causes the man to get angry. "Do you know who he is?"

"I do, but I don't know who you are."

"I'm Victor Rees. I'm the man who can help you," he says, poking Chris's chest but quickly pulling his finger back as if he hurt it. He tries to hide his discomfort, shaking it off. Chris smiles sarcastically and looks down at the spot that he touched. Victor takes a big gulp of his drink, finishing it. "Get me another one," he says and slams the glass on the bar.

"Listen friend, I'm going to ask you to be kind to my bartenders."

"What?" Victor squares up on him. "You know who the fuck you're talking to?"

"Victor Rees," Chris says and smiles with half his lip.

"That's right, bitch. So you better watch your . . ."

Someone knocks into Victor before he can finish his statement. "I'm so sorry," the man says as he keeps Victor from falling. "Hey bro, everything okay here?" Alex appears as if out of nowhere.

"Alex. This gentleman was just letting me know some things," Chris says, showing his irritation that he has been interrupted.

"Oh yeah, what's that?" Alex asks, getting close to Victor. "What are you telling my big brother?" He has his hand placed behind Victor's neck, who is still hunched from the bump Alex gave him. "You got something to tell my brother?"

Victor pulls away, holding his shoulder from the contact. "I told him what I had to," he mumbles.

"What? I couldn't hear you," Alex says, disdainfully.

"Alex, why don't you leave us?" Chris grabs his brother's shoulder to direct him away.

Seeing people watching, Victor stands tall. "I told him what I needed to, but now I'll tell you something . . ." Alex pushes him before he can get out another word. Victor covers his face seeing Alex's hand cocked back to strike him. Chris quickly grabs Alex's arm before he throws his fist at Victor.

Alex looks back at his brother in shock. "What the fuck?"

"Go upstairs." Chris moves Alex in close. Victor, wide-eyed, looks around seeing everyone witnessing what has happened.

"Yeah, go upstairs," he mocks Alex.

"Mr. Rees, I would suggest you gather yourself, and your friends. You should leave."

"I'm not leaving till I get what I came here for," he says, standing bravely.

"Is that right?" Chris moves up close to Victor, letting go of Alex. As he looks down into the other man's eyes, the blue color changes slightly, to a whiter hue. "I will allow you to leave; you don't need to thank me. But appreciate what I'm giving you."

"And what is that?" the other man replies, still trying to act brave. Five men from the other end of the bar jump into action and surround Chris. Vincent comes up from behind the five men, towering over them. "Do we have a problem?" he growls at the men. Chris lifts his arm to his brother, telling him not to engage.

"Mr. Rees, leave," he growls. Victor trembles; looking into Chris's eyes, he sees death. Not wanting anymore action, he motions to his gang, and they leave the club. Chris glares at Alex with fire in his eyes. "You fucking idiot." He grabs his elbow. "Go upstairs," he orders. Vincent walks up to Chris. "I'm sorry, I couldn't stop him," he states worriedly.

"I'll talk with you later," Chris says and heads upstairs.

"Be easy on him. He was just defending you," Vincent calls out.

Chris opens the door to his office to find Alex sitting in his chair again. Rolling his eyes, he motions for him to get up.

"Of course," Alex laughs. "Don't tell me you're mad. Fuck that dude. He's just a punk."

"That punk is Vladimir Taymizyan's nephew."

"So?"

"So, you don't think he's going to be pissed about us knocking around his nephew?"

"Come on, that was the wack'ist of shakedowns. You really think Vladimir sent him?" He takes a seat on the small couch by the window, swinging his right leg over the arm.

"No, I don't. But that doesn't mean that we get into a fight with him. We let him act tough, give him a few drinks, and then let him go." He takes a seat behind the desk.

"But he was totally disrespecting you, disrespecting us," Alex points out.

"Yes, he did. And, yes he was. Who cares?" He starts to look at some receipts.

"Who cares?" Alex gets up. "Are you serious?"

"Did it really hurt us? No. Does it hurt us? No," Chris points out.

"Yes it does! Allowing a weakling like that to push you around shows you are weak," he says and points at his older brother.

"Being calm when someone is attacking you is not weakness."

"That's bullshit. Dad is right about you," Alex states turning to the window and looking down at the club.

"Oh, and what is he right about?"

"You are not right to be leading us," he states, turning to Chris.

"He said that?" Chris looks up at his young brother. "And you agree with him?"

"Yes," he states defiantly. Chris calmly puts the papers down on his desk. He gets up and walks slowly toward Alex. Seeing his older brother's posture change, Alex knows he has said too much.

"You know what?" Chris begins, but before Alex can move, he has grabbed him by the throat and is slamming him into the wall. "I am not weak, little brother," he whispers into his ear. His rage is real, his emotions running wild. His eyes start to tear up. "Our father is the weak one," he says through his teeth. Drool drips from his mouth. "Tell me I'm weak," he hisses, squeezing Alex's throat. His fingernails, growing, cut into Alex's throat. Chris pushes his forehead against Alex's temple.

His every breath can be felt. Alex, in pure terror, struggles to push out the words. "I'm sorry," Alex gasps. "I'm sorry," he garbles, unable to breathe. Blood is flowing out of the puncture wounds. "Brother," escapes his lips as he is about to pass out.

Vincent bursts through the door, having heard the commotion. "Chris, what are you doing?" he screams. Chris releases Alex, who collapses on the floor, retching and holding his throat, blood pooling around him as he gasps for air.

"Get up, I didn't even try to hurt you."

Vincent stands at the door contemplating his next move carefully.

"What?" Chris calls to him, daring him to attack him.

"Nothing," he states and moves to leave.

"Wait," Chris calls out. "Take him with you." He points to Alex.

Vincent offers his hand, but Alex pushes him away. His neck wounds are almost completely healed. "I don't need your help," he says before rushing out and running down to the club.

"Should I go with him?" Vincent asks

"No, let him be." Walking over to the small bar cabinet behind his desk, he grabs two glasses and a perfectly clear crystal decanter filled with a beautiful amber scotch. "Do you share his feelings?" he asks Vincent, motioning for him to close the door and join him.

"He is young," he says and sits. "You know I don't put much stock in Dad's words. But Dad can be very manipulative," Vincent adds.

"True, but his words are dangerous." Chris hands the tumbler to Vincent. "I've built all of this," he says, talking with his hands.

"I know, and so does Alex. He is just confused. He wants to believe in his father." He takes a sip. "At one time you did too," he states.

"True, but I had to grow up," Chris reminds Vincent.

"Someone needed to get us out of that shit. And you did."

"But Alex doesn't see it that way. And neither does our father," Chris points out.

"We can't do anything about Dad. But Alex just needs to be shown that . . ." Vincent, feeling like he may have directed the conversation in the wrong direction, stops his speech.

"Maybe," Chris says, looking through Vincent.

"I'm going to check on Alex." Vincent gets up from his chair and heads for the door. "You okay?" he asks Chris, holding the door open.

"Fine," Chris answers, showing no emotion. Vincent closes the door.

Chris sits there thinking. After a few moments he gets up, grabs his keys and leaves.

CHAPTER SEVEN

The Neurology Center of Los Angeles has a large campus. The main building is known as McCarthy Hall. The man Melisa had transferred is on the sixteenth floor of the building. It took just over an hour to get him transferred. Normally, she works out of the Pacific wing, research and development, which is in another building. But, wanting to be closer to the John Doe, she was able to borrow an office down the hall from the man's room. The view from the office she is using is spectacular. She can see the Hollywood sign and the Griffith Observatory both lit up beautifully.

She has only been in the office twice since she borrowed it. The rest of the time, she's been busy working with patients. The reason for bringing the John Doe to her facility, was the belief she could take better care of him. She was able to get the needed tests done immediately upon his admission to the hospital. All of which came back clear. She knew that if County would have done the tests, it would have taken a few days; here, she can get results back the same day.

They did a TCD, a non-invasive test for visualizing blood flow in the blood vessels of the brain. Usually it's reserved for those who have had a stroke. But with the memory loss, she thought it may help identify something. It didn't, other than inform her that the man has perfect blood flow.

She tried an electroencephalogram, or EEG, a machine that records brainwaves; it was normal. All that is left is the CAT scan. But, with how busy they were, she had to keep moving him down the queue based on the list of cases being triaged. Melisa wanted to move him to the front of the line, but knew that with the status of his current condition being stable, she had no right.

There was a young boy, a toddler. Melisa has been spending lots of time with him. When he came in, he was dazed, throwing up, and inconsolable. His parents had no idea what happened to him. All they knew was he came in the house crying, holding his head. Then as the day went on, his symptoms worsened.

Waiting for the results of the boy's CAT-scan, she sits looking out the window of the borrowed office. Thinking back to the John Doe, she looks toward the hills near her home. Where had he come from? Over the past several hours they have had many conversations. She had asked him why he told her she was not evil. The words triggered a memory and he was then able to remember their first interaction. He couldn't answer as many questions as she would have liked, but they were able to clear a few things up. He couldn't remember what he spoke of, only that he was in immense pain. He remembered that when he saw her, he felt safe. He felt stronger.

When he noticed a red mark on her arm, he apologized. He remembered grabbing her, but could not remember why. Melisa felt the need to assure him she was okay. She couldn't understand her actions. But she continued to forgive the man, withholding any grudge toward or fear of him.

When she told him that, he asked, "What did you do?" though he couldn't remember why he had said that to her. Each time they had spoken, Melisa found herself enjoying his mannerisms and tone. All of her worries for the man, the vision she saw, were fading away. When she ordered for his restraints to be removed, some of the other doctors challenged her. But, she knew this man wasn't going to hurt her. The poor man has been through so much. His demeanor with her never changes. He is always happy to see her. Even after so many hours, he still is willing to go through all the tests she wants done on him.

A man appears in the reflection of the window, a man only standing five foot eight but acting like he was well over six feet. "Mr. McCarthy?" Melisa turns around. "Good evening."

"I see; this is how you take a day off?" He gives her a quick wink, grinning from ear to ear.

"I'm sorry sir, but I just couldn't allow for this poor man . . ." He stops her, shaking his hand in front of his lips. "I just felt a need to help. What are the odds he lands on my property, a doctor who specializes in head trauma?"

"I would say low." He pauses for a moment. "Probably even lower when you consider he lands on the door steps of the best in the country," he adds.

"I don't know about that," she says and looks away and down at her desk.

"I do." He smiles and walks in, taking a seat across from her. "So, why don't you bring me up to speed?"

"Well, I truly don't know how. I'm still baffled by all this. If you would have seen him this morning, you would have thought he would have been dead by now. Instead, he seems to be in the best possible shape of any man I've met before."

"Well, first off, that's not possible. I've met your fiancé," he teases. "And, if I'm not being too presumptuous, I'm in pretty good shape too, for my age, of course." He laughs, getting a smile from Melisa. She would never tell him, but she had noticed Mr. McCarthy's younger man's physique.

"Chris is in fantastic shape." She grins wider.

"Have I told you how happy I am I was able to introduce you two?" He pauses. "How is the build out going? I haven't had a chance to see the bar," he adds, referring to Chris's new project that is being put in one of Mr. McCarthy's high-rises. Mr. McCarthy has property all over the city, and across the country.

"It's going well. He had a meeting there today," she says and smiles with pride.

"That's wonderful. I'm always so impressed with his work ethic. I remember meeting him at his first bar. It says a lot when an owner is working behind the bar."

"He is a workhorse."

"That's why we started using him for all our functions. He sure knows how to get people to have a good time. He's always the one to get a party started," Mr. McCarthy chuckles

"Yes, and that's how I met him. At one of your spectacular parties," Melisa says and waves her hands around sarcastically.

"You don't like my parties?"

"I just don't fit in. So I guess no, I don't."

"That's funny. I always assumed. But lately, I've noticed a change. Chris seems to have brought out your inner socialite."

"How do you mean?" Melisa's eyes widen at the thought.

"Well . . . The last party, you seemed to be enjoying yourself."

"I guess you can say he has changed me for the better, and I would like to say I've done the same for him."

"You see, there it is. That's why I'm so happy I was involved in setting you guys up." Mr. McCarthy claps his hands.

"I'm not going to say thank you again," she adds, with a dismissive smile. Her eyes, tight and worried, glance back at the tablet's screen. Mr. McCarthy takes notice as her hands tighten around the device, telling him more. He leans over to see what she is looking at.

"Anything I could be of help with?" he asks. Her phone rings, and she picks it up without excusing herself from her conversation with Mr. McCarthy. Her eyes widen, as a nurse informs her the boy has gone into a coma. Melisa rushes out of the room. Mr. McCarthy says something to her, but it's just white noise to her.

Melisa rushes into the boy's room. A nurse and another doctor are working on the boy. Melisa moves in and takes over, looking down at his innocent face. "You're going to be okay, sweetheart," she whispers. She places her hand on his head—in a flash, she is there: Standing on top of a washing machine. The young boy is trying to open the door to the back yard. It's something he's done many times in his short life. He loses his balance and falls to the tile floor hitting his head.

"Dr. Castro." Dr. Chan wakes her from the vision. Melisa looks at him, her hand still placed on the boy's head. "What are you doing?" he asks. Melisa has no idea how long she has been standing there. Everyone in the room is looking at her.

"I'm sorry, excuse me." She looks back at the boy. She knows where he hit his head. Without hesitation, she removes her glove and touches the spot where he hit his head. The boy's eyes open and he looks around, confused and scared. Melisa places her hand on his forehead.

"Mommy?" he asks. His panic fades as he looks at Melisa.

"It's okay, sweetheart, she's right outside. You bumped your head and I fixed it." As the words leave her lips, she can't believe what she is saying. *How did I fix it? What will my colleagues think of the words?*

"Where's my mom?" he asks, trying to get up.

"Hold on, we need to make sure you're okay." Melisa places her hand on his chest. "Can you have his mother come in?" she asks the nurse. The others in the room are speechless. Melisa, realizing what she has just done, needs to figure out how to explain her actions. Looking at Dr. Chan, she smiles. "Can we get him another CAT-scan?"

"Yes Doctor." Dr. Chan looks to the assistants confirming her order.

"What is your name, sweetheart?"

"Tommy."

"Well Tommy, no more climbing on the top of the washing machine, okay?"

"Okay." Looking away, he blushes. His mother rushes in as Melisa leaves the boy's room. Dr. Chan is close behind.

"Dr. Castro?"

"Yes."

"What was that?"

"I . . . I don't know. I just had this feeling and went with it."

"That boy, he was totally out when you came in."

"I understand that. I'm sorry, I wish I could explain. But I can't." She cleans her hands and leaves him. Melisa struggles to hold back tears. Her emotions are still running wild.

When she returns to her temporary office, Mr. McCarthy is still there. He is holding her tablet. When she enters he quickly puts it down, apologizing. "What happened?"

"Sorry, a toddler had hit his head. But he's okay now." The boy's vision still in her mind, she thinks about the John Doe. The vision she had with him. Was it as accurate?

"Fantastic."

"Yeah." She walks around her desk, her eyes focused on the tablet Mr.

McCarthy was just using.

"I thought I might be of assistance with your mystery man," he explains, giving her one of his million dollar grins, leaning back in his seat, and clasping his hands together close to his chest.

Melisa takes her seat and opens the tablet. It opens to the man's photo. She had it taken in order to put him in the missing person's data base. "He's handsome," Mr. McCarthy adds. Melisa smiles dismissively looking over his image. His hair is brown and wavy, naturally parting softly in the center. Light brown skin, much lighter than hers. Soft oval eyes of a piercing topaz staring back at her. Now she can see the light green in them. His jaw is square and his cheek bones slightly prominent, making his face a little round, but not too much. She didn't need to look at the picture to remember what he looks like.

"And, if I'm correct, this man has no memory whatsoever?" Mr. McCarthy asks. Watching McCarthy's face as he looks over the image, she sees something in him. He seems to know the man. Melisa looks into his emerald green eyes, hoping for a sign of insight. But nothing comes through.

"None, but his grammar is perfect and he speaks multiple languages."

"Really? Wow. So he's educated?" Mr. McCarthy asks.

"If I had to guess, I would say yes. Except. He doesn't know anything about our technology," she adds, looking back at the John Doe's portrait.

"Interesting. And how did you come across him?"

"He just wandered, or better, fell onto my property."

"Interesting," is all the important man has to say.

"He has a tattoo," Melisa adds.

"Tattoo?" Mr. McCarthy's knuckles turn white as he tightens his grip.

"Yes." She pulls up an image on her computer, turns it for him to view it.

"Interesting. That looks like a beer logo or something," he says.

"So, that's what I got," Melisa says and lets out a deep breath. Something is off, but she can't put her finger on it. The idea of sharing the vision or the vanished hole in the man's chest crosses her mind. She trusts Mr. McCarthy so much, but something inside won't let her say the words.

"You seem tired. Have you eaten anything?" he asks.

"No."

"That's not good. Why don't I take you to dinner downstairs? I hear they make a great meatloaf." He smiles gently. Melisa pictures the food and quickly covers her mouth; a soft burp escapes through her fingers. Her cheeks expand and she runs out of the office for the bathroom. Mr. McCarthy gets up, following to make sure she's okay. Outside of the women's restroom, McCarthy stands with his ear to the door. He gives a soft knock. "Are you okay?" He can hear her heaving heavily. "Oh dear," he mutters.

Standing guard, he asks a group of nurses to go to the other bathroom. Hearing that she is washing up, he gives the door space for her to come out without being overwhelmed. "Are you okay, my dear?" he asks, embracing her.

She softly swings her arms. "Just need a little space."

"Of course, my dear. Can I get you some water?" he offers.

"Yes, that would be nice." She walks back to the office. Mr. McCarthy watches as she walks and nods as if he knows what's going on. He enters the office with two cups, one water, the other, just ice. "I know I'm not allowed to ask, but just so you know. You don't have to feel like you need to hide anything from me," he states with concern in his eyes.

"No, everything is fine, just a little morning sickness." As the words pass her lips she closes her eyes in embarrassment.

"Oh, my!" He turns and closes the office door to give them privacy. "This whole place is all your doing." He places the recyclable cups down. "I just gave the money; you gave the passion," he adds. "You're the expert finding a solution to treat Alzheimer's," he says and then pauses. "Now we have a little one coming, how exciting," he says and smiles.

Melisa smiles, and takes the ice. "It's too early to be telling anyone," she whispers.

"Of course, but can I feel joy to be one of the first to know?" His grin is infectious.

"Please don't make a big deal." She eats a few ice chips. Mr. McCarthy then hurries to her with his arms wide. She gets up and accepts his hug. "I'm so happy for you, my dear. How did Chris take the news?"

"Well, he was excited but sometimes I wonder if his work will get in the way of what I hope we will do," she adds. "He works so late as it is. Now, with the new bar, who knows how things are going to go?"

"Well, you need to give him his due. Remember that men can sometimes surprise you when confronted with a life-altering event," he says, trying to ease her worry. "When did you find out?"

"A few weeks ago, but we got the blood work back yesterday."

"Why did you do blood work?" Mr. McCarthy asks.

"I'm no spring chicken. Women my age need to be careful, especially if it's their first child."

"Oh please, that's ridiculous. You are barely thirty, and Chris is a fine specimen. Those Polish men are made of stone. You're going to have a powerful baby . . . Do you know the sex?"

"Yeah, we're having a boy." She smiles and looks up into Mr. McCarthy's eyes.

"A boy, how exciting," Mr. McCarty says and returns her smile.

"I'm thirty-two, by the way." She feels the need to clarify.

"It's the same. You doctors are all the same. You worry about the silly things and ignore the important things. Always knowing better," he teases her.

"That's not true."

"Sure it's not." He laughs. "Well, with Chris's genes, I'm sure you'll be okay."

"You seem to give him a lot of credit. My bloodline is pretty great too," she teases back.

"So, I say we get out of here. What do you want to eat?"

"No, it's okay. I should get back to the patient. He's scheduled for his CT-scan."

"Please, you don't need to be there; allow the tech to get it done . . . I'll take you anywhere you want. It's my treat," he adds.

"Fine." She laughs softly.

"So, what will it be?" He opens his arms. "Anything at all, nothing is off limits."

"I want nachos."

"Nachos? Well, all right then," he laughs. "Do you know a good spot?"

"Nope."

"Okay, I have one that would work."

"Let's do it. But, I'm driving. I don't want to get car sick."

Mr. McCarthy directs her, taking them to a small hole-in-the-wall restaurant. "Río Dulce Guatemalan Fusion"; the bright blue and white sign illuminates the ground. Melisa smiles at Mr. McCarthy. "You know, I don't mean to be ungrateful, but I was actually hoping for some nachos, like I used to have in high school. You know, the cheese in the large can. Totally unhealthy, but oh so good."

"I'm sure they can make something like that here. This place is pretty clever."

"We'll see." She gets out of the car. Walking in, Mr. McCarthy greets the hostess, speaking to her in fluent Spanish. A small roly-poly woman comes out from the kitchen calling out to Mr. McCarthy.

"*¡Basilio! ¿Cómo estás?*" The round and joyous woman greets him with a hug. "*Es tan maravilloso ver a usted, señor*" she says, telling him how happy she is to see him. He greets her with a soft kiss on her cheek and then introduces her to Melisa.

"Melisa, this is Anna," he says, then turns around, calling her Anita.

"How beautiful," the old woman states with a wide smile. "Come, come. You can sit here." She takes Melisa to a table. "*¿De dónde eres?*" The old woman asks Melisa where she's from.

"*Los Angeles, pero mi padre es de Guatemala.*" She tells her about her father being from Guatemala.

"*¿Y a tu madre?*" Anita asks about Melisa's mother.

"Kentucky," she replies and laughs.

"I, *señor* McCarthy. She is a good one." She taps Melisa's hand. "Sit, sit," she orders.

"She is that, but she is just a colleague, Anita."

"No problem. So what can I get you?"

"Anita makes the best tamales in town," he explains to Melisa. "But, we are here for nachos."

"Nachos? You're loco, okay," she laughs. "I make nachos, you want chicken, steak. *¿Qué quieres?*" She waits for the order.

"*Solamente queso,*" Melisa answers with smile.

"*Dios*, only cheese," Anita teases. "*Basilio?*"

"Melisa, how would you feel about a Guatemalan quesadilla?"

"That's the bread one, right?"

"That is correct, and maybe some plátanos."

"That sounds okay," she answers. The older woman hears and doesn't need anyone to say anything else. She heads off to the kitchen. A young woman drops off some water, some chips with salsa, and a bottle of whiskey. "Geez, who do they think you are?" She crinkles her nose. "I haven't seen this since I was at my uncle's back in Morales," she says and laughs.

"I've known Anita for some time now. She is a wonderful woman. Her husband has helped me with some of my philanthropy. He will be the curator at my museum. Well, that is if we get this drug made."

"Museum?"

"Yes, it will be Central America's largest museum of Mayan culture. And it will be built in Guatemala."

"That's amazing."

"He's the man that inspired me to go after a cure. He has Alzheimer's. He was a brilliant man, but he has lost so many of his skills."

"How come I have never heard of this? We've been working together for almost two years now."

"I honestly can't answer that. I guess it was so personal, I didn't feel I should share. But now that you have shared your pregnancy, I guess I felt I could." He looks around at the framed posters hanging on the walls. They are of different landmarks and cities of Guatemala. "I had no idea you were Guatemalan." He lands his gaze on her.

"Really, how ironic you brought me to this place." She laughs and looks around the small patio. "My father is from an area near there." She points to images of Puerto Barrios. "He came here almost forty years ago."

"How interesting. And how did he meet your mother?"

"She was on vacation with her classmates after graduation. He was their taxi driver."

"How extraordinary. I'm sure it's a great story."

"Not as good as it could have been. My mother passed away six years back." She looks down at the water. "My dad hasn't been the same since."

"I'm sorry."

"It's okay. She inspires me every day." Melisa takes a sip of her water. "Well, you're going to have to drink that bottle all on your own," she says, changing the subject.

"The girl did me a favor; she brought it unopened." He points to the cap. "So since I'm not going to open it, there will be no offense." He smiles. The mood is still heavy. Melisa quickly grabs the bottle.

"Oh man, I really want to mess with you right now, Mr. McCarthy." She pretends to open the bottle, hoping to lighten the mood.

"This is a side of you I haven't had the pleasure of seeing. It's nice to see you with your hair down." He looks deep in her eyes. "Please, when we are out of the office, call me Basil."

"Oh, yeah." Melisa brings her hands close to her chest, and she instantly retreats inside herself. "I don't know if I can do that." She experiences the feeling from what people are saying about her, thinking back to Dr. Franklin's accusation.

"That's ridiculous. I know I'm your superior, but that is only in the office, and even there I never feel I'm the boss. Besides, I think I would enjoy having a person like you be my friend."

"Friend," she says under her breath.

"Yes, friend. Melisa, I could be your father. And, despite the rumors people like to spread, I'm no cradle robber. The reason you are a part of this project is because of your brain, nothing else." He leans back wiping his hands on the table top.

"I know, but sometimes . . ." she begins to explain, but Mr. McCarthy interjects.

"Look, I scoured the world to find a person with your passion and skill. If anyone thinks anything else, they can shove it," he confirms.

"Thank you, I really need to hear that," she says, letting her guard down.

"So, I know you will not be officially announcing, but just so you know, you can take as much time as you need. You have set us up with enough to go on, for some time," he informs her.

"Okay, I guess." The thought of taking time off for the baby had never come to her. The realization that she is pregnant, and all the sacrifices she will need to make, all of a sudden become real. She has been so focused on Chris, and what she needed from him, and never once has she thought about what she will be giving up.

"Did I say too much?" Mr. McCarthy asks, feeling her retreating from him.

"Oh, no. I'm sorry. It just all became so real to me."

"Well. That's going to happen a lot. I promise."

"I can't believe I've never asked. But do you have children?" She looks at him in a new light.

"Alas, no. I was married, but we never had children. I'm not allowed, I mean, I can't have children." He can't help but look down as he speaks.

"I'm sorry. It was thoughtless of me to ask in such a way."

"Don't be ridiculous. I've been all in your business. It was about time you asked something about me." He grabs the bottle off the table and cracks the cap open. "You are driving anyway," he smiles.

Melisa tries to stop him from opening it, but it's too late. "You're going to get wasted."

"No I won't, watch." He calls out to two men at the other end of the patio. "*¿Quieres un shot?*" holding the bottle up. The men smile, agreeing. He calls for the young server to bring a few glasses and he pours them all a stiff drink. The server takes the drinks over and they raise their glasses to him. "This is how I make so many friends," he winks at her. "Plus, I can handle my whiskey."

"We'll see." She rolls her eyes. Mr. McCarthy continues to share his bottle with anyone who will take a shot. He is careful not to finish the bottle too quickly before the food arrives. When it finally does, Melisa is ecstatic. The nachos are exactly what she wanted. The cheese is not from a can, but it is melted perfectly. The bananas and bread don't interest her, and luckily, don't bother her so she can enjoy her nachos.

Mr. McCarthy watches with delight as Melisa eats. She devours every single chip. He sips on his whiskey and doesn't take a bite of his food. She looks up; cheese is stuck to the side of her cheek. Mr. McCarthy tells her about it and hands her a napkin. "What about your food?" she asks him.

"I wasn't all that hungry, and since I'm having dessert already, no need." He sloshes around his glass.

Melisa looks at the bottle, seeing it is three quarters empty. "How you feeling?"

"Me?" he laughs. "I'm great." Anita comes out to check on them. She grabs the bottle and sees that Melisa doesn't have a glass. Quickly she calls to the server to fix the issue, but Mr. McCarthy stops her, letting her know that Melisa is not drinking.

"*¿Por qué?*" she asks why.

"I don't want any," she answers squirming in her seat.

"*¿Está embarazada?*" The old woman doesn't miss a thing.

"No, no . . ." Melisa tries to stop the woman from getting too excited. But it's too late. She leaves to the kitchen and comes back with a special drink. "*Para el bebé,*" saying it's for the baby.

"*Gracias.*" Melisa takes the glass.

"And you, Anita," Mr. McCarthy calls out. "*¿Dónde está el vaso?*" he asks, playfully stern.

"*Ay Dios mío, Espérame,*" she tells him to hold on. Coming back, she has a small shot glass. "*Dame.*" Give me, she calls out in Spanish. She puts her glass out for Mr. McCarthy to pour her a shot. "*Bendiciones.*" She gives blessings, looking up to the heavens. He is able to get her to have two shots. She sits with them for a few minutes talking about her old country and how coming to America was the best and worst thing they have ever done. She loves this country and loves being a citizen, but she misses her home. Melisa is reminded of her father. How sad he is, and that is the moment she decides she needs to get him to go back.

After the short conversation they head back to the hospital. The drive is an interesting one. Mr. McCarthy is drunk, but acting as if he is not. Melisa does her best not to tease him about it, but it's hard since he's acting so out of character. His normally calm and charming self is now a very funny and friendly persona.

No matter how silly he gets, he never makes Melisa feel like she isn't safe with him. The thoughts that he was only after one thing from her have disappeared. He just seems to be an elderly man who wants to do good by everyone. His legacy as being one of the most generous philanthropists and businessmen to live in Los Angeles is already well cemented. But she wonders if that's what he really cares about.

"Sir, I want to thank you," she states.

"For what, my dear?"

"Everything. I would still be in some hospital, dealing with the bureaucrats and all their bullshit, without your offer."

"Oh please, it wasn't that bad." He places his hand on her shoulder for a split second.

"I was just there today. And it is still the same. They didn't run a test and, I bet you, it was because they didn't want to spend the money on a homeless vagabond," she points out.

"I doubt that, Melisa."

"Why?" she asks.

"I know that things in our hospital are different, but that is only because you have more freedom. However, they still have to do whatever is necessary to help the sick and injured. You did when you were there," he points out.

"And I got hell for it. Why do you think they were so happy for me to leave?" she says.

"Be that as it may. Please understand, that it is I, who is grateful to have you with us," he says and smiles.

Melisa pulls the car into the parking lot entrance of the campus. "Are you going to get someone to pick you up, sir? I don't think you should drive home."

"Thank you, I'll be fine. I have some work to do tonight. You're not the only one who works late here," he says with a raised eyebrow. "Tonight was great. I truly hope we can have more evenings like this. And maybe you could even invite Chris."

Going around the McCarthy Hall building, they head to her parking spot. Her phone dings, telling her she has a message. Looking at the screen, it says, "Boy is doing fine. CT-Scan is clear. Obvious change from first. Would like to discuss, Dr. Chan." Melisa's eyes begin to water. The vision from the boy runs through her mind as she drives through the parking lot.

"You know . . ." Without warning, Mr. McCarthy is interrupted, as the front end of the car explodes from an impact coming from above. The whole front of the car is crushed, and shards of windshield glass spray over the two passengers. Looking out the front where the windshield should be, they are frozen by what they see.

The John Doe is lying in the middle of the crumpled hood, nude.

Grimacing in pain, he rolls over and off the front end. He stands, his arms bloody, having used the dented hood to prop himself up, and stares at both people in the car. His eyes are glowing white. He locks eyes with Melisa for what feels like an eternity. A scream from above breaks the trance and there is a loud popping noise, followed by the ping of what Melisa recognizes as the sound of a ricochet.

"Is someone shooting?" Mr. McCarthy cries out. The John Doe continues looking at her. Melisa sees that if he stays he surely will be shot, so she screams for him to run. Mr. McCarthy tells her to be quiet, causing the man to look at him. His eyes are focused on the older gentlemen. Mr. McCarthy feels the man's eyes on him filled with anger. "Run," Melisa screams. The man turns back to her and responds, moving at a speed that is impressive.

Watching the man flee, Mr. McCarthy gets out of the car. Looking up at the building, he sees the officer who was firing his gun. Shaking his head in disbelief, Mr. McCarthy watches as the officer retreats back through the busted window. Screams echo throughout the parking lot. From above, unintelligible words add to the chaotic noise.

Mr. McCarthy turns back to the car; the front end is completely destroyed. Looking in through the shattered windshield he sees Melisa is scared stiff. Her face is full of little cuts. "Are you okay?" He rushes to the other side of the car and opens her door. "I don't know why the airbags didn't go off, but I'm sure glad they didn't," he says. He helps her out of the car and guides her to take a seat on the curb. "How do you feel?" he asks with concern.

"I can't be for sure. But his eyes. I think they were glowing."

"Glowing?" he pauses. "I don't think they were," he tells her. "How do you feel?"

"Yes. Glowing white." She is trembling all over. Mr. McCarthy continues to ignore giving credence to what she saw.

"Let's get you inside. I want someone to check you out. I want to make sure everything is okay," he tells her.

"What for?" she asks, confused.

"Melisa, you were in an accident. We need to get someone to make sure you're okay," he explains. "I think you're in shock. We have to be careful with the baby."

"The baby?"

"Yes."

"That's fine. Can you grab my purse?" she asks as if nothing has happened.

"Of course." He leans her against the car and grabs her purse. He keeps her close, holding her against his right side and walks with her into the hospital.

"I need to call Walter," she states. Her head is nestled on his chest.

"Walter?" Mr. McCarthy is unfamiliar with the name.

"What?" Melisa looks up at him with confusion. "Walter?" She doesn't remember saying his name. Then it comes back. "Yeah, my brother; he's a detective, and he'll help with my car," she clarifies.

"Shouldn't we call Chris?"

"Yeah, of course. He is my fiancé."

"Okay. Let's do that. We'll call both." Mr. McCarthy continues to care for her. When they reach the elevator, it opens to the officer who fired his gun. As he passes them on Mr. McCarthy's left, he grabs the officer before he can run by. The officer instantly tries to pull away, but McCarthy holds tight. Looking him in his eyes, he brings his face close.

"You fucking idiot, you could have killed someone," he whispers through his teeth. "I'll make sure you never work in this field again." He pushes the officer away. Mr. McCarthy doesn't give the officer a second look. He returns his attention to Melisa. "Let's go, dear," he says, almost fatherly.

CHAPTER EIGHT

Halfway up the Coolidge trail, in Griffith Park, a man stands outside the cave John Sullivan spoke about. He wears a zipped-up leather jacket, the round neck snap-tab collar buttoned tight around his pale throat. His eyes are covered by black-lensed sunglasses with silver rims. Black leather side guards make it impossible to see in.

The dark eyewear doesn't affect his ability to navigate in the dark. He enjoys the dark and works best in it. When he first arrived, the whole area was illuminated by work lights. The crew that was working the scene had already called it a night, but it was still being guarded by a couple of officers.

He was quiet in the way he dispatched the two guards. He didn't kill them, but made sure they wouldn't be interfering while he did what he had to do. They didn't put up much of a fight. This is surprising, since they were more than just rent-a-cops, or park rangers. They were actual LAPD.

Facing out over the city of Los Angeles, he smirks. "Oh L.A., how I hate you," he calls out in his thick Scottish accent. Turning to the cave, he enters, stepping over the two men. His shallow breath can be seen in the cold night air.

The cave has police tape up as a warning to keep out. Feeling around the edges of the entrance, he finds a heavy lock of sorts. The main body of the unit is absent. Looking around on the floor, he finds the missing piece. He picks it up. With a quick sniff, he picks up the scent of who or what broke the latch. He feels for the other three locks, finding them in the same shape.

He smiles, looking at the destruction the boulder that was once blocking the entrance has made. He had hoped that when he arrived, he'd find that this was a just a simple accident. But now he is certain; this was done to serve a purpose. But what? He is at a loss. Continuing his investigation, he heads inside.

One arm stretched out, his fingertips rub along the walls as he makes his way down the corridor. A smirk appears on his face as he smears the chalk cave art. *Someone else had their paws on the wall,* he feels with his sensitive fingertips. He whistles, and the echo travels ahead as he strolls along the cave. He reaches a large opening, a room of some kind. A large cathedra sits in the middle. The arm rest has rusty metal shackles with spikes attached. Touching the cathedra, he notes that the restraints are intact. His smile fades.

Everything about the scene gives him pause. How can the restraints be still locked and yet so clean? They are made to hold captives, and when they try to move, the sharp nails puncture the skin. There should be flesh and blood. But, there is nothing. Not one sign that anyone has been locked away here. He was not released, yet he has fled? The man in the leather jacket can't wrap his head around what has happened.

He replaces a look of contemplation with a sinister grin. "So where did you head off to?" he asks. Standing near the throne, he turns in a circle tasting the air, taking everything in. The one who broke the locks at the front of the cave, he came in alone. His lingering scent is much more faded than the rest. The beast stood where the man in the leather jacket is now. Touching the cathedra, he knows the beast did not touch it.

He counts six humans having been in the tomb. All but one has touched the wood and the restraints, some more vigorously than others. Looking down at the shoe marks in the dirt, he finds something interesting. Someone had knelt at the chair. A mound of dirt tells him more. Someone used force from their placed knee. This someone took out the blade. He traces the shoe with his index finger, memorizing everything about it. Bringing his fingers to his lips and tasting, he grins, says, "I got you." Getting up, he slaps the dirt from his hands.

He is relieved, but not excited about his findings. Whoever released the Hunter, had no idea what they were doing. Unless, they worked for the one who opened the tomb. *Has someone tricked some simple humans into unleashing one of the great terrors?* he wonders. That is something he will deal with after he does what he came to do.

"Now, back to my old friend," he says and forces a laugh. He continues on, deeper into the cave. There is a large, smooth, single piece of stone. "Interesting." He examines the stone. The stone is covered in dirt and dust, and there are finger marks on its edges. He grabs the slate from both sides, his long arms stretching wide in order to do so. With the force of an earthmover, he slides the massive stone to the left. The deafening scraping of the dense stone breaching along its channel doesn't bother the man.

He moves it to its carved stoppers, revealing another room. In the center is a pulpit, the wood still in immaculate condition. Placing his hands on the sides, he stands in front of the podium. Opposite to the man in the leather jacket hangs a large wooden crucifix. He nods at the sculpture, giving it respect. The walls are lined with bookcases, filled with old books and scrolls. He runs his finger along the lectern's podium top. The dust outlines where a book was.

"This is not good." He stands, confused. He walks around the small room, running his finger along the books, seeing that they have not been disturbed. "How odd." He stands, turning in a slow circle. Applying his thumb to his index finger, he cleans all the dust it has gathered.

Returning to the pulpit, he investigates the area. A single strand of hair lies where the book should be. "Who would do such a thing?" he asks. Kneeling, he bows his head. "Forgive me, Father, but this time I must kill your child." He raises his right hand up to his face, then down to his chest, and then across his heart, making a cross, ending with a kiss to his hand.

Getting back to his feet, he lights a package of matches. "I'm sorry," he says, then throws the matches onto the books in the bookcase and leaves the room. He doesn't shut the door to the room, fearing that the flame may become a danger once someone finds the room and opens it again. Once again whistling, he calmly leaves the cave.

Once outside, he grabs the two men, who are still out cold. "Sorry, lads." He pulls them far enough away not to be hurt by the flames should they reach the cave entrance. He looks down at the ground. Seeing the hundreds of footprints, he takes in a deep breath. He finds it, the set he needs. He stoops and picks up another scent. Looking around, he tries to find it. Walking to the boulder, he sees another strand of hair. Taking a deep breath, he is puzzled by the scent. But it's familiar. He puts the hair in his jacket.

Taking another deep breath, he shakes his head. "Where are you?" Seeing a set of bare footprints, he tries to gain some information from them, but he cannot. "I hate that about you." He gets up. Looking in both directions, he sees that the barefoot prints do not go any further than where he stands.

Returning to focusing on the first scent, he is directed down the hill. There he finds the spot where the car that the person drove was parked. Six cars have been parked in the same spot. The man in the leather jacket shakes his head. "This could take forever," he says and twitches his nose. "Who has awoken you, my friend?"

This person has the blade. *What is he going to do with it?* he wonders. *What would any normal man do with a blade like this?* He begins to put together a map of where he may have gone. First, he would need to find a place that deals with such items. He knows of a few. One is near, but he would rather not speak with him, unless he truly has to.

With that, he gets into his orange GTO. The engine blares as he tears through the parking lot of the park. Driving through the park after hours, he has to stop and open the road barrier; the locks break easily with a little force from the man.

He jumps on the freeway, heading to his first destination. Making good time, he gets to Echo Park in twenty minutes. "Swords of the Past" is a large bright banner draped across the front of the shop. The shop is open till eleven, which is in two hours. Opening the door, he stands at the entrance and sniffs, looking for the scent. There are only a few customers but no sign of what he is after. The shop keeper, sitting at his desk, notices him. "Can I help you?" he asks suspiciously.

"No, thank you," the man answers. The shop keeper walks around the desk to get a better look at the suspicious man, but he is gone.

"Shoot," the mystery man lets out as he returns to his car. Frustrated, he continues on his search. He drives to a shop in Long Beach, then the Palisades, and even to Malibu, none of which give any sign of the blade. It's late, almost eleven. He knows he has one last place to go, but he truly dreads the idea of having to meet with the old man. He knows that he will be closed, which means he will have to wait till the following night.

Knowing what he must do, he goes to Mr. Hudson's shop anyway. To his surprise, the lights are still on. He peers into the shop, but Mr. Hudson is nowhere to be seen. He pulls the door open, causing the bell to ring out his entry. He reaches his hand into the shop above the door to grab the bell to stop it from ringing, which causes him immense pain. He has not been invited in.

Mr. Hudson turns slowly. A feeling comes over him. He hesitates to leave his back office, but comes out to find the man in the leather jacket standing in the doorway. The two men stare blankly at one another. "Is it here?" the man asks.

"Maybe," Mr. Hudson responds. "How did you know I was here?"

"I've always kept an eye on you. Not too many left from the old days, you know."

"I guess," Mr. Hudson crinkles his forehead. "You know I don't like surprises . . . What name are you going by now?"

"Ha, I haven't decided yet."

"Oh good. The trickster till the end."

"This isn't our end. Or at least I don't think it is," the man in the leather jacket jokes.

"So, what be your business?"

"Is it here?"

"Why don't you remove your shades, Trickster?" Mr. Hudson glares at the man with a smirk as he walks out into the small showroom.

"It's fairly bright in here; I'll go by Ranald." He smiles, showing his teeth. The two stand frozen for a few moments. It's Mr. Hudson who breaks the silence again. "Well, come in." He waves Ranald in. "I've been expecting you." He motions for the man to follow him to the back. "I almost let the boy keep it. I truly don't want to get mixed up in any of this."

"No one will know you were involved." He follows him to the small back office, where he takes a seat on the small leather couch. "No one even knows you're here," he says, trying to ease Mr. Hudson.

"You do." He turns to him, looking over his glasses.

"And I will not tell a soul," Ranald says and smiles.

"And what about those without souls?" Mr. Hudson starts to spin the dial of his safe, his tone firm and annoyed.

"I will not share your whereabouts. I promise."

"I assume you have ten thousand to cover what I spent on this." Mr. Hudson doesn't believe the old trickster.

"Of course." Indicating his excitement, Ranald moves to the edge of the small couch. The safe opens, and the old man pulls out a yellow cloth. He lays it on the small wooden desk. "Here." He unwraps the blade. "It has been completely cleaned."

"Wow, it's been a long time since I've seen this." Ranald drops his shoulders. "Thank you," he says softly. Using the yellow cloth, he picks up the blade, inspecting every edge of it. "It's as beautiful as I remember it."

"Yes, and as disgusting," Mr. Hudson adds, closing the safe. "I assume you are expected to put him back?" Mr. Hudson asks.

"That was the deal." He places the dagger back on the desk. "The Clergy is funny that way. They believe I didn't complete my task." He smiles.

"I told you not to take that deal." Mr. Hudson closes the safe. "You are their lackey, now and forever," he adds.

"True, but I am safe from them," Ranald counters. "I can now roam free; I don't have to look over my shoulder anymore."

"Safe." Mr. Hudson laughs. "When have you felt safe?" Mr. Hudson taunts. "When you went into league with those beasts? When you stabbed that dagger into his heart? When you went underground?"

"I went underground because it was what we agreed to. I am no longer a threat to them," he interrupts, defending himself.

"Were you ever?" Mr. Hudson raises his eyebrow "But you have become a threat to someone," he points out.

"I don't know what you want from me, Mr. Hudson. I did what I had to do, and I will do it again." Ranald pulls out a wad of cash and throws it on the desk.

"Do what again? Put him to sleep?"

"No. This time, I kill him."

"Ha, you make me laugh." Mr. Hudson's deep laugh startles Ranald.

"Mr. Hudson, you know I mean no disrespect. But you are mistaken to believe he is unable to be killed."

"Oh, I'm sure he can be killed. But, I do not think you have the means to do so," Mr. Hudson says and laughs again.

"I chose to let him sleep. I didn't think it right to kill him last time . . . But, this time, I will do what I should have done the first time."

"Ah, you think being able to wield this blade grants you the ability to kill the Hunter?"

"What are you not telling me?" Ranald looks for insight.

"Look at yourself. You are not capable of using this blade in the manner you wish."

"How is that?"

"You helped them stop what they created. And yet they didn't tell you everything." Mr. Hudson picks up the money. "How foolish of all of you to think you could contain such a thing."

"I did what I had to do, but this time, I must not let him live. If I am unable to wield the blade in such a way, who can?"

"That I do not know," Mr. Hudson says and smiles.

"So I will put him back to sleep. Then I will return with him to the Church."

"Church?" Mr. Hudson says and utters a guffaw. He can't help but question the meaning of the trickster. "That is a good idea. Except one thing: What do you think they will do with their amazing weapon?"

"That is not my concern." Ranald heads for the door.

"Not yet." He laughs, counting the money. "Wait," he calls to Ranald who has opened the door. "This is too much."

"Keep it, in case I need more info."

"Oh no. This is a one-time thing. I am not on your payroll . . . Ranald." Mr. Hudson tosses the wad minus his ten thousand.

"Fine." He puts the money back in his jacket pocket. As he turns to leave, Mr. Hudson stops him again. "How did they get into the cave?"

"I'm still working on that."

"The boy said the boulder had given way due to the storm, but how could that be? Did you really leave only a boulder in front of his tomb?"

"It would have taken more than an act of God to move that boulder." He pauses. "Something broke the locks." He reaches into his pocket. Saying, "Someone interfered," he hands him the strand of hair.

"I know this scent," Mr. Hudson confirms. "Is it who I think it is?"

"I wish I could say no, but I will never forget that perfume," Ranald sneers.

"I thought he would have been long dead by now," Mr. Hudson adds.

"Me too," he says and shakes his head. "He agreed to pass his gift, which I know for a fact he did . . . It's been over a hundred years; I can't see how he is still alive."

"Amazing. Are you going to see him?" Mr. Hudson asks.

"I must, but I need to tread carefully." Ranald takes the hair back.

"Oh, and why is that?"

"He took the journal."

"Ah, so the plot thickens," Mr. Hudson says, contemptuously.

"It would appear so. But why would he need it? He is no mystic," Ranald points out.

"Maybe he has met someone who is?"

"But who? Who would be brave enough to work with their kind?"

"Well, it would have to be someone old. Someone who could handle them, if he or she needed to."

"Without the Clergy noticing? A being of such power would have been noticed already."

"You are forgetting all the magic that still exists in this world, and how easy it is to cloak one's self," Mr. Hudson points out.

"Yes, you are right. But who would be here in Los Angeles?"

"That I do not know. But if you would have to guess, who would benefit from having the Hunter awakened? I can't think of any good from such an act."

"I don't think that was the intention of whomever did this; the journal was what it was after."

"So, who would need the journal and why?"

"That's the million-dollar question," Ranald says shaking his head.

"I don't think you have the luxury of staying away from these creatures... You may need them. If you are to accomplish your goal."

"Now that I've had a dialogue with you, I don't suppose I could count on your help in that regard?"

"I'm sorry, I cannot." Mr. Hudson lowers his head. "Go to him; he has many sons. They are powerful, so be careful."

"I have heard." He walks out of the door. "If they are responsible for this deed, I have to talk to them." He pauses. "At least I can bring light to the actions they have taken against us."

"Us?" Mr. Hudson asks scornfully.

"All of us."

CHAPTER NINE

Chris pulls up to an old house atop a long gravel driveway. He hates the area. His father has lived on the outskirts of Newhall since way before they started to build up the area around him. Chris was disappointed that he stayed here all alone in the old house, after Chris purchased a new home for the family closer to their work. His youngest brother Alex was the only one who stayed here with the old man every once in a while.

A dense trail of dust following him, he parks. Not waiting for it to settle, he jumps out. His boots crushing the earth beneath his feet, he walks to the door. Reaching the old wood steps, he kicks at them, and sand and pebbles fall to the ground. The planks creak with every step he takes.

The buzz of his phone stops him. Pulling it out, he sees that Melisa is calling him. He can't handle speaking to her at this moment. He has to keep his mind focused on what he is going to be dealing with.

Knocking twice loudly, he enters the house. "Father," he calls out. No one can be seen. The dark house feels empty. Chris knows it's not, but he must tread carefully, not to surprise anyone. "Father," he calls out as he travels through the house. Coming to his father's room, he sees light shimmering under the door.

He knocks softly, causing the door to swing with an eerie screech. "Dad?" he calls.

"Who's there?" comes the voice of a man, who coughs and then makes scratching sounds. His Slovak accent is harsh at times, but when he chooses he is easily understood.

"It's me, Dad. It's Chris," he calls out, entering the room. The fireplace being the only light in the room, he sees his father wrapped in a blanket sitting in his old chair.

"Oh my, what a treat," he says and waves his son in. "Let me get you a drink." The old man starts to rock in the chair, building up momentum.

"It's okay, Dad, I got it." Chris grabs the bottle of vodka on the shelf that has two glasses next to it. Looking at the bottle, Chris reads, "Sobieski Polish Vodka," and smirks. "You know, Dad, we have some really nice vodka at the bar. I could easily have one of the boys bring you up some to try. I hear Alex has been up here a lot.

"Ha, you kids are so ridiculous. I only drink real vodka from where it was created," he replies, clearing his throat.

"You know, these are Polish, too," Chris says and blows out dust from the two glasses.

"Did you come just to point out how much money you have?" The older man falls back into his chair, rocking it.

"No, Dad, I came to talk about Alex."

"What is it with you? Always complaining about something." His father flicks his hand in disgust.

"I wonder where I got it?" Chris's words float in the air; he knows his father doesn't care about what he has to say about him.

"You never will learn. Always looking to fix things that don't need fixing." His father continues to trail off; Chris is not sure if he understands what he is talking about.

"So, about Alex?" Chris redirects the conversation to his brother.

"What about my dear boy? He is the only one that comes to see me anymore."

"I come to see you," Chris says and hands him the small glass.

"You want a thank you?" The old man takes the drink.

"No, I'm just saying that I come to see you too." He walks over to a small, old fireplace chair. Picking it up, he moves it closer to his father.

"Fine, so what do you want?" The old man sits holding the drink with both hands, as if it is warming him.

"I need you to stop telling Alex that I'm not fit to run things."

"Ha, I haven't said anything of the sort." He waves his hand, dismissing the allegation.

"Dad, I know you like to fill his head with stories of the old days. But those days are long gone. It's been peaceful for some time now." He takes a swig of the vodka, shaking his head from the taste.

"Ha, too strong for you?"

"No, it just has a taste I had forgotten about, and for good reason. How can you drink this?" Chris takes in a deep breath and shakes off the horrid taste.

"Because it's what my father drank, and, unlike your generation, I respected him until and past his demise."

"Yeah, anyway. I need you to stop telling Alex things like that."

"Like what?" He reaches out the glass for Chris to fill it again. "To respect his father? Listen to his father? Trust that his father has been here longer and knows more?"

"Things are not the same. There is no war. There is no blood lust. There is no Hunter killing our kind," he points out, filling his own glass. "I followed you once, believing all your tales. But you almost ended us. You being stuck in the past is dangerous. We have no reason to reignite any old flames." He takes another drink, this time not making a face.

"See, it grows on you. The past is not always bad," he points out. "This future is full of weakness. We were strong before. We had things challenging us, making us united."

"Not this again."

"Yes, this again." The old man tries to get up from the chair. "We had a massive pack; we ruled all the lands of this countryside."

"I've heard the stories."

"Yet you don't listen to them." The old man finally rises from his seat. "I have endured so much, and watching my offspring trying to be one with the humans, it makes me sick."

"Dad. Please sit down." Chris gets up to help him.

"Let me be." The old man walks to the fireplace. He looks up at the large portrait of his younger self. He looked like Chris, with his sharp features. But he has dark eyes. Black, if you ever got close enough to see. His skin is much fairer. "We can live forever, and you are giving it away."

"We can be killed, Dad."

"Ha, hardly." When his father reaches up to touch the image, he notices his wrinkled spotted hands and skin. Trembling, he pulls away. Looking back to his son with narrowed eyes, not wanting him to see his weakness, the feeble old man turns his attention to the smaller portraits, all standing in a row on the mantel, each image showing a different beautiful young woman. Grabbing a picture with force, the old man gazes at it and softly caresses it. "Your mother, she would be ashamed of you."

"Dad, please. You're not making sense."

"You are just like that weakling Aaron. Always talking shit."

"Oh? And what shit am I talking? I'm surprised you even knew which mother was mine"

"Whose scent is on you? Is that Melisa's lips that have been on your neck?" He devilishly watches Chris. "No need to try to hide that from me, son. Your woman is all over you." Chris just stands there, unsure what he can say. In his heart he has no reason to want to defend his actions, but around his father he can't help the feeling.

"My choices are just that, mine. I'm not embarrassed by them either."

"Yet you stand there defending them, eh boy?" He can't help but laugh. "Your young brother continues to bring women like yours to this house. But at least he knows that they are just toys, not his future."

"What does that mean?"

"Nothing. Just funny, is all. Your brother wants to be like you, yet he knows better," the old man sneers and turns his back on Chris.

"What the fuck are you talking about, old man?" Chris's anger builds.

"My poor son. You are so confused. You choose a mate that is at a disadvantage. All of my loves were like us. I never went against our kind, and I wonder: Does your love know who, or what you are?" The old man laughs.

Chris angrily takes his mother's picture out of his father's hands. "She knows what she needs to know," he says, putting the picture back on the mantel. His eyes fixed on the picture, a rush of memories floods his mind. His mother looking down at him when he was a just a little boy. Softly caressing his face, before closing a small door using her fingers to tell him to be quiet.

"You love a mortal, the ones that fear and try to kill us. And you have chosen a life with her over your own kind, over your own brothers."

"That's ridiculous. I am trying to move on, like you did."

"I didn't have a choice."

"I've heard that bullshit before. You had a choice . . . stop stretching the truth."

"I wanted my genes to go on . . . And, like I already told you. I didn't go outside of my kind."

"Stop it, just stop it, Dad." Chris turns to face his father.

"Stop what, telling the truth? I had you and your brothers in order to rebuild. To leave a legacy."

"A legacy?" Chris says, giving a forced laugh. "You were never here. You had us in ruins."

"I could have fixed this, but you are the one who decided to do so. You took this family and made it the weak pack it is now."

"Jesus Christ, that is the most ridiculous thing I've ever heard from your mouth. And that is saying something."

"I was always here," his father hisses in anger.

"Is that why our mothers were here alone to deal with your debt? Is that why they are not here today?" He pauses.

"Your mother's death was a tragedy, but I cannot be blamed for it."

"Oh? And how have you come to that conclusion?"

"It doesn't matter. I took care of those who hurt her, didn't I?"

"What? I was the one who had to deal with them."

"I thought you were the one. But, you have proven you are not," the old man says and slaps Chris across the face. The blow surprises Chris. The pain in his cheek is real. A small drop of blood rolls down his chin from the corner of his lip.

"You are having an abomination and think you can talk down to me, boy?"

"I am not the first to mate with a human, nor will I be the last. Your ways are over, old man. The world has changed, and I am moving with it." He throws his glass in the fireplace, exploding the fire within. "Fuck, Dad. When will you stop this crazy shit?" He clenches his fist.

"You want to hit me?" The old man drops his blanket. "Do it!" he screams at Chris.

"I'm not going to hit you," Chris states simply, a tear building in his eyes. He unclenches his fists.

"Hit me!" His father slaps himself in the face, once on the left side, then on the right. "You fucking coward."

Chris turns and walks away. Clenching the rage inside, knowing he could easily dispatch his father, he heads for the door.

"Oh no you don't." His father grabs his arm, turning him around. "You little shit, you think you can stand up to me?" he growls.

"What? I already have. I don't want to hurt you." Chris begins to cry in pure anger.

"Hit me!" his father demands.

"No." Chris wipes the tears from his face. "I'm not going to touch you," he states, collecting himself.

"So weak are you," his father says, curling his lip.

"Not weak, strong. I promise you. I hate you more than you could ever hate me. And I'm using my strength not to kill you."

"Ha-ha, so confident," the feeble old man laughs. "The one who hides where you come from. Acting like you know how to use the powers I bestowed upon you." He turns away from Chris. "What a waste you are."

"I'm not hiding anything," Chris yells at the old man.

"So, this girl knows what you are?"

"She will," Chris says, meaning his words.

"Ah ha. I'm sure." The old man heads back to his chair. Plopping in it, he points to the vodka. Chris angrily grabs it and fills his glass.

"I will tell her. She needs to know. I am just waiting for the right moment."

"You coward. How could you not tell her what she carries? Do you know what will happen to her?"

"Nothing will happen to her. She's strong." Chris is confused by his father's words. The idea that he has put Melisa in danger makes him scared.

"Physically? What about mentally?"

"Both." Chris narrows his eyes.

"Yet, she will not be prepared for all the changes she will have." The old man is enjoying his knowledge over Chris.

"What changes?"

"God, boy, have you never listened to anything I've ever said?" The old man shakes his head.

"Stop this. Tell me." Chris's anger is building again.

"You just gave your powers to an offspring, and you don't think they will share that?"

"Explain yourself."

"She is one with the baby. She will have everything he has until he is born and they are separated. All of his powers and all of his weaknesses will become hers."

"I don't understand." Chris is shocked by the news. "What does that mean?"

"Do you remember when you discovered your powers? Has it been so long that you have forgotten?"

"No, of course I remember."

"And if it was not for me, how would you have handled them?"

"First off, it was Aaron who taught me how to control my powers." Chris takes a swig of the vodka. "Second, I didn't have my powers until I turned twelve."

"Ah, how much you have forgotten. You didn't transform until you were twelve, but before that, you had strength no mortal has. Not even an adult mortal man was as strong as you when you were just one year old."

"What will happen to her?" Chris's concern is becoming apparent, giving power to his father, which he is enjoying.

"You have cursed her." He reaches out for Chris to fill his glass.

"God damn it, Dad. Why are you this way? Can't you just tell me what to do?" he screams, slamming the bottle on the table. He storms out.

"It's not that bad." Getting out of his chair with ease, he watches with a mischievous smile as Chris drives off in anger.

"I see you are still the same old son of a bitch you always were," a voice calls out from behind the old man. Turning around in surprise, he sees the man in the leather jacket is standing by the fire looking at the pictures of the old man's many wives.

"Get away from them!" He rushes to them, grabbing the one of Chris's mother. "What are you doing here?" He wipes at the glass. "How can you be in here?"

"Oh dear Aleksy, have you forgotten how you invited me in all those years ago? My welcome just doesn't wear off," he says with a smile.

"I see, so I guess I should retract my invite then." The old man cocks his eyebrow with a smirk. "So why are you here?"

"I'm sure you know." Ranald walks to the other end of the room.

"Ha, and what is that?"

"Aleksy, tell me." He pauses. "What are you hoping to achieve, now that you've awoken him?"

"What?" The old man's hands start to tremble. "What are you talking about?" He walks to his chair, gripping the picture tightly. The man in the leather jacket already knows he has something to do with it.

"You expect me to believe you have nothing to do with this?" He laughs.

"He is out?" He looks at the picture. "How?"

"You tell me." Ranald sits in the same chair that Chris was in.

"I have nothing to do with this. You tell the Clergy; I have nothing to do with this," he insists.

"I will do nothing of the sort." He laughs and grabs the bottle of vodka. He sloshes it around, beckoning the old man to join him for a drink. On wobbling legs, he carefully takes his chair. Ranald smirks. He fills the old man's glass, then takes a swig from the bottle.

Pulling out the strand of hair he had found on the boulder, he holds it out to the old man. "How do you explain this?"

Seeing the hair, he tries to get up. "That's not me," he argues.

"Really?" The man in the leather jacket looks at the hair, turning it in all directions.

"No, it is not!" he states firmly and gets up again. "I have nothing to do with the monster. I have been there, but not in some time."

"Why would you go there?" He watches the old man pace.

"I took my son. I wanted him to see what I did for him and his kind," he explains.

"You broke the rules." Ranald rises from his seat. "No one was supposed to know of the location. We made a deal. A deal that kept you alive."

"Alive? You killed me," he screams.

"No, we allowed you to pass your gift. You did it seven times," the man in the leather jacket says.

"We?" The old man's anger builds. "You are just a puppet . . . Edmond."

"Ranald . . . I'm going by Ranald for this journey."

"Fucking vampires, always shrouded with mystery."

"As are you. You knew that the Hunter was here for you and yours. You made a deal. And now it has been broken."

"He was not here for only us. He was here for them, too," he argues.

"Be that as it may. You made your choice."

"For the better of my kind. Yes, I did. But I did not break our agreement," he claims.

"Who did you show?" Ranald asks.

"I will not say."

"Well, if you don't tell me, I will find out myself. And you know what that means."

"No, no. I'll tell you. But please don't hurt him. He will help you. He will help put him away, just as I did."

"Aleksy, your children are not as strong as you. They are too young to help me."

"He can gather many, trust me. All of my sons and other packs are near. My boy has been working to build the clan again."

"Who did you show the Hunter to?"

"I showed Chris." He looks down to the ground. "But this was a long time ago. I have no idea why he would open his tomb. I can't control that boy of mine."

"You didn't show any of the others?" he asks. He knows this old man too well to believe he would give up his son so easily. The old man must be hiding something.

"No." He grabs the bottle from Ranald and takes a swig. Ranald stares the old man down.

"What did you do with the book, old man?"

"Book? What book?" Aleksy asks, but his face tells him he is lying. In a flash, he grabs the old man and lifts him off his feet. Aleksy, holding the bottle, trying not to drop it, just laughs.

"You think you can intimidate me?" He takes a swig of the liquor. Ranald lowers him to his feet, but doesn't release him. He continues holding him face to face. The old man is able to see his reflection in the vampire's glasses. "I wonder, if I flash a light through those things, could I see the holes they left you with?"

With a simple flick, he throws the old man across the room, splintering the wood panels of the wall. The old man lies on his back, his laughter still loud and proud. "Is that all you can do now, beat up an old man?" Still holding the bottle, he takes another drink. "Come help me up." Incensed, Ranald walks up to the old man. "Aleksy, if we find out you had anything to do with this, your whole family will suffer. You have a boy named Alex. That's your name in English, right?" He turns without helping the old man to his feet and heads out the door without saying another word.

The anger in his chest begs for him to go back inside and crush the old man. But he cannot. He needs to find out what happened. Taking a deep breath, he admires the view of the empty field. "Fucking wolves."

CHAPTER TEN

Alex sits on his motorcycle, his helmet off, resting on his knee. His face is stricken with anger, as he watches Victor and his lackeys, stumbling around, hollering at women, making obscene gestures. They are pitiful. Alex can't believe that these men consider themselves tough guys.

The ringleader, Victor, is the saddest to watch. Completely out of control. No discipline. No style. Just a sad sack, which drives Alex nuts. His support system continuously directs him away from traffic, not allowing him to fall or get hurt.

He is obviously the weakest among them, a lightweight. And they allow him to be so. He's a sloppy mess, just stumbling all over the place. How he is in charge dumbfounds Alex. In his own family, the weak was not the leader. The weak were shunned, left to fend for themselves. It was the only way to help them grow stronger.

But here he is watching a weakling order much stronger men around. The role reversal is frustrating. It seems this man's family finds it acceptable for the weak to abuse those around them. *How can you teach a future leader to be so weak?* he wonders. Maybe that's it. They don't see them as leaders, so they let them think they are, so as to build a false confidence.

He couldn't imagine his father allowing any of the brothers to act in such a way, let alone any of his brothers standing for it. The power struggle within his family was real, and constant. Alex understood what his brother Chris was trying to do. But that didn't mean he had to accept or agree with it.

Melisa was beautiful, smart, and a very nice person. She might even make a good mom. But, a mom within his family? His kind would never accept or respect her. It was hard enough for a woman to be respected in their family, let alone that she is not one of them. She would never belong. She was a weak human, a weak human woman. And the child would be weak just like her. A half-blood would never make it in their world.

Watching these fools running around the street, he fears that his brother's child will end up just like them. It was killing Alex to stand by and let his brother make such a big mistake.

Alex plays back all the times he had to cover for his brother, and all the times he cheated on past girlfriends. No woman was a real priority to Chris. Sure, he hadn't done that to Melisa. But in his mind it was firm—not YET.

He couldn't figure it out, nor could he turn to his other brothers for help. Had he really made such a drastic change? His father was the only one who would listen. He explained that Chris was lost. He was trying to be something he wasn't. He wanted to be a human.

His father was the real leader of the family. Yes, he was weakened, but that happens when you do what he did. And now Chris was going to do it, too. The difference was his father had no choice. Chris is doing it on purpose.

The group enter the "Public House," a well-known dive bar in Los Feliz. Focused so strongly on this group of men, he hadn't noticed that he was near Melisa's house. He was just saddened by his brother's decision. How could he be doing what he was doing? How could he choose a woman over his own family, his own kind?

As he gets off his bike, about to head across the street, his phone rings. He looks at the screen, which says "home." His father never called. He wondered why his father would be calling him.

When he answers the phone, the old man instantly begins to yell at him. Alex, trying to calm him, asks what he is talking about.

"You, idiot boy. Have I not taught you anything?" Aleksy, full of anger, asks.

"What are you talking about, Dad?"

"Did you awaken him?"

"Who?"

"You know who."

"No Dad, I didn't even touch him."

"They why am I hearing that he is?"

"I did just as you said. I went inside, and I took the book."

"Did you touch the Hunter?"

"No Dad, I swear."

"Are you sure the cave was sealed when you left?"

"Of course. The rain made it hard, but I closed it. I'm sure."

"Was anyone watching you?"

"No, Dad. I was careful. Do you not believe me?"

"Now I have to explain to our friend that the Hunter is awake. He will not be too happy about that."

"Who cares what he thinks? If he is so powerful, why didn't he go into the cave?"

"Stop your smart mouth, boy!" Aleksy lashed his youngest. "He doesn't need to prove anything to you. I tell you to respect him, and that is all you need to worry about. He is the only way I can be rid of this horrid curse." He pauses. "Do you understand?"

"Yes Dad, I'm sorry." Alex chooses his next words carefully. "So what should I do?"

"The Hunter is free, and he will come looking for his journal. We haven't the time, I had hoped for." He pauses, murmuring to himself. "Where are you, boy?"

Alex knows his dad is annoyed with him. With a smirk he looks over at the bar. "I'm working on something."

"Hurry with whatever it is; I need you here. WE have much to figure out." He hangs up, without saying goodbye.

Leaving his bike, helmet in hand, Alex walks across the street and crosses the large parking lot. The bar is tucked away on the left with other stores to its right, all of which are closed. The bar doesn't allow for him to peer in. The windows have all been painted over. He would normally enjoy such a feature, but today he wishes it were otherwise.

The partyers have been to three other bars since they left Chris's club. Every time, Alex would watch from the outside, gathering as much insight as he could of their intentions. Every time it was the same. The feeble Victor would find the head of the house, and then pull his bullshit. Alex has figured out that the piece of shit is trying to set up a connection to sell drugs.

What a joke. His uncle is connected all across the city; their hands are in everything. He is taken care of and babied because he's part of the family. And here is this little man trying to start his own business on the side. *It's such a disservice to allow the weak to feel like they have power. They never know their place*, he thinks to himself. Having listened in on their conversations, he knows that the uncle is unaware of his nephew's plans. With that, Alex feels like he can do something without any danger of reactions to his family.

Entering the establishment, he places his helmet on the bar. It's quiet, except for the few customers talking with the bartender. Then there are the obnoxious criminals yelling over each other. Everyone in the bar tries their best to ignore them. Alex knows they won't be trying to make any dealings here. This place is just to get Victor off the streets.

Looking around, Alex looks up at the two small box TVs. Both are playing some sport that Alex couldn't care less about. But, he must pretend to take an interest. He positions himself to have a perfect view of the men, using the mirror behind the bar. They've taken a booth toward the back corner. Alex orders a Capt'n and coke. He doesn't like the taste of alcohol, but can handle this.

He waits there, using his peripherals to watch them. His ears are perked, listening in on their conversation. Being as drunk as they are, it isn't that hard. It doesn't take long for Victor to get up for a piss, which he very elegantly points out. One of the delinquents follows him. "What a bitch," Alex mutters.

"Excuse me?" the bartender, hearing him, asks.

"Oh, nothing. I got to use the bathroom. I'll be right back." He places a bar napkin on his drink, leaving his helmet.

As he walks toward the bathroom, the men all watch him. They don't recognize him, but he is someone that demands attention when he walks. Alex stops at the jukebox. "This thing working?" he asks the bartender. "It's too quiet."

"Sure does, fifty cents a song," he answers while cleaning glasses in the sink. Alex puts in a dollar and searches for a song. Finding what he wants, he selects for it to play now, paying the extra credits.

"The Pain That I'm Used To" by Depeche Mode blasts the patrons. Alex looks back at the group of men. The music is not to their taste, which makes him happy. The loud siren sound after the chorus is exactly what Alex wants right now. He walks through the hallway toward the bathroom. The "guard" is standing outside of the men's room. He looks Alex up and down. "Go piss outside," the man tells Alex.

"I'll wait," Alex says and smiles. The man moves toward Alex, not liking his response. Alex doesn't move, he just rocks his head to the beat. He mouths the chorus, looking the protector directly in the eyes. Once the siren plays again he grabs the man by the face, covering his mouth and lifting him off his feet. In an instant they are through the back door.

The back is small, closed in by a wooden fence. A dumpster takes up most of the space. Alex knew it was secluded and free from prying eyes. As he slams the man's head into the ground, blood splatters on the nearby dumpster. Holding his hand over the man's mouth, he digs his fingernails into his skin.

The man tries desperately to free himself, but Alex is too strong. Looking him deep in the eyes, he watches as the life disappears from the man. Needing to dispose of him quickly, he makes use of the dumpster. Covering him with some trash, he heads back inside.

The music slows as Alex enters the bathroom and locks the door. He doesn't turn right away. He keeps his back to Victor, grooving to the music.

"What the fuck, man," Victor screams. "Hey man, I'm still in here," he cries out. "Aram," he cries out to the guard that Alex just ripped the life out of.

"I don't think he'll be of any help to you." Alex turns, grinning and showing his enlarged canines. Victor, seeing them and the blood splatters on Alex's face, begins to freak out.

"Hel . . .!" he screams. Alex interrupts the man's attempt to scream, putting his blood-covered finger up to his lips, staining them. Alex is still bopping to the music, closing his eyes, mouthing the words, as if he is lip syncing a serenade to Victor.

Victor is trembling all over and crying out to his attacker, "What the fuck, du . . ." Alex's eyes, still closed, begin emitting a glow from the creases. "Please," Victor pleads with his assailant. But, it is futile. Alex just keeps the beat, shushing Victor. The chorus finishes once again and the siren blares one last time. Alex opens his lids, exposing brilliant yellow glowing eyes.

In a move too quick for Victor to truly understand, Alex is already on him. The strength and viciousness of the attack is overpowering, though he can't take as much time as he would like. He needs his victim to feel everything. But, he only has the last moments of the song to finish. It doesn't stop him from enjoying every moment of what he is doing to the weak, wannabe gangster.

Once the song ends, he stops the brutal onslaught. Lifting away and taking in a deep breath, blood covering his face, Alex feels rejuvenated. Looking down at his victim, he smiles. Victor is still alive, but barely. His whole body is mauled and bleeding everywhere.

Alex kneels down. "I own you now," he whispers. "You will learn. And I will teach you," he says and touches Victor's face softly. "I will come back when you are ready." He gets up, washes his hands and face. "I got to get you out of here before you make too big of a mess." He opens the door and makes sure no one is around. He grabs the mangled man and takes him outside, dropping him in the dumpster next to his dead friend. "Have a good night," he laughs and covers them with garbage.

He quickly returns to the bathroom. The blood left by Victor is pooled into a small area. Giving it a once over, he sops up the blood with paper towels, which he buries in the small bathroom trash can. He opens the fly of his denim jeans and pisses all over the area. He is marking it, but also concealing himself from the humans. It's a trick his dad taught him when he was younger. Walking back into the lounge, he looks at the men. They are preoccupied with a group of ladies. Raising his eyebrows, he returns to his drink.

"What time is it?" he asks the bartender.

"Eleven thirty," he answers. "Can I get you another?" he offers, noticing Alex is almost finished with his drink.

"No thank you. I got to get out of here. I'll see you later." He smiles and drops a twenty on the bar. Looking through the mirror, he sees that the men are still having a grand time with the ladies, though the ladies don't seem all that entertained. Grabbing his helmet, he heads right for them. "Excuse me, ladies. Are any of you looking for a bar where you wouldn't be bothered by a bunch of douche bags?"

The girls all laugh at the words, but the men are not happy. They quickly get up ready to defend their honor. "You think you're funny?" one of the men calls out.

"I don't know, what do you think, ladies?" he asks.

"You ain't going to be laughing when we're done with you, you stupid guy."

"Stupid guy? Jesus Christ. Who taught you how to curse? Next time, try saying something like . . . are you fuckin' stupid. That would sound a little less lame."

"That's it." As the men rush to get out of the booth, Alex walks backwards, waving at the women, using his thumb and pinky imitating a phone and mouthing for them to call him. He rushes out the door and waits for the men. Once they follow him out, he hits one of them with his helmet in the stomach. He is not trying to hurt them; he just wants them to give chase, which they seem eager to do.

Rounding the corner, he goes about a block, slow enough so they keep coming. Once he feels they are far enough from the bar, he takes off faster than they can keep up with. Running around the block, he returns to the bar. He finds the ladies. "So, you guys want to get out of here?" he asks calmly.

"Dude, are you crazy?" the blonde in the group calls out.

"Nah, I just don't like seeing douche bags like that messing with nice girls like you."

"You think we are nice girls?"

"Well, I was trying to be polite. I say we get out of here before those gorillas come back," he says.

The women all look at each other and decide to join him. "Where we going?"

"I got a great club we can check out. Who wants to ride on the back of my bike?" The blonde quickly jumps at the opportunity. "All right, here." He hands the dark-haired girl a card. "Show this to the bouncer; tell them you're Alex's friends." He smiles and leads his new friend to his bike.

CHAPTER ELEVEN

Melisa has been watching the freeway signs the whole drive. Walter is taking them to their father's house. He didn't waste much time getting to her after she called about the John Doe falling on her car. It wasn't his crime scene, but he was friendly with the lead detective. Being her brother, they gave him extra leeway to help out and be there when they questioned her.

But he was almost escorted off the scene when he punched the officer who discharged his weapon from the window—though most of the other uniforms agreed with his actions.

Now, driving home, he knew she was in shock. But he didn't know how to communicate with her. He was very protective, but never overstepped. When he asked about her choices regarding the John Doe, he never once challenged her reasoning. It was one of the main motives for her to call him.

She didn't call Chris after all. He would have freaked out. He probably would be out hunting down the guy with his brothers. Melisa didn't want anything bad to happen to the man. He was sick and needed help. And Walter would listen to her and try and help.

"Shit." She breaks the silence, startling Walter. "I forgot to call Chris." She searches her purse for her phone.

"God damn, Melisa. You scared the shit out of me," Walter lets out, shaking his head.

"Sorry." She continues to fumble for her phone. "I just can't believe I forgot to call him," she adds. "Damn." She remembers leaving it on her desk, when she was asked to do something. "Can I borrow your phone? I must've left mine in the office."

"Of course." He hands it to her. Melisa dials the number and waits for the sound of Chris's voice. When he answers, a rush comes to her heart. She begins to debate how she forgot to call him. With tears in her eyes, she tells him everything. He is surprisingly sweet. His concern for her wellbeing is number one, followed quickly by their baby growing in her stomach. When she responds about the baby, she instantly realizes she just let Walter know about the pregnancy.

His laugh confirms it. She tells Chris that her brother now knows, which helps the conversation take on a more joyous tone. She tells him that she'll be at her dad's for the night, and gives him his number to call, if he needs to get in touch with her. When she hangs up, she turns to her brother before he can say anything and tells him to "shut up" with a smirk. She tosses his phone on his lap.

"Hey, I wasn't going to say anything," he says and laughs, focusing on the road. Melisa looks out the windshield, seeing they are almost to the destination. Feeling his eyes on her, Melisa feels the need to say something. As she turns to Walter, he turns quickly away, hiding the fact he was just projecting at her.

"So, Dad is excited to see you," Walter gets out, before Melisa has a chance to speak.

"Yeah, I feel bad that I haven't been by lately. I've just been so busy," she tries to explain.

"He understands. I've been staying with him for the last couple of weeks."

"Really? Why? I didn't know that," she admits.

"He's been a little down. He may be closing the shop."

"What! Why?"

"You know all these chumps now. All they want is tricked out, new cars. No one wants the classics. And if they do, they need it dropped and looking nothing like the original."

"What's he going to do?"

"I've told him to go home," Walter tells her.

"What did he say to that?"

"Same thing: this is his home; Guatemala is his past."

"God, how sad. Now I feel like shit." Melisa starts to tear up.

"Come on, prego, no need to cry now," Walter laughs.

"Fuck you," she defends herself, laughing. "Don't tell Dad. He'll never leave if he finds out."

"Well, it's not like I had to pry," he jokes.

"Damn, I'm doing a piss poor job keeping this a secret," she says, joining him making fun of herself.

"Yeah, that's not you. But that's the magic of pregnancy," he says.

"Whatever." She stares out the window. The exit sign on the freeway lets her know they are almost home. A wave of memories rushes through her mind. East Los Angeles was her home for so long. She did whatever she could to get out. She had dreams of getting everyone out. That was why she went to medical school. But now, driving down her old street, it feels like the best place on earth.

After a few turns, they're on the street they grew up on. Parking in the back, they can see their dad cooking in the kitchen. "Damn, I knew he would do this."

"Of course. He was so excited that you were coming over when he was on the phone." Walter opens his door. Melisa stops him, her face focused on her father. A worry he has never seen in her before makes him wonder.

"He should be in bed already."

"That's funny. You actually think he would be in bed knowing his favorite is coming? Once you blab about the baby, he'll stay up all night."

"Please. Don't say anything about it." Melisa slaps the dash of his car.

"Geez, I doubt I'll have to."

"I just hope I don't get sick in front of him," she says as she finally gets out of the car.

"Oh yeah, ha-ha, sucks for you." Walter carries her duffle bag. They had to stop at her house to get it. She didn't have anything in her car when it was totaled. While there, she got Walter a copy of her surveillance video so he could see the difference in the man.

The neighborhood is just as she remembered it. The smells, the sounds, and even the air. As they walk down the small driveway, dogs are barking curiously from behind the gate. When they get closer to the house, the dogs' temperaments change. Walter kicks at the gate, screaming at the dogs to shut up. "When did Dad get the dogs?" Melisa asks.

"He did a job for some guy. He couldn't pay so he gave him the two pits."

"They look mean," she says and moves closer to Walter.

"It's odd, I've never seen them act like this. Dad has them pretty well trained."

"Are they going to be inside?"

"Nah, he'll keep them outside."

Walking to the house, they enjoy the very welcoming aroma. Melisa's worries fall to the wayside. Walter holds the screen door open for her. "Oh Mija," her father rushes to give her a huge hug. "How are you?" Melisa feels the squeeze bringing happiness to her, as she basks in the safety she gains in the presence of the man she calls Daddy.

"Your brother told me about the crazy guy. Did they catch him?" he asks.

"He is not crazy, Dad." She looks at Walter with an eyebrow raised.

"Oh Mija, they're all crazy." If she didn't know her father, she would think him a dangerous man. The tattoos on his arms, the hair in a ponytail. His thin mustache, which drapes down past his lips. He has the look of his past, and doesn't care to hide it. He wears Ben Davis work pants or sometimes Dickies, creased down the center of each leg. A white Stafford tee, ironed smooth. His shoes are the exception.

He wears Crocs. Melisa had gotten him a pair for Christmas some years back, and now that's all he'll wear. He gets a different color whenever he needs a new pair. Today he has orange ones on. But last night he had on ones decorated in the red, white, and blue of the American flag.

He still lived in the neighborhood he moved to when he first came to the United States. He has watched it transform around him. It has gone from very dangerous, to up and coming, back to dangerous. It's currently in an upswing. People are walking around the streets again. It's not the safest, but it isn't that bad.

"Just like you?" she squeezes hard. He lets out a soft noise from the added pressure but doesn't say anything about it.

"Oh Mija, not anymore. I'm too old for that shit." Finally pulling away, still holding her shoulders, he gasps. "Your poor face, look at all those cuts," he states with worry in his eyes.

"Oh, I forgot about those." She tries to laugh it off. "They are nothing, I'm fine," she adds.

With his eyes focused, his worry lines deepen. "How are you, Mija?" he asks again, this time waiting for an answer.

"I'm good, Daddy."

"Good, eh?" He leans his head back to get a better view. Melisa can tell she needs to get him away from focusing on her injuries, or he'll start to get angry and want to do something about it.

"Dad. I'm okay. You made a strong girl. Like Mom."

"That is true."

"Enough about me. How have you been?"

"Oh Mija, I've been good," he smiles as he looks her up and down. "You hungry?"

"It's pretty late, Dad. I've had dinner already."

"Okay, no problem. I'll just give you a little soup." He smiles and walks back to the stove. She can't help but smile. This brute of an old gangster, working the kitchen wearing a flowered apron. She couldn't say no to him.

"Thanks, Dad." She heads to her room, stopping to give him a kiss on the cheek. Walking through the small hallway, she passes framed pictures of each of the family members on one side and diplomas and awards on the other. Walter is coming toward her. "Your shit is on your bed."

"Thanks," she bumps into him with her shoulder as he passes by, causing him to hit the wall softly, almost knocking down her UCSF diploma. Walter shakes his head, remembering their childhood.

"You're going to get it."

"Bring it on." Melisa puts up her hands like a fighter from the olden days.

"Geez, I haven't seen you like this in a long time. It's nice." He reaches up and ruffles her hair. Melisa knocks his hand away, laughing. "Stop it!" She hits him on the shoulder. Walter just turns and heads into the kitchen. Melisa straightens the diploma.

"Dad, what you got going on here?" he hollers as he walks into the kitchen.

She walks into her room and takes a seat on her bed. It's the same old single bed she had from when she was a little girl. It has a new mattress, but the frame is the one her dad made for her when she was ten. Looking around, she sees nothing has changed, including the posters stuck on the walls. One from Oingo Boingo, another from the Smiths, two of her favorite bands growing up. She had a few of a young Jared Leto, Keanu Reeves, and Ricky Martin, her male crushes of that time. And a poster from *The Lost Boys*, one of her favorite movies from when she was young. Melisa feels at home.

Sitting there, pulling out everything from her bag, she grabs her tablet. Opening it, she can't help herself. She turns on the app from her security system. Thoughts of the man have been haunting her. She couldn't be sure, but she thought he had reached out to her. She remembers how he did the same thing when she first helped him. But that time he was accusing her.

He called her something. Chel, she remembers. Using the web browser, she searches the name. Most of the information that comes up is regarding a cartoon about the Quest of El Dorado. She never saw it, but, knowing about the real history of the story, she didn't care to see an adaptation of a tale full of horrible truths.

She was not a fan of the Spanish conquistadors, or how they treated the indigenous people of the Americas; the subject just made her sad. Not wanting to focus on the unrelated subject, she continues her search. On the second page of the search, she finds something that sticks out: Ixchel or Ix Chel. Opening the web page, she finds that is the sixteenth-century title for the ancient jaguar deity. In ancient Mayan culture, she was known as the midwife or the goddess of making children and medicine.

She remembers the short amount of time she spent in Guatemala with her grandmother; she was half Mayan. The sweet old lady would take her into the jungle. She was a nurse and was well loved among the people. The last time Melisa was in Guatemala was for her funeral. Everyone from the hills came down to pay their respects to her.

Her father didn't like talking about the Mayans; he felt that his mother spent too much time helping them and not enough time taking care of herself. But when he saw the mass exodus from the hills, he cried like she never knew he could.

Why would the man call her such a name? Was he implying that she was a doctor? Wait, she remembers. He reached out to her belly. It was as if he knew she was pregnant. But she is barely showing. And for a person that had never seen her before, there was no way he could have noticed.

Playing the footage on her tablet, she watches again. She sees him reach and grab her arm. He wanted something; he wanted to hurt her maybe? He said something to her. He asked why did she do something. Watching the clip again, she sees when everything changed. It was when he looked at her belly. He motioned, reached for her midsection.

She thinks back to him crashing into her car. Raising up and looking at her. His face, it was calm, yet there was something there. She couldn't be sure. But now, looking back, yes he was in pain but not from the fall. It was something else. He didn't act like a man that had fallen twelve stories. He moved like he was at war with himself. He had reached for her, she was certain. But again, was it to hurt her? Or was he reaching for help?

It begins to drive her crazy. The thought that this man was a danger to her and those around her. A loud holler from her brother pulls her from her tablet screen. She has been lost in thought. Suddenly two large dogs appear. One is a dark gray color, almost blue with clipped ears, and the other one is a fawn color, a little thinner with floppy ears.

Both dogs growl at her, the ruff spiked all the way down their spines, and lower themselves ready to attack. She can hear her brother running down the hall. Melisa puts the tablet down slowly. Not sure what to do, she just stares at them. One takes a step into her room. "No," she says. The dog stops instantly. Both raise up, ears perked. "Sit," she commands, and the dogs obey instantly.

Walter arrives and grabs the two dogs by the collar. "Fuck, I'm sorry, sis. I was going to give them food, but they rushed by me," he apologizes, panting.

"It's okay," she calmly states. "What are their names?" she asks. The dogs are focused solely on her.

"Genghis and Geronimo," he tells her, but she feels like she already knows it. Genghis is the larger of the two. Walter struggles to pull them away from her room. "Dad! Can you call these stupid dogs?" he hollers out. Responding to a soft call from the kitchen, the dogs run to their master.

"How did you get them to listen? Those fuckers don't listen to me at all."

"I don't know. Maybe it was that I was calm," she answers.

"Hmm." Walter looks around her room. "Well, food's ready."

"I'll be out in a minute . . . Oh, when can you get me a copy of the tape from the hospital?" She stops him. Walter was privy to more information than she was about the incident at the hospital. He had promised to let her see the tape from the lab, but she didn't know when.

"What? Are you serious?" he asks.

"You said you would. I really want to see what caused him to react like that."

"Fine, I'll email it to you. But don't tell anyone I gave it to you. I'm not even on this case," he reminds her.

Walking down the hall, Melisa stops to say hello to her mother. Her picture, which is on the wall, is cleaned every day. It is from when she was young, a few years after she had Melisa. She was at the park; her dad took the picture. It was her birthday. She looked beautiful and happy. One thing Melisa always admired about her mom: no matter the situation, she found a way to be happy.

"Mija, food's getting cold," her father calls out.

He has the table set. Just like most of the rest of the house, it's the same round old table since when she was little. Everything is old. She sits in her seat, Walter in his, and their father in his. They leave an empty place for the departed mother. The food smells wonderful, and she is surprised that her gag reflex isn't responding. He has made chicken and cheese wrapped in buttered corn tortillas. He calls them enchiladas, but it's his own style. Then there is chicken soup, with avocado slices placed on top. It's like heaven to her.

They all join hands, and her father says grace. He gives thanks for everything, asks for the food to be blessed, for his family to be safe and then finishes with thanks for bringing his children to his home. Melisa can't control herself and tears up.

"Oh great," Walter drops his fork on his plate, "here we go"

"Hey, you keep quiet, Junior," his father orders. Walter's smirk disappears and he starts to eat. "Everything okay, Mija?" he asks.

"Yeah, Dad. It's just been a trying day," she explains.

"Mija, I don't want to be the worrier, but are you okay?"

"It's nothing. I'm just a little sensitive."

"It's okay. Crying is okay. I cry all the time." He laughs.

"I know. I'm sorry." She wipes the tears. "Hey, do you remember anything about the old Mayans?"

"Mayans?" her father answers.

"Yeah. I was curious about the name Ix Chel," she asks, blowing on the spoonful of soup.

"Mija, I don't remember much about those old stories. What are you trying to find out?"

"I heard someone say it. I thought of abuela."

"Your grandmother was a great woman. I'm surprised you remember her talking about those old things," he tells her, tears building in his eyes. "I wish I could help. Maybe you could call your aunt. She remembers all those things."

"Tia Martha?"

"Yes. But make sure she is making tamales."

"It's not tamales season," Melisa says, referring to the fact that most households only make tamales during the holidays because of the massive amount of work it takes to make them.

"Well, if you ask her to show you how to make them, it would be," he says and laughs with his whole body. "Eat, eat. You talk to your aunt." He takes a spoonful of soup to his lips, sucking it down with a loud slurping noise. "That is good." His kids can't help but laugh at their father.

After dinner, Melisa is lying in her room. The dogs are at the foot of her bed. "Oh there you are." Melisa's father walks into the room and points at the dogs. "You okay with them being in here?"

"Yeah, I actually like it. They make me feel safe," she answers.

"Is everything okay, Mija?" her father asks yet again, taking a seat on her bed.

"Yeah, it's just been a hard couple of days."

"Your brother told me more. Your mother would have done the same thing," he points out.

"I know. But I feel so stupid. I put myself in such a position. He could have hurt me," she whines, finding herself reverting back to a little girl in the presence of her father.

"But he did not. You are here and you are safe." He rubs her knee. "Your brother and I are here. And now you have my dumb dogs." He laughs, looking down at them with love. Both dogs perk their ears listening to their master. With a soft tap on their heads, he shares his affection.

"You get some rest. Let me know if you need anything." He gets up and heads for the door.

"Okay Dad, thank you." She remembers she forgot to ask something and calls him back. in. "Dad? Do you think it's possible I can use the Malibu?"

"What?" He is shocked by the request. "You mean your mother's car?"

"Yeah, mine is totaled."

"Oh Mija, but I haven't finished working on it," he tells her. "Why don't you take my truck?"

"Okay, thanks Dad." She looks down, pouting.

"I love you Mija."

"I love you too Dad." A ding sound from her bag catches her attention. "Good night," she says. Looking for her tablet in the bag, she finds that she has missed a few text messages from Chris. "Shoot," she lets out; the two dogs perk up at the outburst.

Grabbing the old-fashioned landline phone, she calls him, thinking about what she is going to tell him.

"Hey babe," Chris's smooth voice answers.

"Hi," is all Melisa mutters.

"What's the matter?" Chris knows something is wrong.

"I'm sorry. I'm just a little emotional, is all."

"Yeah, I would guess so. Would you like me to come over after work? This day has been a nightmare for you."

"No, it would be too late."

"I'm coming over."

"No, don't do that. Look, I haven't seen my dad in a while, and it's nice

113

to be here for the night. I'll stay with you tomorrow," she promises him.

"OK, I guess. But I don't like it."

"I got my dad and brother looking after me," she argues; he can hear her smile.

"Well, I know your dad's got you," he teases, leaving Walter out on purpose. A new ding of her tablet informs her that she has an email. She sees it's from Walter.

"Hey, it's getting real late. Let's talk in the morning," she asks.

"Okay love. I'll call you sometime after ten." Chris blows a kiss at her through the phone.

Pushing the mail box icon, she goes to her email inbox. After a few clicks, she is accessing the video with mixed feelings. She was one of the doctors that rejected the idea of putting cameras in the hospital, feeling it was an invasion of privacy and a HIPPA violation. She ended up losing that fight, but now she was kind of glad she did. The cameras were focused on the CT examination room and another on the tech's room.

The video goes as any exam would go. The tech talks to the John Doe, though without sound she can't hear what is being said. But having been in hundreds of exams herself she has a good idea of what is being discussed. The man has a look of confusion, but is following instructions. The tech leads him to the bed on the table. She can tell by the tech's body language that she is explaining how the bed will move.

The man seems hesitant. The woman moves to the round opening of the machine, showing that it is harmless; she puts her hand in and touches everything on the large white device. Having finally put the man at ease, she walks him to the bed. She helps to put in ear plugs and guides him down without much complaint. After placing a neck brace to hold his head steady, the tech walks around to the controls.

After the tech moves the bed up, the man raises his head, but she is able to get him to calm down. Melisa watches as the woman explains more information to the man. Once the woman has completed her explanation, she starts guiding the machine. A red light crosses the man's face so she can align him in it. He shakes his head and responds poorly to the light. The tech again calms him, showing that the light will not harm him. The man allows for her to continue to set everything up.

Now that everything is ready, she leaves the man. Inside of the computer room, she begins to control the system. Talking into a mic, she is telling the man what to expect. Melisa can see the images that the women is taking. The video doesn't show much of the results. But she can see that the device is taking images.

The man goes in and out a few times. The tech seems agitated, but not upset. She goes back into the room and speaks to the John Doe. Melisa can tell she is asking for the man to be still. The machine needs for him not to move otherwise they won't get a good result.

Again, she operates the machine from the computer room. Her face tells that she is getting better results. The machine goes in and out three times. On the third time the woman stops the machine. Returning to the machine, she acts in an agitated manner. The man is not moving. The tech rushes to him and checks his pulse. She quickly runs out of the room. Within a few seconds a group of men rush in with the tech. The doctor starts to check the man, flashing a light into his eyes, checking his pulse. He is ordering the nurses to go get something. One comes back with a set of paddles, and they quickly strip the man's chest so they can shock him.

At the first strike, the man's lifeless body jumps. The second and third strike produce the same results. Checking the man's vitals again, the doctor seems to relax. An aide pushes a gurney in. The doctor is talking to the nurses about something when the man, without warning, reaches up and grabs him by the throat. He rises from the bed, his eyes reflecting, almost glowing white. With an effortless move he tosses the doctor, slamming him into a wall.

Looking at his body, the John Doe strips off the gown. His rage is easy to see. The nurses all clear the room. Naked, the man, clenching his hands, screams in a fit of anger. Two security guards rush into the room, guns drawn. They give directions to the man. He looks around and leaps at them. One officer takes a shot at him.

The John Doe wipes at the wound, from which blood pours out. The two guards surround the man. In response, the John Doe attacks one of the guards, disarming him. He looks at the gun with curiosity. The other officer shoots him two more times, causing him to fall on the floor.

Melisa gasps and turns away. But she has to continue to watch. The man regains his feet and runs out of the lab. The officers give chase. The video ends there. Melisa starts to cry. The two dogs walk around the bed to comfort her. She strokes their heads. "Come up," she says and pats the bed. Both dogs do as she offers and then cuddle up next to her. She places the tablet on the night stand and rolls over. Spooning Genghis, she falls asleep.

CHAPTER TWELVE

Victor lies in the shadows of death, the burning of his wounds having vanished hours ago. His body is cold and stiff. The stench of the dumpster has long disappeared from his senses. The weight of the trash covering him is a distant memory. He has been motionless for what feels like forever. The sounds of the outside world are replaced with the deafening sounds of silence. He is alone. Life, which he took for granted, has been taken.

Yet he still knows he is in the dumpster. He has thoughts, wonderment about his predicament. How could he be dead if he can ask the simple question, am I alive? His body doesn't respond to any commands he tries to give. His mind screams, but his vocal cords do nothing. Not even a soft hum comes from his lips.

A thump lands on his forehead and liquid continues dripping on him. The continuous thudding sounds like a hammer striking a nail. It echoes in his mind, and the feeling on his face is extreme. Not painful, but very irritating. Victor again tries to move; he needs the knocking to stop, or, he is sure to go mad.

The foreign feeling transcends to that of liquid running down his face. The slow, molasses-like goo passes his lips. Slowly it breaches his mouth and begins rolling down his tongue. It tastes metallic at first. The more the substance touches his tongue, the better he can distinguish other subtle flavors. A rush of energy comes over him, giving him the life that he

117

thought he had lost.

Now able to turn his body slightly, he laps at the pool of life-giving juice. His senses are returning. His eyes open, only he is in complete darkness. Almost in a flash, his eyes adjust to the darkness, and everything is clear. Tinted in a yellow hue, he can see like it is day. Now able to see, he realizes what he has been drinking and where it has come from.

Looking eye to eye, he is face to face with his companion. They weren't close friends, but they had come to know each other. The man had a family, he had children, two of them. The smell of the man transfixes his heart. His whole being is pushing for him to taste the man, to bite into his flesh.

With another adjustment, he is now cheek to cheek with the man. Overwhelmed by the smell of his musk, he can't control the hunger. With new tears in his eyes, he tastes the man's skin. The shame doesn't last. The hunger is too much. With every bite he gains strength, and his inhibitions peel away. Swiftly, he begins to truly enjoy what he is doing. Like a newborn, he falls asleep suckling at the feast.

A loud bang wakes him. More pressure from above weighs down on him. Trash is being thrown atop him. The sour smell of the garbage is strong, causing him to gag. The body next to him no longer tempts him. It is disgusting now, rotten. Another loud thud of trash being thrown into the dumpster erupts, enraging him. The sense of anger builds power. The weight that up to now has felt overwhelming, now feels like feathers. He knows he can escape the vault of the dumpster.

The loud crash of the lid closing on him is the last straw. He needs to be out of the horrid dumpster now. With a quick explosion of power, he leaps out of the metal trash box. Landing on the ground, uneasily on his feet, he holds himself steady, with his hands on the ground. Taking a deep breath, he can smell the man's cologne.

It masks his true fragrance. But not enough that Victor can't make it out; it's intoxicating. "Holy shit, man, are you okay?" the bartender calls out. "What were you doing in the dumpster?" he follows up, moving closer to Victor. Victor looks up at the man, his eyes glowing yellow. "What the fuck!" The man freaks out.

Victor, completely healed from the violence Alex put upon him, rises to his feet; the man back peddles away from him. Victor can smell that the man has pissed himself. Quivering in fear, the bartender drops to the floor. "Please don't hurt me," he begs. With a hunger he has never experienced before, Victor attacks the man's throat. The man can't do anything to stop it. His cry for help is empty. He can only mouth the words as he fades into darkness.

The fever inside the young monster is like a volcano. Finally taking the life of the man, he feels something new inside, a growing pain, starting in his chest. His face covered in blood, he looks up to the moon. He can't stop the urge; he howls loud and hard. His ribs crack; the pain is excruciating. A sudden punch to his chest causes him to fall backwards away from his prey.

His shoulders start to separate, ripping from his collar bone. His traps, a muscle he had never worked out in his life, pulsate. His arms snap forward, and swell. His entire body is changing and he can't do anything but cry out in pain.

"Keep it down, my pet," Alex's voice brings peace to the man. Victor looks for the voice, but with his body wrenching in pain, he can't move to find it. "It will end soon," he adds. "But first, this part is going to suck." And as sure as he spoke, a massive pain to his jaw breaks through Victor. He experiences a tearing of his gums and cheekbones, as his nose cracks and changes and his ears pull away from his head.

The pain has just begun to subside, when a new wave of heat comes over him. It is less violent than before, but itchy. His whole body feels like it is being stung by fire ants. "Almost there, my pet," Alex continues to comfort the changing Victor. "Aw, you see. All done," Alex states.

Victor gets up; the pain is gone. He feels wonderful. Using his hands to push up off the ground, he stops, seeing them for the first time. His hands are covered in fur, and are longer and stronger than the ones God gave him. He gazes at his transformed appendages. Claws reach out six inches from his fingertips. He digs into the ground, amazed at the ease with which his claws break through the concrete.

"Look at what I have bestowed upon you," Alex calls out. Victor turns to see him perched on the wooden fence by the dumpster. Victor looks at him with obedience. "How do you feel?" Alex asks, jumping down to him. Victor tries to speak but can't. "It's okay. It will come back," he says and smiles, pushing his hand out, palm down, in front of Victor. Without knowing why, Victor pushes his nose out to him. "Go ahead," Alex says, allowing Victor to lick his hand. "That's right, you love your master." He smiles, moving his hand and rubbing through Victor's hair. "Come, we have much to discuss," he states almost lovingly.

A soft whimper from Victor causes Alex to laugh. "Don't worry. I will teach you how to transform back." Victor whimpers again in response. "Don't worry about the bodies. They have their own purpose now. Let's see what your new body can do," he states and leaps over the fence.

Victor can hear Alex's thoughts. He is telling him how to control his body. This is the art of jumping with ease and not going too far with it. He jumps and lands on the sidewalk. A loud horn scares him, and he jumps to attack it. Alex quickly grabs him, before they can be seen. "Easy, my pet, we need to learn how not to be seen."

Alex moves quickly, carrying Victor to the roof of the building. "It's late, and there will not be a lot of people out, but there will be someone who would see your foolishness. We need to be able to move through the city, without anyone seeing us." He pauses. No longer speaking, he telepathically communicates, educating Victor further. He explains that his new abilities need to be refined. And the only way to do so, is to listen to everything he is told.

No longer can he just jump and expect to be saved. Alex does not accept failure, and if Victor wants to continue on with this gift, he must do exactly what he is told. The life he now has can be easy, but at the beginning it is always hard. He tries to set Victor's mind at ease.

He is scared, but Victor fully wants this gift. He has never felt power like this before. He had always wanted power, but felt weak inside. He had used his uncle's influence to demand power, but for the first time, he doesn't need anyone. He is the all-powerful one. "Careful, my pet, do not get ahead of yourself," Alex projects, interrupting Victor's thoughts.

"We are one now. I can hear all your thoughts, my pet, and you will hear mine. When I allow it." Victor asks him, what has he become. With a massive grin, Alex says, "Can you not guess?"

Victor whimpers; he is frightened of the answer, but his mind thinks of the monsters he has watched in so many of his favorite movies. "Yes, we are werewolves. Stronger than any other immortals or anything you have ever read or watched before," Alex again responds aloud to Victor's thoughts.

Alex listens to every question Victor has. He answers the ones he finds pertinent to his end goal. Having been a fan of vampires and werewolves, Victor asks about vampires. Alex laughs out loud at the question. "They are amazing creatures. Be careful with the old ones. But the young ones are nothing. We have always been stronger than them. But they are very conniving and not to be trusted."

Victor continues to pepper Alex with questions. No longer in the mood to deal with such things, he commands Victor to be quiet. His education tonight is that of how to use his powers, not that of the immortals that they will have to contend with.

"First, you must understand the most important rule. We are a family; you never turn your back on your family," he instructs, clinching his fist and looking up toward the Los Feliz hills. Victor asks about his own family. "They are no longer your family." Victor has visions of his mother, father, and even his uncle.

The visions are not missed by Alex; he sees how Victor truly felt about his worth. All of his fears of being found out to be a coward, his wanting to be out of the life when he was young. His love for music and dance. A distant memory of Victor as a young boy, walking up to his mother telling her of his dreams of being a dancer. Her laughing at him.

A time in the boy's locker room, when he realized that he was attracted to men. Alex is surprised by the many levels of the man he had judged incorrectly. He wasn't a weakling in the way he had thought before. He was lost, and alone, acting out and trying to find a place in a world that didn't accept him for who he was.

Victor begins to cry, feeling the memories that Alex is viewing. He is ashamed, afraid that he will take the gift now that he knows his inner desires. Whimpering, he falls to his knees; the large beast gives out a heartbreaking sound. Alex kneels down and places his hand on his head. "It's okay, my pet. You do not have to be afraid. My kind does not judge such things. If you desire male or female, it makes no difference."

"I have a brother who prefers the company of men, and it has not interfered with his ability to do his job within the family. I should expect, now that you have shared your secret, you will be even more powerful," Alex adds.

Alex looks across the street; Victor understands that they are supposed to jump from one roof to the other. Alex moves with power and grace, leaping across the great distance. Victor is filled with confidence, and goes for it. His body is not strong enough to make the leap in one jump, but with Alex in his mind, he makes it in two.

Alex holds him tight, embracing the large beast. Alex hears Victor's thoughts, asking if he can see his true form. "Oh my pet, I cannot. You will see me soon, but for now I will be as I am," he states calmly.

"We only have a few hours before the sun comes up. I still have a lot to show you," he says, patting Victor on the side of his face. Alex continues to lead him from rooftop to rooftop. They head up the street toward the hills. Victor understands they are going to see something very important to Alex. Something that he has been working on for some time.

Reaching Melisa's house, Alex explains who the house belongs to. He takes him around back, giving him an article of clothing for him to learn from. He must take in the scent and track it. Knowing that it is a very difficult gift, Alex makes a game of it. Almost like training a dog, he hides the cloth from Victor, having him search for it.

Victor, wanting to please his master, is eager and a quick study. He finds the cloth every time, faster and faster. Alex, hiding the item one last time, notices a horrible smell. Looking for it, he finds the spot where the Hunter had fallen. A big smirk appears on his face. Victor, feeling his happiness, rushes to him.

Alex, feeling him coming, realizes that he is about to run over the blood of the Hunter. He quickly jumps over and drops Victor, stopping him from touching the blood. "You are too young to touch that poison. It will hurt you!" he scolds Victor. "Remember this smell. You must run if you ever pick it up. It is the one thing we must fear."

Victor asks why? "Because, we are still too young to tangle with such a thing. I have a way to stop him, but until that day we need to be careful," he informs him. "Your training is over for today. Come with me," he orders the beast, leading him up to the top of the hill. There they wait for the sun to rise.

The sun's magnificence breaks through the darkness. "Return to your human form," Alex instructs. Victor feels the fire within, his arms slowly returning to their normal state, his face crackling, as it breaks back to normal. The pain is much less than the first transformation. He can hear Alex's voice in his head, soothing him, telling him to relax, reassuring him that his powers are still within him. He is a better self, from now on.

Now back to human form, he looks out upon the world. His clothes are ripped and stretched out. Alex hands him a belt to help with his pants. His eyes are sharper, not as good as when he was in werewolf form, but much better than his mortal eyes were. He looks at his master. The proud new father. He has passed his first test. He is now like Alex, and will be forever.

How do we live like this? Every time we transform, what happens to our clothes? How do we get new clothes when we transform back? Where do I live now? Victor's mind fills with questions.

Alex laughs, reading the man's mind. "You can never go back home. You have a new family. You will live a life with structure and accountability; you will know your place. No longer will you be treated better than you deserve. You earn what you get," he states firmly. "Do you understand, my pet?"

"Yes, my master," Victor states, bowing his head.

"I will teach you of our dens, our many hideouts. The arts of being a werewolf." Alex looks out at Downtown Los Angeles. "Do you not trust me?"

"I do, my master." Victor walks up behind him, taking in the view.

"Great. So let's go get your car and empty your bank account."

CHAPTER THIRTEEN

Walter looks in on his sister before he leaves for work. It's seven in the morning. The two dogs are literally lying on top of her. He smirks, wondering if she can even breathe. His father is up, drinking coffee and reading the paper. "Good morning," he greets him, filling his cup. "How is she?"

"Good, still sleeping."

"Did she let the dogs up on the bed?"

"Of course," he laughs, trying to keep his voice down. His father flips the page of his paper with a light chuckle and straightens the pages with a soft flick of his wrists.

"You have an early one."

"Yeah, got a homicide in Los Feliz."

"Hmm?" His father shakes his head. "This city is getting as bad as it was when I was young."

"Nah, Dad. It's worse."

"You think so? I have a few friends from my time that would debate that."

"I know, Dad. But trust me. Shit is getting really bad."

"Well, you better be safe out; it's raining again," he says and flips to another page.

"All right, love you, Dad." Walter heads out the door.

"Umm hum," he responds. Hearing the door close behind Walter, he looks up, out the window. He watches his son drive off. Turning to the wall with all the pictures, he gazes upon his son's police academy gradation picture. He looks handsome. Darker than Melisa, he has dark, deep-set brown eyes and almost curly dark brown hair. He looks like Melisa. They have their mother's nose and chin. The father smiles as he looks at the image. Seeing his dear departed wife in him. He looks at it only for a few seconds. Then returns to his paper.

Walter drives straight to Los Feliz; he arrives at the bar, which is full of uniformed officers standing around. One of the officers lifts the police tape, allowing him into the parking lot, his face telling him he's about to walk into a scene that's not nice.

His partner, Detective Stephanie Walken, is a short but firm-looking woman. She wears her reddish hair short, lying flat past her ears. She is dressed in a gray pants suit, with a heavy coat, keeping her warm. She is standing under the awning, holding a closed umbrella to her side. Clouds of breath escape as she sips on her sweltering coffee. Her expression doesn't tell him anything, but he learned long ago not to judge a situation by her demeanor. She was hard as stone.

They have been partners for over two years; she transferred from narcotics. She didn't like working undercover and needed a change of pace. She and Walter didn't get along at first. She was so busy proving that a woman could do what he could, she missed that he didn't care about that. He gave everyone the same respect.

It wasn't until she met his sister Melisa that her thoughts on him changed. Melisa and Stephanie are friends. Not close, but they hang out every once in a while. Walter gets invited, but he doesn't go out too often.

Stepping out of his car, he makes a loud splash. He didn't notice he parked next to a puddle, and now his left leg is soaked. "Nice job," Stephanie hollers out to him, as he squeezes out his soaked pant leg. "Crazy weather, eh?" Stephanie walks out to meet him with her umbrella now open.

"Yeah, on and off all week," he adds. "So, what do we got?" he asks, giving in to dealing with a wet leg for the rest of the day.

"Animal attack," she reports without emotion, holding the umbrella so it covers them both. "They got coffee inside; I just got here," she adds while taking another sip.

"The morning shift bartender found him," Stephanie points out as they head inside.

"Who was he?"

"Just the closing bartender."

"His name?"

"Marlin, Marlin Martinez."

"Fuck, I knew him," Walter states. "He was a nice guy."

"Used to come here?" she asks.

"Years ago."

"Not the kind of place I'd expect for you to hang out. Bars that open this early in the morning attract a special kind of drunk."

"You're funny. I was young once too." They walk through the bar passing the men's restroom. The door is open. Little yellow markers are placed around the scene. "What did they find in there?" Walter asks as they walk by.

"Blood, urine, and that's about it."

"Fingerprints?"

"Nothing that they could pull. Too many people have been through that bathroom for them to get a good one."

Reaching the body, he uncovers him. "Fuck." He looks away for a moment in surprise and disgust. Looking back, studying the victim, he notes that the body is broken and mangled. "What kind of animal could do this?"

"We got a specialist on the way."

Walter gets up and looks around. "No cameras?"

"Nope, none inside either."

"That's too bad." Looking at the dumpster, he sees blood splatter on it. "What's that from?" He gets close and investigates. Looking around on the floor he notices a strand of hair. Using a pen, he pulls it up. "Look at this," he exclaims. "Someone else was here."

"Hey, bring that camera over here," Stephanie calls out to the forensics team.

Walter continues to look around. "Anyone check the dumpster?" he asks, looking at the forensics. Walter puts on his blue gloves.

"We've been waiting on you guys," the man with the camera answers.

"Fuck," Walter murmurs. Opening the dumpster, he sees blood. "Shit," he turns to Stephanie. "We got another one," he says and moves a few things around to see the body. The man's face is half eaten. "I don't think this was an animal," Walter adds.

Stephanie peers in, and gasps at the sight. Walter is surprised by her reaction. "What? You okay?"

"I think I know this guy. Back from when I was working gang and narcotics."

"Who is he?"

"He worked for the Taymizyan family, if I'm not mistaken." Flashes of memories from her past days working undercover hit her like a wave. She and this man were friendly. Almost too friendly. She remembers the tattoo on his neck.

"Really? That is interesting." He looks over at the forensics team, specifically the guy carrying the camera. "Can you guys catalog everything in here?" he asks.

Stephanie, using her gloves, moves the man's face. She wants to see his neck. "There you are," she says. "He was a guard. Aram something. He would have been here with a family member."

"Mr. Taymizyan?"

"No, this guy is way too small time." She walks away in thought, taking her gloves off. Walter looks at the forensics men, letting them know they can start. He follows Stephanie through the bar, to the outside parking lot. Seeing the rain falling on her, he takes an umbrella from another police officer who is heading inside.

"What's the deal?" he asks her.

"What?" Stephanie was so deep in thought she hadn't noticed Walter standing next to her. "Shit, I'm sorry. I just knew the man."

"What do you mean, you knew the man?"

"When I was working undercover. He was a good man. Wrong profession, but had a good heart."

"So he was a good, bad guy?"

"Oddly enough, he was. If all the crooks out there were like him, I don't think things would be so bad."

"All right, well, enough about how great he was. What else can you tell me?"

"He worked as a bodyguard."

"Can we find out who he was watching over?" Walters cracks his knuckles with excitement.

"That's easy. The nephew."

"What nephew?"

"Victor Rees, a little dirt bag who loves to throw his bullshit weight around." Stephanie looks around the parking lot in deep thought.

"So, if Aram was here, Victor was here?"

"Absolutely."

"So we put an APB out on him, and there we go."

"Well, that would make sense. But, if the bodyguard of a bed wetter is lying dead, his face half eaten off, you think we are going to find the guy he was supposed to be protecting?"

"Maybe not alive, but absolutely," Walter says and smiles.

"This is a turf war; I know it," Stephanie states, her calm, could-care-less demeanor returning.

"So what do we do, turn it over to Narcotics?" Walter asks.

"Hell no. This is our case."

"That's what I thought. So let's start with what we know. And then work on the things we don't."

"I'm going to make some calls. You make sure we get everything from the scene," Stephanie tells him, as she heads for her car slyly wiping a tear from her face. Walter knows she has a lot more connections in narcotics and gang unit, so he isn't going to challenge her. He heads back inside out of the rain, letting her make her calls.

Pulling a chair from the bar, he sits outside under the tarp watching as they catalog every item in the dumpster and tag the two men's bodies. A uniformed officer calls out to Walter. Inside the bar the representative of the Department of Animal Services, Wild Life division is waiting to speak with him.

He had forgotten Stephanie had called them. But now that she was there he was excited to get some help. He saw an attractive woman, looking to be straight out of college, with dark, sun-bleached hair, tan skin, and an accent shared by many beach goers. He knows she's from either Orange County or San Diego. After a brief introduction, he asks Miss Heather James if she would mind looking at the scene, warning her that it is very gruesome. Acting tough, she shrugs off the suggestion that she can't handle blood. Walter can tell she is in way over her head.

Walter has no problem leading her straight to the back where the bodies are. Even though he warned her of the sight and she acted so brave, upon seeing the bodies, she rushes to the restroom, sick. Stephanie returns just in time to witness the woman's flight. Trying not to get upset by her actions, she looks at Walter with a look of annoyance.

When Heather returns, she's flushed and woozy. "I must admit, I have never seen anything like that before," she states while using a damp paper towel on her forehead.

"It's okay, you never get used to it."

"I have heard of animals attacking, but that was not only an animal."

"Yeah, we figured that. But the other marks were surely those of a large animal," Walter counters.

"Here in Los Angeles, this far from the hills?" she says, straightening her posture, taking a controlled breath.

"It is odd," Walter smiles, watching the animal expert regain her confidence.

"A coyote couldn't have done this; mountain lions, maybe."

"But a lion coming all the way down here?"

"It doesn't make much sense. Unless, maybe if it was rabid," she offers.

"What about getting into the building? That seems odd to me," Walter points out.

"Not really, this fence isn't that high."

"And the dumpster?"

"That wouldn't be a problem for a large cat or other large mammal." She puts the paper towel down. "Wild animals can always find a way," she warns. "Plus, if someone was trying to hide in the dumpster, the animal could have followed them into it. Then just jumped out when they were done eating."

"Now that you make that point, if the bartender was throwing away trash and the animal was inside, maybe it leaped out and attacked him," Stephanie blurts out.

"What other animals do we have around here?" Walter turns back to the animal expert.

"Large cats and coyotes. I can't think of anything else. Bears are in the mountains. But that's not to say that someone may not have an illegal pet that got out."

"What do you mean?" Walter looks to his partner, making sure she is listening.

"We are always dealing with people trying to keep illegal wildlife as pets, bringing them over from other countries and regions."

"Yes, I'm familiar with that. Like having an alligator or monkey as a pet?" He nods.

"Exactly."

"I didn't know that was your department," Walter states, flirtatiously.

"It is, but only limitedly. We still get you guys involved," she flirts back.

"So, if we find that it was someone's pet, should we contact you?"

"That's up to you, chief." She pulls out a card. "My cell number is on it," she adds. Stephanie just shakes her head, watching the two.

"Thank you," he says, giving off a muted, uncomfortable laugh. "I'll use it, if it's needed," he continues, chuckling.

"That's awkward," Stephanie can't help but comment under her breath. Heather gives her a quick glance. Walter pretends not to have heard her.

"One last thing." She pulls out her pen. "Larry Walsh, Chief Veterinarian over at the zoo, may be of better help regarding large animals. He may be able to identify what breed we're dealing with." She writes his number on a card.

"That would be great." Walter smiles and walks her out. As they pass the crime scene photographer, Walter asks the man working the camera who is putting his gear away, "How long before I can have those images?"

"Here." He hands him a digital memory card. "It's all on there. I haven't edited them yet . . . but I have a copy to do that with," he informs him.

"Oh, great." Heather continues to her car, and Walter hurries to catch up to her. He holds her door for her, saying goodbye.

"Walter! What do you say we go see that guy at the zoo?" Stephanie calls out

"Oh yeah," he hollers back. Looking down at Heather and blushing, he closes the door, saying goodbye one last time.

CHAPTER FOURTEEN

The smell of bacon wakes Melisa. She has to push the dogs off; her body is soaked and overheated. "Where were you when I was in Tahoe?" she teases. The dogs stand at the door, waiting. "God, what time is it?" she says out loud. Grabbing her tablet, she sees she has sixteen text messages on the notification screen. She starts to read the first few before noticing the time: "Damn, it's eleven." She quickly pops up from the bed.

"You up?" her father calls out from the kitchen. The dogs both turn to the door, but look back asking for permission to go. "Yeah, I'm up," she hollers back to her dad. "Go ahead," she whispers to the dogs. They rush out of the room, claws scratching at the floor as they run.

"There you guys are?" She can hear her dad talking to the dogs. He lets them out to pee, and has a full conversation with them, asking them how their night was, if they enjoyed lying on the bed, and if they took care of his little girl. Melisa can't help but feel warm inside from his words.

Turning back to the tablet she reads the messages from Chris, ignoring the rest. She can read his worry. She writes a long reply, informing him that everything is fine, and she just slept in. Groggy, she heads to the bathroom. Looking at herself in the mirror, she feels worn out. The last few days are catching up with her. Her stomach hurts, but it's not morning sickness. It's something else. She has been lucky so far, in that regard. Her stomach makes a growling sound, something she'd never heard before.

A sharp pain under her rib, jabs her. "What the heck?" she lets out.

Placing her hand on her abdomen, she feels around. Another poke strikes in the same spot. Pushing hard on her stomach, she finds it. Something is moving in her stomach. Her eyes widen: how could this be? She's only at the beginning of the second trimester.

Her baby is moving, and powerfully enough so she can already feel it. A rush comes over her. Her little boy is strong, and moving. The pain begins to worsen. Melisa feels the baby moving again. Closing her eyes, she can picture his movements within. The agony is too much; she buckles, holding onto the sink, so she doesn't fall. She looks at herself in the mirror, sees her eyes tearing from the pain.

"What's happening?" Suddenly, her whole body begins to writhe, and she can't hold herself upright. Falling to the floor, she holds herself in the fetal position. Her every muscle begins to pulsate. She can hear the dogs scratching at the glass slider, her father calling to them to stop.

"You will be okay, my love," she can hear Chris's voice in her head. He continues to speak to her, comforting her as she goes through the most intense pain of her life. Then, as if nothing had happened, it stops. Her whole body feels normal. Better than normal. The dogs are quiet. Her father is laughing at them for being so silly. She can hear everything outside the house. Getting up, she looks at herself in the mirror. The look of tiredness is gone. Her complexion is perfect, almost youthful. All the cuts are gone. Her eyes are clearer than she has ever seen them before.

Looking over her body, she is amazed. The feeling that Chris was there with her is strong. Something inside her is telling her that she has changed for the betterment of the baby. The endorphins running through her don't let up. She is high and happy. The memories of the events of the past few days recede to the back of her mind, as if everything is great. She brushes her teeth, then heads to the kitchen.

Her father is still outside when she enters the kitchen. He's playing fetch with the dogs. She pours herself some coffee and heads out the sliding door. Looking out on the yard, she says, "I see Mom's garden is doing well."

"Oh yes, Mija. I work on it when I can," he says. But from the look of the yard, she knows he's out there every day.

"Did you leave me any bacon?"

"Of course, Mija. I have it in the oven keeping warm." He smiles, turns his attention back to the dogs, and throws the ball.

"Is that the Malibu?" Melisa asks. The car is under a blue car-cover. But she knows the shape of it well.

"Yes; needed room at the shop." He throws the ball one last time before passing her by. "Come inside, it's cold."

"I thought it was at the shop being worked on?"

"It was, but I couldn't turn away customers," he tells her as he sets a plate for her.

"I heard the shop isn't doing that well."

"Your brother is crazy." He fries a few eggs, and puts them on a plate with bacon and beans. Melisa loves the smell. "Tortillas?" her father asks.

"*Sí*," she answers eagerly, closing the slider. "Where's Walter?"

"He had to go to work early." He drops a couple of tortillas from the flame on her plate.

"Oh."

"Go ahead, Mija, eat," He quickly makes a plate for himself. Sitting at the table, he observes, "Your cuts are cleared up." Melisa just smiles. They make small talk. He focuses mainly on her job; his pride in her being so successful is sometimes overwhelming to Melisa. He asks about her house, living in the fancy Los Feliz neighborhood. If she meets any famous people. He doesn't care too much about that, but finds it funny that she is up there with them.

She answers every question honestly; her voice tends to be a little more high-pitched. The dynamics from the past, her being his little girl coming out as quickly as the conversation began. She keeps everything light, but when he starts to ask about the accident, she has trouble telling him everything. She knows how protective he can be, and the last thing she needs is for him to get riled up. They were having such a good time.

Wanting to redirect the conversation, she talks about the little Guatemalan restaurant Mr. McCarthy took her to. And of course, he knows the place. He knows Los Angeles in a way that most can only pretend to. You couldn't tell by looking at him now, but he was a socialite of his time. Observing his salt and pepper hair. Long, but not too long, pulled back in a ponytail. She knew he was still going to this barber that charges seven dollars for a cut. He loved it. He used to take Walter there when he was little.

"Is Anita still there? I haven't seen her in years."

"Yes, she is very nice," Melisa answers.

"Did you tell here you're my daughter?"

"How was I supposed to know you knew her?"

"Aw, Mija. Because you are Guatemalan," he reminds her.

"Yeah, well, I didn't."

"Okay, okay." He laughs. As he gets up to clear the dishes, Melisa watches him work. As always, he's wearing Ben Davis work pants and a simple t-shirt. She misses hanging out with him. "Do you have work today?" he asks over the running of water.

"No, I'm staying here today."

"Really?" he asks turning to her with a smile. "I have a few things to do at the shop, but I will be back in an hour."

"That's fine. I'll hang out with my new buddies." She points to the dogs that have been watching, still as gargoyles, from the slider.

"Oh my god, how long have they been sitting there?" He laughs. "Can you feed them?" he asks. Which she does.

Her father leaves a few minutes after cleaning the kitchen. Melisa spends her time playing with the dogs, going through her closet, looking over her old pictures. She finds one of her mom, when she was in the hospital. She had a scarf covering her head. Her face was sunken, eyes with black rings. But there was no sadness in her eyes. Melisa tears up from the memory. Her mom was the strongest person she's ever known.

The dogs both brush up against her to comfort her. She holds them and weeps. It's a cry that she hasn't had; she didn't even cry this hard when her mom died. The feeling of letting out the emotions is so new to her, that she almost can't stop. The dogs push on her, getting her attention. Looking at them, she knows everything is okay.

Getting up, she puts the photos back in the closet. She continues to go down memory lane, looking at her old college photos, letters from old boyfriends. Then she finds an old box, something she forgot she had. It's full of letters from her mom. She wrote to her every day while at college. Melisa opens one:

Dear Melisa,

I have some amazing news. Your father and I are going to go to Guatemala! He, finally, is willing to go, I have everything set up with his cousins. They are so nice. Your brother will not be going. I don't think, a month away from school is the right thing for him right now? I'll write about that later. Let's just say he has a lot of his father in him?

I don't want to count on anything before it happens but if things go as I hope, we will finally be buying the coffee farm from your dad's uncle. I'm so excited. Maybe when you're done with school we can open the hospital you always wanted, too.

Before I get ahead of myself, I just want to tell you that we love you. We are so proud of what you are doing. I know things are not always easy. But you are a strong person, who knows who she is. I know that sometimes life can be unfair; you are a woman in a man's world. But don't make excuses. Work twice as hard as the rest. You come from good stock.

Love, Mom

Melisa's transported back to the day she first read the letter. She was sitting in her sorority house bedroom after a horrible meeting with the counselor. He was very dismissive of her idea of going to UCSF Med school. He went as far to tell her to focus her time on getting into a different program, something easier to get in to. She remembered leaving in tears. She had the best test scores in her class, but he felt she wouldn't fit in. Her mother's words could not have come at a better time. It started a fire in her heart, which still burns bright.

Eyes watering, she puts the letter back in the envelope. She starts to laugh, when she remembers sending the counselor a copy of her acceptance letter. The dogs let her know that someone is coming in. Their wagging tails tell her it must be her dad. "Go get him," she tells them, laughing. The dogs rush out of the room, scratching at the floor. Melisa quickly puts everything back into the closet.

"Hey Dad," she says as she comes out.

"Huh." Seeing her puffy eyes, he is immediately on alert. "What happened?"

"Nothing, Dad. I was just reading some letters that Mom sent me, back when I was in college."

"Oh." He lowers his shoulders and puts his keys on the end table. "Are you hungry?"

"No, Dad." She knows he uses food as a way to control things, which makes her laugh. "So, do you remember that time you and Mom went down to Guatemala?"

"Yeah?" he answers, squinting his eyes.

"Who's running the farm?"

"What?"

"The farm you and mom bought, I was wondering who is running it?"

"Oh, your cousin is taking care of it."

"Have you ever thought of going back down there, maybe running it yourself?"

"That was your mother's dream, not mine."

"Well, you seem to do a lot with her garden; that was her dream, not yours, remember?"

"Aw Mija, don't use your brains with me. I have stubbornness."

"What do you say we go?"

"We?"

"Yeah, I have some time I can take off. With everything that has happened I'm sure I can take a couple more weeks off. Maybe Chris can come with us. He's really good with bars and clubs; maybe we can open up a bed and breakfast?"

"This is so unlike you. You don't like to go to places like this. You're too fancy. Everyone is in mud houses." She knows he's full of shit. Her mother explained that his family is wealthy. He had turned his back on them a long time ago, because he didn't think it was fair. But they still cared about him. Yes, he had lots of fights with them over how they treated the poor. But he never did anything about it.

Not wanting to get into it with him she follows the path of talking about her mom. "Dad, Mom wanted that farm so you guys could retire there. Maybe it's time to at least visit it."

"Your mother had a lot of ideas. She didn't understand my country."

"Dad, I don't think that's fair."

"Your mother was a beautiful woman. But she didn't want to see the truth of that country."

"And what is that?"

"People are people. We can't change anything down there. My family has made their minds up."

Melisa knew the truth. Her father left telling everyone he would come back and change the country. He felt there was all this injustice and he was going to cure it. However, when he got to the United States, things didn't go as smoothly as he had hoped. Now, some forty years later, he is embarrassed.

"I'm going to look into tickets. We're going." Melisa decides to use a page out of her mother's playbook. He wouldn't do anything unless he felt like he needed to protect them. He wouldn't let her go by herself.

"You're crazy, Mija. I'm not going." The dogs start barking at the front door. No matter what their master tells them, they won't stop. The barks turn to growls. A loud knock on the door causes them to go wild. Melisa's father grabs them by their collars. "What's wrong with you guys?" He gets them to go with him. Another knock, this time softer, strikes. The dogs again go crazy.

"Sit down," Melisa orders, just before she opens the door. The dogs obey. Her father is surprised by the control she has, especially since he seems to have lost it. Opening the door slowly, she says, "I thought I was going to see you later?" Her father tries to peer over her shoulder. As she opens the door fully, Chris is revealed standing at the door.

"I couldn't help myself," he tells her. "I'm sorry to show up unannounced, Mr. Castro," he hollers over her.

"It's okay, come in. I'll get the dogs." He rushes to round them up again.

"No need, sir, they will be fine," he tells him, returning his gaze to Melisa. She can feel his eyes checking her out. She smiles, knowing he is taking notice of her change. She invites him in. He hands Melisa's phone to her. "I went ahead and picked this up for you."

The dogs keep their distance, looking back and forth between Melisa and Chris, almost confused.

"How did you find it?" She is pleased, but she is suspicious of him. *Did he go to the hospital for the phone or was he looking for the John Doe?*

"Let me put some food on," Melisa's father offers.

"No, Dad, that's okay."

"Chris? You want food? I'm about to make an early dinner."

"I would love some, Mr. Castro," he answers, smiling at Melisa. "I will not be rude to your father," he tells her softly. "These dogs, they are beautiful," he adds, taking a seat on the living room couch. The dogs watch his every move.

"Yeah, he got them a short time ago. Still in training, I guess . . . I'm sorry I didn't text you sooner." She takes a seat next to him.

"I think they were doing the right thing. They didn't know who was at the door." Chris doesn't acknowledge her apology. "You look great."

"Yeah." She looks at him with soft eyes.

"How's the baby?" His caring eyes focus on her belly as he softly caresses it.

"Shush, everything is fine." She moves his hands and makes looks to see if her dad heard him. "I haven't told my dad yet."

"Why not?" He gets up. The dogs quickly move to Melisa's side. "It's okay, I mean no harm," he says very calmly. He takes a knee in front of her, grabbing her hands. "I don't think it's fair. I've told my family."

"Did you tell your dad?"

"He already knew. But we talked about it last night."

"Really? . . . What did he say?"

"He wasn't happy."

"Well, maybe if you had let me meet him he would feel different about it."

"I promise you, that is not the case. He is old school."

"So, it's because I'm Hispanic?"

"Actually, it's deeper than that."

"I'm not Polish?" she asks, eyebrows raised.

"That's closer." He offers a soft kiss, but she gives him her cheek. "I have something we need to discuss," he whispers. Melisa moves away from him; the dogs quickly surround Chris, who smirks while keeping an eye on them. "They are really in tune with you," he points out. "I'm impressed." He closes his eyes for a moment in thought. "That old bastard was telling me." He shakes his head, speaking to himself.

"What?" Melisa asks, not having heard what he said.

"Melisa, I have something I must talk to you about. But we cannot discuss it here." He looks at the dogs, tilting his head. Geronimo begins to growl. Chris breathes deeply, then slowly lowers his hand on the ground.

"I don't think I've ever seen you interact with an animal," she points out as she watches him. Genghis moves around stalking Chris from behind. Geronimo's fur is raised. He is about to attack Chris. Melisa is frozen. It's primal. Chris's every muscle flexes and he touches Genghis and Geronimo at the same time. Both dogs yelp, and nip at his hands, but Chris has them on their backs with one motion.

"Geronimo, Genghis. I mean no harm." He lets go of them, speaking softly. The two dogs jump back up; their growls have lessened but are still present. "These dogs are amazing," he points out. He snaps his fingers. "Sit," he says. The dogs obey.

"How did you know their names?" She looks back in her memory. *Did I call them by their names?* she wonders.

"They told me," he informs her. "We have lots to discuss." He stands. "You keep her safe, when I am not here," he tells the dogs firmly.

"What the heck is going on?" Melisa leans back into the couch cushion.

"Food," her father calls out from the kitchen.

"I will tell you everything. I promise. But first, let's tell your father." He reaches his hand out and she notices his hand is bleeding. "Oh my god, one of them bit you," she quickly places her hand over the wound, putting pressure on it.

"You are going to stay with me tonight," he tells her.

"Look at your hand. Which one bit you?" she asks, holding his hand.

"They both did. I'm very impressed." He looks down at the dogs with a smile. "Good boys," he says pulling his hand away and petting them both. "I'll be okay." He follows her into the kitchen.

"Mr. Castro, your bathroom?" he asks.

"Down the hall," he states, not turning from the food.

"Thank you." He looks at Melisa, eyeing her to tell him their news.

"Dad?"

"Yes love?"

"I got some news to tell you." Melisa begins to explain everything to him.

He is excited by the news. His first question: "Is it a boy?" When Chris comes back into the kitchen, he is greeted with a hug from Melisa's father. Chris towers over the man, but the old mechanic's arms easily hold him tight. He welcomes him to the table and explains that he too knocked up his girlfriend before marriage. But he married her before the baby. He asked when they would get married and where.

Chris informs him that he would like to contribute to the wedding cost, if that would be okay. Melisa father isn't insulted, but declines. He will allow for Chris to pay for the rehearsal dinner, which was their way. After which they enjoy the simple meal her father prepared and Chris and Melisa leave together, with the plan for her to stay with him for the next few nights.

CHAPTER FIFTEEN

The night has come on fast. The rain has built throughout the day. What was once a heavy shower, is now a light drizzle. The man in the leather jacket arrives at the club, parking in between hundred-thousand-dollar sports cars. People have been gushing over the cars all night. The rain doesn't seem to bother any of the club goers. The women are all dressed in short skirts and high heels, the men wearing thousand-dollar suits.

The roar of the classic muscle car catches everyone's attention. The man in the leather jacket getting out of it can hear all the whispers about him and his car. A man in a red Ferrari notices the change. "What year?" the owner of the sports car calls out, trying to make it seem like he doesn't mind the change in attention.

"I beg your pardon?" Ranald, the man in the leather jacket, looks down at the man's shoes, sees he's wearing some kind of colorful slippers. Following up his line, he's not impressed. The man is wearing pants that hug his ankles, yet flare out and are baggy at the top, hanging below his butt. He wears a shimmering black shirt, with some kind of jacket that he has pushed up the sleeves. Not wanting anything to do with the ridiculous man, he continues toward the club.

"Your car, what year is it?"

"If you don't know, no need to converse about it." The group of people around snicker and make fun of the man and his fancy car.

"Fuck you, man," the embarrassed man yells but doesn't get a response from Ranald, infuriating the oddly dressed man further.

Ranald walks to the back, where he meets Aaron for the first time. "Can I speak with Chris?" he asks.

"Fuck, do you guys never stop?" Aaron shakes his head in disbelief and annoyance.

"I beg your pardon . . . ? I believe you are mistaking me for someone else," he tries to explain. His thick Scottish accent becomes softer.

"Oh, and who might that be? Why you wearing those glasses?"

"These?" Ranald points to them. "These are prescription." He smiles. "I have some business with Chris. Is he around?"

"Really? What business? Why don't I know about it?"

"You don't know about it, because he doesn't know about it. I must have misspoken. I have some business that I'd like to share with him."

"I'm getting tired of this shit. I think you best leave," Aaron says and rolls his shoulder.

"I assure you, young man. I came with no intention of causing a problem."

"Well, I would recommend you leave and come back during normal office hours."

"I'm sorry, but that just won't work for me." Ranald moves like a blur. "You are too young to know who I am, but I know who you are," he whispers in his ear. "Days don't really work for me," he says with a smile. He softly kisses him on the cheek, mocking Aaron. "Where is your brother? I would like to speak to him." He lets go of the much larger man.

Aaron smirks, then tries to hit the man but misses. The mysterious man moves back to his original spot. "Relax, young one. Your father and I go way back . . ."

"My father?" His voice deepens, trailing to a growl.

"Aaron, I mean no disrespect. I apologize if I have come on too strong. No need to ruffle your fur. Will you please contact your brother? What I have to share actually can affect all of us."

"How do you know my name?" Aaron's eyes begin to change.

"Wow, no need for this. I assure you, I come in peace. Call me Ranald." He raises his arms, in an attempt to show innocence.

"Whatever." Aaron closes his eyes, and rolls his neck. "My brother isn't here," he states and opens his eyes, which are back to normal.

"Do you know where he is?"

"I do not."

"Could you please call your brother?"

"Fine," Aaron answers, heading into the club.

"Now, please, invite me in," Ranald asks with a light-hearted smile.

Once inside, the visitor sees the bar is being set up by all the workers. The DJ is hard at work, getting his system up. Looking around, he spots the other brothers. "Now Aaron, you have another brother named after your dear father. Is he here?" he asks, following close behind.

"I do, what of it?" Aaron looks at his brother Alex who is talking to a bartender. He does his best not to make eye contact.

"Is he here tonight?" Ranald asks.

"No." Reaching the step to the office, Arron points. "Go up, first door on the right," he tells him.

"Do you think it possible to get a drink?"

"I didn't think your kind drank anything but blood?"

"Oh my dear Aaron. I am not what you think. Maybe once before, but I am now like your father, changed." He smiles, heading up the steps.

"Whiskey?"

"Scotch would be better. But I will take whatever you feel I deserve," he replies. Aaron watches as he traverses up the steps. He waits for him to go into the office. He hurries to Alex.

"You need to get out of here. Something is here, and it looks like trouble."

"Who's here?"

"I don't know, but he asked about you, and he knows Dad."

"Dad?" Alex gets riled up. "I'll . . ." Aaron stops him.

"No, he is not what you think. He is powerful."

"What should I do? Should I talk to him?"

"No . . . He wants Chris; I'll call him." He pulls out his cell phone. "You should leave," he tells him. Alex rushes out the back. Aaron makes the call. The phone rings three times, before Chris answers light-heartedly.

"Hello, Melisa is here with me. So watch what you say," Chris answers from inside his car. "Hi Aaron," Melisa chimes in.

"Hi Melisa," Aaron says. "Chris, do you think we could talk privately?" he asks.

"Why?"

"Trust me. I'm sorry, Melisa, it's not personal," he says to both. Melisa grabs the phone from the center console and hands it to Chris, trying to be helpful. Chris looks at her with love in his eyes. Melisa returns the look, pushing her lips out and blowing a kiss to him.

"What's it about?" Chris turns his attention back to the road.

"A friend of Dad's." Aaron's voice is slightly panicked, an out of character reaction for the strong man.

"What friend of Dad's?" Chris's eyes narrow

"I don't know. He calls himself Ranald; he is someone who knows Dad really well."

"Ranald? I've never heard that name before" His tone is firm, something Melisa has never heard out of him. She touches his shoulder, mouthing if everything is okay. He looks at her and smiles, nodding, for her not to worry. He mouths a kiss in confirmation.

"He's vamp, but not," Aaron begins.

"What?" Chris tries not to show any emotions.

"I can't explain it. He said he doesn't drink blood anymore, something about being like Dad now."

"What's he wearing?"

"A pair of dark sunglasses, a leather jacket, and blue jeans."

"Did he take off the glasses?"

"He said they were prescription."

"I bet they are. Where is he now?"

"In the office."

"Okay, I need to drop off Mel before I come by. Don't let him leave. I actually want to speak with him."

"Do you know who he is?"

"Yes, but only from stories. Don't fuck with him. Don't let Alex, for god's sake; that would be the worst." He gives off a soft chuckle. Melisa is watching intently.

"That's another thing. He asked about Alex."

"What?" He looks at Melisa. "All right, I'm coming now. You'll need to take Mel home when I get there though." He looks at her and mouths that he's sorry. She just smiles and blinks letting him know it's okay. "I'm close. I can be there in twenty," he adds.

Chris arrives fifteen minutes later. He sees the GTO and knows that it must belong to the man in the leather jacket. He parks in his private spot. "I don't know how long this will take. Are you sure it's okay if Aaron takes you home?" he asks.

"That's fine."

"I still need to tell you something very important. So don't go to sleep before I get home." He walks with Melisa in through the front of the club. He is greeted by all the club goers, all wanting to get in favor with him. Melisa can feel all the eyes on her. She's not dressed for a club. She's wearing Hudson skinny jeans, a vintage tee-shirt, a black belted raincoat, and big black patent-looking rain boots.

Once inside, the music is loud. Chris is practically dragging Melisa through the club. She feels every pounce of the bass, the rhythm punching her in the pit of her stomach. The lights on the dance floor are bright. Blue, green, red, and yellow lasers make her head feel pressured. The room starts to spin; pulling back on Chris, she begins to fall over. He is pushing through so quickly that he almost doesn't realize she is collapsing. Aaron comes to greet them, but sees that Melisa has fainted and quickly calls to his other brother, Vincent.

As he can do in any crowded area, Vincent quickly makes a path. He gets to his brothers and soon-to-be sister. The multitude of club goers give different types of response, some mocking, others that of concern. Melisa, coming to, feels sick. Forgetting about the man in the leather jacket, Chris, carrying her, rushes to his office. Ordering ice from his brothers, he charges on alone.

Ranald, having witnessed everything from the vantage point of Chris's office, has the door open. He has used the small bar sink to wet a cloth with cold water. Chris walks through the doorway and sees the man; he almost drops Melisa. The man in the leather jacket raises his hands in peace. "Lay her here," he offers. He takes off his jacket and places it for a pillow for her.

146

His skin is pale white, his arms perfectly smooth. The tone of his thin arms is masterful, like a man made of marble. "She is weak?" he says softly. He uses the wet cloth on her forehead. "Her senses are off," he informs Chris. "Is this the first time this has happened?" he asks Melisa. Her eyes closed, she answers with a nod. "It's okay, my dear. You need some fluids." He looks to Chris to get them. "Cranberry juice and water," he directs. Frightened, Chris follows the order.

"How many weeks are you, Melisa?" he asks.

She opens her eyes. Ranald is looking down at her through his sunglasses. "Who are you?"

"I am nobody, my sweet." He pauses with a smile. "You are with child, no?" he asks.

"Yes, four months," she answers, holding her tummy.

"Amazing," he says under his breath, placing his hand on hers. She instantly feels the coldness of his hand. "I apologize, I run cold," he tells her.

"And you are?"

"I don't have a name, not a real one to share, anyways." It's the first time in a very long time that he has not given a fake name.

"I'm sorry?"

"Oh love, you can call me friend. But it is better you forget me once you feel better." He continues to dab the cloth on her head. "You just relax, my dear." The vampire can't remember a time when he felt like he does with Melisa. "What is your name, my dear?"

She reaches up and slowly touches his face. "How do I know you?" She doesn't answer his question. Her mind races through all the people she's ever met. Somewhere is an image of someone matching this mysterious man tending to her.

He cocks his head to the right in wonder. "You are someone to me," she whispers. She moves her hands to his sunglasses, wanting to see his eyes.

He stops her. "No, love, I'm sorry."

Melisa, not heeding the warning, tries to continue. Surprising himself, he allows her to remove them.

Melisa is shocked but does not turn away. The glasses' removal reveal the man does not have eyes. The skin is dark and scarred, with signs of burning. Melisa touches around them. "I'm so sorry," she whispers. Once she makes contact with the place that should have eyes, a vision appears to her.

She sees the man in the leather jacket; he is being held down. She can see his eyes. Beautiful blue eyes. He is screaming something; she can't understand it. It's a language she doesn't know. The man in the leather jacket hears the brothers rushing up the stairs. Almost like a flash, he has taken the sunglasses, put them back on and is standing by the entrance. The area she touched begins to itch. But the vampire dares not touch them.

Melisa rises up to a seated position on the couch. She is not sure she saw what she did, but doesn't question it aloud. Chris walks past the man suspiciously. He helps Melisa drink the juice. The two brothers, Vincent and Aaron, stand near the man in the leather jacket. Making sure she is doing better, Chris gives his keys to Aaron to take her back to his house.

On her way out, she stops by the man in the leather jacket. He doesn't speak, but he lowers his head in acknowledgment and respect for her. She smiles and does the same, but softer. Not missing a beat, Chris is full of rage. He gives Melisa a kiss goodbye, and watches her leave through the back, away from the crowd and loud music.

"She doesn't know what you are?" the man in the leather jacket inquires.

"No, I was about to tell her. But I had to come here."

"You realize you can be setting her up for death?"

"What is it you want?" Chris is in no mood to be lectured again about his decision.

"I came to talk."

"So talk."

"You know who I am?" Ranald asks.

"Ha, does anyone?"

"I guess that's a fair question."

"I know who you are." Chris begins to crack his knuckles with his thumbs as his hands hang by his side.

"Then, do you know why I am here?"

"I haven't the faintest." He walks to his desk. Pouring a drink, he offers Ranald one, which he accepts. "Why have you asked about my youngest brother?"

"Chris, we are in a very interesting situation. Do you know who the Hunter is?"

"The Hunter." Chris nods his head. "I know of him."

"He has been awoken."

"I see, and you want our help?"

"Well, actually. No," he answers, surprising Chris.

"Then why are you here?"

"Because I need to find out who is responsible for this."

"What are you talking about?"

"I believe your father . . ." he stops himself. "Your father is one of the only people that knew of the Hunter's whereabouts."

"So, you think he told my brother." He gets up from his chair. "You think this why?"

"I found your father's scent," he informs him. Chris shakes his head, not in disbelief but more in the sense of "I hope it's not true." "Where is your brother?"

"If he did anything like what you are suggesting, I'll take care of him."

"Oh my dear boy. It doesn't work that way." He walks up to Chris. "He will have to answer to another power."

"What do you mean?" Chris turns to the man angrily. "No, I will not allow it." He stands, his fists clinched tight. Ranald pulls away; looking at Chris, he knows that he has misjudged his power. "Knowing him, he thought it would be fun," Chris says and raises his eyebrow.

"I understand the need to protect family . . ."

"You do?" Chris interrupts him. "Why don't you tell me what happened to your family?"

"Hmm, I see your father has told you more about me than I would have liked." Ranald moves to the window.

"Yes . . . You are a monster," Chris states, walking up behind him.

"I was, but I am not anymore," Ranald says, looking down in sorrow. "I have been cured of that. But I am also stuck with those memories." He turns back to Chris. "I must take your brother to be judged." His eyes begin to burn. But he continues to hide his discomfort from Chris.

"That will not happen." Chris lowers himself in anger. Just then Ranald realizes why his eyes are burning.

"Maybe, there is another way," he offers. "What if you help me find the Hunter?"

"Find the Hunter, and then what?" Chris laughs.

"Put him down."

"How can we do that? You had twenty the last time you took him. We are only two."

"Your mate, she is special."

"What are you talking about?"

"Have you not noticed?"

"Noticed what?"

"Her touch." Ranald turns to him.

"I don't know what you're talking about. But I will not put her in danger."

"She would be safe, I assure you."

"How can you know that? The Hunter is ruthless. A monster in his own right."

"He is, and he must be stopped."

"And you would have my love, the woman carrying my baby, to help us? How do you see that going?"

"She . . . she has a way. He would not hurt her," Ranald states.

"I would be inclined to agree, but not when she is carrying my child. She is no longer innocent in his eyes. If the stories are true, he does not discriminate, he does not tolerate ignorance."

"You are right. But she would give us enough time."

"Time for what?" Chris asks, his eyes glowing from the anger.

"Time for us to stop him."

"You don't even know where he is." Chris's eyes return to normal. Standing upright, he smiles.

"That is something you and yours could help with, yes."

"Always trying to get a dog to do your dirty work," Chris sneers.

"Your father did what he did for us because he had to; if he didn't he would have been killed. I know he doesn't tell you everything. But like your youngest brother, he doesn't make the best decisions."

"What will happen with him?"

"Your brother?"

"Yes," Chris answers.

"If you help me. If she helps us. I will make it so he is safe. You have my word."

"Like what you did for my father?"

"Oh Chris, how misled you are. Your father was given a life. They allowed for him to pass his gift instead of killing him. He still calls it an injustice, but the truth is, it was mercy. Mercy for a monster who, if not for a more dangerous monster, would have been put down."

"I know my father, and what you are saying doesn't surprise me."

"Then you will help me?"

"I don't know."

"Here." Ranald pulls out a piece of fabric. "It belongs to the Hunter."

Chris takes in a deep breath. His eyes roll back, as he is almost intoxicated. He pauses. "I've smelt this." Taking in another deep breath, he says, "Yes, not that long ago. But I cannot place it," he adds.

"Can you track it?"

"Of course," he states. Ranald is obviously impressed. "I will help. But my woman and brothers are to be left out of this."

"I cannot guarantee we will not need them. But let's cross that bridge when we arrive at it." He smiles. "If you need to get in touch with me, call this number. Leave a message." He hands Chris a dark, reflective card. The front is blank, while the back has only a line of raised numbers.

"What should I call you?"

"Ranald is fine." The man in the leather jacket leaves the room and heads out of the club. Chris watches from the vantage point, his brothers all watching from the club floor. The feeling of wanting to attack the stranger is strong among them. But Chris lets out the thought to keep away from him.

CHAPTER SIXTEEN

Alex sits with Victor in Victor's Mercedes. He watches as Melisa and Aaron leave the bar in Chris's SUV. Communicating telepathically with Victor, he orders him to follow them. He has learned quickly, and Alex is starting to rely on him. This being his first mutt, he wasn't sure how long it would take to teach him. Victor gets out of the car and uses Alex's motorcycle, which is parked in the lot of the club. Alex had enjoyed driving around in a hundred-thousand-dollar car, and doesn't feel like giving it back to his mutt.

Now that he has Melisa being followed by the mutt, he can focus on his new interest. This man in the leather jacket. Why was he asking about him? His father told stories of such a man, a vampire of sorts. The story has changed over the years. First, he was just a vamp, then his father told him he was an immortal, a trickster of sorts. What he knew for sure, he was not to be trusted.

The club is a good five hundred feet away, but Alex can see it clearly. The man in the leather jacket appears, exiting through the main entrance. He stops and looks right at the Mercedes. Alex ducks down, trying to hide. Hearing a soft tap on the window, Alex looks up to the right to see that the man in the leather jacket is standing outside of the car.

He taps on the window again; he isn't looking into the car. He is focused back on the club. Alex turns the key to give power to the windows, then pushes the button to open the window. "Can I help you?"

"That depends. Are you Alex?" the man in the leather jacket asks, still looking away. His hand rests on the roof of the car.

"Yes." As Alex answers, a strange feeling comes over him. He isn't quite sure what it is.

"Were you planning on following me?"

"No." Alex knows what he feels; it's something he hasn't felt in some years.

"That's good. Because if you were, we would have a problem." Ranald moves to be face to face with Alex.

"I wasn't," Alex answers nervously. What he is feeling is fear, which makes him angry. His fight or flight response is telling him to flee, but his heart is telling him to fight.

"You know; I was looking for you."

"Oh yeah, why?"

"I have a few questions; why don't we go for a ride," he states coldly. Before he can answer, Ranald is sitting in the passenger seat.

"What the fuck!" Alex lets out. His fear becomes real. He is frozen, unsure what to do. He closes his eyes.

"Nice car," Ranald smiles, showing his fangs slightly.

"Thanks," Alex answers, unsure what to do next.

"So, let's go somewhere."

"Where?"

"How about Griffith Park?"

"What the fuck you talking about?"

"I see; you are going to act dumb."

"What, motherfucker?"

"What are you going to do?" he laughs.

"Fuck you." Alex moves to strike the man in the leather jacket, but he catches his hand. As he squeezes it, the bones in Alex's hand begin to break, and he cries out in pain.

Ranald lets go. The cry has gotten the attention of his brothers, who all come charging out. Chris stands still, seeing the man in the leather jacket. The two men look at each other for a moment. With a speed that his brothers can't match, Chris is at the car. Ranald moves quickly to get out and prepare to protect himself.

"Hold on boys. This doesn't need to get ugly," he states with his hands in the air, pleading for peace.

"Alex, get out of the car," Chris states firmly. His brothers surround the man in the leather jacket. Chris moves to shield his brother. "You okay?"

"Yeah," Alex, still holding his broken hand, answers bashfully.

"He tried to strike me." Ranald defends his actions in a very calm and soft voice.

"Is that true?" Chris asks his little brother.

"He was trying to take me somewhere."

"Where? . . . I know you think us weak. But I will let you in on a secret," Chris states softly, before moving to strike the man in the leather jacket. The move catches him off guard, and the blow to his face actually hurts. He loses his balance, but doesn't fall.

"Wow, I see you could be of some use to me after all," Ranald states, holding his face. "You are more powerful than I would have guessed." His eyes stop burning, and the pain he had quickly become accustomed to disappears.

"There is a lot about me that you don't know," Chris smirks. "Shall I transform and show you my true power?" he asks. The brothers all move away, expecting him to do so.

"No, no. I think the lesson has been learned," Ranald laughs. "I like you, Chris. So let's keep things civil from now on." He walks up to Chris slowly. "I see us becoming good friends" He pats him on the shoulder. "You have my card, call me," he states, walking through the brothers to his car. "What's the best way to get to Glendale at this hour?" he asks as he walks away.

They watch as he leaves. Chris turns to Alex. "Whose car is this?" he asks firmly.

"A friend's."

"Which friend?"

"You don't know him."

"Alex, I'm going to ask you this just once. Do you have anything to do with this creature being here?"

"No."

"Alex, you are my brother. If you are in trouble, you need to tell me. I will help you."

"I'm fine, I can take care of myself," he yells, running to the car and driving off. The four brothers watch. All are quiet waiting for Chris to give instructions. He just waves them back into the club. He can't understand what his brother's issues are. He is young, but he is acting so weird.

Alex drives as fast as the car can handle. He weaves in and out of traffic; his anger at the embarrassment he just endured is too much. Why did his brother need to be such a dick to him? He appreciated his help, but did he need to make him feel bad about it? He is conflicted about how he should feel about his brother.

His reckless driving and wandering mind do not go unnoticed. He doesn't notice the police car behind him flashing its lights for him to pull over. The loud buzz of the horn finally gets his attention. Looking through the rearview mirror, he sees there are two officers in the squad car. "Fuck," he mutters under his breath. This is the last thing he needs to deal with. Hesitantly, he pulls over. It takes him a moment to realize that he is driving Victor's car.

Pulled over to the side of the road, he watches as the driving officer gets out of his car first. He can't see the other officer; they have their flood light beaming in through his rear window. "Turn off your engine," one of the officers orders through a loud speaker. Alex follows the instruction. It dawns on him; the car is hot. Victor Rees is a wanted man. How stupid of him to be driving in such a way.

The loud speaker continues to bark orders at him. Alex debates his options. He can follow their instructions, or he could drive off. He has another option, but he doesn't want to think about it. He has too many things going on to make this a worse situation than it already is. He will obey these men.

Getting out of the car slowly, arms raised high, he walks to the back of the car. He is ordered to turn around and walk backwards. Once to a place the officers feel comfortable, they have him get down on his knees, then to the ground, flat on his face. Alex does everything they say without any further delays.

The first officer is quick to put his knee on Alex's back and calls out a bunch of questions, asking if he has any weapons, what is his name, whose car is he driving, and why does he have it. The second officer goes and checks on the car.

Alex, maintaining a calm demeanor, just answers the questions the best he can. He tells the officer he bought the car from Victor Rees a few days ago. He paid cash for it. He apologizes for driving recklessly, informing the officers that he was angry from a situation at work and was driving around to clear his head.

The first officer is surprised by his statements and follows up with more questions. Alex informs him that the papers are in the car. He mailed in the bill of sales, but made a copy. The second officer comes back with the papers Alex was talking about. Picking him up, the first officer dusts him off. Their attitude toward him changes.

"So, have you had anything to drink tonight?" the first officer asks, dusting Alex off.

"I have, but only a few," Alex answers. "I will not object to taking a field sobriety test, if you would like." He knows that he would never be caught for being drunk. His body flushes alcohol through so quickly, that he could literally drink a bottle of vodka and pass the test.

"We're going to have to," the first officer informs him. The second officer goes back to the squad car; Alex can see he is working with the onboard computer. Watching the second officer's facial expressions, he sees that he may not be off the hook. The two officers make eye contact, and with that, the first officer pulls out his handcuffs and shackles them around Alex's wrists.

"Sorry pal, but looks like we need to take this off the streets."

"What is this about?"

"The car is tagged, and any drivers need to be taken in for questioning."

"That's bullshit. You telling me that I'm in trouble because I bought a car that is stolen?"

"No, the car is not marked stolen, sir. It may have been used in a crime."

"Shit, so it's worse?" Alex asks. His surprise is convincing, but the officers need to take him. The second officer informs him they will be impounding the vehicle. Alex continues his act of ignorance. Inside he is laughing as they take him into custody.

CHAPTER SEVENTEEN

John has met up with his friends at a small brewery on the border of Glendale and Los Angeles. It's trivia night, something that happens every Thursday. The crew has been taking up two booths, and had already lost miserably during trivia. Now, they just work on having a good time drinking.

The group was close, none more than John and Bernadette had been. But, she hasn't said a word to him all night. Every time he gets close to her, she finds a way to move or speak to someone else. He even went so far as to buy her a beer, but it just sits on the table getting warm. All he wants to do is clear things up with her, but she is not having it. He doesn't believe she'll rat him out. But he needs to be sure.

Frustrated, he stews in his seat. "Damn, John, you really sucked tonight," Monica calls out. During the game he wasn't paying attention. Normally a great resource for useless facts, he couldn't focus enough to help.

She surprises him; he has been so focused on Bernadette that he didn't even notice her sit next to him. "Yeah, sorry. Got a lot on my mind," he finally responds.

"B?" Pulling her blonde hair back she makes a quick bun. John sometimes forgets how pretty Monica is, but is reminded every time she pulls her hair back from her face.

"What?" he blushes. "No!"

"Well, you haven't taken your eyes off her all night. What happened? Did you finally tell her your feelings?" She looks at Bernadette who is looking the other direction.

"What the heck you talking about? I don't have feelings for her."

"Please, everyone knows." Monica rubs up against him, rubbing her shoulder to his.

"Well, if I did, I sure don't anymore." John slams back his beer finishing it off.

"Then why are you here moping in the corner?" Monica asks with a smirk.

"That's a great question." He starts to get up, but Monica stops him.

"Hold on, why are you in such a bad mood?"

"Look, I don't need to hang out with you guys anymore. I'm going to be moving."

"Geez, John. I don't know what's going on, but no need to be mean to me." Monica pulls away.

"I'm sorry, Monica. Come with me to the bar." He offers his hand. "I'll tell you."

He buys her a drink, and she doesn't fail to notice the wad of hundreds. She doesn't say anything, but her facial expression tells him she saw it. "I sold some things," he tells her, trying to stop her from questioning it.

"No worries, not my business . . . So what's up with you and B?"

"I'm leaving," he starts. "I sold some stuff and now I have enough to take off."

"Wow, when are you going to tell everyone?"

"I wasn't. Only you and Bernadette know."

"When?" she asks.

"Tomorrow."

"Wow, that's crazy. I don't get why she would be upset. How annoying, if I'm being honest."

"That's what I want to figure out, plus I need to make sure . . ." He stops himself from divulging anything about the cave or the blade.

"Make sure what?"

"Nothing, I just need to talk to her before I leave. But she's acting like a bitch."

"Why?"

"I, I don't want her . . . I can't leave with her mad at me."

"Well? I guess it may be too late."

"That's what I'm afraid of," he says.

"So, since you're leaving. Should I buy you a goodbye shot then?"

"Nah, I'll buy you one." He orders them. Monica spins on her bar stool. Now watching Bernadette, she giggles. "What's up?" John asks, turning around too.

"Look at the guy talking to B; she seems to be enjoying him," she points out.

John stares at the man. "What the fuck, why is he wearing sunglasses at night? I hate that shit," he states. "What's up with the leather jacket too? What is he? Some kind of greaser?"

Without a clue, he is making fun of the man in the leather jacket, who is listening to every word he is saying. John takes his shot and walks over to them. "Bernadette, I need to speak to you," he says, stepping in between them.

"Bernadette, I knew I would get your name," Ranald flirts.

"Yes, my name is Bernadette. You win," she laughs, flirting back.

"Can I buy you a drink? That way you can take a moment to talk with your friend John here."

"Sure, I'll have an . . ."

"IPA?"

"Yes, how did you know?" She half smiles

"I can smell it. I also caught your lotion. What is that?"

"What? I didn't put anything on tonight." She leans away from him.

"Are you sure? I can swear I smell fig," he says, leaning close but not too close.

"Wow, that's from my sunblock. I was wearing it earlier," she says and smiles.

"Oh, well. It's nice nonetheless," he replies, likewise smiling.

"I don't know about that. You're making me feel like I didn't shower well," she laughs.

"Well, if you smell this nice at the end of a long day, I'm impressed," he softly touches her elbow. "I'll get the beer, and how about you, John? Can I get you something?"

"What the fuck, dude, how do you know my name?"

"Excuse me?"

"Do we know each other?" John barks.

"I beg your pardon. Bernadette said it aloud. I didn't mean anything by it." He turns and walks away to get Bernadette her beer. Bernadette turns, fuming at John. She pushes him away from her.

"What the fuck, John?"

"What?"

"I don't have anything to say to you. You're leaving and we are all going to be glad when you do. No more hearing you complain about how nothing works out for you. Especially when you don't do anything to move forward."

"Hold on, B, I came here to apologize."

"I don't want it. Just get out of here," she orders. Just then Ranald returns with the beer for her.

"I'm sorry, but I got called and need to leave. Please enjoy your beer. I wish I could have spent more time talking with you," Ranald says and makes his exit, passing the bouncer at the door and shaking his hand goodbye as if they were old friends.

"Thanks a lot, John." Bernadette hits him in the arm. "That guy was nice."

"Looking for another one-nighter?"

"Yup, as long as it's not you. I'm so glad I never lowered myself enough to get with you," she blasts him back. Pissed, John knocks her beer, spilling it on her. The guys in the group quickly jump to her aid, pushing John away from her, cursing at him. They take him all the way out of the bar, telling him not to come back. He can hear Bernadette laughing in the background.

Once outside, John tries to collect himself. Wiping off the beer that he splattered on himself, he can't believe what he just did. He has never been so angry. Never would he think he could strike a woman. Even if it was just to knock a glass out of her hand. Upset with himself, he heads to his car.

As he walks through the parking lot, he feels the sting of a bite on his neck. He slaps at it. The lights go out. Looking around, he sees that the street is dead. Not another soul is visible. Unnerved, he rushes to his car. Reaching for his keys, he stops. He can't find them. Looking at his hand he sees blood on his fingers. "What the fuck?" Rubbing the blood, he begins to feel light-headed. His mind spinning, he dizzily runs around in a circle.

The spell dissipates. John collects himself, and turns back to his car. He freezes, seeing the man in the leather jacket sitting on the hood of his car. In his hands are John's keys. Wanting to run, his whole body feels stuck. The man hops off the hood and walks slowly to him. His walk is smooth, almost gliding.

"I'm sorry I had to pick your pocket. I wanted to make sure you didn't leave before we talked," Ranald starts.

"What do you want?" John struggles to speak. Every muscle in his body is tense and unresponsive to his commands.

"John, I want you. And how perfect it is that you put on that show."

"What?" John's feels his body release its tension, and he falls to the ground.

"I need your help. I need someone like you."

"What did you do to me?" John asks, trying to stand up again. "What are you?"

"Me? I'm nothing of consequence," Ranald states, taking a knee next to John. "Why don't you get up so we can have a man to man conversation." John feels his body return to his control. He quickly gets up and tries to run. Ranald snaps his fingers and John is frozen again.

"You need to listen for a change." Ranald's words are only in John's heads. Tears building, John tries to shout. "That is useless. John, you work for me now. You should feel lucky; back in the day you would have been dead already," he muses, still communicating telepathically with John. "Now, follow me to my car," he tells John. All the lights turn back on, and John sees that he is seated in the man in the leather jacket's GTO. People are all around, going about their business. "What did you do?"

"What I do best," Ranald informs him with a smile and turning on his car's throaty v-eight engine.

"John, why did you go into that cave?"

"What?"

"Really? I need to repeat the question?" Ranald looks in his direction with a smirk.

"No. I was trying to show her I was brave."

"Bernadette?"

"Yes."

"Ha, well you fucked that up pretty good." Ranald taps his steering wheel in amusement. John looks at Ranald with disdain. "So, I have a woman you need to keep an eye on for me." The vampire is now explaining what he wishes of John. They drive around the local neighborhood.

"Why would I do that?"

"Don't trouble your head with thoughts like that. Her name is Melisa Castro. She is a doctor."

"Where is she?"

"She's with her father now. But her home is in Los Feliz. You'll have to follow her." As he speaks, John gets a flash of information directly to his mind. He knows the address and everything about the woman that the man in the leather jacket knows.

"She's beautiful," John can't help but state.

"That she is. I need you to help keep her safe. Don't fall in love with her. The last thing we need is you trying to go into another cave." He can't help but laugh at the man. John turns and looks out the window, biting his inner lip. "I'm just teasing you, kid."

"How am I going to keep her safe?" John answers, trying to show what the vampire is saying doesn't bother him.

"If you see her, I will see her. If she needs help, I will allow you to help her. I will give you powers you have only read about."

"I don't understand."

"You will."

"How long will I have to do this?"

"Until my task is complete."

"Will you kill me?"

"What? No." Ranald laughs.

"Will you erase my mind?"

"Erase your mind? Geez, kid, how much TV do you watch?" He laughs. "No, you will go on with your life. And hopefully you will have learned how to be a good human being," he says, and laughs again.

"Is that why you can control me? Because I'm a bad person?"

"God damn, kid. Please don't ask me anymore questions like that." Ranald stops his car. John hadn't noticed that they were back at the brewery. "Now, get out. And don't tell anyone anything about me or what you are doing. Keep up the idea that you are leaving tomorrow."

"What if someone comes to my apartment?"

"Don't be there anymore. Use some of that money in your pocket to get a hotel room. That will be all," he orders. John is outside of the car, but doesn't remember making any moves to do so. Looking around, he sees the GTO and the man in the leather jacket are both gone. His keys are in his hand.

"What the fuck was that?" Looking around, he heads for his car. Not sure if it was real or not, he gets in his little red car. Starting the car, he looks around, checking the mirror, then he shakes his head, laughing to himself. "What the fuck happened?" he laughs again.

Suddenly the man in the leather jacket's reflection replaces his own. "Get a move on," the voice states in his mind. John clamps his eyes closed; he can't believe what is happening. Opening his eyes slowly, he sees himself. The stinging on his neck returns. Looking in the mirror, he sees two small punctures. Feeling them, they are sensitive to the touch. "Go," the voice of Ranald calls to him. Turning on his car as if he has no control, he starts to drive. Instead of making the left he normally makes toward his home, he makes a right.

Almost on autopilot he drives to Los Feliz, his little hatchback struggling up the hills, black smoke pouring behind leaving a thick trail. He makes lefts and rights through the narrow streets, going to a place he has never been before. Finally, he pulls up to a dramatic Mediterranean villa-style home. The large metal fence in the front doesn't allow for John to scale it.

Walking around the property and trespassing on her neighbor's property, John squeezes along their wall. Finding a spot where he can climb a tree, he is able to leap over the fence to soft dirt on her grounds.

Now able to walk around her yard, he sees that no one is home. He doesn't know what else to do. A new destination appears to him. Melisa's father's house. He looks around and sees he doesn't have a way out.

Desperate, he tries to climb the wrought iron fence, but falls, bumping his knee.

As he is rubbing the pain away, a light appears. A large black SUV pulls up to the gate. The driver types in a code on the keypad opening the main entrance. John hurries away and finds a place under some bushes to hide. The SUV pulls up into the driveway stopping at the garage.

Melisa exits the passenger side; she is talking to someone. John can't make out what she's saying; they are too far away. A sudden pain overtakes his ears. A loud pop erupts, causing his ears to ring. As he clutches them in pain, a dizziness comes over him.

"Come inside, I don't know how long this will take." John hears Melisa's words as if he was standing right next to her.

"Fine. Do you have anything to eat?" a deep voice replies. John can't even see the man who is speaking, but he is picking up every inflection of his voice. The man speaking has a slight accent. Polish, John can feel the man in the leather jacket informing him. Peering under the car from his hiding place, he sees the man's feet land on the ground. The sound is like a metal plate landing on a gym floor, rattling his ears.

The man walks, each step echoing in John's ears. He rounds the front of the truck meeting up with Melisa. He can't hear her walk; wearing ballerina flats, she floats as she moves across her pathway. The lights around her house make it hard for him to make out more than a silhouette, making it impossible to make out the man.

Suddenly, like his ears, his eyes begin to burn. Rubbing at the pain, he opens them again. Everything has changed. The lights no longer cause a problem. He can see everything as if it was day time, only with a slight blue tint.

The man is large. His broad shoulders and thick chest are visible through his coat. With a square chin, and deep-set eyes, he still has a very delicate face.

Melisa and her companion head up the path to the front of the house, and John needs to move in order to continue his infiltration. His own moves cause pain in his ears, as he hears every brush of a leaf against his own body and the dirt crumbling under his knees as he crawls. He wants to stop, but can't.

Finally reaching a point where he can see the couple at the door, he freezes. The large man is staring directly at him. John knows he's under cover, but the large man's eyes are looking right at John's. Even though he is over two hundred feet away, he can make out every shade of the man's brown eyes.

"What's the matter, Aaron?" Melisa asks.

"Nothing, I just thought I heard a rodent," he answers, narrowing his eyes, focused still on John.

"Don't move." John can clearly hear Ranald. "Stay right there," he continues. "Wait till they go inside, then you need to get out of there," the voice continues to direct with a sense of worry.

Following his instructions, John runs to the gate and without hesitation he leaps over the fence. He runs to his car and turns it on. He drives up the hill. Looking in his rearview mirror he sees Aaron appear, having jumped the gate too. Pushing his old VW as fast as it will go up the hill, he is relieved to see the man does not make chase.

"You will need to ditch this car. And change your clothes. Go to the Los Feliz Hotel. Room 3."

CHAPTER EIGHTEEN

"Aaron?" Melisa calls out coming from her bedroom. Walking down the stairs carrying a small bag, she looks for the man. "Aaron, where are you?" she calls out again. Hearing her front door open, she asks, "Where did you go?"

"I had to make a call. Service wasn't working in the house." He walks along the platform walkway, his face showing he is in deep thought.

"Oh." She pauses and drops the bag. "I have to get a few more things." She hurries back up the steps.

"Take your time . . . Chris wants me to take you to your father's house; he has something he has to do tonight."

"Why didn't he call me?" she hollers from her room.

"He was going to, but I was already talking to him. I'm sorry"

"So who was that guy?" Melisa asks, she has been trying to figure out how she knew him ever since they left the club. He was nice. But there is something else there. Something she doesn't trust.

"I honestly don't know."

"What did he want with Chris?"

"I don't know that either."

"Hmm. Well he seemed nice." She returns with another bag, and drops it down to Aaron who catches the heavy bag as if it was nothing. "So, I have some leftovers in the fridge if you want?" she offers but he doesn't respond. "Aaron, are you okay?" She peeks her head around the corner. She can't help herself. They have always gotten along. Of all of Chris's brothers, it was Aaron who she could most be around.

"I'm sorry, Mel. Forgive me for being rude." He quickly smiles. "I was just thinking about the va . . . I mean man."

"What?"

"Nothing, never mind."

"Are you guys in trouble?" Melisa starts to assume the worst. She hasn't forgotten where she came from, nor the streets. A man like the one wanting to talk to Chris could easily be something bad.

"No, no. We are all fine. What do you have that you'd like to eat?"

"I have some Indian. I would love some tikka masala in a tortilla," she laughs. "God, my stomach is asking for the craziest of things."

"That's not that bad. Naan is close to a flour tortilla."

"Yeah, but I only have corn tortillas." She turns and hurries back to her room, giggling. He has always enjoyed her dorkiness. Now that she is pregnant he feels it to be more extreme. He picks up all the bags with his powerful hands. He walks back to the entry, dropping them by the door.

Aaron turns to the kitchen. The brightness of the white room is almost overwhelming. Looking around, he is truly impressed. The massive sub-zero fridge is built into the wall, with a pantry on each side. The cabinets all match, with high-gloss fronts. He had been in Melisa's house before, but he had never been in her kitchen.

Every time he was over, it was quick. He was either dropping something off or picking his brother up. Chris was protective like that. He didn't like for his brothers to be around Melisa too often, and never invited them over to her house. Aaron has been the only one to actually enter her home thus far.

Opening the fridge, he finds the leftovers. The fridge is a mess. All the food seems to be from some restaurant or a quick heat and eat type meal. He sees that she has a well-stocked vegetable drawer. He remembers Chris talking about how she uses a blending machine to make vegetable drinks. He can't help but smile. Pulling out the bag marked Indian, he closes the door and places it on the white stone countertop.

He marvels at the Wolf range stove. Four feet wide, he has never seen such a massive thing within a home before. Its stainless steel metal, blue knobs, and double griddle in the center make him feel like he is in a professional kitchen. The heavy duty cast iron grates are level and continuous. He starts to get excited about cooking in the beautifully untouched kitchen. He wonders if she has ever cooked in it.

Grabbing a nonstick frying pan, he turns on the modern-looking wall hood to ventilate the air. He opens the container and takes in the smell of the food. The bright orange-ish tikka masala cream sauce covering the bits of chicken are beautiful to him. He dumps the food in and starts to warm it.

As the food begins to sizzle, a beautiful mixture of fragrances flows out, into his nostrils. The smells are welcomed. A lover of food, he mixes it, making sure not to scorch any of it. Returning to the fridge, he pulls out the tortillas. Turning on another burner, he lays the tortillas one at a time directly on the flame. Allowing them to slightly blacken around the edges, he flips them, making sure to cook them evenly.

Checking on the Indian food, he feels like he would like something else to go with what he is cooking. Returning to the fridge, he pulls out other ingredients. The pickings are slim, but he can make magic happen.

Meanwhile, Melisa is making a mess in her closet. She has pulled everything out and is trying to figure out what she'll need for the next few days. She doesn't want to leave her home. But with the stranger still out there, she feels better not having to deal with him showing up at her front door.

She doesn't believe he would hurt her, but she doesn't want to take the chance. His actions at the hospital were enough for her not to trust her gut. Looking down at her arm, she sees that where she was bruised from when he grabbed her has completely healed. Then it hits her. How come she hasn't thought about the man's fall? He fell twelve stories and then ran off, like it was nothing. Her mind has been ignoring so many things, so many scary things. She knew baby brain was a real thing, but this was getting ridiculous.

The recent visions she's had start to replay in her mind. All the things she's been seeing. The things she's been doing. All out of character. A strange stench penetrates her nostrils. *What the hell is that?* she asks herself. Smelling her clothes, she can't find it. Then it hits her. The food. Has Aaron burnt it? She rushes out to investigate. Aaron is in the kitchen; he is wearing her apron with his sweater sleeves pulled up. The aroma hits her in the stomach; she feels sick instantly, and kneels in pain.

Noticing her, Aaron quickly turns off the stove and moves and catches her before she falls to the tiles. His jacket is on the nearby stool. He quickly grabs it. "Here, lie on this," he urges her. He hurries to the sink and grabs some water for her. "Here, drink this."

The taste of the water is so metallic that she pushes it away. "Don't move, I'll be right back." He lays her on his jacket and runs out. He reappears holding a small jar of baby food. Using a small spoon, he places it to her lips. "Eat this," he instructs her. "My mother taught me this trick."

Within a few seconds her head stops spinning and her stomach ache is softening. "What is it?" she asks; she holds his arm as he feeds her.

"It's just some sweet potatoes. Is it helping?" he asks.

"Yes." She looks down at the food. "When did you get that?"

"Keep eating. I'll finish the food." He hands her the spoon and helps her to sit up. Melisa can't figure out the massive, gentle man. Realizing what he is about to do, she quickly gets up, trying to stop him.

"No, please, it will make me throw up," she says, holding him.

"No it won't. You'll be great in a few minutes," he says as he carefully removes her grasp. He returns to the stove and continues to cook. The smell no longer heavy on her, Melisa finishes the jar. Aaron is busy cutting fresh vegetables. He has three pans cooking. Getting up to see what he is doing, she sees that he has taken the leftover Indian food and is now making an original dish.

"I didn't know you could cook," she laughs.

"My mother taught me."

"Your brother never talks about your mom," Melisa gets up. "Where is she?"

"She passed." He pauses his knife work.

"I'm sorry." She picks up his coat and places it on the counter. Taking a seat on the stool, she watches as he cooks. "What happened?"

"She and my father didn't get along," he states. He tightens his jaw. She gets up and rubs him on his left shoulder. "She taught me many things. She and I were close."

"Was she close with your other brothers?"

"Not really. She was not their mother."

"Oh, I had no idea."

"My father has had many mates, that's why we all have different mothers" he states, grinding his teeth.

"Really?"

"I'm talking out of turn." He turns back to the food.

"Aaron, it's okay if you don't want to talk about it."

"My family is not like yours; there is no respect for women," he says and looks at her. "But, I did not agree . . . My mother was an angel."

"What happened?"

"It was before Chris was born. Back in my home country. He doesn't even know most of what I endured."

"I'm so sorry, Aaron." She squeezes his arm. It's the first time she has ever touched his bare skin. Thinking about it, she had never seen him without a long sleeve shirt on. He is like stone, but covered by scar tissue. She flips his arm around to see that he has markings going up his arm. He has been burned. Her mind takes her there. To when the burns happened.

Aaron is fighting; he looks just as he does today. There is fire all around him. He is screaming for his mother. He is trying to find her. The fire engulfs him. He can't stand it any longer. His arms catch fire, and he runs out. Melisa's vision ends. The visions are becoming more frequent, but she doesn't understand them.

She had never heard that anyone in Chris's family was a burn victim. Aaron pulls away from her and lowers his sleeves, covering his arms. "Wait a minute. What is that?" she asks. This is the first time she has a chance to get some clarification. Was she just hallucinating or was she really having visions?

"Nothing."

"No, Aaron. Please tell me."

"If Chris ever hurts you, I will kill him," he states as tears form in his eyes. Melisa just grabs onto the large man.

"Who did that?" she asks him. "Aaron, who started the fire?" she asks. Aaron, spaced out remembering the past, has forgotten the food.

"I did," he states, eyes glassed over.

"How?" she asks. Noticing the food, she rushes and takes over the cooking duty.

"I had to show him, that what he was doing was wrong," he says. "I stood up to him, and in the process, a fire broke out."

"Was anyone else hurt?"

"Just one."

"Your mother?"

"Yes."

"How old were you?" she asks as she plates the food.

"I had just had my thirtieth birthday . . ." He freezes, realizing what he just said.

"Thirtieth?" she pauses. "I'm confused." She crinkles her eyebrows. "You said it was before Chris was born?"

"Melisa, Chris has much to discuss with you. I cannot say anymore."

"Aaron, I have been feeling lost for the last few days, the more I think about it. I've been feeling off ever since this pregnancy."

"I would have assumed that. Believe me when I say, I will not let anything happen to you or the baby." He begins to eat.

"I'm sorry, I need more than that, Aaron."

"We are not what we seem. But I cannot be the one to explain it."

"Aaron. This isn't funny." Melisa gets up and calls Chris. Aaron gets up and grabs the phone.

"I'm sorry. I will tell you. But first have some food." He takes a seat, placing the phone on the counter. Melisa begrudgingly takes a seat. Her eyes focused on the large man, she starts to eat, wrapping the food in the tortilla she was craving. Her eyes close as she takes her first bite, letting out a moan.

"This is delicious," she lets out.

"I'm glad you like it."

"Now tell me what's going on," Melisa asks, continuing to eat.

"My family is special. We have abilities unlike you or anyone else you know," he starts. Choosing his word carefully, he continues, "We don't age like normal people. We are of a time long forgotten."

"So, what are you then?"

"I'm sorry, Melisa. I can't say anymore. It will be better to come from Chris."

171

"Are you serious?"

"Quite."

"This is getting ridiculous. You know what? . . . take me to my dad's. I'm done talking to you." She gets up, leaving the plate. She starts to grab her bags, Aaron tries to help, but she tells him to leave her be. He backs off and looks at her.

"Melisa. Respect that I cannot betray my brother. And trust me, when I say he will tell you everything," he pleads.

"Fine. Let's go." She walks off letting him take her bags. They don't speak the whole drive. Once at her father's, she ignores him, going straight inside leaving her bags behind. Aaron carries them to the porch and heads back to the car. Pulling out his phone, he texts Chris about what happened. Chris just tells him to stay there and watch over her. He'll talk to her in the morning.

CHAPTER NINETEEN

The sun is about to rise. Chris sits looking out onto the city. His face is stoic. Arms resting on his knees, he rolls a patch of hair between his fingers. It is blonde, short, and thick. Single strands have laid the trail to where he now sits.

It didn't take him long to find or track the scent of the Hunter. It was unique so that he could trace it for a mile easily. What troubles him is the other scent that followed the same path. The hair that led the monster to Melisa's back door.

Visions of Alex, mischievously leaving behind hair, rush through his mind. An anger builds inside him. Why would his brother have done such a thing? The feeling of betrayal overwhelms him. His stomach aches from the thought that someone in his own family has deceived him. He knew that Aaron wasn't a worry, but what of the others? He has six brothers in all.

Looking at his watch, he sees it's almost five A.M. Taking out his phone, he texts his brother Aaron, but he doesn't tell him what he found. Instead, he informs him that he will need to keep an eye on Melisa for a bit longer, Chris having already asked him to watch over her through the night. Picturing his big brother sitting outside her home, trying to be inconspicuous, brings a smile to his face. The large black SUV, holding a six-foot-five, two-hundred-forty-pound man.

Melisa would be waking up in thirty to forty minutes. She always was up before six, usually about the time Chris was finally relaxing from work and going to bed. Even when he stayed with her, he had trouble falling asleep when she did. She would surely notice him. But Chris didn't care. She needed the protection.

He knew Alex didn't like his beloved. But he never in a million years thought his own flesh and blood would have directed the Hunter to her. Their father would tell them horror stories about the Hunter. How he had no mercy. No feelings for anyone or anything. A butcher born of hate and savagery.

Questions emerge regarding his father. He would talk about taking the Hunter down many times. Alex loved the story, but would he be so reckless as to think he could release him? How did he plan to put him back? Alex wasn't clever enough for such actions. It must be his father. But why?

Were the rest of his brothers in on it? He texts Aaron again; he doesn't ask directly but needs to know what he thinks of the Hunter being released. "We need help" is all he writes back. Aaron, being a man of few words, makes it clear that he was not part of this. And like always, he is right. They need help.

Aaron let Chris know of his worries about the man in the leather jacket, about having seen his lackey at Melisa's house earlier that night. And, he knew he was still watching her. Aaron offered to kill the person following them, but Chris wasn't sure of the repercussions of such an action. He must be keeping an eye on her, in case he decides he needs her, is his thought.

Pulling out the card, he dials the number of the mysterious vampire. The phone rings just once. A woman answers. It's an answering service. Not sure what to say, he hangs up. Chris knows he could be a great help, but would he? How can he make an alliance with him? The Hunter is after his love, yes. But, Alex and his father had plans to hurt her, too.

It's the first time he realizes that he could have been there the morning the Hunter appeared to Melisa. He didn't hurt her then, but if he had felt Chris, he would have. He doesn't understand the limits of the Hunter's powers. No one does. Melisa didn't tell him much of the encounter. All she shared was he was lost and confused. Was that a ploy? Was the Hunter trying to trick her?

Looking down at her home, he sees the cameras. She records everything. He made fun of her for having such a radical surveillance system. But, now he is excited. He can go down and see what happened. Full of anger, he calls on his powers, but does not transform. The ground trembles under his feet. He pushes down with his legs, leaping from the hillside down to Melisa's property.

He lands hard, bending his knees to absorb the shock. Walking around to the front, he leaves deep indentations in the ground. He can smell the Hunter everywhere. His mind plays out what happened. He sees where the man fell. How Melisa tried to help him. How he got up and went around through the orchard.

Once inside the home, he can see what happened in real time. He trusts his senses, but he needs to see the emotions. See her face, see his. He walks up to the screen on her wall in the kitchen. He sees the same dried blood Aaron had noticed. The stench is too much for him to work the device.

Going into the living room, he grabs Melisa's wireless tablet controller. After pushing a few buttons, he has what he wants on the screen. Feeling the need to see it on a larger screen, he activates the TV to display what is on the tablet. He selects the time just after his leaving of the house.

Setting the sixty-five-inch TV to show all nine cameras at the same time, he takes a seat on the immaculate white couch. Fast-forwarding the video, he sees Melisa. The sight of her brings tears to his eyes. He slows the video feed to play normally, selecting the feed focused on her, with a viewing angle looking inward from the hillside.

Her movement is magnetic, her grin devilish as she strips off her clothes. Chris can't help but smile. Slightly aroused, he watches his love move about in the water. Transfixed, he forgets for a moment the situation they are in. In that moment he realizes just how much he loves her. The feeling that he needs to change, needs to be there for her, causes him to weep.

She gets out of the water, looking innocent. Watching, as she takes in everything around her. He sees what his dad was talking about. She is changing. She is able to gather the environment around her, just like his kind can. The excitement is short-lived. Melisa's whole body language changes. She focuses to an area not on his screen.

Returning the screen to show all nine video feeds, he sees it. The Hunter is in view for the first time. Melisa is helping him. Chris gets up from the couch, leaving marks from the dirt he had on his butt. Walking up to the large screen, he changes the image to focus on their interactions.

Reaching out to touch the man's image, he can't believe what he is seeing. He is so weak, so small. Nothing like what his father had described in his stories. Something about him is not right. Suddenly, when Melisa moves to do something, the Hunter reaches out and points to her stomach.

Chris's eyes begin to change. The rage is returning in full force. Continuing to watch, he sees the Hunter changing too. Something has caused him to react. And Chris knows what. He sees the baby. A baby that the Hunter will kill when he gets a chance. Chris crushes the tablet in his hands as he watches the scene unravel. When the Hunter grabs at her arm, the pain in Melisa's face is almost more than he can take.

He punches the screen where the Hunter lay. A large pop followed by electrical sparks surrounds his arm. Pulling his arm out from the hole he has made, he sees that he went through to the outside. He shakes off the plaster that covers his hand. Shrugging his shoulders, he has no idea what he will tell Mel. But fuck it. He has bigger things to worry about.

The Hunter knows she is carrying his baby. And he will be after her. His father had told stories of how he had no remorse, no mercy. The Hunter would surely kill her, because in his mind she is a sinner. No matter how innocent she was, he wouldn't care. Their kind were not permitted to live.

Chris hurries out of the home, leaving the mess for another day. He needs to get to his car and be in contact with the man in the leather jacket before daybreak. Having only a bullshit card, he can only call the mysterious man through the answering service. Chris leaves the message that he needs to meet with him right away. He has information. He tells him to meet at his bar in downtown. No one will be there.

Twenty minutes after the call, Chris arrives at his small bar. Unsurprisingly the man in the leather jacket has beat him there. They don't shake hands, but they acknowledge one another. Chris's anger is still very visible to the man in the leather jacket. He walks up cautiously. "What did you find out?"

"I need your help."

"Help? That's what you were supposed to be doing for me," Ranald states.

"You were right to suspect my brother, but I don't believe he could have done this alone. My father is behind this."

"Are you going to tell me something I do not know?"

"He was at Melisa's."

"Who was at Melisa's?" Ranald's face tightens.

"The Hunter." Chris grinds his teeth.

"Interesting."

"Interesting? I don't think so. My brother led him to her doorstep," Chris explains. Ranald rubs his chin in thought. "You need to help me protect her."

"My dear lad, I can't promise to do that."

"She is innocent; you know she is," Chris pleads.

"Is she? I'm pretty sure you took that from her."

"Don't give me that crap. She and my child are innocent." He walks to the entrance of the bar. Stopping, he looks down in thought. "My child will not have to do the things I did. I'm trying to do what others like me have been able to do."

"And what's that?"

"Change." Chris unlocks the door.

"What changes are you talking about?"

"My people are not bad."

"Not in the eyes of the Hunter."

"We will show him. Not all of us want bloodshed. We too want to live in peace. Build a life. I've shown that by having a child, haven't I?"

"I can see what you are talking about. But how would you be able to explain that to the Hunter? He doesn't care what you wish to do," Ranald explains.

"Why?"

"He was not created to do that."

"We are not all demons. We can change. I know it."

"Like your brother Alex?"

"That is not his fault. My father got to him. I can work with him."

"And if you can't?"

"Then I will kill him," he says firmly, holding the door open for the man in the leather jacket. "Please come in."

"I do not have much time," he says and looks up at the sky.

"Can I count on your help?" He lets the door go, staying outside with him. "Please. I will do whatever I need to do. I will find the Hunter, but I can't do that knowing that my brothers may try to hurt her."

"I have someone watching her."

"I know. Aaron spotted him."

"I'm surprised he is still alive."

"I told him to leave him be," Chris explains.

"Thank you." The man in the leather jacket's alarm goes off. Looking up at the sky, he knows the sun is about to rise. "I need to go; I will keep an eye on her. She is worth more alive than dead. Find the Hunter." He returns to his car and drives off quickly. Chris, feeling tired, knows he can't rest. He must find the Hunter.

Going into the bar, he heads to the office. Taking a seat at the desk, he opens the drawer and pulls out a bottle of whiskey. What is he going to do? He feels better about having the man in the leather jacket protect Melisa. But can he trust him?

What did he mean, she's worth more alive than dead? It's the second time he said something of that nature about her. He pointed out that she is special. But how? Was he going to use her to draw out the Hunter? Was he talking about being able to manipulate him? Use her to get him to do his bidding?

Filling a glass and not putting down the bottle, he drinks it quickly. Doing this two more times, he knows he must continue his search. The Hunter is out there and he needs to find him. He knows where the trail is going to be fresh: Melisa's hospital. He was there just the other night. Chris felt stupid, thinking that Melisa had told him about this man, with glowing eyes, falling from a building, and then running off.

All the signs of a specialness, and yet he didn't put two and two together. With trying to keep the business going and his brothers in line and the thought of the new baby, Chris's mind is just not right. Taking another swig, he puts the bottle away. "Time to get back to work," he tells himself aloud.

CHAPTER TWENTY

Parked on a short street in the Glendale hills, Detective Walken sits in her car, sipping on a hot cup of coffee. She is reading a file that her friend over in Narcotics shared with her. A file of the man she believed to be responsible for the homicide: Victor Rees. Victor has been an informant for the narcs for the past two years.

After getting picked up for soliciting sex from a transsexual, he quickly offered up everything he knew, and he knew a lot. He was a small fish, but they were hoping he would bring them to the much larger fish in the city. He never gave up his uncle, but he was instrumental in taking down some large outfits.

Now reading about the man, she has a hard time believing he was responsible for killing and eating anyone. Everything in the file suggests he was just a lackey. He was always surrounded by guards, but from what was gathered about the relationship, they were there to keep him out of trouble, not be his enforcers. Even the little drug distribution he was trying to set up. It was all a ploy by the detectives to get others.

To think she came up to the Glendale hills to investigate him, only to come upon a new set of murders. She had found multiple homicides within, only hours before. She couldn't be sure if Victor was inside. But she hoped he wasn't. He would be a good resource to find out who is doing all this.

She called it in right away, not even going in to investigate. It didn't stop her from getting in trouble. She has been ordered to stay on the outside of the crime scene. Two officers stand by her car, there to keep her from interfering.

She didn't call ahead for permission to work outside of her department, and the locals were pretty upset with her for it. Having worked with them on many cases back in her Narcotics days, she felt it wasn't a big deal. But Glendale can be strict when they want to be, especially when it comes to a mass homicide.

So, now she is being treated with lots of hostility. They didn't want to hear what she had to say, even when she tried to explain that the victims have the same markings as the ones in the case she's been working. She only got a glimpse of the scene before calling it in, but now she feels like she should have taken her time.

Two detectives exit the home; one is looking directly at her. She quickly texts her partner the address of Victor Rees. She puts the file under her seat and gets out of her car. The two officers standing by her car tell her to get back in her car. She just tells them to fuck off, and walks up to the detective, making eye contact with him. "What's going on, Phil?" she greets the man familiarly.

"Why were you here, Walken?" Detective Phil Garrett and Stephanie go way back. The other detective gives Stephanie the stink eye as he walks by. She just smirks at him, not caring.

"I had a lead. I know I should have called, but I didn't think I would be walking into a scene like this."

"That doesn't make it okay."

"Yeah, I got the earful already from my chief." She sips her coffee, showing she doesn't care about the reprimand. "So, was Victor in there?"

"No."

"Damn it. We need to find him."

"I put out the BOLO. For everyone to be on the lookout for him," Phil says.

"This is either someone muscling in or someone taking over," she points out.

"It's hard to take over when you don't have anyone to follow you. Whoever did this, is thinking replacement," he states.

"Can I go in now?"

"Yeah, but watch your step." He leads her into the crime scene. The blood-covered walls are a sight to behold. The home is riddled with bullet holes. The floor is coated with the thick dark red pooling around the corpses.

"Have they I.D.-ed everyone?" she asks,

"Yes . . . And, no."

"What do you mean?"

"Bodies are missing."

"What do you mean, bodies are missing?"

"Here, look." He guides her to a spot on the ground; it has blood all over it, except a spot that looks like someone was lying there. "Whoever was lying there has been moved."

"There are no signs of someone being dragged though?"

"Yeah, but do you think anyone who lost this much blood could just get up and walk away?"

"I guess not." She pauses, looking at the scene. "How many did you find like that?"

"Twelve."

"How many bodies in total?"

"We figure forty, including the missing."

"I've heard of hits like this before. They must want to use the bodies for some show of power." She uses her gloves and gets a sample of the blood around a bullet hole. "I don't think what did this returned fire."

"What are you talking about?"

"Our case has only two bodies, but they were mauled just like this," she reports. "So far the only ideas we have, is it's some kind of large wolf or jackal. Something from another country."

"The bodies definitely were mauled; we have an expert coming in, too."

"I'm happy to share what we got, but I'm going to need access to this scene."

"Look, you really fucked up; people are not happy you found this scene."

"Well, if it wasn't me, who would have? God knows how long these bodies would have been here. Then tell me, how would you guys feel?"

"I understand what you're saying, but just understand that people don't want you here. I can keep you in the loop, but as for complete access, I doubt it."

"That is bullshit, and you know it."

"Bullshit or not, they have rules for a reason," he says, trying to get her to be understanding.

"Fine. Then let me look around now, with you."

"That's what we're doing," he says. Stephanie continues on, looking around. She sees tracks leading away from the only body on the stairway. "Do the rest of the missing bodies lead somewhere?" she asks. "Look at these markings on the floor." She points out claw marks.

"We found a few of those."

"Did you note the nail marks on the banister?" she asks, noticing a small indentation.

"Not sure. But our team is good. They take as many shots as needed so we don't miss anything."

"Good." She pulls out her phone and snaps a quick picture. "Just in case."

"Don't do that, Steph, you're already in enough trouble."

"The only one, I promise." She puts her phone back in her pocket. Getting up, she looks at the scene from the new vantage point.

"This one set of footprints is all we have. We believe he was the last one. The last one mauled."

"Really?" she asks, not expecting a response. Following the trail, she carefully navigates through the corpses, all marked with numbers.

"You want to know where they lead?"

"I think I will find out soon." She doesn't even look back at him as she continues to follow the blood. Reaching the top of the stairs, she finds the end of the trail. A heavy-set man lay, completely disfigured. "Is this who I think it is?"

"Yes," Detective Garrett replies. "They identified him by his wallet. They took prints to be sure, but I'm confident it's him."

"Me too," Stephanie replies looking down at Vladimir Taymizyan's body. "They stood right here." She notes the pool of blood at his feet. "He wasn't mauled either. Look." She kneels by the corpse. "All blunt trauma." Something about this makes her think of the movies she loves. She recollects the last thing Walter had told her. The DNA was inconclusive. It was contaminated. A mix of both wolf and human. She didn't want to share that with anyone. Shit, Walter didn't want to tell her.

But now looking at this scene, all she can think is that they are dealing with something supernatural. Detective Garrett, getting a call, leaves her in the scene alone. She takes the opportunity to take a few more pictures with her phone. She can't count on getting all the information about this homicide later.

Looking down at the former head of the house, something strikes her. He was the only one treated in such a way. It was personal. She didn't have much insight about the relationship between Victor and Vladimir Taymizyan. But now she had a hunch, it wasn't all roses and wine. Maybe he is the one doing all this.

Hurrying back to her car, she opens the file. She remembered reading something about his father; there was something about Victor's father he spoke about in an interview. Flipping through the papers, she finds it. Victor was caught for being gay. His uncle beat him half to death. *There it is. That's as personal as it gets*, she thinks.

Victor is finally coming out of his shell, she realizes. The animal he is using, though. Where did he get such an idea? Where would he be keeping it? Too many questions remain, but her new lead suspect is Victor Rees. Stephanie catches Detective Garrett approaching, and she quickly hides the file under the seat.

"What do you think?" he asks.

Stephanie jumps up out of the car, her face flushed.

"I don't know. It looks like what we dealt with, but different on a lot of levels."

"I see."

"I'll send you what we got; I hope you guys do the same," she states, taking a seat back in her car. Detective Garret holds the door, looking down at her. He wants to say something, but seems unable. Stephanie smiles and pulls the door closed. As she drives away, she laughs at her thoughts that the scene seemed supernatural. She can't believe she would even consider something so crazy. This scene and the file on Victor has really helped clear up what they are dealing with.

They have a young man, upset with his family, who is trying to take over. Now they just need to find out who. And what in the hell kind of animal are they using?

CHAPTER TWENTY-ONE

Larry Walsh, the Chief Veterinarian of the Los Angeles Zoo, is not squeamish. Walter could show him the crime scene photos without much of a reaction. He is a tall, thin man, his long salt and pepper hair tied in a bun, like an old hippie. He is very knowledgeable, but unfortunately not helpful to Walter. Larry thought the bites and cuts were more in line with a bear attack. However, the lab results showed wolf DNA.

Larry was adamant that wolves are not in this county and that the marks on the bodies were not those of wolves. He went as far as getting images of bite marks from the two animals. That's when things got even more confusing for the two. The bear marks didn't coincide with the mauled men either. The victims' wounds were like a cross between the two. However, the claw mark images were more in line with a bear. But again, nothing was concrete.

He needed to see more than the photos. He felt they did not give a good representation of the wounds. He also offered to look at the crime scene. He would like to see if he could find something the forensics missed. Having helped in other countries with animal attacks like this before, he knows that they miss things that he would not.

Walter drives the animal expert to the crime scene. The whole back of the bar is covered with a tarp to protect it. The rain is pooling in one small area and forming a ball. Worrying that the water will affect the scene, Walter fashions a makeshift scoop and pushes the water out of the tarp.

Larry, using his flashlight hat, crawls around on the floor. He stops at the dumpster and feels around on the metal.

"What are you looking for?" His antics cause Walter to pause. The man is now looking in the large metal garbage bin. "This," he calls out. Walter jumps down from scooping water. Larry, holding the lid open, has his head lamp illuminating a mark on the interior of the metal.

"This is a claw mark. And it is not that of a wolf or a bear," he informs him. "Hold the lid?" he asks Walter. In an instant, he is inside the dumpster. It is empty; everything that was inside has been taken into custody by the police department.

Pulling out a small vial and spray, he takes a sample from the marks. He continues to investigate the metal. "Here we go," he says aloud. He takes another sample. "Wow, whatever did this went through the metal with ease."

Jumping out of the bin, he has Walter help him move the large bulky box away from the wall. "Nice." Using a pair of plyers, he finds a claw stuck in the wall. "This is concrete," he laughs. "Wow, this is amazing."

"What are you talking about?"

"Whatever did this was able to break through steel and penetrate through concrete . . . This is truly special."

"Yeah, well, whatever did this, is dangerous and not special," Walter adds.

"Forgive me, Detective Castro, I only mean that this could be a species that shouldn't be here."

"A new tack by these new age gangsters—get wild dangerous animals from other regions and use them to intimidate."

"Surely this animal did its job."

"I don't agree with your attitude about this, but I understand your statement." A buzz from Walter's phone tells him he has a text message. Looking over the message, he sees it's from the Chief Medical Examiner.

"Please call, found something interesting."

Walter puts his phone away after reading the message. "I need to make a call."

"I think you misread me. I'm not happy that an animal like this is here. I prefer them out in the wild." He stops himself. "Before you ask why I work at a zoo, I will tell you." Larry walks around, still investigating the scene. "I work there so I can help these poor animals get the best treatment possible. I could easily be out in a desert, or jungle, but then who would be here for these creatures. Who would champion them?"

"It's fine. I'll be right back," Walter tells him.

"Ah, yes, I have gone on, haven't I?" He stops moving. "Detective, I don't like animals to be used to hurt people. But, I am never angry with the animal when it does. It is in their nature."

"Everything is okay. I have to make a call."

Walter leaves the defensive Larry in the back. Inside the bar, he calls the doctor. "Hi, it's Detective Castro."

"Hi, detective. How long would it take you to come down to my office?"

"Not long, I'm in Los Feliz."

"Then do so. I found something; it would be better to discuss in person."

After a brief discussion, Larry offers his services further. Walter drives them to the department of medical examiner-coroner building on Mission Road. All the dead come through the doors of this massive building.

The entire drive, Larry has his laptop open. Using his cell phone as a hot spot, he is able to access the Internet. A glance or two from Walter shows that Larry is conversing with a colleague. He had asked permission to share the images from the scene, which Walter allowed.

"There seems to be lots of encounters like this throughout the country" Larry informs him, as he continues to interact with his computer. "I think we have something, though."

"What's that?"

"My colleague in Egypt has been on the trail of an animal that matches these markings. He too has a claw that is very similar to ours. Once we get it to the lab we can be for certain."

"Egypt?"

"Yes, one of the two countries in Africa that has wolves."

"So we're back to wolves?"

"No, not necessarily."

"Then what are we talking about?"

"You're right, I guess we are talking about wolves," Larry answers without looking away from his laptop.

Pulling alongside the large brick building, Walter parks in front. "We have to check you in. I'm friends with the chief medical examiner, but he doesn't take kindly to me bringing in someone to challenge his findings."

"I assure you, I will treat him with the respect that he deserves."

Dr. Roth, a heavy-set, balding man, greets the two men as they enter the main lobby. "Detective! How's your sister?"

"I forget sometimes how small the community is," Walter says as he shakes the man's hand. "She is doing well."

"Did they find the man?"

"No, not yet. I'm keeping tabs on it, but not able to help."

"I understand that. So, is this the animal expert? I'm Dr. Roth."

"Doctor, I'm Larry Walsh, the Chief Veterinarian at the LA Zoo." Larry shakes his hand.

"Let me show you the bodies." He leads them past the sign in, not bothering with it. "I have found something, and I think you will be of some help to me, Dr. Walsh," the doctor tells Larry.

"We were sure that an animal did this. But, after the lab results came back, I'm at a loss," Dr. Roth points out.

"You'll have to explain," Larry replies.

"I've found human DNA with traces of wolf."

"Excuse me?" both Larry and Walter blurt out at the same time.

"I thought you said it was wolf DNA," Walter says.

"I did, but that was initial results. Once I sent it upstairs we got these results."

"Did anyone tamper with them?"

"That's what I was wondering, so I had them do a second and third sample." Dr. Roth pushes the dual swinging doors. "Here we are." The large room has six tables, but only two have bodies on them. The change in temperature is reflected by the clouds coming out as they breathe.

Larry follows closely, helping the doctor uncover the bodies. "This one... he was found in the dumpster. He has two sets of saliva residue." Using an examination stick, he points out that the body also has two separate types of bite marks.

Larry gets close to the body's face. "My goodness. This is not a predator . . . That looks human."

The doctor quickly puts a light on the area that Larry is talking about. "Yes, that's what I found too."

"Human?" Walter asks, trying to get a good view of what the two doctors are looking at.

"Here again," the doctor points out to Larry. They are now working together to reexamine the body. "I found three."

"Look at this one here. It is almost human, but the canines are much more enlarged," Larry points out.

"I've been wracking my brain. I've never seen anything like this. I had a guy in here who was bitten by another man who was on bath salts, closest match I can make."

"You see the marks here?" He points to the nose of the victim. "Whatever did this tried to suffocate while biting."

"How do you know that?"

"Look at the marks; it was not trying to tear. It was holding on. This is a wolf tactic."

"What are you saying?"

"These teeth marks, they are neither man nor wolf. But, they are held in place. The bruising around the bite shows that the animal stayed latched while he was trying not to let the man breathe," Larry continues. "Did the man have any signs of asphyxiation?" The examiner, intrigued, grabs the lungs that are in a silver dish, and, using a microscope, checks.

"Interesting," Dr. Roth says, then adds, "He's right."

"You see here," he says and points to the neck area. "Whatever did this, placed its paw on his throat, too." He pauses. "But the claw indention shows it's not a wolf. Wolves don't have claws like these. Plus, there are five marks; wolves only have four and a dewclaw." He points to a place high on his arm showing them where it would be. "Either way, they are not used for attacking prey. Their feet are for running; only their mouth is for biting," he adds.

"I'm confused; what are you saying?" Walter asks.

"I'm saying that whatever did this, acts like a wolf, but is not a wolf." He stands between the two victims. "These men were killed by two different animals." He pulls out the claw he found in the wall. He points out the second victim: the bartender. He marks the teeth marks and the claw marks; they are much smaller and very messy.

"This is from one of the animals," he says, holding out the claw.

"What is that?" the doctor asks.

"I found it stuck in the wall outside the bar." The doctor takes it and quickly puts it up against the wounds, he finds that it matches those used on both men.

"This is from the smaller animal?"

"Yes, can we get it analyzed here?" Larry asks.

"Of course," the doctor replies. "I will take it upstairs right away," he says and heads for the door. Walter's phone rings; excusing himself, he answers the call. Larry watches as Walter's eyes light up.

"You're kidding me?" Walter states, the shock of information being given to him telling Larry he has just got some good news. "Thank you, I'll be there in ten. Have Detective Walken meet me there," he states. Hanging up the phone, he looks at Larry. "I got to head to County," referring to the county jail house. "Will you be okay here for a couple of hours?"

"Sure, there is still plenty to figure out," he states with a smile.

CHAPTER TWENTY-TWO

As Walter arrives at the county jail, Stephanie is on her way to join him, but he doesn't want anyone else talking with Alex. Walking in, he spends a few moments checking in. He makes small talk, but doesn't engage directly with anyone. He needs to get in there; Alex is the only connection to Victor they have been able to find alive.

The fear of this turning into a cold case is real. With the lack of witnesses, and no clues connecting them to a suspect, the theory that Victor was responsible was all they had. But they had no proof that he had anything to do with it. He was both a missing person and a key suspect. All Walter has, are the crime scene photos and a theory.

Walking the wide halls, Walter is led to the interrogation room. He takes a seat and lays his file on the table. He waits a few minutes for Alex to come in. He is not in handcuffs, when he enters. He hasn't been charged, but they have kept him as a person of interest. Taking a seat, he smiles at Walter. "How you doing, Walt?" he asks, extending his hand to shake it.

"Good. You all right, Alex?"

"Yeah, this is some bullshit, though."

"I bet. I came right away, when I heard it was you." He pauses. "They told me you didn't want any counsel?"

"Yeah, why would I need counsel? I didn't do nothing wrong. I should be dealing with a ticket is all."

"I don't think it wise, you talk with anyone without a lawyer with you, including me."

"Hey, I got nothing to hide, except the fact that I got picked up. I don't want my brothers to know about this. They don't know I spent my bonus on that stupid car."

"Since you bring it up, when did you buy it?" Walter asks.

"Two days ago, now." Alex leans back in his chair, lifting its front legs off the ground.

"Do you remember who from?"

"Yeah, some little dude named Victor. Armenian, I think."

"Did he tell you why he was selling it?"

"Listen, Walt, I don't know what's going on here. But you got to get them to let me out of here. I need to get to the club, before they start to worry about me."

"Did you not call anyone, when you got arrested?"

"Nah, I told you. I don't want them to know about what's going on. You won't tell your sister, right?" Alex leans forward, the chairs legs hit hard, making a scraping noise.

"No, I will not. I don't talk about my work with her."

"God, that's good. You know she'll tell Chris, and then that's it." He laughs.

"Yeah, I guess so. She's not one with secrets." Walter smiles, wanting to disarm Alex.

"So, what else do you want to know?"

"When you bought the car from Victor, did he have anyone with him?"

"Nope." He sits back, thinking. "There was some bigger dude watching us. Now that you ask, I remember thinking it was a set up."

"What do you mean?"

"You know, they get someone out to buy a car, then once they see the cash, they rob you."

"Oh, so you thought Victor had someone waiting to do that with you?"

"I did, but nothing happened."

"How much did he sell the car to you for?"

"Hey, will I get in trouble if I put a different price on the regs than what I actually paid?" Alex asks, leaning in, trying to be secretive.

"I'm not the IRS. You're good," Walter laughs.

"Then, I paid thirty K. The guy was desperate for cash."

"Thirty-thousand for a ninety-thousand-dollar car?" Walter pulls away in shock. "You didn't think anything was fishy about that?"

"He had it listed for thirty-six, and I was able to talk him down."

"But still. That's pretty low, Alex."

"Hey, I wasn't going to challenge it. I figured these kind of guys are rolling in dough, and don't care."

"It didn't worry you, that it may be hot?"

"The papers looked good. He had the pink, so I figured it was all good."

"Not smart, Alex." Walter takes a deep breath.

"Yeah, guess not. So, what now?"

"Have you ever been to the Public House?"

"The bar in Los Feliz?"

"Yes."

"Not in years, why?"

"Here, is this the man that you noticed when you bought the car?" He shows a mug shot of Aram.

"No, wait . . . Yeah, I think so."

"What about this guy?" He shows a picture of Victor.

"Yup, that's Victor. Never forget that little jerk."

"He was a jerk?"

"Just rude," Alex says and looks up at Walter.

"Had you seen him, or Aram, before you purchased the car?"

"Nope, not that I can remember."

"Had they ever been at your club?"

"Oh, I have no idea. Everyone likes our club."

"I bet. You guys doing well over there?"

"We could be doing better."

"Can't we all." Walter puts the pictures away.

"So, you going to tell them to let me go?"

"Yeah, and I appreciate all your help." Walter gets up and heads for the heavy locked door. He bangs on it, letting them know he is ready to leave.

"Yeah, no problem," Alex gets up too.

"One last thing, where did you buy the car?"

"What's that?"

"Where did you meet?"

"Oh, in a parking lot."

"Which parking lot?"

"Somewhere in Santa Monica."

"Do you have the address?"

"Oh, no. It's the one by the promenade."

"Who gave you a ride?"

"What? No one. I took a ride share."

"Great, when we get you released, could you give the address from the app?"

"Sure, but he just told me to go to the promenade, then we walked to the car." Alex hesitates.

"So you have his number. That would be so helpful to me."

"Sure, no problem. I just hope I didn't erase it." The large door opens, and the two men walk out. The sheriff leads Alex in another direction, so he can be released.

Walter pulls out his phone, sending a simple text to Stephanie: "Meet me at Victor's apartment." Walking out of the county jail, he blocks out the change from indoors to bright sun light. His eyes adapt, and he is surprised to see Vincent, Alex's brother leaning against a half-wall. Walter has made a point to meet all the brothers, once he found out Melisa was getting serious with Chris. He never really trusted Chris.

"Are you here for your brother?"

"My father told me to pick him up."

"I was under the impression he didn't want his brothers to know what happened."

"Our father thought differently." The large man pushes off from the wall. "Why are you here?"

"I wanted to make sure he was taken care of properly. You guys are almost family," Walter smiles and greats Vincent with a hand shake. The two men stare at each other for a moment, sizing each other up. Vincent lets out a soft huff, and smiles. Walter's grip tightens, but it doesn't get a reaction from Vincent.

"We appreciate that."

"I bet. Have a good one." Walter pulls his hand from the much larger man's and leaves.

CHAPTER TWENTY-THREE

Melisa wakes in a cold sweat. The dogs are covering her, but their heat isn't the cause. She easily pushes them off and sits up in the bed. She has been having horrible dreams all night. Her anger at Aaron never left her. The feeling of being betrayed was strong. There was also this feeling about Chris. Grabbing her phone from the bedside, she is disappointed that there isn't a message from him.

She dials his number, but the phone goes straight to voicemail. It's odd; he has never done anything like this before. Her mind races, conjuring all the horrible things that could have happened to him. The man in the leather jacket becomes a strong focus for her. Who was that mysterious man? An emptiness hits her stomach.

She is hungry, to a degree that she has never felt in her life before. Getting out of bed, she joins her dad in the kitchen. He has newspapers covering half the table with his tools laid out in order, as well as gaskets and other fittings and holds a carburetor in his blackened hands. With a smile, Melisa comes up from behind and kisses him on the cheek. Saying "Good morning," she walks to the stove and fixes herself a plate.

"You never stay in bed this late, Mija . . . Everything okay?"

"Yeah, Dad. All good." She takes her seat at the table. The blank face she wears is not lost on her father. He knows something is troubling her. He asked her once; he won't again.

"Who's the guy in the car?"

"What?" She quickly looks out the window to see Aaron sitting asleep in Chris's SUV. "What the fuck?" she whispers. Melisa knows her father must have stayed up all night watching the car. He was old school. If things were out of place, he wouldn't ask questions or call for help. He would just watch and wait. He wasn't afraid of anything, having come from a third world country and survived its civil war.

"He stayed out there all night, no?" He looks up for a second, then continues on with his task.

"I think so. He must have been worried about that John Doe." As she says the words the only person she pictures is the man with the sunglasses.

"Which John Doe? What aren't you telling me, Mija?"

"The one who I was trying to help." She tries to pretend it's no big deal. "Who you rebuilding the carb for?" She changes the subject.

"Just a little side project; should have had this done a long time ago," he states, not looking up from the metal object. "Are you worried about the man coming here?"

"No. Chris is. But I'm not."

"Did you give him my address?" His expression is solemn as he looks directly into her eyes.

"No, Dad, nothing like that."

"Well, you should have. Is that why you are staying here?"

"Kind of."

"Really? Well, maybe we should stay at your house. Then I can introduce myself to this John Don."

"John Doe," Melisa says and grins widely. "Dad, everything is okay. Everyone is just acting macho; I don't need you to, too . . . Did Walter come home last night?"

"No, he's really busy with his case." Pausing, he looks out the window. "Why don't you invite him in . . . I made enough food for him."

"I don't think so, Dad." Melisa still feeling annoyed with Aaron.

"Well, at least take him some food. I don't want it to go to waste."

"Okay Dad." She makes a plate for him. Carefully carrying a plate for each of them outside, she walks straight to Aaron's SUV. Half asleep, he wakes when he hears the gate close. Knocking on the tinted window, she smiles and lifts the plate for him to see. Aaron reluctantly unlocks the door.

Melisa opens the door but doesn't get in.

"My dad figured you might be hungry," Melisa says and hands Aaron the food. "You know; it looks pretty odd to him that you stayed out here all night."

"I'm sorry." He takes the food, taking in the aroma. "Wow, he made this? Tell him, thank you."

"I will," Melisa smiles. "So you want to come in?"

"I would rather not."

"Look, it's weird that you stayed out here all night, and my dad is asking questions. So, let's forget about what happened."

She smiles, but her eyes are heavy. "My dad's about to head to work. Maybe, you can come in for a few minutes until he leaves."

"No, I was told to stay here," he says, looking up at her. "Thank you for the food. I love bacon." He starts to put a taco together with the ingredients.

"Gringos always make tacos with tortillas," she says and lets out a chuckle.

"How should I use them?" he asks, stuffing an already made taco in his mouth.

"Like bread. Roll them up and dip them in the juice." She continues to laugh. "Use the fork to eat the food, and then bite into the tortilla," she continues, showing him with her own food.

"Gringo, eh? I don't think Poles fall under the gringo status," he teases back.

"What do you mean?"

"You haven't heard all the Polish jokes?"

"Oh, yeah. I'm a little slow right now." She raises an eyebrow. He finishes his taco, then rolls his second tortilla and finishes the food the way she suggested

"Have you heard from Chris?" Melisa asks.

"Not since earlier this morning, sometime around five."

"What did he say?"

"To stay here with you."

"Why?"

"He is worried."

"You guys are way too overprotective. My dad almost started in on me too."

"Have you tried to call him?"

"I have, but no answer."

"That's odd. I'm sure he must be sleeping. You know how he can't sleep at night."

"Sounds like it's a family thing." She looks out in front of the vehicle.

"Yeah, I guess so."

"It's really cold out here. Can we please go inside?" Melisa crosses her arms rubbing them for warmth. Reluctantly, he agrees. Carrying the food, he continues to eat as he walks. Once they are inside, the dogs come barreling over, barking. Aaron jumps in front of Melisa, lowering himself to protect her.

"Hey," her father calls from the kitchen. The dogs both stop. "Get over here," he commands them back into the kitchen. He leads them outside, then heads to the living room and introduces himself to Aaron. "Hello, I'm Almir." He offers his hand.

"Mr. Castro. It's a pleasure to meet you. I am Aaron."

"Aaron, my home is your home. Please eat in the kitchen. I will make way with my junk," he says and leads them to the kitchen.

"Your food is delicious, sir. Thank you."

"My pleasure. My mother was an amazing cook. I hoped my little girl here would have taken up her recipes, but I don't think she can brown meat," he says and laughs whole-heartedly.

"Thanks, Dad. I'm not that bad." She takes a seat at the table.

"Please, sit." Aaron does and continues to eat.

"Well, I'll be outside. I got to put in this carburetor." Her father gets up and heads outside.

"I knew it! That's to the Malibu," Melisa erupts in excitement.

"Yes, when it's done, maybe you can help me test it." He smiles. Melisa jumps up from her seat and gives him a huge hug.

"Thank you!" She kisses him. A buzz on Aaron's phone draws his attention from the family bonding. Looking down, he sees it's from Alex. It reads:

"Come home, something happened to Chris, go to dads."

Aaron looks up at the father and daughter. He knows that if Alex is sending this message, something is wrong. He should never be sending messages to him. He was at the bottom of the hierarchy. "Excuse me, but I need to be leaving. Melisa, may I have a moment," he asks, getting up from the table and putting his phone in his pocket.

"What's up?" she follows him to the front door.

"Please, stay here. Do not go anywhere until I come back, please."

"I don't understand," she says and looks down to his pocket. "Was that Chris?"

"No. And that is the reason. Please. Listen to me. You need to stay here. Keep those dogs close."

"You're scaring me, Aaron. What the hell!"

"Melisa. I'm sure it's nothing, but to be on the safe side . . . Stay here!" he states. Melisa doesn't like being put in situations like this. It reminds her of when she was a kid. Her father had some people from his past that liked to show up unannounced. When they did, her mother would always have her and Walter stay in their rooms.

They finally stopped coming by when her mother laid down the law. And when she did so, her father had to make a choice. She never saw those friends of his again. Looking into Aaron's eyes, she can now see the same fear. Something bad has happened. She just prays it wasn't Chris.

"Aaron, if you think I'm going to stay here without an explanation, you're crazy."

"Melisa. Trust me . . . Just keep those dogs close." Closing the door behind himself, he never looks back. He goes straight to the SUV, gets in, and drives off.

It takes Aaron an hour and a half to get to his dad's house. It gives him time to collect himself. He knows something isn't right about the situation. He tried to call Vincent, but only got his voicemail. He ended up calling Alex, something that left a bad taste in his mouth. Talking with Alex angered Aaron. He couldn't stand to have the baby in the family call him, telling him what to do. There was a hierarchy in his family, and Alex was at the bottom.

Driving down the dirt road, he can see his brothers' cars. Now his worries begin to compound. Having all the brothers at his father's can mean only one thing . . . Chris is no longer in charge. From the way Alex had just talked to him, he knew who he would now be following.

He knows what is going to happen next: either Chris has been hurt to the point he can no longer lead, or he is going to die. He knows that Alex could never beat Chris, but then again, he is very cunning and complex.

Parking, he sees his brother Jesse standing at the door, his red hair waving in the wind. Walking up to him, Aaron see tears in his eyes. All of Aaron's fears are building up within. Aaron walks past him with only a nod. He knows that Jesse adores Chris. For him to be so sad means the worst.

Entering the house, he walks to the main room. His other brothers are spread out around the room. Alex is kneeling next to their father, talking. He stops once Aaron enters.

"Where's Chris?"

"He is downstairs," he says, referring to the basement. Alex moves away from his father. "But before you say anything, you need to know things are changing around here."

"Why is he downstairs?" Aaron asks in a low growl.

"Listen to your brother," his father calls out, flicking his fingers about.

"You do not speak to me," he growls harshly at the old man. The other brothers quickly move around their father, shielding him from Aaron.

"Hold on, guys. Let me talk to Aaron." Alex walks up to Aaron. "You need to respect our ways. You know what is happening here."

"I know you are a snake in the grass, little one," Aaron states firmly. "Why is Chris downstairs?"

"He is infected."

"What?"

"He got into a fight, and he is sick," Alex points out with a smile.

"With who?"

"The Hunter," Alex says with a smirk.

"You did this," he replies and lowers himself to attack. A large hand touches his shoulder. Aaron doesn't need to look. He knows whose it is.

"You need to calm yourself, brother. You are not doing anyone any good," Vincent states from behind.

"I did nothing but start to fix the situation that Chris started," Alex says.

"You started? Or did he start?" Aaron points at their father. "Chris was creating a great life for us all."

"How is that, by playing human?" Aleksy calls out. He gets up from his chair, using the arms of Greg and Jim for leverage, neither of whom are as large as Aaron, though each stand over six foot tall. "Your foolish brother was sending us down a road that we would have not been able to recover from."

"What road? What are you talking about? You crazy old man. I already warned you. Do not speak to me again." Aaron's eyes begin to glow. His brothers, feeling Aaron's anger, again quickly go to defend their father. Vincent grabs ahold of Aaron's shoulder.

"Please, Aaron. We need you," Vincent tells him.

"You've agreed to this? I can't believe what I'm hearing. You all speak of respect and family this and that. And yet our brother is downstairs hurt and all we are doing is arguing over who is in charge." He flexes his shoulders showing his strength. His brothers back up, lowering themselves in preparation. "Chris is the pack leader."

"Not while he is in that cage."

"What cage?"

"Oh please, stop being such a drama queen." Alex waves his hands about, like his father does. Before he can react, Aaron has him by the throat and is slamming him into the wall, breaking the wood around him.

"Don't ever speak to me that way. I can end you," he growls, pushing his forehead against Alex's. Vincent crashes his fist into the back of Aaron's head and slams him to the floor. Instantly, the other brothers pounce, but Aaron leaps to the wall, causing them to miss.

"You fools! You chose this little shit? You think he knows anything? He is weak." Aaron is ready to keep the fight going.

"We did not choose him. We are following our father," Jim says. The third oldest, he is a brother that Aaron doesn't know that well. He was born when Aaron had left after the fire. Looking at him now, he knows that was a mistake. He has no connection with him.

Aaron looks around at his brothers. The feeling of betrayal causes tears to build. "I can't believe you. This is not right, and you all know it."

"Please brother, move on with us," Vincent says calmly, rubbing his hand.

"Yes, all will be forgiven," Alex adds, sending sparks down Aaron's spine.

"Forgiven? What about Chris?"

"He will be fine. It will take time, but he will be okay," Aleksy informs him. Aaron looks at him with spite.

"You won't stop until you get us all killed. Telling your stories. You think we can deal with the Hunter? Even with Chris we are no match for him," Aaron points out.

"True, but we are not alone. Follow me downstairs." Alex chuckles and rubs his throat. Feeling it's a trap, Aaron goes anyway. He needs to see Chris, make sure he is okay.

The stairs creak with each step. He follows Alex, knowing his other brothers are following close behind. His ears perked, he can hear Chris, but he is not alone.

Aaron can't believe what he is seeing. There are a dozen men, all chained. From their scent, he can tell they've all been turned into "mutts." A large cage sits in the center of the room. Aaron's eyes widen, seeing Chris inside, lying curled up in pain.

Aaron moves to him but is stopped by Vincent. "Leave him. The mutts are still wild," he warns.

"So, I will destroy them all if even one touches me." Aaron shakes Vincent's arm off.

"That's not the point. We need them."

"Ha, you think they will be of any help, you're crazier than I thought."

"They will be a great distraction."

"For who? The Hunter? What about the man without a name?" Aaron says, keeping his eyes on Chris. "He is here. He will not leave until he gets his job done."

"That vampire is no concern," Alex snaps back.

"What vampire?" one of the other brothers calls out. The rest begin to murmur at the thought of him. They all know the stories of such a man. A mysterious man, who has no name.

At the sound of a soft tap on the floor, a familiar rhythm catches Aaron's attention. Looking at his other brothers, he knows they don't recognize it. It's something from when Chris was a child. He used to do it when he was happy. A little beat, telling Aaron he is okay. Aaron hides his happiness. He can't let them know his brother is healing. He knows Chris is strong, and now he has to do what is best for him.

"Listen, I will help. But I must protect Melisa."

"No!" Aleksy shouts, as he walks down the stairs, using the rails for balance. "She is not one of us."

"But her child is."

"That bastard is not of my blood."

"I promise: you will not breathe another breath if you speak of that child again," he growls. His focus on his father brings chills to all the brothers. They all know that he means what he is saying. Aaron would protect the innocent with his life. He has already done it once before.

His brother Jim turns and walks backwards toward Aaron in agreement. The other brothers, except for Alex, all make their move toward Aaron. Aleksy smirks, shaking his head. "Fine, bring her here." He smiles and heads back upstairs followed by Alex. Halfway, he pauses. "Only Aaron," he adds, followed by a cough, which quickly turns into a fit. Alex grabs hold of him, helping him the rest of the way back upstairs.

"That's what you are following. An old man, bitter from his own mistakes," Aaron says, waving off his father. "You all sicken me," he states and leaves the basement.

CHAPTER TWENTY-FOUR

Walter arrives at Victor's apartment. Stephanie had gotten the address from one of her sources. It was a place no one knew about, his private place, away from his family. He stopped at the apartment manager's residence, getting him to go up with him. Stephanie was sure that Victor was behind all the murders, but Walter had to anticipate that he too might be a victim of the string of homicides. That's how he was able to procure a warrant so quickly.

Warrant in hand, he knocks loudly. The apartment manager stands nervously behind him. Walter can feel the worry of the older man. Trying to calm him, he offers to take the keys, so he can go back downstairs and not be seen. The manager jumps at the idea and hands over the keys, hurrying away.

Not one to be fearful of thugs, Walter doesn't care to wait for back up. He knocks again. A woman pops her head out screaming at him in Armenian. Walter just smirks, knowing the neighborhood well. He expected nothing less. He shows his badge, pointing for her to go back inside. She curses him but follows his instructions.

Banging harder on the door, he puts the key into the deadbolt. Pulling out his sidearm, he quickly unlocks and opens the door wide, turning his body and using the wall as cover. "LAPD," he hollers out. "I have a warrant," not sure who may be inside.

The room is silent. Taking a quick peek, he looks inside. His gun pointing into the room, he carefully enters, with his left arm holding a flashlight under his gun arm. He checks his blind spots. The entrance is only a few feet wide. To the right is the living room; the left is a dining room. Straight ahead is a short hallway with a door directly in front of him, which looks to be the bathroom.

"LAPD," he calls out again. The room is dark; all the windows are covered. He enters the living room first, taking mental images of everything. A small gray square couch is set up under a large window. A coffee table, something you would pick up at a European furniture store. There are books on the table. From the look, they seem to be more decorative, than something someone would be reading.

Turning to the dining room, he sees a small modern orange round high-top table with four stools surrounding it. Walter actually likes it. Keeping his gun pointed toward the hallway, he continues to look at the small common area of the apartment. It's not what he would have expected from Victor. He prejudged him, expecting to find everything gold and gaudy.

The dining room has a direct line into the kitchen, which is small but well kept. Everything is organized in its own plastic container, labeled and dated. The man who lives here is obviously compulsive. Thinking of what Stephanie had told him about Victor, it all makes sense. If this was his hidden world, of course he would keep it pristine. He wondered if he ever had anyone up here.

Looking at the entrance, he notices slippers sitting against the wall. Then, looking down at the carpets, he sees that they are very light colored; he must have taken his shoes off every time he came in.

He heads through the kitchen, which leads to the hallway as well. There is a door on the right of the hallway, sharing a wall with the living room. It must be the bedroom, he figures. Keeping his back to the opposite wall, he sidewalks toward the open bathroom. Using his flashlight, he pushes it open. It's empty, just as he thought.

Now standing directly in front of the bedroom door, he readies himself. He leverages himself, so he can kick it in. As he is about to strike, Detective Walken opens the front door, startling him. Walter dives to the floor, pointing his gun at her. She has her gun drawn on him. He puts his index finger to his lips, telling her to be quiet. He waves her in, pointing to the bedroom.

He gives her the sign that he has not checked it yet. She hurries to him, and positions herself to the side of the door. Walter readies himself again, and this time he quickly kicks the door in; Stephanie moves in checking to the left, and he follows checking to the right. The room is empty. Holstering their weapons, Walter shakes his head at Stephanie.

"What?" she laughs.

"You scared the shit out of me."

"Well, what do you expect? You left the door cracked, and I had no idea what to expect."

"I thought I closed it all the way, whew." He lets out a deep breath, shaking his head.

"It's a nice place, eh?" Stephanie looks around the room. "Where's the super?"

"He didn't want nothing to do with this apartment, so I told him to go back to his apartment."

"Bunch of scaredy-cats in this building, present company included," she laughs.

"Fuck off. I don't know why I was freaked out . . . I guess I was expecting to unleash a wild animal or something."

"Shit, this whole thing is pretty freaky," she says, still snickering. "I get it."

Walter turns off his flashlight, and turns on the lights. The two begin to look for clues. Victor's bedroom is immaculate, like the rest of the house. His bed looks like it was done by an ex-marine. Tight and solid. His clothes are organized by color and style.

"This guy is a neat freak; I doubt we will find anything here."

"Yeah, you're probably right. Except maybe that." Walter points to the laptop on the small corner desk. Opening it, he sees it has a password. Looking under the drawer he finds a list of passwords. He smiles at Stephanie. "God, I wish I was so organized," he states with a grin.

Logging on to the computer, he goes to the web history. "Take a look at this," he states. "Looks like our friend was trying to get out of town," he shows her. "Dancing was more than a hobby."

"I hope he was good. These schools are no joke."

"Well, he was little and fem; I'm sure he had it in him."

"Don't be that way." Stephanie taps him on the shoulder.

"What?" he laughs. "Let's head to the club. I really would like to see those brothers again."

Stephanie and Walter arrive together at the club. Walter has pushed hard for Stephanie to follow his suspicion. He doesn't know how Alex and Victor are connected, but he knows they are. It's still early enough that the club is not quite open. There is a line at the door, which is still closed.

Walter leads the way, knocking heavily on the door. A large black man wearing a security shirt opens the door. Walter, showing his badge, asks if he can come in. The security guard allows them in without protest, but informs them that no real manager is on site. Walter politely asks for whomever has been left in charge.

Inside is quiet. The DJ is still getting his set ready, moving different milk crates around. The bartenders are prepping all the produce for the night, and the bar-backs are setting up all the glasses.

The security guard leads them to the manager on duty. "Hey Valerie, these two cops would like to talk with you," the large man calls out, annoyed. His tone tells the detectives more than they could have hoped. The manager is wearing a seductive little outfit, which both detectives can't help but check out.

"Hi, I'm Detective Castro, and this is Detective Walken . . . Are the owners in?"

"No," she rudely states without introducing herself. Stephanie looks her up and down, with spite. Walter looks back at her, turning the conversation over to her.

"So, you're the manager of this place?" Stephanie moves closer to the woman.

"Yeah, so?" Valerie rolls her head with attitude.

"Well, since you are being so helpful, I'm going to do the same. From what I can see, this place is breaking a few fire codes." Stephanie smiles. "You should go outside and tell everyone waiting to go home."

"What? You can't do that."

"Oh, is that right?" She pulls out her phone and calls someone. Valerie begins to panic. She reaches out to touch Stephanie, trying to get her attention. "You touch me again, I'm going to arrest you, you little bitch."

"What?" Valerie has no idea what to do. She watches and listens to Stephanie begin her conversation. She is talking to the fire chief and informing him that they need to come out to the club and check it out. The girl just stands there whimpering and trying to get Stephanie to stop. She looks at Walter, who just shrugs his shoulders.

"You shouldn't have been so rude," Walter says and raises his eyebrows.

"Wait, wait. I'm sorry." Valerie again tries to touch Stephanie, but pulls her arm back remembering what Stephanie told her. "I'm sorry I was rude. How can I help?"

"Hold on," Stephanie tells the person on the other line. "What was that?"

"I'm sorry. How can I help you?"

"Oh, yeah. Let me finish this call, then we can deal with that," Stephanie rudely states. She tells the person on the line to hurry up.

"So, where is Alex?"

"Alex? I don't know," Valerie replies.

"What about Chris?"

"I don't know."

"I see. Can you get in touch with them?"

"Yes."

"God, I'm really starting to hate this little bitch . . . You talk to her, I can't."

"Listen, I'm sorry. I just don't know what to say."

"Hey, listen. We came in looking to see if this guy has been in here. He may have been trying to set up shop here." Walter shows Valerie a picture of Victor Rees.

"I wouldn't know anything about that. Alex never tells me anything."

"How well do you know Alex?"

"I know him good."

"You guys a couple?"

"Not that it's any of your business, but yes," she responds, her attitude beginning to come back. Stephanie turns back around looking at her with fire in her eyes. "We have been dating for a few months now," Valerie says as her eyes widen.

"So he put you in charge pretty quick, eh?" Walter asks.

"He thought I would be a good manager."

"When did he do this?" Stephanie chimes in.

"Today."

"And how long you been working here?"

"Two months."

"Must be real good, eh?" Stephanie winks and blows a kiss at the young woman.

"What? Fuck you," she responds.

"What! Little bitch." Stephanie moves close to her. "Fuck this cunt, I'm taking her in." She starts to move close to her. The girl hides behind Walter, who looks at Stephanie and with his eyes tells her she's acting too harsh. The game is about to go the wrong way.

"Hey, look. You don't have to worry. We won't be taking you in. We just need some answers. Do you know or recognize this man?" he again asks and shows her the picture of Victor.

"Yeah, he was in here the other night."

"Do you remember anything about him?"

"He was a dick. I was bartending, and he wanted free drinks."

"I see. Then what happened?"

"He got into it with Chris, then Alex got involved. But nothing happened. He just left with his entourage."

"I bet. Was this man with them?" Walter shows a picture of Aram.

"Yeah, I remember him. He was nice."

"Well. These guys are pretty mad about all this. We are trying to help Alex. Do you know where Alex is?" Walter continues to work her feelings for Alex.

"I think he is at home."

"Do you have an address? I would like to get to them before the bad guys do."

"Yeah, it's his father's house. It's the only house he's taken me to. Let me write it down."

"Okay, you can put it on this piece of paper," Walter says and hands her a small card.

"What about closing the club? Can you guys not do that?" she asks as she writes the address on the card. "I'm really sorry I was a bitch. Alex told me not to take shit from anyone who comes in here."

"Well, that wasn't smart. But we will tell the fire chief to let it go . . . this time," Walter says to comfort her.

Once outside, Walter can't help but laugh. Stephanie has a self-serving grin on her face. "I couldn't have done any better," he blurts out.

"I can't stand little bitches like that. You know she's sucking someone's cock . . . She is why women can't get ahead in this world."

"Wow. All her?"

"Yeah. That one girl is responsible for it all," she says, laughing. "So, what's the play?"

"Well, traffic will be a nightmare. I say we pick this up first thing in the morning."

"Sounds good. Do you want to grab a drink?"

"Yeah. After today, I can actually use one." Walter's response surprises Stephanie.

"Really? Well, all right then," she says with a smile. "I can't remember the last time we had a drink together. Or the last time I heard you had a drink."

"Yeah, let's not make a big deal out of it. Don't make me regret this already."

"Hey, I'm done. Let's go get this drink."

CHAPTER TWENTY-FIVE

"Give it a try," Melisa's father hollers, half his body reaching over and under the hood of the Malibu. A nineteen-sixty-seven, two-door, the metallic, light blue car is immaculate. Melisa is turning the ignition, helping to get the car started. The engine cranks, but never turns over. She gives it three tries, the gas pedal under her foot being controlled by her dad, as he chokes the carburetor.

"Give me a minute; I'm going to try some starter fluid," he calls out. Melisa can't hide her excitement. The dogs are sitting in the back seat, tongues out, as excited as Melisa, drooling and looking around. The Malibu hasn't run in eight years. Her father wouldn't even start it so he could move it. He would put it in neutral and push. Remembering the last time it ran brings tears to her eyes. They had a family trip to the beach.

Her mom loved the car. It didn't look then like it does now. When she drove it, it was a mess. The whole car was painted with primer, with a few rust spots waiting to be worked. The rims were just a basic metal cylinder. When it ran, the back of the car bounced from the old suspension. The engine was loud, but not in a cool way.

Melisa remembered ducking down when her mom took her to school. This little white woman, driving this boat of a car, the neighborhood predominantly Hispanic. She was cool. Melisa smiles, thinking about her mother. Nothing got to her. She just did her thing.

"Give it another try," her dad calls out, shaking her away from memory lane. With one turn the car rumbles on. He uses the lever on the carburetor to rev the engine. The loud, throaty engine shakes the whole car. It's not the engine she was used to. Her dad has completely rebuilt the car.

She knew it was a way for him to be close to his wife. Sometimes she wondered if it was some kind of apology. He always wanted to fix her car up, but with work, he never got the chance. But her mom never complained. She couldn't even remember a time when she got mad about the car. The thing was breaking down all the time, and, funny to think, Melisa's mom probably knew more about it than her dad.

The engine idling smoothly, her dad slams the hood. "You want to take it for a test?" he asks with a smile.

"Sure, where do you want to go?" she asks. He walks up to the driver's side door.

"You go, Mija, I have some things to do around here."

"Are you sure it's street ready?"

"Oh yeah, the papers are good on it too. I never let it lapse; just take it around the block," he says, slapping his towel on the roof. "Let me open the gate." He calls for the dogs to go with him, but they stay in the car.

"Okay, hold on, I have to get my wallet." She hurries inside and grabs a few things. She feels like a little girl. She's always wanted to drive the car and can barely contain herself. A loud boom of thunder catches her off guard. Running outside, she sees the sky is turning gray, and the first drops of rain start to fall. Her father hurries into the house to get away from the shower.

"I don't think it's a good time to test drive a car, Mija," he says sadly.

"Shoot, I really wanted to." She whacks her small clutch on her thigh.

"The tires are new, and the brakes work great; I tested them before I had to replace the carb. Maybe you'll be okay." Her father tries to make her happy. "You go, just stay off the freeways."

"You sure?" she asks.

"Yeah, go ahead." His action reminds her of the first time she drove a car by herself. She was just sixteen, with only a learner's permit. She had a date with a guy she really liked. It was a double date. His car broke down, and she called her dad. He came and helped, but it was taking so long, and her girlfriend needed to get home.

Believing he had taught her well, he allowed her to drive his car and take the kids home. He stayed behind and worked on the car. Thinking back, she believes it may have been raining that day too. Looking back at her father, she can't help but run up and give him a huge hug and a kiss. "I love you, Dad," she whispers into his ear.

With a yelp, Melisa runs under the cold rain. She slips slightly when she makes the turn around the front end. Catching herself on the hood of the car, she laughs, shouts, "I'm okay." Continuing the rush, she rounds the door, and starts to laugh. "Hey, I thought Dad told you to get out?" she calls out to the dogs.

"Just take them, Mija; they're stubborn, like me. You'll never get them out of there." Melisa doesn't debate it. She just takes her seat and turns the ignition. The boom of the engine rattles the whole car, and she revs the engine with a few soft pumps, until the idle is smooth. Looking at her dad, she gives a wave and puts the car in drive. He returns the wave as he watches her leave.

After a few turns onto different streets, she passes a restaurant called El Tepeyac. Manny the owner had been amazing. She and her dad loved to share a meal there. Manny was always so nice, and a big flirt. He would take her by the hand and lead her to a table. It's been years since he passed; she can't even remember the last time she's been inside the restaurant.

The old neighborhood gave her some good memories. Melisa passes the old cemetery; an eerie feeling comes over her. She pulls over. If she makes the next left, she'll be heading back to her father's. If she goes right, she'll be heading into downtown. The first bar Chris opened is in the financial district.

Looking into the cemetery she remembers the first funeral she ever attended. It was a good friend of her dad's. To this day, she doesn't know how he died. She thinks back to the night it happened. It was raining, like it had been the last few days. Melisa's aunt showed up unannounced. She was panicked and started telling her mom all kinds of things about Melisa's dad.

In those days, her dad was always getting in trouble because he wanted to be a good friend. She can't remember what was said. But, she understood that her dad was in trouble. Melisa's mom left her and Walter with their aunt, while she went out looking for her husband. Melisa was no older than seven at the time. Walter was two.

Her memory is fuzzy on the details, but she does know that her mother found him and brought him home. Melisa has images in her head, of her little white mother walking up to a bunch of thugs and pulling her father away. She was so brave. But, she was also married to a man that would have killed anyone who would have talked bad to her.

Aaron's words start to play back in her head. She can't explain it, but she knows Chris is in trouble. It's more than just a feeling. *That man in the sunglasses, the one without eyes.* She starts to wonder about him. *Who was he? Most likely that dumb shit Alex got his brother in trouble.* The stranger didn't look or act like a bad guy, but from her own experiences, that doesn't mean anything. Either way, she needs to focus. *No more what if's. Just find Chris.*

With that, Melisa knows what she must do. She looks at Genghis, who has sneaked into the front leaving Geronimo in the back seat. "What do you think?" she asks him. Genghis gives her a sloppy lick on her face. Eyes closed and smiling, Melisa wipes the slobber off her face. "Well, all right then." She heads right at the stop sign, the strength of her mother in her heart as she goes out to find her man.

The rain begins to pick up, and luckily the wipers are doing a good job. After a few more turns, she is driving by the front of the bar. It's almost five. The bar was always open from eight in the morning till two in the morning. Chris called it his dive. She always made fun, because it was anything but. The bar had its regulars, but they were all white collar, yuppie types. He chose the location specifically because of its proximity to the financial district, and it was paying off big time. It is what paved the way for him to open the club and now the restaurant bar in Mr. McCarthy's high-rise.

Stopping out in front, she tries to see through the front door, which is propped open. She can't tell who's inside, so she parks and pushes the hazards, being in a no-parking spot. It was the first place Chris opened; he doesn't spend much time there anymore, leaving the day-to-day to his younger brother Jesse. But, knowing that he sometimes comes in before the night shift to check on things, she feels it is a good place to start. Melisa tells the dogs to stay, and hurries through the rain.

A young girl is tending the bar. She's petite and really cute, almost elfin in her appearance. Melisa smirks. Chris always seemed to hire the same type of woman. She wondered how he could be with such a tall girl as herself, when he obviously likes that type.

"Hi, is Chris around?" she asks, almost out of breath. Her hair and clothes are wet from the rain.

"No, sorry," she answers, continuing to cut limes and lemons.

"Have you heard from him?"

"Nope, been here all day."

"I'm Melisa, I don't know if we met before . . ."

"Yeah, I know who you are . . . You came in here last month. I'm Hannah," she says and smiles. "Can I get you something?"

"Oh, no thank you. If you see him, tell him I came by."

"Sure thing," she replies. "Actually, I haven't heard from Jesse either. He was supposed to be here an hour ago." Taking in the information, Melisa doesn't know how to process it. Chris's brothers were all known for never missing work. She had met Jesse a few times at events Chris catered. He was very nice.

"Okay, well, if I see Chris, I'll tell him." Melisa leaves, unsure of her next move. Something is off, for sure, but she can't tell what. She closes her eyes, looking inside for guidance. But it never comes. The closeness she had felt the last few days to Chris is gone. The soft voice comforting her is missing. She feels completely alone.

The falling rain is freezing cold. Melisa rushes back to the illegally parked Malibu and accidentally peels out from the curb. Now both dogs are in the front seat with her. She shivers from the wet clothes. She turns on the old heater and is excited to see that it works. She goes down an old short cut, one that she would use when she didn't want to take the freeway.

The drive takes her up through Elysian Park where the baseball stadium is. Driving through the hills, she remembers her dad teaching her how to drive on the wide roads. It wasn't nearly as busy back then. Going around the hill, she thinks, *Lucky there isn't a baseball game.* Driving down the long hill she decides she should just head back to her house, she is so close. All the worries of the men in her life bombard her mind. She doesn't want to live in fear, and she truly doesn't fear the "John Doe." She needs a change of clothes so she can continue to search for Chris.

As she drives along the freeway, she sees the traffic on it is building up already. She passes a small park. It's empty, but that doesn't prevent her from slowing down to the required fifteen miles an hour. She hates to drive fast when kids could be around. She continues on down Riverside Drive, where she slows down again to pass Allesandro, an elementary school. A big electric board illuminates its name and highlights different students that are now in college. She wonders if her school ever did that. It makes her happy to see that the community is trying to build confidence in their youth, especially an under-privileged neighborhood like this. Now she needs to check with her old school. If they don't have something like this, she is going to make sure they do.

When she makes it past Rick's Burgers, she looks up to the small hillside, she remembers when people were able to ride their dirt bikes, before they built the apartment buildings at the end. The rain is really coming down, and she slows the car again. "Hold on," she calls out to the dogs to brace themselves.

With all of the Malibu's horse-power and super easy power steering, she doesn't feel completely comfortable behind the wheel yet. She stops at a red light and looks up at the Hyperion Bridge; she can picture the old motel that used to be there. It was in the movie about the gangsters. She could never remember the name of the movie. All she could remember was the guy on a motorcycle and the phrase about a gimp.

Not being a movie buff, she didn't even know it was in the movie until Chris had it on, and she noticed the old blue motel. Now there is some ugly cinder block building in its place. Looking to the right, she sees something leaning up against the fence of the freeway. It's a man, dressed in tattered dirty clothes, sheltering from the rain. The homeless problem in the area is getting worse. And when the weather got like this, it was dangerous.

It didn't rain a lot, but when it did, the laughable LA River would become rapids. She doesn't notice missing the light turning green. She sits through the light, and almost sits through another, but a car pulls up behind her and honks. The sound startles her, but also catches the homeless man's attention. He looks up, and to Melisa's surprise—it's the John Doe.

Melisa drives through the intersection and pulls over. Looking back through her mirror, she can see the man holding himself. His body is shivering. Her mind tells her to call the cops, but her heart won't let her. This man needs help, and so far, she has failed him. Turning off the car and grabbing her coat, she again tells the dogs to stay. She covers her head and runs across the street to the man.

"Hello," she calls out when she gets close enough. Looking down at the man, she can see he has cuts and bruises. "Oh my god, what happened?" she asks and moves closer. The man looks up at her in pain. He recognizes her. "I'm not going to hurt you," she says, reaching out for him.

"I'm so lost," he says.

"It's okay. I just want to help." She touches his hand. A sudden shock stings her fingertips. "Sorry, the weather can create electricity," she says, trying to ease him. "Come on, let's get you out of the rain," she says and softly tugs on his arm. She doesn't know why she's doing what she is. But the fact that this man just so happened to be here doesn't seem like a coincidence. She feels like she was supposed to find him. And, she is supposed to help him.

The man goes without much of a fight. He is sore all over, and it shows. They slowly cross the street. The dogs are looking through the back window. They start to bark as she gets close. She tells them to be quiet, and they listen. The man stops and looks at them. "They won't do anything," she assures him.

"I'm not sure how I feel about dogs," he says, his focus only on them.

"I promise; they listen to me." She moves him closer to the car. He doesn't resist again. Once in the car, she helps put his seat belt on. She explains everything that is happening; the last they spoke, he had expressed concern over not knowing things about his surroundings and from what she can gather, that hasn't improved.

Closing the door after him, she looks out into the distance. She can't believe what she's doing. She knows she can't take him to the hospital, nor can she take him to her dad's. She decides to take him to her own house, where this all began. The thunder strikes again, and the man jumps. The dogs bark, but Melisa quickly calls to them and they both lie down. She gets in and drives them. The man is holding his chest and the lower part of his neck.

"What happened?" she finally asks.

"I was attacked."

"This area can be rough. I'm sorry . . . I'll get you to my house and see if I can tend to those wounds."

"Thank you, Miss Castro; you have been the only constant," he says. His words give her a little smile.

Pulling up to her house, she pushes the button to open the gate. The man watches in amazement. "My whole house is automated. The lights are about to turn on," she explains. He smiles seeing what she predicted happen.

"Magic," he whispers.

"Technology," she replies. The garage door opens and she pulls the car in. The car is so long that she has to get out and make sure it fits. Once everything is set, she helps the man out and into the house. The dogs run in, passing them by, exploring the new surroundings and sniffing everything.

She leads him to the first room, the guest room, which is the only room on the east wing. The room is bright, with white oak furniture. The only color in the room is from a painting on the wall. It's a piece of plywood painted black with a red rose.

The man follows her as she takes him into the bathroom. It's similar with its white tones. He doesn't particularly like the brightness of the rooms, but he feels welcomed. She has him sit on the closed toilet, washes her hands, and begins to examine him.

She checks his head first then moves down, clearing off any dried blood. Having him move his hand from his neck, she can see what looks like a bite mark, but it's almost healed. "What did this?"

"I don't know," he says, looking down. Melisa opens the cabinet and pulls out some alcohol. "This may sting," she warns as she begins to apply it to his wound. The man flinches but takes the pain. "Can you take off your shirt?" she asks. The man does so. She can't help but admire the man's physique. He is not the same as when she found him just two days ago.

His upper body is riddled with bruises and cuts. "Did this all happen from the fight?" she asks.

"No," he says. "I had some pain from something I do not remember." He watches her hands as she touches his skin, ever so carefully.

219

"Do you remember falling?" she asks, not looking up at him. She is careful not to agitate the man. He is definitely working through some head trauma.

"Falling?" he asks, confused.

"Oh, nothing. This is an interesting tattoo; I've been trying to figure it out." She points out the small brand on his left arm, just under his bicep.

"I do not know what it means," he says. Melisa traces the black markings, her index finger following the cross first, then the antler that starts off black but fades going up his arm. The more she follows it, the more she notices that it is a larger brand than she first noticed.

Suddenly there's a flash—another vision strikes her. She sees the man lying on a wooden table. He is covered with blood everywhere. His chest wounds are open. It's not the same vision she had when she touched his chest on their first encounter. This time, there is another man. He is short and wears a cloak. A large rosary hangs from his neck. It's the same priest from the first vision.

Speaking in a language she doesn't understand, the monk pulls out a blade. Holding the man's left arm down, he cuts into him, using the blade to etch the tattoo she has been outlining. He makes the cross only. He trades the blade for a small wooden bowl. Inside is a black liquid, which he rubs into the exposed flesh. The man screams in pain.

Melisa is horrified by what she is witnessing. The antlers she had just thought reminded her of a beer logo appear, on their own, burning into the man's skin. As the priest continues chanting, the antlers branch out around the man's arm, infecting it and moving over his chest. Reaching the deep wounds on his chest, they start to heal, while the man continues crying out in pain.

Melisa pulls her hand away from the man. She is back to reality. Looking up at her, he notices the change in her face. "Are you all right, miss?" he asks.

"Why don't you take a shower?" she replies, holding back tears and turning away from him so he doesn't notice. Pushing the light switch, she illuminates the area. "Let me get you some clothes. I think you and my fiancé are about the same size," she says, her voice breaking. "I'll leave the clothes on the bed for you." She slyly wipes a tear away as she walks through the doorway.

The man looks around at the area she just lit, by pressing a light switch on the wall. His eyes reflect his wonder, taking in the magnificent display. Everything is shimmering. A twelve-inch, fixed, square showerhead hangs from the ceiling, its shining chrome reflecting the bright lights illuminating the shower. Six metallic body sprays poke out through the bright white tile. The man has no idea what he is looking at, including the slide rail with hand-shower, hose, and outlet elbow. "Miss?" he calls out softly.

"Yeah?" Melisa turns around. Her eyes are watery.

"I do not understand how to use this device," he states sheepishly.

"The shower valve supplies water at a pre-set maximum temperature to the hand shower, body sprays, or fixed head," she instructs. The man just looks at her. Melisa smiles gently. "I'm so sorry." She shakes her head. "I don't even realize how I'm talking, sometimes." She laughs.

Moving back into the bathroom, she reaches in the shower and starts the water, adjusting it to a nice hot stream from the ceiling showerhead. "That should do it," she says and uses her hand to gauge the temperature. "Good thing we're not in my shower," she teases, turning back to the man. "It has even more buttons."

"Thank you, Miss Melisa. I appreciate your patience with me," he says and nods.

"Yeah, well. You take your shower; use any towel. Just push this button when you're done." She points to the center unit. "All right, well, enjoy your shower." She leaves and has to stop herself from touching his shoulder.

Stepping outside of the bathroom, she closes the door behind her and leans up against the wall. Unable to hold back the tears any longer, she slides down to her butt, holding her face and muffling her sobs. This is the fourth time she has seen a vision of this nature. First with this stranger now using her shower, then, with the man who was missing his eyes. Then Aaron, and now this.

Overwhelmed by the psychic episodes, she grabs the pillow from the bed and screams into it. The dogs come into the room to investigate. Melisa grabs hold of them, squeezing them tight, holding on until she calms herself.

CHAPTER TWENTY-SIX

John has been following Melisa. The man in the leather jacket, having seen everything through his eyes, can't believe what he is witnessing. Melisa has taken the Hunter into her home. Making John move in closer, Ranald can hear their conversations.

Watching her help the Hunter and hearing him speak, he senses that something is not right. The Hunter is acting off. Taking into account some of the other things that have happened, it dawns on Ranald: The Hunter doesn't know who or what he is.

It makes sense. That's why Melisa was not hurt before. Why there have not been any deaths among the immortal community. For now, the Hunter is just a man. Knowing the Hunter's past, Ranald worries for Melisa. Who knows what will cause him to revert to the monster the man in the leather jacket and his kind know him to be?

This new knowledge perplexes him. He needs to strike while his enemy is weak, but at the same time . . . If he fails, he could be the one responsible for awakening the beast. What would his employers do, if that was the case? He has John move around the house, to find the best viewing point.

Now looking in through the kitchen, staying out of the light and using her large windows, he is able to watch everything through John's eyes. The thought of contacting Chris comes to mind. But given the worries that come with their kind's wild antics and unpredictability, he worries about endangering Melisa.

Listening in, he hears the Hunter speak of being attacked. *Hmm, was it Chris? Did Chris try and fight the Hunter?* He hasn't heard from him since early this morning. Though the sun is down, the man in the leather jacket is still in his hotel. He debates his next move.

When Melisa leaves the Hunter, she is crying. She noticed his tattoo, the branding of the Hunter. *Why was she crying? Did she see it? Did she see who he is?* The man in the leather jacket's excitement can be felt by John.

"You're hurting me," John says aloud, speaking to the man in the leather jacket. The pain building in his head stops. Ranald apologizes. He hasn't controlled someone in some time. He forgot that losing his focus could hurt his puppet.

When he allowed her to see under his sunglasses, her touch was that of someone he knew very long ago. Now he is sure of it. She has the gift. *But was that gift able to touch the Hunter?* he wonders. *Was that why he was so subdued?* He couldn't bet on that. He needed to get her away from the Hunter.

John, being one with the man in the leather jacket, doesn't like what he is hearing. He knows he doesn't have a choice, but he had hoped the man in the leather jacket wasn't going to have him do something that would get him killed. "Don't worry, I still need you. I have no plans of killing you," Ranald transmits to John.

The words don't bring comfort. He knows something is going to happen, and he will be the first one to experience it. In the last few days, John has seen enough to know that he is a very small fish in a very large pond.

When Melisa gets up and leaves the room, John tracks her from the outside and finds her in the kitchen. After pouring herself some water, she takes a seat at the counter, phone in her hand. John is pushed to go back and view the Hunter. The bath only has a small window, positioned about six feet high.

Looking up at it, John shrugs his shoulders. A pain in his feet and fingertips lets him know that the man in the leather jacket is giving him another power. He knows what he can do and what to do. Softly touching the wall, he can feel every bump and crack in the surface. Gripping the wall, he is able to scale it.

Soundlessly, he climbs. Looking into the bathroom, he sees the Hunter standing in front of the mirror. He is looking at his bare chest. Using his hands, he is touching his scars. John's ears ring; the man in the leather jacket is concentrating on being able to hear what the Hunter is saying to himself.

His force on John's body is starting to take its toll. His ears start to bleed. John, about to cry out in pain, feels his mouth closing. Ranald has locked John's mouth closed. His neck contracts and he cannot make a sound. His body is no longer his.

"Who are you?" he hears the Hunter asking. That's what he needs to hear. Relinquishing some of the control back to John, Ranald is now sure the Hunter is without memory.

John begs to be let go, but he is still much needed. A sudden numbness comes over him. John is told it will not last long, but relax.

The Hunter disrobes and steps into the shower. Though John is not happy to be peeping in on a man, he watches, nonetheless. Ranald, the puppeteer, lets him know that he is not gay for watching a man bathe—unless he is enjoying it. John grimaces, not liking the joke at his expense.

The Hunter investigates everything in the shower. He looks over all the bottles, reading them. Some are in French, which he speaks fluently. It's almost charming to see. He takes in all the scented perfumes, looking for one he finds pleasant. He stands under the water for some ten minutes.

It's amazing to be watching this man, someone so fierce, acting so innocently. Ranald remembers the time when he was changed, when he was cured of his blood lust. Remembers the joy of indulgence. Seeing things for the first time again. Learning his powers. He allows John to share in the memory.

John sees it all. Ranald, being left for dead. Waking to the touch of a small, native American-looking woman. His face burnt from the sun. His beautiful blue eyes looking up at her. His body burnt all over.

This woman was not afraid of the creature, the monster he was. She helped him. She treated him. She brought him back. He should have been killed, but he was alive. He didn't know exactly what she did for him, but he was never the same.

Looking down at the Hunter, he remembers seeing the woman's dead body. John begins to tear up; he can't tell if they are his or those of the vampires. He experiences the image of holding the old woman's lifeless body, feels the pain he felt, and feels even today.

The Hunter killed her because she helped a vampire. It didn't matter that she changed him; the Hunter was one without remorse for any sympathizers. The Hunter was of one mind and one purpose, to eliminate all immortals.

One thing that the man in the leather jacket could never forget. She died differently than any others in the Hunter's wake. With her he killed her quickly. He also left her to be buried. The Hunter had never done things like that.

After her death, things changed. The Hunter no longer only hunted those connected to the immortal kind. He started going after the Church itself and the very people that created him.

Ranald never returned to his old ways. He didn't have the lust, but it was hard to change so completely. He did not want to dishonor the woman who saved him, but he couldn't stop being who he was, a trickster. So he hatched a plan to put the Hunter away. He traced down the overseers of the Hunter and offered a solution. A chance for peace. They were the ones that gave him the blade, the only thing that could stop the Hunter.

A loud scream comes from inside the house. The Hunter has been out of the bath for some time and is wearing only the pants that Melisa gave him. Ranald hadn't even noticed any of these things. But luckily he had given John back control of his body, so he had been following the Hunter.

The Hunter runs to investigate and John follows. Moving to a view of the living room, he sees Melisa is standing in front of her TV. There is a hole in the center of it, through which the backyard can be seen. Laughing in embarrassment, Melisa apologizes to the Hunter and tells him that she is okay. The dogs are pacing back and forth, sniffing the area.

Picking up the pieces of plastic and plaster from the floor, she places them on the coffee table. "It looks like a post came through here," she says and laughs. "Have you ever seen the movie *Christmas Vacation?*" she asks. "When the ice goes through the window and breaks the neighbor's audio system?" She can't stop laughing. "Something came through the window, something crashed into the stereo," she chatters, trying to repeat the lines from the movie.

The Hunter just watches, a strange grin on his face. Melisa realizes she is alone in the joke and stops her laughter. "I guess you've never seen the movie?" she asks rhetorically. "Fuck it." Giving up on picking up all the pieces of plastic and glass, she gets up from the floor. The Hunter can see something is not right with the woman. Her ambivalent attitude toward such an alarming incident is odd. He knows something with immense power caused the hole. But what could he say to her? Her actions tell him she is unwilling to care about such things.

"The pants fit, that's good. How about the shirt?" Melisa's question confirms the Hunter's feelings.

"I apologize for my attire; I hurried when I heard the scream. I will return in proper garb," he tells her. Melisa just nods, not sure how to respond to the formality of his words. Melisa walks to her small bar. She reaches in and grabs a bottle of wine. It's a red varietal, as are most of the bottles on the shelf.

Using a mounted wine opener, she pulls the lever and pops the bottle open. Grabbing a wine tumbler glass, she pours the dark burgundy liquid into it. Bringing it to her nose, she takes in the aroma's bouquet. Almost putting the glass to her lips, she remembers that she is pregnant. At the same time, she knows a sip won't hurt, that people in many other cultures drink during pregnancy. Still, she decides not to do it.

The Hunter walks back into the room. He is wearing the button-down shirt, tucked into his trousers. The clothes fit, though a little tightly. Melisa, seeing him, smiles and puts the glass down. The Hunter, seeing it, asks if he could have a glass. Melisa thinks it may be a bad idea, but goes ahead and gives it to him. She leaves him, so she can get a glass of water. The dogs follow her.

John continues to watch the Hunter through the window, as he walks around the room. He is looking at the pictures Melisa has scattered around the house. He smiles looking at her as a little girl. He picks one up. It's of her and her mom. Melisa is wearing her graduation gown. Putting it back down, he stops and focuses hard on a picture. Picking it up, his demeanor changes. Melisa returns to the room. "That's my boyfriend," she calls out.

"This man?"

"Yes. Chris."

"He is the man that attacked me," he declares. The dogs begin to growl.

"What?" Melisa is dumbfounded. "Chris went after you?"

"He tried."

"What?" Melisa's eyes widen "What did you do to him?" she calls out in anger. The dogs lower themselves preparing to fight. The Hunter looks at them for only a moment. His anger returns its focus on Melisa

"I didn't have to do much. The monster was too weak. Trying to sneak up on me; he was a fool." The Hunter spits on the floor in anger.

"Chris would never have done that!" Melisa knows her words are desperate. She could recall many times his hot temper got him into a fight.

"What is your game? Have you been planning this?" He throws the picture to the floor and slowly stalks toward her.

"Hold on, just wait right there." Melisa's fear is real. Back peddling, she doesn't understand the quick change in the man. "I'm sorry, I didn't do anything." The dogs move in front of her, blocking the man.

"You had him try and hurt me, didn't you?" he shouts. He pushes the large couch out of his way like it is nothing. The dogs leap at him, tearing into his flesh. The Hunter tosses them off and jumps toward Melisa.

"No, I swear," Melisa pleads.

"What is your end game? Where is he?" he yells, blood dripping from the dog bites. Genghis again jumps at him, but the Hunter catches him midflight and throws him against the wall. The dog let out a gut-wrenching yelp.

"Look, I don't know what you are talking about. I didn't do anything. I promise." She moves to the right, keeping the living room furniture between them. Geronimo comes to her side, ready to give his life for hers.

Ranald has John hurry to the front door. John resists, and the man in the leather jacket is forced to take complete control of the young man. He forcefully knocks on the door.

He can hear Melisa scream, so he breaks down the door. The Hunter turns his attention to John. John's internal voice begs the man in the leather jacket, but it is no use. John is controlled to move inside and confront the Hunter.

"Who are you?" The Hunter moves in close, lowering his body. "Who's in there?" he asks. Ranald knows he can be seen by the Hunter.

"Leave her be, she is innocent."

"Innocent? Is that why you are here? Here to hurt me?"

"I am not here to hurt you. This body cannot hurt you."

"Why are you here? Why is everyone following me? Trying to trick me." The Hunter grabs his head in pain and confusion. Melisa takes this opportunity to flee, heading upstairs to her room with Geronimo following close behind.

"We are not trying to hurt you. We . . ."

"Enough. Leave me alone." The Hunter leaps at John, striking him in the face and knocking him across the room. Ranald tried to block the pain from the strike but it was too much. The rattle of the force almost severed his connection with John completely. Bleeding from the mouth, John falls in a heap. Through John's open eyes, he is able to see the Hunter hurry in the direction Melisa went.

The vampire pleads with John. One thing he cannot do, is force him to invite him into the home. John must do it of his own volition. In utter pain, John knows his life is ending and asks Ranald if he can save him. He is told he cannot. He doesn't wish to lie to John.

"Please come in, save her," he says out loud. John feels the vampire leave his body. John is left alone in his final minutes.

The Hunter breaks through Melisa's heavy bedroom door. As she cringes in the corner of her room, Geronimo charges the Hunter, and leaps, biting him on his defending arm. Melisa pleads with the Hunter to leave her alone.

"You have betrayed me. You are a monster just like those creatures that have been following and attacking me," the Hunter hits the dog and throws him to the side.

"Please, I'm pregnant," she begs.

"I know; I can see the monster inside you."

"What are you talking about? Sir, please. You need help. Let me help you," she begs, crying.

"Help? Is that what you have been trying to do?"

"Yes."

"I wish I could believe you," the Hunter says and shakes his head.

"I've only tried to help. I promise."

"Enough with your lies." Enraged, the Hunter charges her. Before he can touch her, the window explodes with a blur that crashes into the aggressor. The man in the leather jacket now stands between Melisa and the Hunter.

Dusting himself off, he looks at the man in the leather jacket. "So, another beast. You are surrounded by these foul things," he says and looks at Melisa.

"The only thing foul is you, Hunter," the vampire says, standing defiant.

"Ah, you are the puppeteer?" The Hunter moves toward him. The two men circle each other, Ranald moving Melisa with him, never giving up enough space for the Hunter to get close to her.

"You may not know who you are, but I do," Ranald states and attacks the Hunter. The force of his contact with the Hunter is like steel crashing against steel. The men engage in a fierce battle.

Melisa is unable to make out what is happening. The sheer speed and viciousness of the two men cause her to cover her eyes. Terrified by the sounds of the men exchanging pain and inflicting terror upon each other, Melisa screams for them to stop, but they ignore her.

The fight continues; she can feel the force of the men as they strike one another. Suddenly, like when a barometer drops, silence strikes. Melisa opens her eyes and sees the man in the leather jacket, with black blood dripping down from his wounds, standing over the Hunter, bleeding all over.

Melisa stands up and walks slowly toward the fighters. "Is he?" Melisa asks.

"Stay back, Melisa. He is not dead. This time, I will do what I should have the first time," he states, pulling out the blade from his jacket.

"What are you doing?" Melisa's eyes enlarge. Ranald reaches back for the final blow. "No!" Melisa screams and dives in between the man and the blade. She cannot just stand there and allow someone to be killed. The thud of the blade and the sound of Melisa's gasp of breath is all that echoes in the ears of the vampire.

Melisa looks down at the blade, which has been plunged deep into her chest. It has missed her heart. Ranald steps back in horror. The Hunter's eyes are large. He feels the sting of the blade, which has punctured him just slightly. The wetness of her blood covers his own chest, mixing with his own.

The woman he was going to hurt just saved him. The two men watch as Melisa slowly pulls the blade out from her chest. The Hunter looks at the vampire. He doesn't need to say anything.

Melisa looks at the blood-covered blade and drops it next to her. "I'm sorry," is all she says before fainting. The vampire grabs her and picks her up. He looks down at the Hunter, seeing the blade lying next to him.

The Hunter rolls over in pain, then reaches and picks up the blade. In that moment everything seems to stand still. As the Hunter stares at the blade, a strange wave of information courses through his veins. His mind opens up to who he really is, who he used to be and what this blade means to him. Ranald realizes that the one tool he had to stop the Hunter is now in the Hunter's hands.

"I am not the Hunter; I am a monster," the Hunter murmurs. Without looking up at Ranald, he holds the blade up with an opened hand. Ranald takes the blade. As a surprised look lasting only a moment crosses his face, he puts the blade away. With a push of force, he flies out through the window, carrying in his arms Melisa, who is clutching her chest in pain, leaving the Hunter lying on the floor sunk in despair.

CHAPTER TWENTY-SEVEN

Melisa's father is in his front yard picking some vegetables from the garden, when Aaron pulls up and parks. Getting out of the SUV, Aaron looks around; the overwhelming feeling of being watched is strong. He makes eye contact with Mr. Castro, who continues to gather his produce.

Mr. Castro gets up and waves Aaron onto the property. He pulls the bandana from his back pocket and cleans his hand off, before offering it to shake Aaron's hand. "Aaron? Correct?" Mr. Castro smiles.

"Yes. I apologize for showing up unannounced, sir, but I have been trying to get in touch with your daughter."

"Well, I'm sorry. But she is not here."

"I see. Did someone pick her up?"

"No, I gave her the Malibu." Mr. Castro smiles.

"Do you know where she was going?" Aaron asks.

"I'm sorry, but I do not. Is everything okay?" he asks, worry beginning to show on his face.

"Oh no sir. I felt bad for the way I left earlier. I just wanted to apologize. To both of you, actually," Aaron says, trying to reassure the protective father.

"Well, that's nice of you. We all have lives and sometimes, those lives need us to be a little rude. No harm," he laughs. "Would you like to come in for some food?" Mr. Castro offers with his great smile. Aaron can't help but laugh with the old man.

"No thank you, sir. I must be going. Please tell her I came by though."

"I will." They shake hands and Aaron heads to his car. Aaron opens the car door, but halts, perking his ears. He knows someone is following him, but he can't seem to pinpoint their location. As Aaron turns, he sees Walter pulling into the driveway. The two men make eye contact. By the time Walter realizes who he is, Aaron has already jumped in his car and taken off. The last thing Aaron needs is to get into a conversation with Walter.

Walter parks and, using his mirror, watches Aaron. Getting out of his car, he looks at his dad, who is heading back into the house. Walter's mind roils with curiosity. A motorcycle comes racing up the small hill, going the same direction as Aaron. Walter almost drops his keys when he sees who is on the bike. Frozen, Walter watches Victor race past, most likely to follow Aaron.

Without a second thought, Walter jumps into his car and gives chase. He calls Stephanie and lets her know that he is in pursuit of Victor. He gives her the plate number for her to find out who it belongs to. He tells her that the motorcyclist is tailing Aaron, Alex's brother. Stephanie informs him that the motorcycle belongs to Alex. Walter knows the information is a bombshell, but he just doesn't have the capacity to understand what it is at the moment.

Walter continues to follow them, making sure not to be noticed by Victor. The way he is weaving in and out of traffic, he is shocked that Aaron hasn't noticed Victor as it is. Then again, Aaron is driving erratically too. Walter just hopes that the two men don't cause an accident. Or worse, get pulled over. He needs to know what these guys are doing. *Why is Victor following Aaron? And why does he have Alex's bike?*

Then it comes to him. Alex and Victor are working together; that part is easy enough. But, if Alex is working with Victor against his brothers, then what would their plan be? *Is Alex trying to build his own outfit? Is Victor in debt to Alex? Is Alex in trouble with someone?* The ideas and questions start to stack up.

Walter knows the information is there for him to figure out. But something is missing. There is no central idea or motive that would connect any of the theories. *Why would they kill everyone? Maybe they were lovers and just had enough?* Walter starts to wonder. But it passes quickly; with the money they had, they could have just taken off. It was something else.

As the chase continues, Walter notices that they are heading to Melisa's house. He hadn't even thought about her getting mixed up in all this. She has been dating the ringleader of one of the groups. Chris isn't the best guy, but Walter never thought of him as a crime kingpin. He is just an arrogant club owner, used to getting his way.

Walter calls Melisa, but she doesn't answer. He leaves a simple message. He calls her house line. He made her get it when she had the house built. She complained about the bill, but he just laughed about it. She could afford twenty dollars a month. God, he starts to think about the amount of money she makes.

Walter laughs at himself. Why is he thinking about the most obscure things, while in a car chase? Her answering machine picks up. Walter curses and tosses the phone on the seat next to him. Looking at the freeway signs he sees that they are two exits away from Los Feliz. Walter knows they are going to Melisa's. He pulls back a little farther. He watches as they move to the right, changing to the exit lane just past Glendale Blvd. Walter's suspicions are confirmed. With that, he decides to take the Glendale exit; he knows the area well and knows he can come around and not be seen.

Making a few simple turns, Walter is now on the same road on which Melisa had picked up the Hunter just hours before. He heads toward her home. Reaching the stop light at Los Feliz, He gets into the left turn lane to go up the hill. Walter is shocked to see Aaron's car at the cross street, waiting on his own red. Walter ducks down, hoping he wasn't seen.

Aaron, who looks preoccupied, has no idea that he's being followed. Realizing that his light is next, Walter changes lanes so he will go straight through the intersection instead of turning, so as not to end up alongside of Aaron. He uses the car next to him as cover as he proceeds through the intersection, driving into Griffith Park. The north and south lanes are divided by a small hill, forcing Walter to go past the old pony riding circle and then down a ways before he can make a U-turn.

Aaron, still oblivious to his pursuers, heads up the hill to Melisa's. He hopes for the best, but is so used to dealing with the worst, he can't stop thinking that Melisa is in trouble. He turns up Commonwealth and takes the road up the steep hill, making a quick right followed by a left. He is now on Melisa's street. Going up slowly, he parks on the outside. He walks to the main gate and looks in. All the first floor lights are turned on. The second floor is dark, except for a small flashing light coming from what he knows is Melisa's room.

The feeling that he is too late kicks him in the stomach. With a leap, Aaron soars over the eight-foot tall wrought iron fence. He lands softly, his knees bending slightly from the impact. Taking a few inhalations through his nostrils, he picks up four different scents: Melisa, her dogs, a man's musk, and another man. But that second man, his scent has a new aroma he has never smelled before.

Aaron walks carefully, following the trails. Two scents lead straight into the house, and the third moves around chaotically. Following the lone scent, he recognizes the man's odor. His mind races with different faces. His memory works unlike that of anyone else in his family. Every single scent he has smelled, has a face to match.

It comes to him. Aaron memorized it the other night. It is of the man who drives the ugly red car, who was following Melisa. The man in the leather jacket's puppet. The vampire that had Chris follow the Hunter. Walking around the outside of the house, Aaron detects every one of the man's movements. Aaron touches the wall, where he had climbed up to look into the house. *Why would he be spying?* Aaron wonders.

The trail leads him back to the front of the house. Reaching the front door, he sees it has been forced open. The wood is splintered and the deadbolt has ripped through the door frame. Taking in the air of the house, he smells death. He can't pick up anything or anyone else. He knows there is a dead body within.

The fear that he is about to come across Melisa's dead body, sickens him. His eyes begin to swell; he doesn't know if he can go through the entrance. He can't bear to see Melisa this way. He peers in, conflicted. If he doesn't go in, someone else will. *What if she is still alive, but just barely?* He knows that it is wishful thinking. He knows when he smells a rotting corpse.

Ever since he was a little boy, Aaron has spent most of his time honing his tracking skill. To do that, he had to learn to detect animals, both living and dead. And, to be able to tell the difference. Summoning all his bravery, Aaron takes the first step into the home. He draws in a deep breath. His eyes closed, he traces out the home. Like a bat uses echoes, he is able to do the same with smells. He knows the entire layout of the home, and knows where the dead body is. He also knows it's not Melisa.

Relieved, Aaron walks into the living room, where he sees the signs of a struggle. The blood on the wall is that of the man whose track he has been following. He follows the trail and finds John lying on the floor. He had dragged himself three feet from where he had fallen. Looking at the man's body, Aaron sees that whatever did this was not one of his kind, nor was it a vampire.

The other scent is now known to him. He is smelling the Hunter. A rage builds inside. The Hunter is not there, neither is Melisa. He must have taken her. Aaron hurries to where the smells lead him. He freezes, seeing Melisa's bedroom door in pieces.

He knows that the Hunter broke through here. A growl comes from the door. Aaron knows instantly it's Geronimo, Melisa's pit-bull. Slowly walking in, he is horrified by the sight. The room is covered in blood and broken furniture. The two dogs, hurt and weak, are both in the room; Aaron takes hold of them.

He listens to them. They tell him what happened. How, the Hunter was the one who attacked Melisa. How they couldn't stop him. Aaron holds them tight, telling them they did good. Seeing the pool of blood, Aaron closes his eyes in fear. The dogs confirm it to be Melisa's. They inform him of another being in the room. How he came in and protected her. Aaron sniffs at the air, taking it in the scents. Aaron quickly finds that the scent belongs to the man in the leather jacket.

The puppet must have invited him in, Aaron discerns. The dogs tell him of Melisa's sacrifice. How she saved the Hunter from the vampire's weapon. Aaron shakes his head in disbelief. They continue, telling him of the vampire taking Melisa away and the Hunter fleeing up the hill.

Aaron, full of rage, needs to find the Hunter. Once he has, he will call on his brothers; surely, they will help him take down the monster. Then, he will find Melisa. He promises the dogs he'll be back and leaps from the second floor down to the lawn below. He follows the trail up the hill. He makes his way along the pitch-black hiking path, until he reaches the cave that the Hunter has gone into. Five armed security guards stand at the mouth of the cave. Aaron takes in his surroundings, confirming the Hunter is surely inside the cave. He has entered undetected by the officers.

Aaron pulls out his cell phone and dials his brother Alex. A soft snap of a twig behind him gives him notice that someone is following him. He takes in the scent, finding it to be a "mutt." He already knows whose: Alex. He looks to the guards, making sure they have not noticed the clumsy mutt's approach.

With a move too fast for Victor to respond, Aaron is behind him, holding his hand over his mouth preventing him from making a sound. "You shouldn't be following me," he whispers. "I'm going to let you go, but do not make a sound," he warns. "Why is Alex having me followed?" he asks.

"He wanted me to help you," he says, matching Aaron's soft whisper. Aaron can't help but give off a soft, quiet chuckle.

"You shouldn't lie. Especially to a creature such as myself. I can smell it," he states coldly. "Why is my brother having me followed? This is your last chance."

"I am to find Melisa," Victor admits.

"Why?" Aaron asks, with narrowed eyes.

"I do not know," Victor answers.

"Well, since you can communicate with him, tell Alex I have found the Hunter. Have him send my brothers to help me," he tells the mutt. Victor reluctantly sends Alex the message.

"Alex said no."

"What? Why?"

"We do not have the blade," the mutt reminds Aaron. Aaron can't believe in his rage he had forgotten such a thing. He looks at the mutt, realizing he has just shown weakness. He debates killing him to show he is not weak.

"Alex is sending your brothers to us. They will help. We are to take down the Hunter."

"What, that is not possible. We do not have the blade."

"He says that we are to take him down, and the brothers are bringing a special chain that will be able to hold him," Victor explains.

"What, that's crazy. What special chain?" Aaron doesn't believe a word the mutt is telling him.

"Alex says to be patient; your brothers will be here shortly."

"This is crazy. We do not have a special chain for the Hunter," Aaron mutters to himself. "Fine, we will be here. But tell them to be quick. I don't know how long we have."

CHAPTER TWENTY-EIGHT

Walter arrived at Melisa's house just moments after Aaron had left. He was horrified by the scene he found. He called it in and created a missing person alert. When Stephanie arrived, she found Walter sitting on the front steps, petting the two dogs lying next to him, lost in thought. He didn't even notice her walking up to him.

The sun is rising over the mountains; Stephanie can see the pain and anger in her partner. She takes a seat next to him. Waiting for him to speak first, she sits for ten minutes. "There is a pool of blood up there," he states evenly.

"Is it Mel's?"

"No one knows." He continues to look out into the distance.

"What do you want to do?" Stephanie asks, concerned.

"Find these fuckers," Walter states coldly.

"Do we know who did it?"

"I followed Aaron here. Victor was following him, so I think we have a good idea."

"Then let's go," Stephanie says.

"Where?"

"We've got Alex's home address. Let's go see what we can find there," Stephanie reminds him.

"Yes, let's do that," Walter agrees, rising from the concrete step. "You'll need to drive." He lifts his hand, showing it shaking from anger. "Hey, can you get these guys to a vet?" he calls out to one of the officers.

Stephanie follows Walter's direction the whole drive. He uses his phone's navigation to get them in the vicinity of the property, but since the house is built on a large lot, they could only find the address on the maps. Pulling up the long driveway, they see a single light is on by the door. The sun is now illuminating the whole valley. The land is dry, mostly dirt and sand.

The home is something out of a horror movie. It's dark, and looks as if no one is living within. Paint is chipping off the sides, and the roof is weathered and missing tiles. It's nothing Walter would expect from Chris's family. They always seemed so clean and fancy. The porch wraps around most of the house. The pillars show more wear, telling them more and more that the home has not been taken care of.

Parking, Stephanie and Walter look up at the house. The home is not what either expected. Walter rolls his shoulders and moves his neck, cracking it, simultaneously opening and closing his hands and making a fist. Stephanie grabs Walter's wrist. "Are you going to be okay to do this?" she asks.

"Of course. I'm good," Walter declares. But the fire in his eyes is plain to see.

"Why don't you let me go up first."

"Fuck that, I'm good." He hurries out of the car and heads quickly to the front door. Pressing his ear to the door, he can hear the sounds of a TV. With a heavy hand, Walter bangs on the door.

"Walter, take it easy."

"There is a TV going; I want to make sure they can hear me," Walter says. She knows it's more than that. But there is no stopping him now. Stephanie looks around the property. She can see that there have been many cars up on the dirt road, but only her car is there now.

Walter bangs again, and the door flies open before he can finish his antagonizing attack on it.

"What!" Aleksy answers the door. "Why are you banging on my door, so early in the morning, god dammit?" the decrepit man screams at the two detectives.

"Detective Castro and Detective Walken. We are looking for your son."

"What, are you guys some kind of TV show or something?" the old man replies. "Castro and Walken," he further gibes.

"Is your son here?" Walter asks.

"Which son?"

"Alex."

"No."

"What about Chris?"

"No," the old man says, and smiles.

"Aaron?"

"No." The old man's eyes tighten.

"Are any of your son's home?"

"No." Aleksy moves to close the door.

"Then why did you ask which one?" Walter uses his arm to stop the door from closing.

"Because I wanted to know which one of those dumb boys you wanted to talk to."

"Is anyone here with you?"

"No." Aleksy shakes his head with a satisfied grin.

"Do you mind if I take a look inside?"

"Only if the lady asks. And then, maybe she would be the only one I let in."

"Listen, sir. No need to be rude," Walter starts but is interrupted by the old man.

"Fine, fine. Come in. Dust off your feet first, god dammit!" Aleksy yells. Walter and Stephanie follow the old man. They keep their eyes sharp, not sure what to expect. "Lock the door!" Aleksy orders, walking back to his bedroom with the fireplace. He takes a seat in his old recliner, focusing on the TV.

Walter looks around the room. "What's in that room, sir?" he asks, pointing to a closed door.

"The shitter, you need to go?"

"No, sir." Walter just shakes his head, looking at Stephanie and giving a look like this is a waste. Stephanie points to the area they had come from, and she shows him two fingers, telling him there are two rooms she wants to check out. Walter nods, telling her to go for it.

"So, when was the last time you saw your son?" Walter begins.

"Which one?"

"For fuck's sake." Walter can't help but laugh at the belligerent old man. "Look, if I ask a question about your son, just assume I'm talking about Alex."

"You know what they say, sport. Assuming makes an ass out of you and me." Aleksy chuckles at his own joke. "Why do you want my boy? What did he do?"

"He may have been getting mixed up with some bad apples."

"I'm sure his brothers will straighten him out," Aleksy asserts.

"Yeah, well, I'm also interested in Aaron," Walter states, as he moves around the room.

"I thought to assume Alex."

"Yeah, well I guess I like to be made an ass of," Walter wise cracks back. The old man explodes in laughter.

"You're not too bad, cop'er. I like you." Aleksy grabs his almost empty bottle of vodka. He lifts it to Walter, offering him some.

"No thanks."

"Oh come on, don't be a pussy. I bet your lady partner would have some," he laughs, teasing the detective. "Hey, where did she go?"

"Fine, just one." He walks up to the old man, taking a glass that he fills for him quickly. Stephanie walks back into the room, just in time to see Walter take the shot. The old man watches her from the corner of his eye.

"Don't worry, hon, I got some for you too."

"No thank you, I'm fine."

"Bullshit, I can tell you're a drinker, aren't you, sweets?" Aleksy winks at her. Stephanie looks at Walter with a face of pure annoyance. "I don't think she likes me much. Does she, Detective Castro?" Aleksy takes another swig of his vodka. "Castro. You know, my son is messing around with a nice little Latino girl called Castro. You wouldn't happen to be related?" he asks, laughing.

"Actually, yes," Walter answers, keeping his calm. The old man erupts in laughter again.

"You got to be kidding me. What are the odds?" Aleksy shakes the bottle at Stephanie while he laughs.

"That's the reason I'm here instead of someone else," Walter says, trying to gain favor with the old man.

"How do you mean?"

"I would prefer to be the one who takes him in."

"You know what, I've never actually met your sister. But I hear my son really likes her."

"Yeah, well. That's not why I'm here." Walter grinds his teeth. "When do you expect Alex to be home?"

"Well, you know kids. I have no idea. They don't always come home at night." The old man pours himself another drink. Walter walks over to Stephanie for advice on how to continue with the old man. What they do not know is, they are standing directly over Chris, who is still in his cage.

Chris woke up when they arrived. He is still very sick but getting better. Listening to the conversation, he is worried for Walter. Chris tries to get up in the cage, but the sting of the silver on the bars is too much for him to bear. He is still too weak to help. He needs to warn the two detectives. Knowing his father as he does, Chris knows that any minute, Aleksy will grow tired of teasing them.

Once that happens, his father will have no problem killing them. Aleksy has no care for human life and takes it without remorse, a trait Chris doesn't share with his father. Listening, Chris can hear the two detectives walking around. They are leaving. Chris begins to relax, but it is short lived.

His father has risen from his chair and is walking toward the two detectives. Aleksy is offering them more vodka. Aleksy tells them that his son Alex will be home shortly and if they would like to wait for him, they can take a seat on the small couch or wait in the kitchen at the table.

Aleksy continuously points out to Walter how much he likes him. And how he is excited about the possibility of them all being family. Walter placates the old man, just agreeing with him. Chris knows that his father is up to something. He is leading them to the kitchen, passing the basement door. "You guys want to see something really special?" the old man asks the two detectives.

"Sure," Walter answers.

The old man opens the basement door for the two detectives and leads them down the dark stairs. A single light at the bottom is all that gives them the ability to see. Having descended the stairs, Walter is the first to see Chris. He is lying in a cage, the light hanging above him. It's plain to see Chris is in pain and unable to move or speak. But his eyes tell them they are in danger.

The two detectives whip out their guns, pointing them at the old man. They are shouting at Aleksy, but the old man just smiles, and laughs at their orders. He walks slowly backwards to the hanging light. Hands raised, he doesn't say a word. He stands next to his son's cage, with Chris looking up at him. Aleksy smiles at his weakened son. With a quick move he grabs and pulls the small chain, turning off the light.

The dark room throws the detectives into a panic. A low growling of animals surrounds them, telling them they are not alone. They turn in every direction, pointing their weapons at the sounds of the animals near them. A yelp in Stephanie's ear causes her to fire her weapon. The flash of the gunpowder lights the room for a moment.

They are surrounded by men, or what can be assumed to be men. The moving of chains and rustling of feet tells the detectives that whoever is there with them, they are chained up. "You know what, Detective Castro, I wasn't kidding when I thought you would be a good addition to the family," the old man speaks, his voice traveling like an echo in the pitch-black room.

A flash erupts from the small light, as Aleksy turns it back on. "I want you to know, that I do not take any pleasure in what I'm about to do. But we always do what we must to make our children happy," he states, lowering his body. In an instant he leaps at the two detectives. He tosses them both in different directions. Stephanie slams against a metal pipe, almost knocking her out. Walter lands against the foundation wall. Aleksy jumps on him, biting into his flesh and covering his mouth with his powerful left hand. Walter can't scream. The sound of muffled breaths wheezing through is all anyone can hear.

Stephanie, finally able to get back up, picks her gun up and shoots the old man. Aleksy turns to her as he takes the bullets, laughingly. "Wow, you're a much stronger woman than I thought. You'll be a good first for him," Aleksy devilishly explains. Stephanie continues to pelt him with bullets, but they don't even slow him. The old man charges her with a speed she can't respond to.

With a grip like a vise, Aleksy grabs her arms and lifts her up. He looks at her face, lowering it to him until they are nose to nose. He pushes his lips, blowing a kiss to her, his eyes glowing yellow. He head-butts her, knocking her out.

Chris, having seen the whole thing, is disgusted with his father. He turns his back to him. "Oh come on, boy, you know that was funny," he mocks Chris. "At least you'll have company," Aleksy continues with his antagonistic remarks.

Carrying Stephanie like a sack of potatoes, Aleksy drops her next to Chris's cage. Grabbing a set of shackles, he locks them around her ankles. He leaves her and walks slowly to Walter's lifeless body. Grabbing him by the leg, he drags him, placing him next to Stephanie. "When he wakes up hungry, make sure he eats her," Aleksy laughs, speaking to Chris, who is trying not to look at his father. "Don't be such a baby. This is good. You wanted Melisa to be part of our family, and look, I'm making it so she has her brother too," he teases.

"You are not my family," Chris says weakly, barely able to speak.

"That's not true. I'm your daddy, and that will never change. Everything I'm doing is for you, boy. You'll see soon enough."

"I don't want anything to do with you." Chris struggles to get the words out.

"I know you're upset now. But once my plan comes together, you will see," Aleksy tries to reassure him.

"You let out the Hunter; you have killed us all," Chris growls.

"That was a mistake, yes. But what can I say, your brother is an idiot." He laughs. "But he got me what I needed. We will handle the Hunter, like we did before." He smiles. "I do love you, boy. Even if you hate me," the old man states, his voice full of sincerity. "You rest up. I know how that poisoned blood of the Hunter can really fuck you up." He smiles. "You're young yet; maybe if you were a little older it wouldn't burn so bad." Aleksy laughs as he heads off. Chris listens to every step he takes, until he finally sits back down in his chair to watch TV.

Chris knew something else was going on. No way his father was just trying to set his kids up. Aleksy didn't care about his children. He was doing something for himself, but what? Chris lay in the darkness waiting for the old man to tell him more. And, as luck would have it, he didn't have long to wait. The phone rings. His father turns off the TV and answers it.

"We have the book; I've already told you that." Aleksy is talking on the phone. Chris strains, using his spectacular hearing to catch the words of the person his father is conversing with.

"What are you doing about the Hunter?" the voice on the other end passionately demands of the old man. The voice is deep, familiar, but not one he can place right offhand.

"We are working on that."

"Where is the blade now?"

"I think with that meddler, that damn vampire. The one that wears that stupid leather jacket," Aleksy points out mockingly.

"Hmm. That is a problem. Your boys are not strong enough to take him."

"Yes, they are."

"We shall see." The voice disappears. The old man murmurs to himself, telling Chris he is agitated. The voice, who is he? Why would he be working with his father?

CHAPTER TWENTY-NINE

A loud crash of pots falling startles Melisa awake. The room is slightly dark, but she can make out the subtle details. As she pulls off the covers, a sharp pain strikes her in the chest. Taking a breath, she calmly and slowly turns to get out of the small bed. She places her feet on a soft fur rug.

The room, though unfamiliar, is welcoming. The walls are dressed with many pieces of art and tapestry. Looking down at her feet, Melisa flexes her toes in the fur, bringing her a little smile. Its takes a few rocks for her to get to her feet without straining too much. The pain in her chest is not constant, but she knows it's there.

Melisa's memory is a little fuzzy, but she doesn't have any feeling of fear. She knows she is safe in the room, but she has no idea where she is. Walking on unsure legs, she moves to get a better look at the art.

Now face to face with one of the paintings, she sees it's something very old. The first to admit it, Melisa doesn't know or understand art. But as she looks at the symbols, they become clear to her, changing so she can read the words, the hieroglyphics, telling her the story. She begins to read them out loud in a tongue she doesn't know.

Mr. Hudson is in another room. The lights around him begin to flicker. Hearing the words from Melisa's room, he charges in and stops her from finishing the incantation. The small cabin's lights go back to normal once he is able to get her mind focused on him. Melisa falls faint in his arms for a moment. Coming to, she looks up at a man she recognizes but can't remember how or why. "What happened?" she asks, confused.

"Do you not remember?"

"I was . . ." she looks up at the papyrus. "I was looking at the art, and then everything went black."

"That piece is from what is called *The Book of Coming Forth by Day*."

"What does that mean?" Melisa asks, looking up at the image. Mr. Hudson doesn't want her to mistakenly begin to read from it again, and starts to explain the image. What he doesn't know is Melisa's eidetic memory has already memorized the image and the words.

"Some would call it The Book of the Dead. This is just a piece of the story."

"Oh, it's beautiful," Melisa answers, keeping her hands behind her back.

"How are you feeling?" he asks.

"I'm doing okay."

"Would you like some food?"

"No, thank you. I'm not hungry," Melisa replies sheepishly.

"Can I offer you some tea? It's important to get some fluids in you," he states softly.

"Yes, that would be nice," she says and smiles. A sharp poke under her rib reminds her of something she can't believe she had not thought of. "Oh my god, I'm so sorry baby. I can't believe I forgot about you," she speaks to her belly as she rubs it. The pain from his movement is comforting.

"I'm sure he'll understand. Why don't you come with me?" Mr. Hudson offers her his arm. He leads her to the other room, where she helps him set the small tea table. The floral pattern on the mats reminds her of things her mom would use. She watches as he moves. Mr. Hudson acts old and slow, but something about him tells her that he is not. His body looks sturdy to her.

Taking a seat at the table, she places the napkin on her lap and waits for him to finish what he's doing. Examining the room, she wonders where she is. She knows she's in a cabin, but where? As she is about to ask, Mr. Hudson brings the tea tray into the room, placing it in front of her on the table. "Do you take honey, milk, or lemon?" he asks as he sets the three options down.

The man is obviously a man of formality, so Melisa will do her best to respect him. She thinks back to her sorority days, which was the last time she actually had to practice acting in such a way. Being a Tri-delta, they made her and the rest of the girls take an etiquette course. The sorority days weren't something she cared about, but with the chance to save money on housing, she would have done anything.

"Just honey and lemon, please," she answers. Mr. Hudson coughs softly, telling her that something is wrong with what she asked for, but he doesn't object further. He pours the tea and places the tea and honey next to the small cup. She watches as he pours, and starts to make his cup. He pours the milk into the cup first, then the tea. Once he is done pouring, he finally takes a seat, almost falling into the chair.

"Where are we?" she asks.

"My home," Mr. Hudson answers with a smile. "We're high in the mountains of Big Bear," he adds.

"I haven't been up here in years . . . I'm sorry, but I do not know your name," Melisa points out as she squeezes the lemon into her drink.

"I would assume not. You came here not in the best of conditions. My name is Tobias Hudson, your host for as long as you like," he states in the most charming of ways. Melisa chuckles softly at the man's manner of speech.

"My name is Melisa."

"I know, my dear, your friend told me."

"Which friend?"

"The man in the leather jacket," he answers, taking a sip from his tea. Melisa looks down and to the left, thinking about whom Mr. Hudson is speaking. "I see you are still having trouble remembering things; that will pass soon. I had to give you a sedative; I was afraid you might wake and panic being in such a strange predicament."

Melisa looks at her hands and moves her fingers. She is drugged. Looking up at Mr. Hudson, she begins to worry about the baby, looking down at her belly.

"Melisa, please do not panic; the baby will be fine. But, if you begin to raise your stress levels, you may cause the drug to act the opposite way."

"Mr. Hudson, I'm sorry but I don't know if I can," she says, starting to shake.

"I see; well, can I tell you a little about the piece of art you were looking at?" he asks. Melisa nods, needing him to help her from freaking out. "Well, it's a scene, from the Papyrus of Hunefer. It dates back to 1275 BC. Do you know who Hunefer is?" he asks. Melisa, still trying to get her mind right, shakes her head no. The image is clear in her head. There is something being weighed on a scale against what looks like a vase. A dog-like creature is under it and there are three men wearing masks, representing dogs too.

"Well, Hunefer was a scribe, a kind of writer in his day. He was part of the nineteenth dynasty," he informs her. Melisa is looking Mr. Hudson directly in the eyes as he speaks to her. The drugs are starting to have a relaxing effect. Her mind is no longer rattled.

"So, Hunefer's heart is being weighed on the scale of Maat against the feather of truth. Anubis, also known as Anpu or Inpu, depending on who you ask, is the one wearing a jackal-headed mask. Thoth, the one wearing a mask that looks like an ibis—it's a long-beaked bird, before you ask," he laughs to himself. "Now, Thoth is the scribe of the gods, and he is there to record the results."

"What results?" Melisa asks. Mr. Hudson's face shows great relief, seeing Melisa engage again.

"If his heart equals exactly the weight of the feather, Hunefer is allowed to pass into the afterlife. If not, he is eaten by Ammit, a female demon in the ancient Egyptian religion; she was part lion, hippopotamus, and crocodile, the three largest man-eating animals known to ancient Egyptians." He laughs at the thought.

"Did he make it?"

"He certainly did. My papyrus does not have the whole vignettes, sorry. Images such as these were a common illustration in Egyptian books of the dead," he adds.

"How do you know so much about this?" Melisa asks, taking a sip of tea for the first time.

"I have always loved it. I guess you could say it's my history."

"You're Egyptian?" Melisa asks.

"Yes, you could say that," Mr. Hudson replies as he watches Melisa's movements. Seeing she can handle the situation better, he starts to talk about why she is there. "Do you think we can discuss why you are here?"

he asks carefully.

"I remember being at my home. I was with the John Doe," she starts. "He became angry with me about something." Melisa pauses, "Oh my god, he attacked me. My poor dogs." She again starts to shiver.

"It's okay, you are safe here. I promise." Mr. Hudson reaches out and touches her hand. Once he does, she is instantly transported to a desert. Mr. Hudson is standing in front of a large marble statue. He is young, and built like a muscleman. His dark body shimmers in the harsh sunlight. He looks at Melisa with puzzlement.

"How are you seeing me?" the deep voice of the young Mr. Hudson asks. In a flash, she is back in his cabin. Mr. Hudson is holding his hand away from her. "How did you do that?" he asks impatiently.

"I'm sorry, I didn't mean to." She starts to shake. The feeling she had when she was attacked by the Hunter comes back, and she begins to panic.

"Please, please. Calm down. I am not angry; I am the one that should be sorry." He gets up and kneels next to her. "I was surprised, is all," Mr. Hudson states.

"I'm so confused." She begins to weep.

"I know, sweetheart." Mr. Hudson shows a side of himself that he had forgotten he had. "Is this the first time you've seen something like that?"

"No," she states, sniffing from crying.

"When did it start?"

"When I met the man."

"Which man?"

"The one who fell on my property the other day."

"The Hunter?"

"The what?" She wipes her nose, with a loud sniff.

"I'm sorry. The man you are talking about is called the Hunter."

"The Hunter?"

"I'm assuming no one has shared with you the situation you are in," Mr. Hudson states, looking down at the floor. "Those beasts," he mutters.

"I keep being told that someone else will tell, or the time is not right." She shakes her head in frustration. "I can't stand to be left in the dark anymore."

"Melisa. I'm sorry to be the one to tell you this. But, the life you have been working for, is no longer," Mr. Hudson states, looking directly into her eyes.

"What do you mean?" Melisa asks with reflective eyes.

"You have wandered into a world of fairytales. You are carrying a child that is special."

"What?"

"You have what we would call a half-breed."

"Half-breed?" Melisa is incensed by the word. "I fucking hate that kind of talk. People asked my mom how she felt that I was a half-breed, being half white and half Hispanic. It's bullshit."

"Melisa, please." Mr. Hudson places his finger on her lip. "I do not mean what you are thinking. A race is one thing, but a breed is something else. The child you carrying in your belly is not only a man."

"What are you talking about?" Melisa begins to get angry at what the old man is telling her. However, as he tells her more, she already knows what he is going to say. Memories of Chris's odd traits, things she had just ignored, all start to rush through her mind.

"The father of your child. He is not a man."

"What is he?" she asks, not wanting to know the answer.

"He is a werewolf," Mr. Hudson states calmly.

"You got to be fucking kidding me." Melisa laughs at the idea. But then stops, knowing it is true. Every ounce of her being tells her so. Feeling her belly, she looks down in thought.

"I appreciate the humor in what I'm saying. But this is no laughing matter. You will be giving birth to a man, who, when he turns of age, will have powers beyond any normal human."

"I don't get it. Why didn't he tell me?" Melisa looks up at the ceiling reflecting on their whole relationship. "So he can live forever, and he thinks I wouldn't notice or something," she asks aloud, but is really talking to herself.

"Actually. When a werewolf passes on his or her gift . . . by having a child. They begin to age. They grow old."

"So he is giving up his youth?"

"That is one way of putting it."

"So why didn't he tell me any of this?"

"Maybe he wanted to protect you?"

"You call this protecting me? I'm in a stranger's home, my chest is on fire. I'm being told that I'm pregnant with a fucking werewolf . . . Jesus Christ, I don't even know what to say right now." A sharp poke at her side turns her attention to the baby growing in her stomach. Her eyes start to water. "I'm so sorry my love. I didn't mean it. I love you no matter what," she says, addressing the unborn child.

Mr. Hudson takes his tea and walks into another room, giving her time to come to terms with her situation. When she finally comes to talk to him, she has a smile on her face. "Tobias, I don't mean any offense, but this all seems like a load of crap."

"I assure you, what I have said is all true . . . Think about your chest, or how you came to be here. Do you remember being stabbed?" he asks as puts away the book he was reading. Looking down, she touches the area. Instantly, she is transported back to when the man in the leather jacket pierced her chest. She can see him, his face. Almost frozen in time, she sees his mouth, his fangs, his bone structure. None of it is how she saw it before. When he grabbed her and takes her away, they are flying. The man in the leather jacket takes her over the city, floating like angels. "Do you remember?" Mr. Hudson asks, pulling her from the vision.

"I do."

"That is no drug, or any trickery. Those are your memories."

"But . . ."

"You can see things now. You probably could your whole life. But the baby inside you has awakened your abilities. These powers have been passed down from your grandparents or great grandparents."

"My abuela, she was said to be able to see the future."

"I don't doubt that. But your real gift, Melisa, is the gift of sight. You can see into people, see what they were, what they are, and what they should be," he explains. Melisa just looks at him, waiting for more information. She is having a hard time believing what he is saying. But she knows there is truth within his words.

"Did you touch the Hunter?"

"What?"

"The man, the one I call the Hunter. Did you ever touch him?"

"Yes."

"Did you ever get a vision from him?"

"Yes," she states, not wanting to play this game, but unable to stop herself.

"Let me guess. You saw him in a jungle perhaps or in Spain maybe?"

"Yes. The jungle."

"Did you see him being marked with a blade?" He gets up and walks to a bookshelf. He reaches behind a book and pulls out a cloth-covered item. "This blade," he says as he unwraps the dagger.

"Oh my god, yes." She reaches out to touch it. Mr. Hudson recoils, moving the blade away from her.

"I'm sorry. I don't think it's a good idea. I don't know what you may see," he states.

"What do you mean?" Melisa asks.

"Melisa, this is the blade that struck you. I have had to use some ancient magic to save you. I do not want you to fall into another vision if you touch it," he says worriedly.

"What is it?"

"This was created a long time ago. It was made for those that hunted werewolves and witches."

"I don't mean to be rude, but can you stop being so cryptic? I do better with facts."

"Of course, forgive me." He takes his seat back in his chair. "Many years ago, when the world was new . . . when God made man, he left his angels here to help guide them. They were to learn how to fend for themselves and how to be good. All without directly interfering with their prosperity.

"However, some of his angels saw in man something God did not. They saw that they needed to do more than just influence man. They needed to control them. So, these few angels began interfering with how man was creating his civilization." Mr. Hudson pauses, the thoughts bringing him sadness.

"You won't read about anything I'm telling you now in a book. Sadly, they have all been destroyed," he informs her.

"As I was saying." Mr. Hudson clears his throat. "Now these angels were working to build civilizations, and the people doing the work mistook them for gods. This is where the angels made their second mistake; they didn't correct the people. The angels actually began to believe they were gods, too. You may know of one; they called him Ra." He looks at Melisa, who is deep in the story.

"He is the god of the sun, right?" Melisa asks.

"Kind of; sometimes he's called the king of gods." Mr. Hudson smiles. "So, Ra, was just like all the other angels helping to build civilization, but he took it upon himself to lead man in what he felt they should be. He was able to get other angels to follow his lead, disregarding God's warnings not to influence man." Mr. Hudson takes another sip of his tea. "The first thing God did was to banish the angels, stripping them of the ability to return to heaven."

"How sad," Melisa whispers.

"Oh, but it does not end there."

"What?"

"Two of the angels, angry with the Lord, did something that changed this world forever. They made a deal with one of the most powerful angels, the first banished angel. God's first favorite."

"You mean the Devil?" Melisa raises her eyebrow.

"Sure, let's call him that. Or Lucifer." Mr. Hudson smiles. "As I was saying." He clears his throat again. "These two angels mated with two demons. They birthed the first werewolf and the first vampire, creating demons on earth who grew as they spread their curse upon man. Taking them from God."

"You have got to be kidding me. Where did the demons come from?" Melisa can't help but laugh.

"That is a story for another day," he smiles. "Now, unable to interfere directly, God had to give the task to another group of angels, ones who could instruct man on how to fight these monsters."

"The Hunter?" Melisa asks.

"No. These were just men and women, who fought as best they could." He smiles. "And sadly, they were not strong enough."

"So what happened?"

"Well, God decided to punish the angels for their deeds, with a show of force that would put the beast at bay."

"What?"

"He called on Anpu, kind of an archangel. He created a creature that could kill angels, sending them to an afterlife that was neither heaven nor hell. This beast was stronger than anything ever to touch the sacred ground of earth. He killed the two angels in such a fashion that the monsters, fearful, quickly went into hiding, as well as did the last remaining banished angels."

"So then what happened?"

"Most of Anpu's powers left him once he was done with his task." Mr. Hudson takes another sip. "Once evil learned he was not there for them, they came out in full force. Man was ready though. They were able to fight off the attack of the monsters and keep claim of the earth. But, like all things, power shifts. And the monsters, working together, began to win, trying to claim earth once again." Mr. Hudson finishes his tea. Looking at Melisa, he can see she is speechless.

"As things happen so often in our world, a fortunate accident gave humans another chance. A man was struck by a werewolf and was in the process of turning into one of them, when a mystic used a spell to save him. The spell created something no one expected."

"The Hunter?"

"Yes. They created a man who could fight the monsters."

"Werewolves and vampires?"

"Yes, but sadly, he too became corrupt."

"So they buried him?"

"Yes."

"This is getting a little ridiculous." Melisa gets up from the table.

"I understand where you are coming from. But please understand that things are not as you would hope. You are in grave danger," Mr. Hudson explains.

"Why is this happening to me?"

"That I do not know. You fell in love with the wrong man, is all."

"Chris," she states, looking away. "The man, the John Doe. He did something to him. Didn't he?" The feelings about his true nature are second to the idea that he may be hurt. "Where is he? Where is my Chris?"

Her eyes begin to water.

"I cannot say. I have tried to stay away from all this. Your friend in the leather jacket seems to have dragged me into it," he states unemotionally.

"We need to find him; he needs me," she pleads, hoping for the old man to help her.

"I cannot. We cannot; we must stay here." The old man rises from his chair and grabs a handkerchief for Melisa. Melisa sees he is not one who will change his mind once it is set and pulls her emotions back inside her.

"Thank you." Melisa calmly takes the cloth and wipes her eyes. "Why are you even involved?" Melisa asks suspiciously though calmly.

"Let's focus on keeping you safe until tonight."

CHAPTER THIRTY

Alex is the first brother Aaron sees coming out through the trees off the trail. The other brothers appear single file after Alex. The pecking order change is drastic in Aaron's eyes. It is strange not to see Chris leading the pack. How can they be "The Seven," if there are only six? It brings tears to Aaron's eyes. Chris not being there is weighing heavily on him. He hopes the six will be enough to avenge their hurt brother and his unborn child.

It strikes him hard, to realize that he has no idea how Melisa is. She could be dead for all he knows. And Chris's legacy would be gone as well. His temperature rises at the thought—the helpless Melisa being stabbed by the monster they know as the Hunter. A ruthless man, who kills his kind without mercy.

He hides his emotions as the brothers greet him. Quietly, Aaron grips hands with his brothers, one by one, in their special way, overlapping the arm holding the elbow of the counterpart. Alex is showing his rise in the hierarchy with a firm grip. Aaron's eyes narrow, when he feels the pressure Alex tries to squeeze on his elbow. It doesn't hurt, but the feeling tells Aaron he is trying to hurt him.

Holding in his laughter, Aaron ignores his baby brother's attempt to show dominance, turning to greet his other brothers. He notices that there is a definite change within the family. Aaron's fears are realized. "Where is he?" Alex asks, without even looking at Aaron. He knows something is coming, but doesn't want to give it power over him. His family feels like strangers, and he knows he's unsafe with them.

"The Hunter's inside. Do you really have something that can stop him?" Aaron asks worriedly. His senses are telling him to be ready. His fist is clenched, waiting for something that never comes. Finally looking at Alex, Aaron sees that things are different between them. Alex turns away from Aaron and looks at the cave. Knowing something isn't right, Aaron takes in a deep breath from his nostrils. Closing his eyes for a second, he maps the area. He knows who is in the woods and who has been there before. A scent surprises him. Alex! He has been here before.

"We don't need it. All we need to do is to bury him in the cave. It would take him a hundred years to escape the tomb," Alex explains.

"Hell, how many of those filthy things have you made?" Aaron asks, already knowing that there are more mutts in the wooded area surrounding him.

"Enough," Alex smiles.

"You've been busy, little brother... Dad seems to have been teaching you a lot, eh? So, what's the plan?" Aaron is careful not to challenge too strongly. He already knows he is at a disadvantage, but if he can come up with a better plan than his little brother, he can get his other brothers to listen to him, and maybe he can sway them to rethink their alliance.

"We have this." He opens a small bag filled with explosives.

"Where did you get that? . . . What about the chain your mutt spoke of?"

"That's for someone else."

"Who gave you the explosives?"

"A friend of Dad's. Don't worry about it," Alex states with a smirk. Now Aaron knows. Alex is working with their father and someone else. Someone who has helped to create this whole situation, Aaron is sure. He knows his father has been making things difficult for Chris, but now it's clear. Aleksy is working to rebuild the family. He means to take out all who would stand up to him. Aaron knows he must tread carefully; betrayal is near. His brothers are listening to Alex, but it's not Alex they are following; they are following their father who has never forgiven Aaron for standing up to him.

"Jesus, I don't know about this." Aaron looks at the mountainside. "We could bring down the whole mountain on us all."

"Nah, but we will for sure bury the Hunter." Alex laughs softly. Aaron quickly shushes him.

"Fine, let's do it, but you need to get those officers away from the entrance."

"Fuck them. Collateral damage."

"No. We are not animals, brother. We must not kill indiscriminately; think about all Chris says."

"Chris? You see him here?" Alex looks around at his other brothers who all laugh with him.

"Alex. Do what is right . . . We have evolved; we are not the old mindless beasts humans portray us as."

"Fine." Alex motions for his mutts to take out the guards, which they do quickly and quietly. "Happy?"

Aaron is shocked at his youngest brother's abilities. *How has he changed so much without me noticing? Where is this confidence coming from?* he wonders.

"All right, you and Vincent need to go inside. In case the Hunter tries to come out before we finish setting the explosives up," Alex says. Aaron is already unhappy with the plan. "Look, you two are the only ones who could even stand a chance of slowing the Hunter down," Alex says with a grin.

"This is crazy." Aaron looks at Vincent, who is unfazed by the idea. "You're okay with this?"

"I am. Our family needs this to happen," he states matter-of-factly without looking Aaron in the eyes.

"Fine. Then let's get going." Aaron leads Vincent into the cave. The other brothers follow Alex to the mouth of the cave, so they can set the explosives. Vincent stays close behind Aaron. The two brothers walk stealthily along the rocky floor. The stench from the fire set by the man in the leather jacket is thick. Their night vision ability allows them to see everything perfectly. The markings on the walls are beautiful and untouched by the flames. Aaron can't help but look at them with amazement, but Vincent doesn't even care to look at them.

Aaron turns to his brother; something isn't right with him. He stops him. "What's up?" Aaron whispers.

"Nothing, we need to stay quiet. He can hear us," Vincent replies. His eyes tell Aaron more than he is letting on. "Let's keep going." Vincent passes Aaron by. Aaron looks back to the cave entrance, which is already becoming a small bright circle in the distance. Going against his better judgement, Aaron hurries to follow close behind Vincent. He doesn't want him to get caught by the Hunter without him there to help.

"Brother, we are family. You know I love you and my other siblings?" Aaron states without regard for being heard. The worry of what his brothers may be planning to do to him is great, but the careless way things are happening really worries him.

"Of course," Vincent replies, not turning to look at his brother. Frustrated with Vincent's response, Aaron grabs his shoulder and forces him to look at him. Aaron is shocked to see tears in his older brother's eyes. Vincent never cries.

"Vincent, what has happened?"

"I'm sorry, brother. But I cannot disobey our father," he states, looking down at the floor.

"What are you talking about?"

"Melisa and the child will be protected. I swear," Vincent says, looking up from his hunched position at Aaron; he is now crying a flood of tears.

"I don't understand."

"You should not have challenged him. I'm sorry," is all Vincent says, then a loud thud is all that is heard. Alex has snuck up behind Aaron and broken a stone over his head.

"Do it!" Alex commands Vincent, who, with the force of a jack hammer, punches Aaron across the jaw, breaking it and knocking him down.

Aaron, unconscious for only moments, wakes to the sound of the brothers screaming for them to blow the cave.

In immense pain, he rises and runs in the opposite direction deeper into the cave. The explosion is deafening. The concussive power from the blast knocks Aaron off his feet and throws him forward. His body slides over the rough dirt and gravel floor.

"Betrayal seems to be the norm these days," a voice states, coming from above Aaron. He doesn't need to look up to know who it is. Aaron lies there waiting for the Hunter to kill him, but it doesn't come. He hears the sound of the Hunter's footsteps walking away from him.

Aaron gets up, dusts himself off, and, with a loud popping sound, re-hinges his jaw. The pain of betrayal is worse than that of his jaw. He follows the Hunter; the person he is there to kill. Aaron is led into a large open space. Two torches light the area, more for decoration than anything else. The Hunter takes a seat on his throne. The fire from the man in the leather jacket didn't reach out from the secret room. Aaron nervously approaches him. "I am Aaron," he states casually.

"You and yours call me the Hunter, but my name is Fernando," he states with a stone face.

"Fernando?"

"Yes, I was blessed to regain my memory, thanks to a wonderful woman," he tells Aaron, his face showing his sadness.

"Are you going to kill me?" Aaron asks.

"No," the Hunter replies.

"I don't mean to sound masochistic, but why not?"

"You are not the monster: I am." A single tear rolls down the Hunter's cheek.

"What does that mean?"

"I remember; I remember it all," he laments. "I have done much worse than those I was charged to destroy. So how can I sit here in judgment, when it is I, who needs to be judged?"

"Are you okay?" Aaron asks, not believing that he is asking such a thing of the man known as the Hunter.

"I have killed the innocent," he states. "I have no purpose now." The Hunter gets up from his chair and walks to the wall, looking at all the cave drawings painted on it.

"Did you kill Melisa?" Aaron asks. He can't help but expect the worse. The Hunter looks back at him, his eyes red from the tears. Aaron moves closer to him; the fear he once had is gone.

"I do not know. But I am responsible for whatever happens to her now." He wipes a tear from his face. "She saved me, she saved a monster, and may have sacrificed her own life for me," he states, dropping to his knees and grabbing Aaron's hand. "I may have killed that amazing creature of God." He weeps.

"She may yet be alive?"

"The dagger kills your kind, and it was plunged within her," he states, choked up from the tears. "The baby makes her susceptible to the blade's venom," the Hunter explains.

"Yet, the vampire took her. Did he say anything?"

"No." The Hunter is too tormented to listen to Aaron's words of hope.

"He is old. Maybe he knows things . . . like if there's a cure. Do you think there is a way to save her?"

"I know nothing of saving; all I do is kill," the Hunter weeps.

"How can you be so weak? You are the Hunter!" Aaron cries out, picking the man up by his shoulders. The Hunter looks him deep in the eyes.

"Am I the Hunter? Or am I the monster?" he asks with grief. Aaron is dumbstruck by the Hunter's disposition. How could this man of infinite power be so weak, so emotional? All the stories he knew were wrong. Aaron now knows he is going to have to do this alone.

"Is there another way out of here?" he asks, letting the man go, who collapses back down to his knees.

"Of course. Through my library. Or what is left of it."

"So, you'll let me leave?"

"I will," the Hunter states, his depression still deep.

"Then come with me. Help me try and save her."

"I cannot. I am going to waste away here. I don't deserve to be anyone's hero."

"You wouldn't be the hero. You would be repaying a debt. Melisa deserves that, and you know it." The Hunter looks up at him, his eyes changing to a blue glow. Aaron's confidence is quickly disappearing.

"You need to leave. I no longer wish to speak about this. I have made my decision," the Hunter states with anguish in his eyes.

"Please, help me." Aaron can't stop himself. The Hunter rises, looking Aaron eye to eye.

"I'm sorry. But I have failed already. I will take my judgment when it finally comes. But, I will not add to it." He grabs Aaron by the arm, and in a show of force he tosses him to the left, toward the library. Aaron catches himself from falling. The Hunter walks away back toward the entrance of the cave where it has collapsed.

"She deserves better and you know it," Aaron calls out. He leaves through the secret exit of the cave.

Aaron is rejuvenated once he makes it through the small access hole, escaping the Hunter's den. The sun is now overhead. The feeling of freedom gives him calm, which is short lived. Looking around the vast canyons of the park, he knows it's time. He needs to move on and find Melisa.

Using speed and power, he runs through the hills, rushing to Melisa's house. He needs to find the trail of the man in the leather jacket and find it soon. He knows his brothers are not as proficient as he is when it comes to tracking, but that doesn't mean they can't find her. Using all of his senses, Aaron is able to pick up the scents of the man in the leather jacket and Melisa again. Melisa's scent is more dominant, because she is bleeding.

He can't pick up any of his brothers' scents. *Why wouldn't they have started here?* he wonders. The thought passes quickly. He knows what he must do. With that he moves, running and leaping in such a way that anyone can see him. He cares little if anyone does; if he doesn't make it soon, who knows what people will be seeing. Melisa is his only concern, and he will find her first.

CHAPTER THIRTY-ONE

Stephanie's eyes begin to flutter, the swaying light above annoying her closed eyes. Her head hurts, and she reaches up to feel the lump on the back of her skull. She's relieved that there isn't a cut. The headache becomes sharp when she finally opens her eyes. Shading the light, she looks for Walter. "Walter?" she whispers, trying not to get the attention of any of the monsters in the room.

"Keep quiet," a soft voice whispers. It's not Walter, but the voice is familiar.

"Who's there?" she calls out.

"Shush, my name is Chris. I'm Melisa's fiancé," the man's voice answers.

"Where are you?"

"I'm next to you. I'm stuck in the cage." He pushes on the steel of the cage, showing himself to her. His face still shows he is in pain.

"Where is Walter?"

"He is close. But we need to be careful not to wake him. He is still changing, but he could wake any moment," Chris informs Stephanie.

"What the fuck is going on?"

"I'll explain later. First release me; I will break your chains." He points to an area on the wall. Stephanie's eyes are adapting to the dark room, and she can see the outline of a key.

"But the chains will make noise as I move," she argues.

"You are right. Let me think; there has to be another way." Chris focuses.

"What is happening to Walter?"

"He is dying."

"What?" Stephanie can't control the volume of her voice. Chris shushes her again. They both stay frozen, waiting to see if anyone responds to the outburst.

"He is transforming; first he will die, but then he will be reborn," Chris tries to clarify.

"What are you talking about?" Stephanie tries to control the volume of her voice.

"Your friend is no longer like you. He is closer to me." Chris tries to explain.

"And what are you?"

"I am a werewolf," Chris states proudly.

"Ha!" Stephanie can't help but let out the fake laugh. "You're a werewolf? And you need me to help get you out of a cage. That's rich."

"I am sick. And this cage is made of silver."

"Seriously?" Stephanie can't wrap her head around anything that is happening.

"We are both in danger, and once your friend wakes up, you will be dead. He will have to kill you; it is his final stage of his new . . ." Chris stops mid-sentence. He puts his finger across his lips, warning Stephanie to be quiet. He listens, looking up to the ceiling above. He motions for Stephanie to pretend to be asleep.

The basement door bangs open. The loud stomps of Aleksy and Alex come crashing down the steps. "You awake yet?" Alex calls out. Chris is lying down facing Stephanie; she is wide eyed looking at him. He squeezes his eyes, blinking, telling her to do the same. Once she does, Chris rolls over.

"Are you going to let me out, or what?" Chris's voice cracks as he speaks.

"Oh brother, why are you so angry with us?" Alex asks

"Maybe because I am in a cage, like an animal."

"That's your fault. How were we to know if you were contagious; the venom of that blade and the blood of the Hunter are so awful," Alex laughs.

"Maybe you should have asked your father if I was." Chris looks at Aleksy.

"I did; that's why you're in there." Alex continues to laugh. Walking closer to Chris's cage, he looks over him and sees Stephanie's body lying next to it. "Is she still out?" he asks

"Who?" Chris acts as if he has forgotten about the woman.

"That nosy bitch, your girl's brother's partner."

"I have no idea. I woke up hearing you two loud asses." Chris tries to get the focus back on him. Alex can't help but laugh.

"You are so confused. Look at all I'm doing for you," Aleksy finally adds to the conversation.

"Awakening the Hunter, and having me almost killed by him. Yeah, thank you, so much."

"It was not my plan to awaken the Hunter. That was an accident. All I wanted was the book."

"Book?" Chris is unsure what he is talking about.

"Yes, the Hunter's journal," Aleksy clarifies.

"You want a book; that's a first." Chris coughs as he chuckles.

"I may not read, but I have a friend that does. And that is all that matters."

"Oh, and what of this person? What does he think he can do with the book you have?" Chris tries to get more information out of his father.

"I will tell you, but not now."

"Where is this book?" Chris asks.

"None of your business, brother," Alex jumps in.

"It is safe," Aleksy laughs. "Your brother is right. But he doesn't need to be so rude." He looks at Alex as he speaks.

"Who is the reader? Do I know him?"

"Perhaps. He is on his way. And once he arrives I will be returned to my old self."

"What old self? You've always been a horrible son of a bitch."

"Oh, Chris. We all came from bitches. You of all people know that. Your son will surely be coming from one." Aleksy smiles.

"Where is Melisa?"

"She will be here shortly," Alex answers the question. Aleksy looks at him, not liking him answering without being told to.

"I swear, if she is hurt I will . . ." Chris is interrupted by his father, who hits the cage with a stick. The mutts all get up from their slumbers. Chris looks at Walter, hoping he is not awakened.

"You will what? You are stuck in a cage. If you don't start to think of your family first—you will never be let out. You'll watch that bitch of yours have the baby, then I'll feed her to these new ugly mutts." Aleksy smacks the cage again in anger. Alex looks at the mutts, offended by the remark about his creations.

"Father, do not do anything to her. Kill me, if you must. But please do not hurt her or my child," Chris pleads.

"I have no plans to hurt any of you. I will honor the family, but I will not take any more of your disobedience," he snarls.

"I swear; I will follow whomever is now pack leader." Chris lowers his head in shame. The pride of being pack leader is less important than the new family he is trying to build.

"You see?" Aleksy looks at Alex, his youngest. "He can learn. I told you." He hands the stick to Alex. "I'm going to take a nap. Make sure there are no more mistakes, Alex."

"Yes father." Alex and Chris watch as their father heads back upstairs. Alex purposefully walks up to Chris's cage, kneeling next to it. Chris knows his brother means him harm, but he cannot move away from him. His father has claimed the pack, and Chris allowed it without a challenge. But now Chris cannot give too much respect to Alex. Otherwise he will be treated even worse than he already has been.

"So, you fucked up and released the Hunter." Chris decides to go on the offensive against Alex.

"What?" Not expecting the allegation, Alex leans back, but stays on his knees. "I didn't do anything. I did just as Dad said. I got the book. How was I supposed to know that the boulder would move from the rain?" he defends himself.

"I guess I understand. But why didn't you come to me, brother? I would have helped you."

"I don't always need your help. I can do things on my own." He places his hand on the cage, forgetting what it was made of. The sting of the silver causes him to recoil in pain. Chris laughs at his thoughtlessness. "Stings, doesn't it"

"Fuck you." Alex holds his wounded hand to his mouth.

"Why did you want Melisa killed?" Chris asks, needing to understand why his brother hates him so.

"What?" Alex's face tells Chris he is telling the truth.

"I followed your trail. You led him straight to Melisa's."

"No, I didn't." Alex is still confused by the allegation.

"You don't have to lie; I'm no longer mad at you, brother . . . But tell me why?"

"I didn't do that. Yes, I went to her house after getting the book. But I just wanted to look down on the house. I knew you were there."

"Why would you do that?" Chris is so conflicted by what his brother is sharing. Had he been wrong all along?

"Because. Because I wanted to see you acting like a mortal. I wanted to see what you wanted to be."

"Why don't you understand what I'm trying to do? I was never going to leave you."

"You would have," Alex answers. "That woman has changed you. You are throwing it all away for her!" Alex stands up "We could have anything we want. And now you want to live a normal life with that woman, give up your immortality?" Alex shakes his head at the thought. "I love you brother, and I always will."

"What are you going to do?"

"Nothing."

"Alex. Don't hurt her. I beg you."

"Chris. You will thank me later."

"Alex, please. Dad already said," Chris pleads. Alex throws the stick at the nearby wall.

"No. Dad did not say anything. Soon, he is not going to be in charge. He promised me the pack, and I will not have you with that human." He storms out of the basement. Chris watches him leave, then looks at the wall. Alex had knocked the key off its hook, and the stick was close enough that Stephanie might be able to grab it without having to be near the mutts. He listens to Alex's footsteps, hearing him head out the front door. He can hear Alex's car start and drive away.

Chris calls to Stephanie with a soft tap of the cage. He points at the objects with a smile. Stephanie looks at him and sees that his eyes are red, as he holds back tears. Having heard everything, she carefully moves to get the keys. Crawling, she grabs the stick and uses it to hook the key ring and drag it to her past the mutts, who are all lying down again.

Once the keys are close enough, Stephanie picks them up and carefully opens the lock. Chris inches himself out of the tight space. His whole body aches. Once outside, he stands up. His legs are weak, and his back is in agonizing pain. Stephanie calls his attention with a cough. Chris smiles and reaches down to the chains.

With a simple snap, he separates the shackles from her ankles. He stops her from getting up. "Before you leave, you need to find the book," he tells her in a whisper close to her ear.

"What book?" she whispers back into his ear. They continue the conversation in this manner.

"It's like a book of stories. It is also said to have writing of spells and other incantations," Chris explains.

"Jesus. This is getting stranger by the moment." Stephanie shakes her head.

"I understand. But you need to find it. And take it with you."

"Where is it?" Stephanie doesn't need to debate anymore. She just wants out.

"It is probably in my father's study."

"Are you fucking kidding me?"

"Listen, once he falls asleep, he will be out. We all have the same trait. We sleep hard during the day," Chris reassures her.

"Why don't you get it?" Stephanie asks.

"I'm too weak. I'm having a hard enough time just standing here, right now."

"This is bat shit crazy. I can't believe I'm going to do this." She looks at the stairs. "Fuck, all right. How do you I get to his study?" Chris gives her the exact steps she will need to take to get to the study. His father will be in the living room sleeping in his recliner. He knows he is there because he counted his steps when he left.

Stephanie, holding the stick, navigates through the mutts. None move as she carefully steps between them. Looking down, she recognizes some of their faces. Unnerved, she stops and looks around the basement. The men chained are all those missing from the Taymizyan murders. Wide-eyed, she takes it all in. But, she has no idea how to process it all.

Reaching the stairs, she puts a foot on the first step, and the creaking of the old wood almost gives her a heart attack. Stephanie looks at Chris who motions for her to continue.

Once on the main floor, she takes a deep breath and, using all her bravery, heads through the house. Following Chris's earlier directions, Stephanie goes across the living room, which the old man uses as his bedroom. She sees him sleeping, snoring louder than anyone she has ever heard before. He stirs only once as she passes through the room. She doesn't linger, in case he wakes.

Going through the hall, Stephanie reaches the front door. Reaching for the door knob, she stops herself. She truly wants to run to her car and just drive off. But she can't leave Walter like this. If any of this shit is real, maybe there is a spell in this crazy book that can bring him back to them. Taking another deep breath, Stephanie heads to the study. The bookshelves are mostly empty. None of the books look like the one Chris told her to look for.

Reaching the desk, she finds a locked drawer. She laughs to herself. Why would these monsters lock a simple drawer that any of them could break with a simple pull? Not wanting to dwell on it, she looks for something to help her unlock the latch. She finds a letter opener, and jams it into the small slot. The noise worries her. She looks to the doorway, hoping not to see the old man.

Waiting a few moments, she returns to unlocking the drawer. After a little finagling, she breaks the lock. She slides the drawer open and sees a large, leather-bound book. The cover has a symbol of antlers with a cross in the center. Stephanie picks it up and heads back to the basement.

When she walks into the living room, she sees that the old man is no longer lying in his recliner. Stephanie, about to run, hears a noise coming from the small bathroom that Walter had asked about when they first arrived. She moves back into the hall, hoping he doesn't notice her.

The old man comes out of the bathroom, crudely burping as he crashes back into his recliner. His actions and movements tell her he has been pretending to be feeble. There is no sign of him having been shot. She knew she struck him many times. She listens to him grumble about something, then he quickly returns to his snoring. Her heart in her throat, she peeks into the living room. The old man is asleep again. Tiptoeing across the room, she quickly returns to Chris in the basement.

His eyes are huge when he sees the book. Stephanie hands it to him, and he opens it. "I was worried when I heard him go to the bathroom."

"I almost peed my pants," Stephanie says. Cocking his head, Chris picks out a sound from the road. What sounds like a van, is pulling up to the house. A loud crash of the door from upstairs, tells him that Alex is back.

"Shit, you need to put the shackles back on. It's Alex, he's back. If he comes down, he needs to think everything is the same," Chris tells her. The pair return to their respective restraints. Alex walks down into the basement.

"All right boys, it's time you get out there and do some work. We have the trail," Alex claims excitedly. He walks around the mutts, unlatching them one by one. He places a necklace over each of their heads, but Chris can't make out what it is. "Do your father proud, your brothers are doing so well," he says, looking at Chris.

"You have no idea what you have done to us all," Chris tells him.

"I do. And you will too. I promise you, brother, you will be happy with what happens," he says and heads back upstairs. Listening to his movements, Chris hears Alex load the mutts into the van. Aleksy walks through the house. The old man paces back and forth.

Stephanie turns around to him, but Chris shakes his head and places his finger on his mouth, telling her not to make a sound. He points to the ceiling letting her know that they are still up there and awake. She drops her shoulders in disappointment. Looking at Walter's lifeless body, she feels the despair that he may wake before she can do anything.

Chris uses his fingers to wave Stephanie to him. He leans to the edge of the cage, and waits for her ear to be close enough. "Something has my father worried. He is right above us. When he walks to the other side of the room, you need to move toward that wall. There is a small access hole, an air vent. Look at me; I will hit the cage and, depending on my father's response, I will do a second hit, which means you need to open the hatch. If I do not, we must wait," he explains.

Stephanie nods in understanding. Chris points to her shackles telling her to take them off. He looks at the ceiling above, his sharp hearing focused on the sounds of the man standing above them, then he points to the wall. Stephanie doesn't think twice; she quickly takes off the shackles and stands waiting at the wall, under the small air vent. Chris lifts his back hard against the cage. With the adrenaline pumping through her, Stephanie knows she'll be able to break the wood around the vent no problem, once Chris gives her the sign.

She waits and nothing happens. Chris is still focused on the activity above. Chris looks at her, with purpose in his eyes. Stephanie, about to run back to her shackles, is stopped by Chris. "You fucking old man. You've killed us all," Chris screams. The deep-throated cry echoes in the small dark room.

A loud banging on the floor, from the old man, makes Chris smile. "Where is Melisa!" Chris replies with a scream, while pointing to the access hole next to Stephanie. The old man again hits the floor, and Stephanie sharply breaks the wood, opening the bright world to her. The light of the moon resurrects the whole room. "Let me out!" Chris screams, gesturing for Stephanie to leave. When the banging hits again, she pushes the book through and squeezes her slight frame through the small opening.

Once she is outside Chris opens the cage, and heads for the opening. His body is too big for the small hole. He knows the only way he can make it, is if he breaks the wood frame, which would make even more noise.

"Hurry up," Stephanie whispers.

"Yes, hurry up boy. We can't wait out here forever," Aleksy growls from behind Stephanie. "Clever girl, aren't you," he laughs and knocks her down. "Chris, what were you going to do with this?" he asks, lowering himself to see through the vent.

Chris looks up at him, his inner voice telling him to give up and prepare for the beating that is about to come from Aleksy. Chris listens for his brothers, expecting them to enter, but they do not. He is alone in the basement.

"Don't worry, son. I would have done the same. It's true what they say. You always have the most trouble with the son that is most like you." The old man laughs. "Why don't you get in your cage like a good boy? I'll take care of this brave girl. Don't worry, I won't hurt her; that's for your brother-in-law to do. You're the one that wanted this family." The old man laughs with even more veracity and watches as Chris obeys.

CHAPTER THIRTY-TWO

Melisa has been lying on the couch, resting her eyes. Mr. Hudson has a small TV set up and has been watching an old movie. She liked hearing all the monotonous dialog, which helped her doze off. When Mr. Hudson gets up from the couch, she opens her eyes. He walks over to the door and opens it.

To her surprise the man in the leather jacket is standing there. She can't remember hearing a knock, but maybe that's what woke her up, she thinks to herself. Mr. Hudson invites him in, and the two men walk into the small room in the back. Melisa rises from the couch and follows.

"I'm going to lead them away," Ranald says.

"Are they close?" Mr. Hudson replies.

"Close enough, but still far enough for you to cloak the area," Ranald informs him. Melisa, standing behind the two men, doesn't know what they are talking about. But she knows it has something to do with her.

"You go then. I will continue to watch over her," Mr. Hudson tells the man in the leather jacket.

"What's going on?" Melisa asks, concerned.

"Nothing, my dear, you shouldn't be walking around. Please go back to the couch," Mr. Hudson says sweetly.

"I don't mean to be rude, but if I'm in danger, I would appreciate knowing," she interjects. Ranald turns to Melisa and gives his million-dollar smile. Melisa notices his fangs protruding.

"You are right." He reaches out to take her hand. Melisa pulls her hands to her chest.

"What are you?"

"Take a seat."

"God damn, I'm tired of everyone telling me to take a seat. Just answer my fucking question."

"Wow, all right then . . . I'm a vampire. I've killed hundreds of people in my five-hundred-year existence. And, I have no idea what my name is. How's that?" The vampire takes a seat at the table. Melisa is frozen. "Now, will you please take a seat. I have something to discuss with you." He pulls out a chair for her, patting its seat. Melisa looks at Mr. Hudson, who can't hide his enjoyment, of watching his old friend. Reluctantly, she sits.

"What's left of The Seven are coming; they want you."

"Who?"

"The brothers . . . Chris's family. I assume Mr. Hudson has filled you in about some of the situation."

"Wait, if Chris is coming for me, why the theatrics?"

"Because Chris is not with his brothers. I don't know what has happened to him, but he is not with his brothers anymore. The family has shifted, and you are now in danger," he explains.

"So what do you want from me?"

"You did something, something that resonated with the Hunter."

"What?"

"You sacrificed yourself." Ranald reaches for her hand, and this time she lets him take it. "My dear. You are special. I can't explain it, but you may have changed everything." He turns to Mr. Hudson. "I need Mr. Hudson to help you learn your power. Learn how to continue being you. He will also protect you."

Mr. Hudson nods, agreeing to help. Melisa looks at the older man standing behind the vampire. She doesn't feel that confident about his ability to protect her, but at the same time her vision is still fresh in her mind. He is hiding something, and that something may be able to protect her.

"I must go; got to lead some dogs away from here," the vampire smiles. "Do you mind?" he points to her shirt. He rips a piece from the sleeve.

"For them to track me."

Mr. Hudson follows him outside. He has a strange red herb with him, which he sprinkles around the area of the cabin. The vampire leaps into the air, leaving them behind. His worry for them is strong, but he hopes that the old man will keep his word. He knows Mr. Hudson's power, but he also knows that he may not use it.

Ranald lands; he needs to find a location nearby but not too close to the cabin. If Mr. Hudson's cloaking spells work as he hopes, he will be able to redirect the trail away from Melisa easily. Landing on the main drag of Big Bear Lake Road, he works a path for the brothers to follow. He hurries to the docks of the lake.

He finds a large boat that is not occupied. He heads to the engine room and jump starts the vessel. He captains the boat to the other side of the lake, where he slows the motor, but he doesn't stop it. He turns the boat so it passes close to the dock, so he can step off onto it. He leaves the boat running heading back into the center of the lake, leaving behind the cloth from Melisa's shirt. He heads for an uninhabited area.

He hopes all of his tactics work; having dealt with their kind before, he knows their tendencies when it comes to tracking. He makes a trail to an empty forest, where he sits crossed legged waiting for the brothers. He is happy when he hears them before they see him. His plan has worked.

The brothers are hunched over, walking slowly toward him. He counts only four. The others are missing. Focusing his senses, the man in the leather jacket can't feel the fifth or sixth anywhere near him.

Vincent, the largest brother, cautiously leads the smaller pack toward the vampire. "Where is she?" he asks in a deep-pitched growl sniffing the air.

"Not here," Ranald answers, staying crossed legged.

"Where is the blade?" Vincent follows up.

"What blade?" Ranald wears a sarcastic smile as he converses with his captives.

"No games, we know you have both. Now give them to us," Vincent continues.

"Why? So you can put the Hunter away?" Ranald flexes his arms, making fun of massive Vincent.

"Ha, we have already taken care of the Hunter," Vincent boasts.

"Really? And how did you do that?"

"We buried him."

"That should work for about a week. You idiots don't have any idea how powerful the Hunter is, do you?" Ranald slowly gets to his feet. A sound attracts his attention. At first he thinks it is the missing brother, but, with the clumsy movements and smells, he can tell it is mutts. About twelve of them. He smiles at Vincent. "I see you brought your big guns."

"I won't need them."

"Well, let's get on with it then." Ranald claps his hands and follows the act with shaking out his arms getting ready to fight. The brothers quickly swarm him. Vincent lets out a shivering howl.

"This will make it a little fairer," the vampire jokes, knowing what the call means. He watches with amusement as the brothers all transform into massive beasts.

The first to attack is Greg, a smaller beast, but still a foot taller than the vampire. The strike misses. Ranald moves much quicker than the monster. Two of the other brothers attempt to strike him too, but his reflexes are too quick for them to make contact.

Vincent howls again. The mutts come charging out from the tree line. Ranald looks at them with a smile, knowing they can't hurt him. However, the second he takes his focus off Vincent is all that is needed for him to make the first strike on the wise-cracking vampire.

The thunderclap of the hit across Ranald's face knocks him twenty feet away. His glasses almost fall off, but he quickly adjusts them to normal. Doing so allows for another hit, this time by the brother Jim, followed by another strike from a different brother. The brothers swarm at the opportunity. The vampire is overwhelmed by the onslaught of hits. He drops to his knees, being pummeled.

The pain is real, and he realizes he has underestimated the brothers. He tries to fight back, but the attack is so overwhelming that he can't do much in defense. Using their claws and sharp teeth, the werewolves rip at him, tearing into his flesh. Using the last of his strength, Ranald explodes upward with a powerful leap into the air.

Two of the brothers hold onto him, as he lifts them high up into the air. The brothers relentlessly rip at the vampire, forcing him to give up his escape. He falls to the ground in a heap. The brothers again jump on him, beating him until he stops trying to move.

Ranald lies, bleeding and weak, facing up at the sky. "So now what?" the vampire asks, with a laugh, his mouth spitting out his black, oil-like blood.

Vincent stands over him, looking down at him breathing the fire out of his lungs. "You will have to answer to our father now."

"Great, let's go see Aleksy." Though pain stricken, Ranald continues to laugh.

"Pick him up. Put him in my car," Vincent orders. Greg and Jim grab hold of the vampire and place silver chains around his wrists and neck. The metal stings as it makes contact with his skin.

Above the brothers, hiding in the trees, Aaron sits, perched on a large branch, holding a special flower cloaking his location. He witnessed the battle. It took all his strength not to interfere. Something inside him told him that the man in the leather jacket should not have been taking the fight so lightly. At the same time, everything he knows about the vampire, tells him that he allowed them to take him.

He watches as Greg and Jim load the vampire into the back of Vincent's car. Alex is sitting in the driver's seat of the large cargo van parked next to Vincent's car. The coward didn't even get out to help his brothers. Are they so unaware of what they are dealing with? Has his family truly been manipulated to believe such falseness?

Barking orders for everyone to hurry up, Alex slaps the door of the van. Aaron waits for his brothers and their mutts to file in and leave. Once the area is clear he leaps down from the tree and hurries to the area.

Taking in a deep breath, he isolates the vampire's scent. He turns around in a circle, finding where it came from. The path leads him to the lake. There, he sees the boat bobbing up and down in the water, moving slowly without a pilot. He knows that it was used. Jumping from the shore, he lands on the boat. He finds the remnant of Melisa's shirt.

Taking in the scent, he finds that the man in the leather jacket was there too, just as he thought. He leaps to the dock on the other side of the lake, where the vampire got the boat. He follows the scent to where he landed on the main road. Closing his eyes, Aaron picks up the scent in the air. He can almost see the particle line of where he flew from, falling to the ground.

Unlike the vampire, he cannot take to the air, but he can follow it from the ground fairly easily. The scent is pushed by the air, but being so high up, the altitude is helping him.

As he tracks the vampire, hoping the trail leads him to Melisa, he thinks about how lucky he is. He had tried to train his brothers in the art of tracking, but none were interested. Only Chris was eager to learn. How ironic they were fighting to return to the glory of a past they knew nothing about, nor cared enough to learn about. They had adapted to this modern world, and lost touch with so many of their abilities. *How can they want it to be like it once was, when they don't even understand their true past?* he wonders.

Moving through the small mountain town, he enjoys being so close to nature. He had tried many times to get Chris to buy land in the Big Bear Mountain area, but Chris wanted to wait. It was always wait with Chris. Aaron understood his motives. But he did have issues sometimes with his frugal nature.

He didn't challenge it, knowing how well he has done with the little money he had. It was Chris who got the family the cars, the new house, the bar, and club. Aaron knew Chris did everything. The other brothers didn't appreciate what he did to get the money, which explained how they could so easily turn against him. Aaron had asked Chris to tell the brothers of his sacrifice, but he didn't think it important. Now, he was sure Chris regretted not telling them.

Aaron stops in his tracks. The scent has changed direction. It leads back to the city. Looking around, he sees that the man in the leather jacket stopped here. He walked around somewhere, but his scent is being masked.

Taking a deep breath, he picks up a scent, something that is not supposed to grow in this area at this time of the year. It's a Snow Plant. A plant that feeds off decaying pines, it's rare and only comes out after a snow. Looking around, he doesn't see any of the plants around. They are hard to find but easy to recognize. They are red, absent of any other color.

Aaron follows the faint scent. He walks into the middle of the road; the streets here don't have sidewalks. The few cars driving by, flash their headlights at him; he just waves them on. He will not allow himself to lose the scent. Reaching the peak, he comes to a small cabin.

The cabin has smoke coming from the chimney. Nervous, he heads for the door. He checks around to make sure he is not being followed. Reaching the wooden door, he is about to knock when Mr. Hudson opens the door. "Can I help you?" he asks. Aaron is impressed by the old man's stature. His aura is immense.

"I'm, I'm sorry. Is Melisa here?"

"Aaron?" Melisa calls out from the other room.

"Melisa, thank God." Aaron moves to pass the old man. Mr. Hudson places a hand on his shoulder and Aaron stops instantly. He does not want him to enter, and Aaron can feel he can't force himself in. Not wanting to escalate things, he steps back. "I apologize. May I come in?" he asks Mr. Hudson.

"No. You fool," Mr. Hudson states sharply. "You have led them right to her," he says. He slams the door. Confused, Aaron looks around but can't sense anything that the old man stated. Breathing in deep, his ears perked, he waits.

In the moonlight shining down on the mountain range, he sees something. It's a mutt in the tree line. Its eyes are reflecting. *Shit, they followed me. But how?* he asks himself. He still can't smell them. How could they do it? He is better than that. Looking at the tree line, he sees more eyes reflecting. He counts twelve. Listening carefully, he finally can pick up their breathing. And it's getting louder.

He knows he can handle a few mutts, but he doesn't know how many are really out there. And if his brothers are too, he can't fight them all. He turns to knock on the door. Mr. Hudson calls out from behind the door: "Handle your business." Already, Aaron doesn't like this man. If that's what he is.

Aaron takes a step off the patio and walks up the drive facing the monsters that have surrounded the cabin. If the mutts are there, so must be his brothers. He knows it's going to be a losing battle. But he will give his last breath to protect Melisa. "Well, let's go then!" he calls. The mutts all howl at him, accepting the challenge.

A yelp is heard coming from the left. It's the sound of a mutt crying out in pain. Aaron waits for the attack, but instead he hears another yelp, and another, until he counts twelve in total. All the yelps come from the area where he assumed the mutts were stationed.

Aaron waits. Taking a deep breath, he picks up a scent he never thought he would have to deal with again. Someone he hoped would have helped but had said no. Aaron watches as the Hunter appears to him, walking out from the bushes. His arms are covered in blood, with little splatters on his clothes and face. He walks right up to Aaron. He stops and looks him up and down. "I believe this is yours," he says and hands Aaron a necklace made from his hair. "They all had these on," he informs him. Aaron breaks the necklace and throws it to the ground. "They reek of magic," the Hunter says.

"That's how they hid from me," Aaron reflects. The Hunter just looks at him, emotionlessly.

"Where is she?" the Hunter asks.

"She's inside."

"May I speak with her?"

"I don't know," Aaron answers. Just then Mr. Hudson opens the door. The two men stare at each other for a moment.

"You are the one they call the Hunter?" Mr. Hudson asks.

"Yes, but please call me Fernando."

"What is your purpose for speaking to her?"

"To know she is okay." The Hunter's eyes plead with Mr. Hudson.

"She is," Mr. Hudson says, giving the Hunter a tone that is firm and unafraid. "You may enter my home, but no funny business." Mr. Hudson moves from the door, holding it open for the Hunter to enter.

"Thank you, sir." The Hunter walks past the old man. He stops to look him in the eyes, needing to figure out the mysterious old man.

"Don't waste your time, young man. Just go on in." Mr. Hudson ushers the Hunter through, to where he waits in the living room. Mr. Hudson looks out into the hills. He knows someone is out there watching. As Aaron walks past him, he tells him they need to leave. Aaron looks back, trying to see what the old man is seeing, but he cannot.

"How is she?" Aaron asks once inside.

"Well enough, but she needs more time; the blade's venom is still dangerous. She is lucky that the baby is still not more present in her blood," Mr. Hudson tells him. "But, I'm afraid you do not have the luxury of more time," he adds, closing the door.

"I'm Aaron. I didn't catch your name."

"Call me Mr. Hudson."

"Mr. Hudson." Aaron acknowledges the formality in the older man's introductions.

"Yes." Mr. Hudson nods and walks to the kitchen, where he pulls off a set of keys from a hook and tosses them to Aaron. "You need to take her somewhere safe. The car is in the back, and the one watching, I'll keep him busy."

Turning to see who he is talking about, Aaron can't make it out. "Who is it?"

"Just a watcher, left behind I'm sure to keep its creature apprised of our goings on," the old man says as he ushers him into the house. Aaron looks down at the key ring, sees the keys belong to an old Cadillac. "Mr. Hudson, thank you. I wish I had a way to . . ."

Mr. Hudson waves Aaron off from giving him any more thanks. "We need to get her out of here now," he says, walking through the living room. "Well, come along," he says and taps the Hunter on the shoulder. He knocks on the bedroom door where she is resting. He peeks in, asking if it's okay to come in.

"Of course, please do," she smiles, carefully sitting up.

"We have some guests. Please stay calm, I promise no ill will come to you," he tells her with his hands up in a calming matter. The Hunter enters, and Melisa's eyes enlarge, just about popping out of her head. She doesn't notice his sheepish look.

"What is he doing here?" she screams, about to run. Mr. Hudson quickly moves to her side, still trying to calm her.

"Melisa, I'm here too," Aaron calls out, moving past the Hunter, bumping him. Seeing her in such a condition causes the Hunter to drop to his knees.

"Aaron, what the fuck?" Melisa is so confused.

"It's okay, honey. We are here to help you," Aaron tries to reassure her.

"Where is Chris?" she asks. A slew of memories come flooding through her. The peace that she had earlier, is now gone. The sedative no longer works to keep her calm. Melisa is now inconsolable and cries out hysterically.

The Hunter can't handle her this way; he gets up and attempts to leaves the room. As he is about to leave, Mr. Hudson stops him. "You must face all you have done, boy. You might as well start with her," he states, looking him firmly in the eyes.

"What are you?" The Hunter looks deep into Mr. Hudson's eyes.

"That is not your concern. Like you, I have my demons. But I am no coward. I faced them."

"What should I do?" the Hunter asks.

"Put yourself at her mercy"

"How?"

"Give this to her." He hands the Hunter the dagger. Taking it, the Hunter looks at it with understanding and walks back into the room.

Melisa is slightly calmer, but seeing him with the blade causes her to tremble. Aaron gets up, ready to protect her. Mr. Hudson, standing behind the Hunter, uses his hand to encourage them to be calm. The Hunter walks up to Melisa slowly, kneels and offers her the blade, holding it above his lowered head.

With fear in her eyes, she takes it. The thought to plunge it into the back of his head is strong. Not being able to, she looks to Aaron, thinking to offer it to him, in order to kill the beast before her.

"Give it to him, if you wish," the Hunter states, shocking her. "I will not protest. I accept your judgment. You have been nothing but kind to me. I am the one who betrayed you. I will gladly go to the next life by your judgement." The Hunter places his hands on the floor, exposing his neck, as an offering.

Melisa looks at Aaron; his eyes tell her he will do whatever she asks. She places the dagger on the mattress. "I do not wish anyone dead, because of me." She wipes the tears from her eyes.

"Now that that's settled, can we get going?" Mr. Hudson calls out from the doorway.

CHAPTER THIRTY-THREE

Chris has been sitting in his cage, awake and broken, the whole night. Vincent's car pulling up catches his ear. The car parks quickly, and he can hear his brothers tumbling out in a big fuss. They have someone with them, who is chained up. He tries to use his sense of smell to figure out who it is but fails. His nose is still not working the way he needs. Still relying heavily on his ears, he listens. Another car pulls up. It's the cargo van that Alex was driving.

The ruckus makes it easy for Chris to figure out that things have not gone according to plan for the brothers. The anger the brothers have is amazing. Alex is calling out about losing his mutts. The Hunter is called out as well. Chris waits for them to enter the house so he can make out exactly what they are talking about.

Exploding into the home, Alex is the first one to enter. The brothers are outside dealing with the prisoner. "The fucking Hunter let Aaron live," Alex cries out as he enters the house. Chris can't believe the words. They have tried to kill Aaron. This was not the family he knew. Something horrible has influenced this. They would never act in such a way, unless for some outside influence.

"Where are the mutts?" Aleksy asks.

"Dead. The fucking Hunter killed them."

"And he let Aaron live?" Aleksy demands.

"Yes." Alex is stomping around the house above Chris, forcing dirt and small pieces of wood to fall on his face. "I thought he hated our kind?" Alex asks, frustrated.

"He does." Aleksy can be heard pacing above Chris. "Where are they?"

"Some cabin in Big Bear," Alex answers. Aleksy is walking toward the front door.

"Who do you have here?" Aleksy asks. Chris can only assume he's referring to the prisoner.

"The only good thing to come from tonight," Alex says and hits a wall in frustration. The other brothers walk into the house. Two are walking with the prisoner. They hold up outside of the door. Aleksy greets them. "So, I hope they weren't too rough on you. You know how boys can be," Aleksy starts.

"Of course not. They acted in the way one would expect, knowing they are from your loins," the prisoner answers. His thick Scottish accent tells Chris it is the man in the leather jacket. Chris can't believe how out of the loop he has been through this whole thing.

"That's great," the old man says, continuing the banter.

"Well, I know you got things to do. Should we end the pleasantries and get to business?" Ranald offers.

"Oh no. We are waiting for someone." Aleksy laughs, as if the secret will trouble the vampire. Chris doesn't need to be able to see, but he knows his father is giving Ranald one of his devilish smiles. "So, why don't you come in. No need to have you wait outside all night."

Chris can't stop wondering who his father is talking about. He heard the conversation. Was the voice coming to their home? And if so, who is he? A feeling of nausea comes over Chris; his nerves are overwhelming. Whatever his father had planned, he has been working on it for some time. But how could he have done so under his nose?

The feeling of failing his family is strong and is intensified by being helpless in a cage, which he put himself in. It doesn't even have a lock on it anymore, yet Chris doesn't dare leave again. The sound of a new car pulling up catches his attention. The engine sounds like it powers something elegant, most likely European . . . something expensive.

"Wow, he's early," Aleksy calls out. He walks across sturdily, dirt falling with his steps above Chris's cage. Upon opening the door, Chris hears

Aleksy greet the visitor with flattering admiration. The voice comes from the stranger that was on the phone call with Aleksy earlier.

"Come in, come in," the jovial Aleksy invites the voice in.

"So, where is my old pal?" the voice asks, using what sounds like a cloth to dust off his shoes. Chris imagines a man dressed in fancy clothes. Most likely using his gloves. His brothers are all whispering to each other, letting Chris know this is the first time they are seeing the owner of the voice.

"Wow, this is a surprise," the vampire exclaims.

"Oh Andrews, you look amazing. I like the sunglasses," the voice calls out. Chris gasps. *Andrews? Is that his real name?* he wonders.

"Ha, that was never my name," the vampire tells everyone, taking the small satisfaction away.

"But it was the one I gave you," the voice asserts.

"Sure, only while in your employment. I go by Ranald right now."

"Ranald? I like Andrews better."

"And what should I call you?" the vampire asks. Chris's excitement is hard to control.

"Oh Andrews. I have many names, but not because I find it fun to hide who I really am. It's because I actually have many names."

"I like Itzamna," Ranald calls out. Chris's puzzlement continues. He has never heard a name like that before.

"Well," the mysterious man's voice breaks. "I haven't heard that in some time."

"I'm sure you haven't. But I have. And I've heard about what you did," the vampire states.

"Well, I guess you do know some things," the mysterious man agrees. "How did you come across this information?" he asks.

"Really? You think I'm going to share? How long have you known me?" Ranald laughs.

"Andrews, I truly missed you." The voice joins him in laughter.

"I should have expected you were behind this. Still trying to get all the books, eh?"

"Hmm." The voice chuckles.

"You guys are lucky; you could have been left to die in the jungle like I was."

"Oh Andrews, I left you because you failed. But look at how things turned out. You are a better you," the voice offers. "You should be happy."

"I am. I'm here to witness you explain to these morons that the book will not be any good to them."

"What?" Aleksy calls out.

"Don't pay any attention to him," the voice reassures the old man. Turning his attention back to Ranald, he says, "You know, you are the real architect in all this. It was you who put the Hunter in his tomb, you who worked with these fine creatures." He pauses. "You, my dear Andrews, helped to make all this happen," the voice sincerely states.

"God, who has a stake? I'm ready. I can't listen to this guy anymore," Ranald lets out, frustrated. The brothers all roar in laughter.

"You still got it, Andrews. Able to make anyone laugh," the voice chuckles in a sadistic tone.

"The only mistake I made, was allowing a fool like Aleksy to help," the vampire volleys back.

"You let the Hunter live on. By doing so, you allowed me to find it."

"Not true. I allowed him to live, because he is better than all of us. He was just manipulated, just like you manipulated me. And, just like you are now manipulating this stupid pack."

"I have not manipulated anyone," the voice defends himself.

"I know the truth. I know the real you. And, I know why you need the book," Ranald states. His confidence is strong, and powerful.

"Oh, and what is it you think you know?" the voice asks, his tone showing he is smiling, calling out a bluff.

"Stuff, lots of stuff," Ranald says and erupts in laughter. The brothers can't help but laugh with him.

"Where is the book?" the voice asks.

"I have it safe," Aleksy answers. Chris listens as one of the brothers hurries away and then returns with what he assumes is the book.

"It's as beautiful as I dreamed. It's only fitting you are here to experience this with me, Andrews."

"Remember, you promised to fix my curse, before you do anything else," Aleksy interjects. The vampire laughs at the notion.

"Ha, you think this guy can make you immortal again?"

"Don't be so cynical, Andrews. This book can do many things," the voice calls out.

"Sure, but not that." A growl from the old man gets his sons to follow the lead. "And definitely not now."

"Is he telling the truth?" Aleksy asks the voice.

"Of course not. Here, let's look at the book together," the voice offers. "Right here. This spell. This will grant what you are asking for." The voice then reads the words in a tongue that Chris doesn't understand. The vampire's laughter continues as the voice reads aloud.

"Thank you for allowing me to see this. I'm actually in your debt for this," Ranald says and continues to laugh. The old man strikes the vampire down, growling at him. "Oh please don't. I still need to see the rest. Go on, tell them what it says. Read the words." Ranald continues to aggravate the situation. Chris can hear the spitting out of the vampire. Hearing the splatter, Chris can guess it's blood.

"What is he talking about?" Aleksy growls.

"Only a select few can read the words in this book. And, have the words work for them." The voice pauses. "But do not worry. I already have someone lined up."

"Is that all?" Ranald laughs again.

"What is he talking about?"

"Well. It may be a problem that the Hunter is awake."

"You've lied to me," Aleksy growls

"I told you not to wake him. I was explicit about that," the voice replies, calm and collected.

"Oh no. Now what?" the vampire is relentless in his mocking. Aleksy roars, striking him again, yelling for him to shut up. "What's the plan, big guy?" Ranald spits out while still laughing.

"Shut up." Aleksy smacks the vampire. "Take him downstairs. I can't listen to his stupid voice anymore." Two of the brothers comply with their father's request. They drag the vampire through the house to the basement door. The whole time he is teasing them, begging for them to let him stay.

Once at the door of the basement, they toss him down the steps. He tumbles, but Chris can see that every move is controlled. It's at that moment, that he realizes that the man in the leather jacket has been playing them all. He was just letting them think he was weak. It's Vincent and Greg who walk down after him.

Chris tries to talk to them, but they both ignore him. They grab Ranald and drag him near Walter's body. They hook him to a set of chains, which are made of the same silver they have wrapped around his body. Chris can't remember a time when he saw them there before. It's like they had installed them just for this purpose.

Ranald is able to get himself up, although the discomfort caused by the chains shows on his face. The two immortals look at each other for a few minutes, then return their attention to the conversation upstairs. "What about the blade? Who has it?" the voice asks.

"That piece of shit had it." Aleksy must be referring to the vampire.

"I see," is all the voice says.

"It has to be with the girl," Aleksy points out.

"What girl?" the voice asks. It's the first time he has sounded actually surprised.

"My other son's human. Melisa," Aleksy explains.

"Melisa?" the voice's tone changes. "What does she have to do with any of this?" the voice asks, as if he knows her.

"She is being protected," Aleksy adds.

"By whom?" the voice asks. Chris is sure the voice knows Melisa.

"The Hunter and my other son Aaron."

"I see. So out of the seven, two have turned against you? Did I make a mistake offering you this?" the voice says, challenging his own decision.

"Of course not."

"And how do you expect for this to play out?" the voice asks.

"I will get the blade, I promise," Aleksy claims loudly.

"How?"

"With force. My sons will take the Hunter down."

"That is a mighty bold objective. I don't see that happening."

"My boys are stronger than you think," Aleksy boasts.

"I'm sure they are, but not strong enough, Aleksy. I will take care of things from now on. I no longer think you are up to the task." The voice heads for the door, his steps soft and firm.

"You think you're leaving with that book, you can just think again,"

Aleksy growls. His sons all join in, echoing the warning.

"Oh, I see." The voice's tone is confident, yet subdued. "Here. I will return for it, once I have accomplished my goal," the voice states, leaving the house. Aleksy follows him outside. The luxurious car's engine starts and drives off slowly. The brothers all walk across and head outside to join their father.

No one returns into the house until the sounds of the car are long gone. Aleksy is the first one to enter. Alex stays outside while the brothers all follow their father. Aleksy has to call Alex inside.

"We need to get that blade before he does," is all Aleksy says, before walking to his recliner and sitting down. The brothers seem to be stuck without guidance, and just stand in the same spot.

"Don't tell me we got to go back up that mountain?" Alex whines. A loud slap catches everyone by surprise. Their father moved from his chair and is now standing in front of Alex.

"You do what I say boy. If you lost me my life, I'll fucking kill you," Aleksy snarls.

CHAPTER THIRTY-FOUR

Aaron is driving Mr. Hudson's Cadillac. Next to him, the Hunter is riding shotgun. Melisa is lying in back, in visible discomfort. Aaron has no idea where to take her; all he was told is he needs to get her somewhere she can heal in peace. The next two nights are crucial.

Before they left, Mr. Hudson sprinkled an odd-smelling liquid all over the car. Aaron asked what it was, but the old man didn't want to share. All he stated was that it would shield them from being tracked. With that knowledge, Aaron knew he had to get somewhere quick but far enough away that they would feel safe.

Melisa was the one who gave the idea of going to Las Vegas. She had an uncle there; he would be able to give them a place to hide without using their names. And nobody knew about it, except family. He lived off the strip in a high-rise.

Aaron took the winding highway down, through the back side of the mountains. Knowing that he is likely to be tailed again, he keeps a keen eye behind him. He is moving at a good pace. But, with Melisa in the back, he takes special care when moving along the twists and curves. She never complains once.

Reaching Barstow, they fuel up and have a straight shot to Las Vegas. The Hunter is quiet the whole drive. He cleaned up at Mr. Hudson's and borrowed some clothes. He hadn't even noticed his appearance until Mr. Hudson offered the clothes. Now he sits there, like a normal man. Aaron can't help but keep his peripherals on his every move, even though he hasn't moved the whole drive.

"So, that Mr. Hudson is some character." It is Melisa who is the first to speak. "What do you think he is?" She needs to lighten the mood. Aaron looks at the Hunter, who is still focused only on the path ahead. "Aaron?"

"I have no idea. But he seems powerful," Aaron finally responds.

"What about you?" she asks the Hunter.

"He is old. I wish I knew," he states coldly. The words speak more truth than the two could ever guess. It's at that moment, they realize the Hunter has been trying to figure out the old man the whole time.

"He is a good man," Melisa states.

"I believe that to be true," the Hunter agrees.

"I heard you say your name is Fernando. I'm glad you've regained your memory," Melisa says.

"I wish I could join you in that feeling," the Hunter replies.

"Can you tell me where you come from?" Melisa asks. "Your accent is beautiful."

"Not all my memories are back, but I can tell you I was born in Spain," the Hunter answers.

"Beautiful. I love Spain." Melisa smiles, looking up at the ceiling of the car, remembering the time she spent there.

"I cannot join you in that sentiment; those are the memories I am lacking,"

"You mean feelings?"

"I mean memories of joy. All I remember is pain and suffering."

"I'm so sorry." Melisa moves, emitting a little sound of pain as she shifts her position. "May I?" Melisa asks, lifting her hand up near the Hunter's face.

"What is this?" The Hunter moves forward away from her.

"Mr. Hudson showed me something."

"What?" The Hunter looks back and forth between her and the man next to him.

"I can see; I can see inside the real you. If you allow it."

"You are a witch?"

"That is not what Mr. Hudson called it. He said I was blessed. Something from my heritage."

"I'm allowing a werewolf to drive me, why not allow a witch to read my thoughts." The Hunter's statement is not lost on his two companions. Aaron lets out a deep-throated laugh, which the Hunter finds amusing. He shows a slight smile.

"I'm not sure if that is a yes or a no," Melisa teases back.

"Please, go ahead. You never seem to stop trying to help me; why is that?" The Hunter smiles and moves back a proper seated position, looking out the front window.

"I don't know. I just see something in you," Melisa answers, looking at his reflection in the windshield.

"I worry; maybe after you see what I'm seeing you will change your mind," the Hunter adds.

"I can't promise that I won't find things to be horrible, but I believe that is not who or what you stand for," Melisa adds, reaching her hand next to his temples. "I will start if you are ready."

"You may proceed." The Hunter closes his eyes. Aaron is in doubt about the action, but doesn't say anything. Closing her eyes, Melisa makes contact. The words of what Mr. Hudson had told her play back in her mind.

"Concentrate, yet leave your mind blank. Look for the door, but remember you are a guest. You cannot change what you see, but you can see what is not wanted to be seen," Mr. Hudson had explained to her.

"Fernando, tell me of your father?" Melisa asks. Another thing Mr. Hudson taught her. If the door is closed tight, have the person answer a few questions about their past.

"My father was a soldier." The image of the Hunter's father appears. He is dressed in sixteenth-century service garb. Melisa only knows this because the Hunter is telling her so, through his thoughts.

"What else can you tell me?" Melisa asks.

"He was a good father. He loved me and my mother very much." The words draw up another image: the Hunter's mother. She is beautiful, fair skinned, dressed in elegant clothes from the same era.

"She is beautiful," Melisa adds. The words open more images. It is the

Hunter when he was a child. He is playing in a field. Looking around, she can see that they are in a vineyard. "Fernando, don't go too far," his mother calls out in Spanish. She is walking holding her husband's hand.

The young Fernando doesn't listen; he continues to run farther from his parents' view. The loud thunder of a stampede can be heard. Loud clashing sounds of metal and wood travel and grow with the animals charging in his direction. The ground begins to shake. The young Fernando is frightened. He begins to shiver. He is alone. The despair in his heart is so powerful, Melisa begins to tremble herself.

He screams out to his mother. The pounding is coming closer to him. He lowers himself to the ground unaware of what to do. The frightened child is unable to move from the danger. He hears the screeching of the oncoming horses, pulling a carriage as it climbs into view over the small hill. The boy screams, frozen, as the driver of the carriage fails to see him there.

As the horses are about to run over the helpless boy, his father grabs him, pulling him out of harm's way. The carriage doesn't even slow. Looking at the rear of the carriage, with tears in his eyes, the boy sees the emblem of the holy cross.

"What were you thinking, my son? You know they are on official business and cannot divert from their task, even for a little boy."

"I'm sorry, Father. I was scared," he cries. Melisa feels tears building in her own eyes.

"It's okay, my son. I love you; you just scared me." Holding him tight, he pulls him away to look him in the eyes. "You are my only son. You are my everything." His father begins to cry. His mother comes rushing to their side. She joins them and takes a knee.

"Oh my Fernando, you must not do that to us." She is smiling, helping to make the young boy feel better.

Melisa removes her fingers. Still teary-eyed, she sits back in her seat.

"They died shortly after that," the Hunter says.

"What happened?" Melisa asks from reflex.

"A beast took them from me." The Hunter lowers his head at the memory. Both Aaron and Melisa know he is referring to a werewolf. Aaron wants to say something, but knows it wouldn't be right.

"I'm sorry, Fernando." Melisa places her hand on his shoulder.

"Is that why you hunted my kind so feverishly?" Aaron finally speaks.

"It was why I became a Knight of Prosperitas," the Hunter tells him. "I wanted to kill all your kind." Aaron returns to his silence. Melisa feels she may have created a problem between the two men. It's the Hunter who clears the air.

"I found out some years later, that it was all by design," the Hunter tells them.

"What do you mean?" Aaron asks, surprised by the revelation.

"My uncle. He was to blame. My father had turned his back on what he wanted to do. He thought his actions were flawed," the Hunter adds.

"What happened to your uncle?" Aaron asks.

"He helped lead the Inquisition," the Hunter states frankly. Melisa and Aaron stay quiet for a moment.

"The Spanish Inquisition?" Melisa is shocked.

"Yes," the Hunter answers.

"What is your family name?" Melisa asks.

"de la Torre." He pauses. "But my uncle went by de Castella," he clarifies.

"I don't know the name. Sorry. My history has always been off," Melisa apologizes.

"I don't know if the names are of any consequence in your day. But, they were well known in mine."

"The vision you shared, where was that?"

"Africa. My father did not want to give up his wife, or his child."

"What do you mean?"

"The Pope put de Cisneros in the church and he established the revolutionizing Franciscan order in Spain. He forced the friars to become celibate, giving up the practice of taking a wife, or wives known as concubines would be more accurate. They had to be living in the parish where they would be present for confession, and preach every Sunday.

"He wanted to clean up the filth he found in the church. However, he was punishing all, not just the ones he thought to be using their powers for bad. My father, for example. He took one wife. He had one child. But he was forced to withdraw from us. The resistance was so fierce that four hundred men of the cloth fled to Africa with their wives and concubines, then converted to Islam.

"My father did not go that far. He left but did not follow those men. He cared about me and my mother. My uncle, a true believer and confidant of de Cisneros, didn't see it that way. As I was to find out many, many years later," the Hunter explains.

"Oh dear. So what happened to your uncle?" Melisa asks, fascinated.

"He died of old age. It would have been sooner had I found out the truth earlier. Instead, I followed him to the ends of the earth, and inflicted horrible pain onto those that opposed him and the kingdom."

"Jesus," is all Melisa can say.

"And that was before I became the monster I am now." The Hunter can't help but put himself down.

"I do not agree with vengeance, but it is understandable." Melisa tries to be understanding of the Hunter's plight.

"No, it is not. It is blind and unjust. There is never an excuse for vengeance," the Hunter adds. "I was mistaken, like most who go after such a thing. There is only one truth; forgiveness is the only redemption." Tears run down his face.

"How did you become the Hunter?" Aaron can't help himself. The Hunter wipes his tears away.

"I was ambushed by your kind. I escaped with my life, but I was struck by your venom. I was in the jungles of Valle de Panchoy, the new capital of the Kingdom of Guatemala. It was a beautiful place."

"Guatemala? My family is from there." The Hunter turns to look at her, then turns back quickly.

"The Franciscan monks were the first to move there," he adds. "I would assume you do not know the history I will share with you now," the Hunter says. "When I arrived there, my knights and I went through killing and destroying all that opposed the Church. We helped it burn and destroy all the markings of the people. We killed many, thinking it was for the good of our Lord." He pauses. "I truly hated that part. I did not agree with destroying their history," he adds.

"I made friends with an elder, a man who denounced his many gods to become a man of the cloth himself," the Hunter continues. "On one journey, my militias and I had to investigate a temple in a remote area. Most of the area would be considered remote. But this location was special. We knew it was a place that helped protect an immortal." The Hunter pauses. He chooses his words carefully. "My men got sick; a plant was toxic. We lost many men that day. The elder saved us. He used his knowledge to counteract the venom of the plants. I never spoke of his kindness, for fear he would be killed for being a witch. It was the first time I went against my oath." He stops.

"What do you mean?" Melisa asks, enthralled by the story.

"He used means outside that of our teachings. He was a witch," the Hunter explains.

"So even if he saved you, he was to be burned on the cross?" Melisa asks, unable to understand the logic.

"The Inquisition believed that only God was supposed to deliver miracles," the Hunter explains.

"So what about Jesus?"

"Jesus was one of his miracles."

"But how could anyone know that?"

"Melisa. I don't wish to get into a debate about the thoughts of the people from my time. I am just telling you about what transpired. I would rather not continue, if it is going to make you upset."

"No, I'm sorry. When I hear of things that are unjust, I get angry. Please continue," Melisa insists.

"Where was I . . . ah, yes. My guard was saved; the mystic cured us. I was fascinated by his gift. He showed me that all he was doing was using the earth to supply him with the cure from the earth's own poisons. It was beautiful. He had a true love for the Scriptures, but never gave up his past." The Hunter pauses, looking at Melisa. "I made him promise to keep all this a secret. And to never practice his arts again."

"How did he help you then?" Melisa asks.

"I was caught, ambushed. A werewolf got me. I was dead, going to turn into the very thing I hated. This shaman, a holy man, he saved me. He risked everything to save me. He used the two worlds. He found a knowledge in the great book and those prayers of the saints before us. Then he added the magic that was his heritage. And, putting that all together, he cursed me."

"Cursed?"

"If you live long enough, it's easy to lose sight of who and what you are. I was blind with power, and vengeance. It wasn't until I killed one like the monk who saved me. This elderly woman saved a vampire. I took her life, without even a second thought."

"Vampire?" Melisa knows he is talking about the man in the leather jacket.

"With her last breath, she gave me a glimpse. The image of what she had done. It was too late, but I understood that she made the vampire different. I was never the same after that."

"How?" Melisa asks.

"I realized the men I was following were wrong."

CHAPTER THIRTY-FIVE

It is noon when the brothers arrive at the cabin. They are surprised to find it burnt to the ground. The firemen working the closed off area wave them by. The brothers can't believe what they are seeing. Alex slams his hand on the steering wheel in anger. "I knew we should have attacked last night. Now how are we going to find them?"

"It's okay, brother; call Father, he will know what to do," Greg chimes in. Alex looks at him with disdain.

"No shit." Alex shakes his head in annoyance.

"Calm down, brothers, no need to get nasty with one another." Vincent tries to calm the situation. Alex pulls the van over. The smell of ash is strong. The brothers make their complaints, asking Alex to park somewhere else. But he doesn't care. He made a decision to park there and that's where they will stay until he moves.

The phone rings five times before the old man answers the phone. Alex explains the situation to him, the whole time expecting him to get angry. Surprisingly, Aleksy had expected this. He tells them to sit tight, he will find out where they are going.

Alex waits, hearing the old man walking through the house. A door opens, and the sound of footsteps going down steps tell him his father is coming into the basement. "Don't mind me, boys. I need to wake our sleeping beauty. He sure likes his down time," the old man calls out to his prisoners.

"Aleksy, I was hoping you would come down here. I have something I need to share with you. I'm willing to give everyone up," the vampire declares.

"Shut up," the old man laughs. "I have ways to find things out too, Andrews," he taunts back.

"No!" The vampire sarcastically acts like the word hurts. "Don't call me that." There is the sound of chains, followed by a rustling around. Aleksy is back on the phone. "What's this guy's name?" he asks Alex on the phone.

"What guy?" Alex asks, confused.

"Melisa's brother," his father clarifies.

"Walter?" Alex is unsure he is answering correctly.

"Ah, yes." The old man puts the phone to his side. "So, Walter. Let's get you on my page." Alex can still hear everything and knows right away what his dad is doing. He had wondered why he was keeping him around. Now it is all clear. "Walter, where is your sister going?" Aleksy can be heard moving the man around.

Alex knows his father is connecting to the future mutt. He was better at transforming humans than he. Alex needed them to change completely in order to mirror minds, but his father could do it while the other was still in gestation.

"She has an uncle in Las Vegas. That is the only place close enough for them to go. Anything else would take too long. And if she is hurt like the blood would indicate, she can't be on the road that long," the old man tells Alex.

"Okay Dad, we are on our way," Alex says excitedly.

"She'll be off the strip. They have a loft in one of the tall apartments," Aleksy adds.

"Thank you, Father." Alex can be heard smiling.

"Alex?" Aleksy speaks his son's name softly.

"Yes?"

"Don't fail me again," Aleksy states coldly. Visibly rattled, Alex hangs up the phone. It is the first time his father has ever threatened him.

"All right brothers, we are going to Vegas."

"Are you serious?" Greg interjects.

"Is there a problem?"

"No, I just don't have the clothes for Vegas. This is going to suck."

"We have more important things to worry about than your wardrobe, Greg." The brothers all join in laughing at their brother.

Aleksy is not happy about where this is leading his sons. Looking at the three people in his basement, he is disappointed at how things have gone. His plan is slowly falling apart; what else could he do? He knows deep down his boys are no match for the Hunter. Maybe if Chris was with them, but there is no way he could convert his son now.

He has only one solution. He needs to join his children. He needs to come out of hiding. The idea is frightening. The weakness of being mortal has held him captive. Looking at the three men, he feels in the same situation as the men. He is the fourth captive. It was different when he was with his boys; they could protect him.

"What's wrong?" Ranald can't help himself.

"God, you really never shut up. You know, I have another gift for you." The old man walks up to the vent hole that Stephanie used for her failed escape. He moves the board from it, allowing the sun to penetrate. The beam of light shines through like a laser, focused ten feet away from the vampire.

The old man looks at his watch: "I say you have 'til about three before the sun reaches you."

"Shit, that long?" Ranald doesn't show his fear. Aleksy heads upstairs. The men listen as he walks above them. His steps are solid, not like the feeble old man they have come to know. The old man starts to talk. He is on the phone.

"I know where they are going," he states. Ranald can't hear the voice on the other line. His hearing isn't as sensitive as Chris's. He looks to him, hoping he is listening. Chris is. "I'll meet you in Van Nuys; get your fancy private jet ready. I need a ride," Aleksy hisses. "Just get me there; I'll take care of the rest. I've put him down once, I can do it again," the old man brags. He hangs up the phone and stomps around the house.

"You think you can help me out here?" Ranald asks Chris.

"I'm not supposed to leave the cage. It's the only thing I can do now to protect Melisa," he states shamefully.

301

"You're kidding me, right?"

"If I obey, at least she has a chance. If I try and fight, she is all but killed."

"You realize she is being watched by the Hunter."

"That doesn't make me feel any better. You know what he does to our kind."

"I do. But like I told you before. She is special. And she . . ." he stops talking, hearing the old man returning. Stephanie's muffled cries can be heard as the old man carries her to the basement. He is holding her with one arm. Her mouth is gagged, her hands and feet bound. He drops her under the beaming sun.

"Just in case you get any ideas," he smiles at the vampire. "Walter, it's time for you to wake up, my pet," the old man says softly. A whimper comes from the almost dead Walter. The old man laughs as he leaves the basement. The sound of him leaving the house is a surprise. Both immortals know he is going out to help his sons.

"Who was he talking to?" Ranald asks.

"The voice. I still cannot place it." Chris slumps down in his prison.

"Fuck." Ranald can't believe the situation. Stephanie is wiggling around like a fish out of water, desperate to get free. "Hey, Stephanie. You need to calm down," he calls out to her.

She tries to see who is calling out to her, but the sun's rays are making it impossible. She bites and moves her head, forcing the gag to move, until she is finally able to free her mouth. "Who's there?"

"You do not know me. But I am a friend. You need to stay calm. The more you move, the more you will perspire," he warns her. Stephanie can't see anyone, but she knows that the man talking to her is talking about Walter.

"What should I do? Just lie here until he kills me?" she asks rhetorically. "Fuck that." She again struggles to free herself. The vampire smiles at her attitude.

"Fine. If that's the case, you might as well squirm your way to me. I can help you." He can't help but laugh at the predicament.

"I can't see shit," she lashes out.

"Just push your legs. Listen to my voice. I will guide you as best I can," the vampire offers.

"God damn it. Why do I feel like I'm jumping out of the pot into the fire, right now?" She can't believe she is listening to the stranger.

"I hope this isn't too forward, but I think I like you." Ranald makes light of the situation. Stephanie moves across the ground, following every move the man calls out. She isn't that nimble, but she is able to maneuver around the basement's retaining posts. She feels the scrapes and bruises being caused by the rough surface.

The vampire can smell the blood. He looks over at Walter; he is being called to it too. He is still asleep but starting to stir. "I don't mean to rush you, but I would move a little faster if I were you," he calls out.

"Dude, if you think you can do better, I can lie here and watch," she calls out. The vampire can't help but laugh. Walter begins to move more frequently; which information he keeps to himself. He just continues to guide Stephanie toward him.

"I'm directly behind you. One more heavy push and you will be reaching my feet," he explains. Stephanie, completely spent, gives the final push, until her head touches what she hopes is the man who has been directing her.

"How the fuck, are you able to see anything with those glasses on?" is the first thing that she says when she sees him.

"I promise to tell you anything you want. But first you need to get up so I can help you with your ropes," he states, looking past her. He uses his legs to help leverage her up, so she is in a seated position.

Once there, she sees what the man is looking at. Walter is beginning to rise. A deep growl is coming from him. "Oh fuck," she can't help but gasp.

"Um, I would hurry if I were you," Ranald encourages her. He continues to use his legs to help her up, until she is on her feet. "Hop around, put your hands by mine. I will cut through the ropes." Stephanie does what he says. She doesn't question anything anymore.

She can feel his ice cold skin as his fingers run up her arms, looking for the rope. She helps by getting on her tip toes. It takes him just a moment to cut through the rope with his fingernails. "Now hurry up," he calls out. Walter is standing up, his back to them. Sniffing the air, he is looking for Stephanie.

"Where are the keys to your shackles?" Stephanie asks the man.

"They are upstairs. I heard one of the brothers put it on the mantel," he tells her. Walter turns around at the sound of their voices. "Don't move. Let him come to you," Ranald instructs. "Call to him," he tells her.

"Walter?" She does what he asks. Walter cocks his head, looking right at her.

"Call him over here," he continues to instruct.

"Are you kidding me?" She can't believe she is going to do what he is asking. "Walter, come here," she calls. "I'm right here, Walter," she continues to call to him.

Walter walks on unsteady legs straight to her. The vampire waits for the right moment. Once Walter is close enough, he swings his shoulder, crashing into Walter and throwing him across the room.

"Run, now get those keys," he orders. Stephanie moves right away. She closes the door behind her and locks the door. She doesn't know how much that will slow him down, but she had to do something. She runs into the kitchen, looking for a knife to protect herself with.

Walter is close behind. Slamming into the door, he bangs on it screaming out in a fit of rage. Terrified, she runs for the keys, which she finds exactly where the man in the leather jacket told her they would be. Once she grabs them, she runs for the front door, just as Walter bursts through the basement door.

He sniffs out her direction and follows her outside. Stephanie rounds the house and heads for the vent hole she used before for her escape. This time she uses it to get back into the house. Squeezing her body through the small hole, she drops to the floor. The fall knocks the air out of her.

Close behind, Walter tries to make it through the same hole, but he is too big to do so. He gives up and takes off, coming back around into the house. Stephanie gets to her feet, though the pain in her chest is so bad that she almost falls right away. "Fantastic, you made it. I'm impressed," Ranald calls out.

"Motherfucker," Stephanie lets out, her hands on her knees.

"That's the spirit . . . Now get over here and unchain me; he's coming," Ranald hollers out. With her last ounce of strength, she staggers over to him.

"I don't mean to worry you, but he's inside the house," Ranald says, keeping her apprised. Stephanie looks up hearing his heavy steps above confirming what she is being told. "Come on, sweetheart. I know you can do it." Stephanie makes it to the vampire. She struggles to get the key into the lock. "Take your time. He's almost here," the vampire calmly states.

Stephanie tightens her lips. Puts the key into his lock and clicks it free. Walter leaps down the steps in one jump crashing into the wall. Shaking off the hit, he charges at Stephanie.

She drops to the ground, covering up, bracing for him to land on her. A shriek is all she hears. Opening her eyes, she sees the vampire has Walter by the throat. He holds him up, as he is still freeing the rest of his body. With a powerful squeeze he crushes Walter's throat and drops the still-alive mutt. Then he walks out of the silver chains. "Close your eyes," he tells Stephanie. She does as he says. Her ears tell her what he does next. The dragging of the body is saddening, but the hard crack of bones breaking is what breaks her heart. She knows that it wasn't Walter anymore. But that doesn't make it any easier.

"All right, let's get out of here." Ranald touches Stephanie on the shoulder. "Do you have some heavy moving blankets or any heavy clothes?"

"Why?" Stephanie asks, allowing him to help her up.

"I can't really be in the sun," he says with a smile.

"For fuck's sake," is all she can let out.

"Yeah, and you thought that mutt was bad, right?" The vampire tries to make light of the situation.

"What about him?" she points to Chris who has been silent through the whole ordeal.

"He's coming with us." He pauses and looks down at her. "You like Vegas?" he asks Stephanie with his devilish grin.

CHAPTER THIRTY-SIX

Melisa relies on Aaron to help her walk up to the concierge. She asks for her uncle's room. He gives her the courtesy phone. Calling up to him, he tells her he'll come down to meet them.

"Hi Tio." Melisa greets the short, well-dressed man with a hug.

"Hi Melisa, how are you, my darling." Her uncle smiles from ear to ear at the sight of his niece. "What a surprise. Why didn't you call first? The building isn't even finished yet," he adds.

"I'm sorry, Tio, it wasn't planned. I hope it's okay we are here?" she asks.

"Of course. So, are you going to introduce me to your friends?" he asks, offering his hand to the men to shake.

"Of course, this is Aaron, and um, Fernando." It all feels surreal to be talking about these two men with such a regular tone. "This is my Uncle Alberto."

"What a pleasure." Her uncle takes their hand one after the other. "Do you need a place to stay, honey?" he asks her.

"Yes, Tio. Is that okay?"

"Of course. I have work, then I'm heading out to party. So I'll be out late. The rentals aren't ready, but you can stay in my apartment; there's plenty of room." He went in early as an investor in the building. It's still being remodeled and only has a few residences. The property is made up of two towers, and his tower is the only one finished. It will be a time-share when it's all complete.

Melisa remembers when he tried to get her to invest. She even asked Mr. McCarthy if it was a good deal. He liked it, but thought she should wait on such an endeavor. She always trusted anything he said when it came to investing or buying property. He was the one who showed her the home she lives in now.

"That's not a problem. We will be just hanging out here today. We had a long trip."

"Sounds good to me. Call downstairs if you need any takeout. They are really helpful." He kisses her on the cheek and leaves, giving her the key card to go upstairs.

"Thanks, Tio."

The elevator is quiet and fast. The door opens up to his apartment, which occupies the whole top floor. Being one of the hottest chefs in Las Vegas, with three restaurants, he has made a comfortable living. The apartment is decorated with gold leaf everywhere, from the fixtures to the picture frames. Even the chandelier is plated with gold leaf. The sun is coming down from above a massive sky light, reflecting on the gaudy, shining chandelier. Melisa looks like she's about to faint.

The Hunter is the one who catches her, before she can hit the floor. He takes her to the nearest room, which holds a king-size bed. He lays her down and leaves her. Aaron comes in with some water and a fruit that Mr. Hudson wants her to eat. It is supposed to help her heal. He leaves her to rest, joining the Hunter in the main common area.

He is looking out from the massive floor-to-ceiling windows. Aaron walks up behind him and takes in the view with him. "This world has so many wonders. Looking out over this land, reminds me of the old Mayan city of Tikal. They focused on building structures as high as they could," the Hunter tells Aaron.

"If we survive all this, what will you do?" Aaron asks.

"I do not know. My heart tells me I still have much to remember. The life that I left behind before I became the tool of destruction."

"You keep saying things like that. What do you mean?" Aaron is truly curious. "If you were a tool or weapon, who was wielding you?" he asks.

"At first, the Church. But soon, it was just a man."

"I don't understand. How? You're so powerful."

"I may be powerful. But my greatest strength was my greatest weakness."

"What's that?"

"Faith," he says, turning his gaze to Aaron. "I was manipulated, until I became as corrupt as those that were supposed to be guiding man's salvation."

"So the Church betrayed you?"

"Oh no. The Church never once betrayed me. It was the men who worked for the Church. Those are the ones responsible."

"What will you do?"

"Forgive them. Something I learned from the amazing woman I almost killed," he says, looking toward Melisa's room. "You should rest. I don't believe we will be safe here for much longer."

"Why are we running? You could take them out by yourself."

"A long time ago, yes. But I am still very weak. I am only a fraction of my past self," he explains. "Your family will be able to find us. Your kin have many clever abilities. My memory is still not complete. But I have flashes of what I've had to contend with. They will be able to feel the baby, or maybe you are the key. Something, there is always something that leaves a trace."

The night comes quickly. Melisa has been up and about for an hour. The Hunter hasn't rested; he has been busy building weapons to slow and kill the beasts. Taking the legs from the dining room chairs, he has whittled them into points. Using the limited materials and tools in the loft apartment and having found a small propane torch and a cast iron pan in the kitchen, he has been able to melt the fancy silver flatware Melisa's uncle had in his dish cabinet. He worked outside on the patio, keeping the horrible stench away from Melisa. She had offered to help, and he showed her how to place the silver on the tips of the wooden stakes.

Aaron took some time to find a comfortable place to rest. But once he did his snoring was loud enough to be heard throughout the residence. The Hunter and Melisa enjoyed the tasks, giving them a moment to take their minds off the confrontation they know is coming.

Melisa never spoke to the Hunter, other than offering him some food or drink whenever she was fixing herself something. What she didn't realize, was he was just focused, mentally preparing for the pending attack. He worked out every angle he could think of.

Aaron was very helpful. He had told the Hunter a good deal about his family, describing in detail every brother's ability and weakness. He hoped that being so high up, they would be able to respond to any attack quicker, knowing that any attempt to scale the tower would make enough noise that they could thwart all interlopers.

When the elevator door bell rings and opens, it catches the Hunter off guard. He had forgotten about the technology of this new world. He turns, seeing Melisa walking past the heavy metal door. He moves in a flash, to protect her.

The doors open, and the Hunter shields her from any threats. However, the elevator is completely empty. "That's odd. You can only access this floor with a key and a code," Melisa states.

"It's time. They are here," the Hunter reports. "You need to go to your room," the Hunter tells Melisa. He walks behind her, his eyes sharp. He stops at Aaron's room. He is dead asleep, but is instantly awake when the Hunter tells him it's time.

Aaron hurries to the main room. The elevator door is closing. He looks around knowingly, suspiciously. His ears are perked. He looks up; they are on the roof. The Hunter joins him. Aaron puts his finger to his lips and points up.

"You may need to change now," the Hunter tells Aaron. In a violent display, Aaron's body transforms into a massive hellhound, his human features all but gone. The beast stands upright, clothing ripped and torn from the massive shift in size. The floor tiles beneath him crack from the shock of the change in weight. He roars with acceptance of the battle. His brothers answer the call from the roof. They can't make out how many are up there. "Protect her," the Hunter tells Aaron and runs out to the balcony. He jumps, grabbing the patio cover, and pulls himself up to the roof in one fluid move.

Aaron turns to Melisa's room. She screams and runs when she sees Aaron for the first time. Her eyes focus on only the magnificent weapons that are his hands and teeth. He changes back to his human form and catches her, covering her mouth. He tries to comfort her, holding her tight and keeping her silent. A loud crash, followed by the rattling of the chandelier above, tells them the battle has begun. Thunder-like booms shake the whole apartment. The two look up following the horrifying noises. Aaron, using his keen hearing, figures out that the Hunter is fighting three of his brothers.

The other two must be coming for Melisa. Aaron, prepared to fight, looks at Melisa, telling her to stay put. He slowly moves around the apartment, looking at the windows expecting anything to come at him. It is Vincent who shows up first. Having scaled the side of the building, he leaps over the balcony railing and now stands on the outside of the heavy glass windows looking in on him.

His massive werewolf form towers over eight feet tall. His red matted fur and yellow glowing eyes, are focused on Aaron. The heat from his breath fogs the glass and then disappears. Aaron knows Vincent. He must challenge his ego. Feeling like he is stronger than any other, he will respond wildly if Aaron doesn't transform for the fight.

Aaron squares up and lowers himself, ready to take him on without changing. Vincent blasts through the window and leaps at Aaron. Aaron knows the brute is slow, so he must use his superior speed against the beast. All the while leading him away from Melisa's room.

Vincent does what Aaron expects. He charges in madly, swiping at him with his massive claws with all his might. Aaron moves and dodges the first onslaught, aggravating his larger brother. In a fit of rage, he cries out and grabs a nearby book shelf and throws it at Aaron. Aaron eludes the object, but it leaves him vulnerable to Vincent. Finally, he makes contact with him. Vincent rips into Aaron's flesh, splattering blood everywhere. The wounds are deep. In human form, Aaron is no match for Vincent. He transforms in a vicious manner, attacking Vincent with a fury he had not expected. Aaron's speed is too much for Vincent, but Vincent can take the hits.

The two exchange heavy blows. Aaron, working on the defensive, moves to keep Vincent focused on his attack. A roar from above causes both brothers to stop. It's the call of a fallen brother. The Hunter has killed one of them. Vincent howls in anger and charges past Aaron. He leaps up to the roof to help his other brothers. Aaron takes a breath. His wounds are severe. He needs time to heal. But he knows he doesn't have it.

A loud crash is heard from above. The Hunter comes crashing through the skylight breaking the chandelier, slamming down, with Vincent and Jim on him, biting and ripping at his body. When they land, the Hunter loses his grip on his silver-tipped wooden weapon. The brothers see the death stick and move to keep it away from the Hunter. The Hunter kicks Jim off and contends with Vincent one on one, all the while trying to break away and retrieve his silver-tipped stake.

Aaron moves to help, but Alex and Greg jump down and intercept him. "Traitor!" Alex roars. The two leap at Aaron. He dodges their attack, but is quickly run down. He takes Alex down easily, but Greg grabs hold of him. The two werewolves are much smaller than Aaron, but with all the damage inflicted by Vincent, he is not able to handle them.

The Hunter has the upper hand on Vincent. Holding his jaws, he is about to break them apart. Jim charges back into the fight causing the Hunter to let go. The Hunter slams his fist into Jim's head, knocking him to the floor, dazed. The Hunter leaps for his stake and turns to Jim who attacks, diving at the Hunter.

Aaron is pinned; his two brothers are biting at his arms and throat. In a fit of desperation, he calls out for help, knowing that he doesn't have any. The two brothers just laugh as they continue to rip the life from him.

A loud howling cry stops the two brothers. Looking up, they see Jim is dead, his human form all that is left of him. The Hunter is holding his lifeless body in his bloody arms. He pulls the stake from his victim. With a force like thunder, he flings the dead body at the two brothers, pushing them through the window out onto the balcony. He rushes to Aaron's aid. "Are you okay?" he asks.

Aaron can't answer him. But his return to a fighting stance is all the Hunter needs to be ready himself. The two stand back to back. The three remaining brothers surround them. For the first time Aaron feels like they can win the fight. A loud scream from Melisa's room catches them all by surprise. The Hunter leaves the fight and runs to her room. Aleksy has snuck into the apartment, cutting through the window with his sharp claws, using the sounds of the battle to mask his entry. He is still in human form except for his arm, which is holding Melisa by the throat. "Stop right there," he orders the Hunter. The Hunter recognizes his face.

Melisa is gasping for breath. The Hunter leans in, about to attack, but Aleksy squeezes, letting him know that he can kill her before he makes it to him. "Don't even try it," he states. The brothers, hearing their father's voice, all come running in. All are shocked to see him, standing so strong.

"Boys, why don't you come over here," he calls to them. All four walk toward him. "Not you, Aaron. You've made your choice," Aleksy states firmly. "So, where is the blade?" he asks. Aaron transforms to human form, as the other brothers do too.

"We don't have it," Aaron pleads with him. "Let her go, Father."

"Oh my son. I can't do that. She is the only thing keeping that monster by your side at bay," he laughs. "Now, I'll ask one more time. Where is the blade?" he growls, his eyes beginning to change to his werewolf color.

"We do not have it, I swear." Aaron drops to his knees. "Please do not kill her."

"How did I raise such weaklings?" The old man shakes his head. He moves out of the room, using the door that leads to the living room. The Hunter and Aaron follow through a different door, which leads to the entrance. They can see the old man the whole time.

He heads toward the outside. The Hunter moves closer to him, ready to stop them, if they try to leave. "Last chance," Aleksy calls out, picking her up and dangling her over the edge of the balcony.

"If you drop her, I will destroy you," the Hunter finally speaks.

"That I am sure of, since I will be dead soon anyway. I could think of worse ways," the old man admits. "So, what will it be, the blade for the girl, or killing me, for the blade?" the old man asks.

"I don't have the blade. She does," the Hunter states. His eyes are locked on her. Melisa pulls the blade out from her pants and plunges it into Aleksy's chest. The old man cries out in pain, dropping Melisa over the balcony to the street below.

The Hunter moves like a bolt of lightning, passing the old man before he can hit the floor. He grips the edge of the balcony, his fingers breaking the cement. He pulls with all his might, propelling himself down toward Melisa's falling body. She is already halfway down the twenty-story building

His fast-falling body is plummeting to the earth below. She feels the Hunter's strong hands grip her waist. He flips her around so she is facing the sky above. His back facing the earth, he holds her tight. Looking back to the rapidly approaching ground, he knows he must absorb her fall. He focuses on his whole body. All of his energy set to take the force, he pushes his arms out, away from his body, creating a separation between them.

Melisa feels something inside her. A force, protecting her child in her belly. They break through plastic tarps covering the construction zone, slamming into the earth and breaking the concrete around them. His arms collapse, absorbing the force so she lands on his chest with a thud. They have landed in an empty construction area.

The adrenaline is immense, as she rolls off her savior. "How did you do that?" she asks with a raspy voice; the air is still knocked from her lungs. She had forgotten the pain in her throat. She looks down at the Hunter. His head is bleeding, and blood is spilling out from his ears and mouth. Melisa drops down to him.

Checking his neck, she can't find a heartbeat. A soft thump a few feet away scares her. Aaron has jumped down and is standing next to her. Melisa is in tears and looking down at the Hunter's body. She is covered in blood. Melisa can't believe what is happening. She rushes into Aaron's arms. "He is dead," Melisa says.

"What?" Aaron can't believe the words she is speaking, even remembering how the Hunter told him he was not at full strength. But could it really be true?

"Look," she says, pointing to the spot where they had landed. The blood and cracked cement are all that are left. The Hunter is nowhere to be seen. Aaron holds her tight, as they both look around, knowing he is alive. Aaron is still trembling.

"What's wrong?"

"I need to get you to the hospital."

High above, the brothers all stand looking down at their slain father. Alex walks over to him and kneels by his side. The others are in shock. Looking down at his father's face, Alex removes the blade from his chest. "I'm sorry father," he whispers.

Alex turns to his remaining brothers. Jim and Jesse are both dead leaving only Greg and Vincent. "We will have our revenge on them," he says, holding the blade tightly at his side.

CHAPTER THIRTY-SEVEN

Melisa sits up in the hospital bed, in a daze, still trying to piece together the events of the night. She has the TV on but is not paying attention to it. The sounds of the late-night talk show are just noise in the background. Her eyes are focused on the large cross in the room. Aaron is sleeping in the small chair next to her. She has an I.V. in her arm. Her neck is bandaged, along with some other minor bumps and bruises. Aaron is still showing signs of his fight, but he looks almost healed.

Over and over in her head, Melisa continuously plays back her fall from the high-rise. Everything she had ever learned, every thought now has been put into question. How had this whole world been kept hidden for so long? How could a man fall from such heights and walk away?

The thought of the Hunter is weighing heavily on her. The fear of what could have happened. Not only from the fall, but the whole situation. She had wanted to help a man who was hurt. What if she hadn't? What if she had let County Hospital keep him? What if he had never been transferred? What if she had not spent the few minutes trying to understand him, when he was lost?

It's overwhelming to work out all the what-ifs. Looking back, she knows she would have done the same thing all over again—she places the highest value on saving lives—and that is why she is still alive. A sharp pain in her chest reminds her of her injury. A burning sensation grows from the center of where the blade struck her. She places her hand over the bandage; it feels

315

like it's on fire.

Melisa jumps out of bed and pulls the bandage down. The wound is ablaze, fusing closed. The pain is crippling. Melisa falls to her knees. She puts her hands over the wound, burning them. She screams in horror. She is unable to soothe the flame, as it begins to spread. She closes her eyes in agony. She hears the voice of the Hunter calling to her, saying her name. His hands are gripping her shoulders, moving her back and forth.

Melisa opens her eyes, and she realizes she was dreaming. Looking up, she sees Chris for the first time. He is gently holding her shoulders. "Melisa, wake up. You're having a nightmare," he explains. Groggily, she wipes her eyes. The sun is peeking in through the shades. Seeing her love is confusing. *How long has he been there?* she wonders. Looking to where Aaron had been sitting asleep, she sees he is not there. The TV is off. The idea that she was dreaming is hard for her to understand at first.

"How did you get here?" Melisa is in a state of disbelief. She had not thought of Chris this whole time. Her own safety, and that of her baby, was the only concern she had. Something inside kept telling her not to worry about Chris. Looking at him now, she feels like he had been communicating with her the whole time. Staring at each other, she feels like she can read his thoughts. And, he can read hers. For the first time, she understands all. She is changing too. The baby inside her has made her something new. The lack of fear, the ability to survive . . . all of this is coming from the boy growing inside her.

"I came in early this morning," he tells her.

"How long have I been out?"

"At least ten hours. They have been pushing fluids in you," he tells her.

"The baby?" she asks in terror.

"Fine. Your dehydration was a worry, but the doctors say you are in perfect shape." Melisa looks over her body. She is dressed in a hospital gown, not like in the dream. Looking up at Chris, she is not sure what to think is real or not.

"Where have you been?"

"I'm so sorry, my love." He begins to cry. His emotions are on his sleeve. "This is all my fault."

"Where is everyone?"

"They are here, waiting to see you"

"I need to go to the bathroom," she says and moves off the bed, passing Chris in a cold manner. She pushes the stand for the still-attached I.V. along with her. He doesn't take offense, but he is worried he has lost her. Once in the bathroom, she splashes water on her face. Looking at herself in the mirror, she realizes she doesn't have any pain. Pulling off the bandage from her neck, she sees the bruises are all gone. Pulling down at her gown, she pulls off the bandage covering her chest wound. The scar looks just like the one from her dream.

Placing her hand on it, her mind flashes to the moment when she jumped under the blade. Her hand pulls away quickly. A knock at the door startles her.

"Are you okay, love?" Chris calls out.

"Yes, I'm fine." She leaves the bathroom. Chris tries to touch her, but she moves away from the contact. He may have to come to grips with his greatest fear, that he's lost her. Getting back in bed, she looks up at Chris, who looks pitiful. It makes her angry to see him acting in such a way. A knock comes on the main door, taking her focus off Chris.

Stephanie asks if she can come in. Melisa is excited to see her. Expecting to see Walter walk in behind her, she sits up. "Where's Walter?" she asks. Her excitement is turning to worry.

Stephanie walks slowly up to Melisa. Her face tells Melisa something has happened. She places her hand on Melisa's hand. "I have something I must tell you," she says, keeping a solemn face. "I've had to do this many times before, but never with someone I care about," Stephanie adds.

"What is it?" Melisa already knows what she is going to say before she does.

"I'm sorry to tell you, but Walter is dead."

"What? But he was . . ." Melisa stops, hearing the words resonate in her head. The blunt words are what they all taught when breaking news such as this. "How?" she asks.

"My father," Chris interjects. "I'm so sorry, my love."

"What?" Melisa pulls her hands away from the two people. "I think I need some time alone," she tells them.

"Mel." Chris tries to explain.

"Chris. I can't talk to you right now. I don't want to talk to anyone right now," Melisa says, looking down in thought. He and Stephanie leave her be.

Alone in her room, now, she sits in silence, playing back all that has happened. The knowledge that her brother is dead feels like an unseen force crushing her; she can't seem to process the information. "Who's going to tell Dad?" she asks herself aloud. At that moment, a rush of her anger is focused on Chris's father. She remembers killing the man, his beastly hand holding her, causing such pain. The feeling of stabbing the blade deep into the man, penetrating his skin and breaking through the bones of his chest and piercing his heart.

Like a hard kick to the stomach, she realizes she has taken a life. The feeling travels up to her throat. The taste of bile engulfs her mouth. Getting up, she rushes to the bathroom dragging the annoying I.V. with her again. Melisa clutches the toilet bowl as she dry heaves. The bile is disgusting, but nothing else is coming up.

A warm sensation comes from her chest. Like before, in her father's bathroom. Her whole body begins to spasm. Falling to the floor in the fetal position, she cries out in pain. Then, as if nothing had happened, she is fine. The memories of taking the man's life fade to the back of her mind.

She gets up and rinses her mouth out. Her body feels wonderful. She takes the I.V. out from her arm and presses on the puncture wound. Within a moment it is completely closed. Leaving the bathroom, she walks up to the blinds. Using the cord, she lifts them up, blasting her room with natural light.

Eyes closed, she opens her arms enjoying the warmth of the sun beaming down on her. Rejuvenated, she turns around. A package wrapped in Mother's Day wrapping paper sits on her side table with flowers. The card on the gift reads:

"Melisa, I'm glad you're okay. Ever since meeting you, I've known you were much stronger then you appeared. Inside you will find something I think will help you in the future. Keep it safe, and don't let anyone know you have it. Be careful what you read aloud. Remember, this all started because an old man wanted to live forever. You have a man willing to give up immortality for you.

Your Friend without a name, Cheers"

Melisa's eyes swell with tears. She remembers what Mr. Hudson had told her about Chris giving up his youth. She still can't believe any of this. Or the fact he has kept so much from her. Looking at the package, she is filled with wonder. She peels back the corner exposing the leather of an old book. A knock on the door surprises her. Putting the book down on her bed she answers the door. To her surprise, Mr. McCarthy is standing there holding flowers and a card. "Mr. McCarthy?"

"Basil, please . . . Melisa, how are you, my dear?"

"I'm doing better." Melisa turns and walks back to her bed. "How did you know I was here?" She gets in, pulling the covers over herself. Distracted, she forgets about the book, and it falls. Melisa tries to reach for it. But, it's Mr. McCarthy who catches it before it hits the floor.

"I got it," he smiles. Holding the package, he looks at the opening. His eyes are focused intensely on it.

"I'll take that," Melisa says and reaches out for the book.

"Oh, of course my dear," he says and hands it over to her. "What wonderful wrapping. I feel bad that I didn't bring a gift. I just brought flowers." Melisa puts the book under her blanket with her.

"So, what are you doing here?"

"I got word from Chris. I had called him when he didn't show up for a meeting. He told me everything," Mr. McCarthy explains. Wide-eyed, Melisa watches his every move. He hands her the flowers with a caring smile. "I flew out as soon as he told me."

"What did he tell you?" she asks

"That you got sick." He takes a seat on the bed.

"Oh, yeah."

"I just want you to know, take as much time as you need. Everything will be okay until you're better."

"Thank you sir."

"Well, I should be going. I have a meeting with a developer. Was supposed to be next week, but since I'm here, I might as well take care of it now." He smiles at her, tapping her on the knee. "Now get some rest." He gets up, and kisses her softly on her forehead. She watches him leave. Melisa is taken aback by the whole encounter. After all she has gone through, she doesn't feel she can trust anyone. She is suspicious about why he turned to the package while he was there. *Why was he so interested in it?* she wonders. Looking at the gift, she wonders if she is just being paranoid. The wrapping is funny. Maybe he was just enjoying the humor of it.

She gets up from her bed and checks outside her door to see if anyone is coming. She doesn't want to be surprised again. Tentatively, she slowly rips the rest of paper exposing the whole book. The cover has the Hunter's tattoo branded into it. The first page is written in Spanish. "The year of our lord, fifteen hundred and one," she says aloud. Reading the page, it tells her it's a journal. Some kind of travel log. There is a name at the end of the entry. "Fernando Jiménez de la Torre." Melisa almost drops the book when she realizes what she is holding.

The vampire just gave her the journal of the Hunter. She flips through the pages, seeing depictions of symbols from the Mayan people, as well as Egyptian symbols like the ones Mr. Hudson had hanging on his wall. Why did he give it to her? All she wanted was to be done with all of this. But now she is stuck in the middle of it again. What is she supposed to do with this book? This journal of a man she doesn't know.

The feeling that they are connected grows. She can't help but wonder where he is at that moment. Looking out the window, she feels as if he is watching at that moment.

There's a knock on the door. Melisa puts the journal back in its wrapping and places it under her pillow, for safe keeping. "Come in," she calls out. It's Chris. He looks at her with a hangdog expression. A flood of emotions rolls over her. He has lied about so much. Her whole life has been turned upside down all because of his lies. He walks up to her slowly.

"I know there is so much to say . . . but I'm just so glad you're okay." Beginning to weep, he drops to his knees and takes her hand. "This is all my fault. I fell in love with you and thought I could make all these changes. All I did was ruin your life." He buries his face in her blanket.

Melisa places her other hand on his head. Looking out through the window, she can't help but feel what she feels. Even after everything that has happened, something inside her tells her to forgive him. Trust him. Love him. Placing her hand under his chin, she raises his head. She notices the bruises on his face.

"Oh my god, what happened to you?" she asks. Chris just smiles.

"It's nothing." He doesn't allow for her to make a big deal over them.

"It doesn't look like nothing."

"I'm fine." He smiles softly. "How's my son?" he asks, placing his hand on her belly.

"Strong," she says placing her hand on his.

"That is all I needed to hear."

"Are you really giving up your gift to have a family with me?"

"What?"

"Tell me what you've been holding from me all this time. I already know, but I still need to hear the words from your mouth."

"Yes, you are right. I am so sorry."

"Enough with the sorry."

"I am a werewolf . . . But I am a man too," he says defensively, looking deep into her eyes. Melisa is focused on his, taking in everything he is saying. No matter what she already knows, hearing it from him is making it all feel more real.

"And we are having a baby, which means what for you?"

"I will age. I will grow old with you."

"How old are you now?"

"I will be aging from twenty-five," he says and smiles.

"Great, now I'm a cradle robber," she says, making light of the news he has just shared. "So, now what?"

"I think we should discuss names?"

"How about we name him after his father?" Melisa smiles.

"I thought you didn't like him much and wanted to name him after me?" They laugh together, knowing that this happiness is only a short luxury. Looking back out the window, Melisa's eyes suddenly widen. *Holy Shit, I'm pregnant with a werewolf.*

Nicholas Arriaza